By Pierre Salinger

A TRIBUTE TO JOHN F. KENNEDY
WITH KENNEDY
AN HONORABLE PROFESSION
ON INSTRUCTIONS OF MY GOVERNMENT

ON INSTRUCTIONS OF MY GOVERNMENT

Pierre Salinger

ON INSTRUCTIONS OF MY GOVERNMENT

Doubleday & Company, Inc.
Garden City, New York

Except for those persons prominent in recent history who are identified by name, all characters in this work are the products of the author's imagination. Some of the events, however, are based on actual occurrences.

To Guy and Ghislaine and, of course, Nicole

CHARACTERS

The President of the United States
Samuel V. Hood, Ambassador to the Republic of Santa Clara
Burgess Rand, Secretary of Defense
Sterling Adams, Secretary of State
James Halverson, Secretary of the Air Force
Leverett Rhodes, Secretary of the Army
Boyd Wright, Secretary of the Navy
General Mark Courtland, Chairman of the Joint Chiefs of Staff
Martin Trask, Director of the Central Intelligence Agency
Edward O'Farrell, Assistant Secretary of State for Inter-American
    Affairs
Gene Haas, Special Assistant to the President for Latin American
    Affairs
Senator Harlan Grant of Illinois, candidate for President
Senator Robert E. Breckinridge, Chairman of the Senate Foreign
    Relations Committee
Palmer Joyce, commentator for Universal Broadcasting Company
Donald Marston, president of Heli-Commuter Corporation

General Leonard Moody, military adviser to the President
Colonel William Gruver, military attaché, American embassy, Ciudad Alarcon
Carl Reasons, press attaché, American embassy, Ciudad Alarcon
Bennett Cullers, American consul, Ariella

THE SANTA CLARANS

Constanzia Novarese, widow of the thirty-sixth President of the Republic of Santa Clara
Jorge Luchengo, the thirty-seventh President of the Republic of Santa Clara
Francisco (Paco) Jiminez, revolutionary
Arturo Lara, Foreign Minister
General Carlos Silvera-Guzman, Defense Minister

THE MAFIA FUGITIVES

Giovanni Petracci alias Johnny Partridge
Bruno Cassavettes, the capo
Mario Cassavettes, his son

JUNE

THE PRESIDENT was in a black humor this humid June morning in 1976. A Cabinet conference on the budget, a stubborn nineteen billion dollars out of balance, had kept him up until long after midnight, and a cold caught at the last summit in Moscow had given him little sleep. But the focus of his irascibility was a front-page headline in the Washington *Post:* PRESIDENT'S POPULARITY AT NEW LOW IN HARRIS POLL.

He was, perhaps, the last traditional politician who would hold the nation's highest office. The veterans of campus dissent, now approaching their thirties, had taken much of their impatience, if not their militancy, into the suburbs. The blacks, formidable in their new sophistication, were the new power in the cities. The browns, from the Puerto Ricans in the East to the Chicanos in the Southwest, were an emergent and aggressive elective force. And all were contemptuous of the old politics and its practitioners and deaf to banal appeals to party loyalty.

But the man in the upstairs bedroom in the East Wing of the White House read none of this into the statistic that only one voter in three could presently support him for re-election. He was convinced that the voters were, and would always be, divisible into blocs of Democrats, Republicans, and Independents; young and old; black, brown, yellow and white; blue collar and white collar, and ghetto, suburb and farm. And when they went to the polls they would vote as they always had, for the man and party most likely to serve their self-interests; most able to calm their fears; most willing to absolve them of prejudice, and most wary of change. It was not a question of bringing them together. To the contrary, wasn't its very diversity the strength of America? For him, it was a question of keeping them apart—proud of their differences, respectful of the rule of law, and identifiable in the pre-election canvass.

The President's first call was to National Party Chairman James J. Mallory. He hadn't seen the poll yet and the President read it to him. "It couldn't be much worse, Jim."

"It could be a hell of a lot worse, Mr. President. We've still got five months to go before the election and right now it's you against every one of their possible nominees. Wait until it narrows down, one to one, after the conventions. You'll be all right."

The President's next call caught his press secretary, Maxwell Busby, just entering his office in the West Wing.

"If the correspondents start hounding you this morning for a reaction from me to that Harris poll, I haven't given you one," the President told him.

His schedule for the day came up with his breakfast tray. His first appointment was at 10 A.M.: "Secretary Adams, Ambassador Hood, Haas." He would tell his appointment secretary to cut this one short. Fifteen minutes—no more.

Sam Hood was shaving in his suite at the Mayflower. He had flown in from Santa Clara the night before and had not left the hotel. Washington was no longer his town, nor did he like summonses from four thousand miles away to consultations where his presence would be no more than a formality. He, too, had read the Harris poll in the paper sent up with his breakfast and could anticipate the President's mood. Polls! It was a hell of a way to run a country.

Secretary of State Sterling Adams was already at his desk. He had thought, but only briefly, of calling Hood to reassure him that the President was still willing to listen. But no, the ambassador might expect too much support from him this morning. He would, of course, go along with Hood as far as he could. He *was* State and it *was* his embassy. But Adams' own summons to the White House from Haas left no doubt of the President's intention. An "urgent review of the Santa Claran allocation" was in order.

In his home in Bethesda, Gene Haas, Special Assistant to the President for Latin American Affairs, had been up since five-thirty, drafting and redrafting the statement he would clear with the President and then deliver to Press Secretary Busby for his afternoon briefing of the press—*after* Hood was airborne from Dulles. The ambassador could be unpredictable.

The driver of the State Department limousine had orders to drop Ambassador Hood off at the west basement entrance to the White House, where Secretary Adams would be waiting. Later the President would ask them to leave the same way—invisible and unavailable to the press corps.

The guard at the basement entrance knew Adams by sight but had to check Hood's identification against the appointment schedule on his desk. The Secret Service agents in the corridor outside the Oval Office let them pass with only a curt nod to Adams, nor was there a delay in the appointment secretary's office. The President was waiting.

If the choice of entrances to the White House did not tell Hood that he had come to listen, not to be heard, his first sight of the President did. He was standing behind his massive desk and the gilt seal on its facing and the array of service flags behind it were intimidating assertions of authority. If the Chief Executive actually did want a free exchange of opinions on options he was still holding open, the white leather conversational unit facing the fireplace on the opposite wall was much more amenable to informality and candor. But on this morning he came out only briefly from behind his desk.

"It was good of you to come up here on such short notice, Sam. But Adams here will have to go before Foreign Relations next week, and they'll want verse and chapter on what we're planning to spend and where."

"I understand that, sir."

Haas, as always, came into the office precisely thirty seconds after the principals—his one deference to rank. "Mr. Secretary . . . Ambassador." He took the staff chair to the right of the desk, facing Hood and Adams, but obliquely.

"We're having difficulties up here, Sam, and not just on the Hill. The whole country's up in arms against inflation."

"I saw the poll, Mr. President."

"The poll doesn't bother me, Sam." His tone was chiding. "You should know that. The fact is that I've got a budget that's nineteen billion out of whack, and the question is where do I start cutting? Now I've had Haas here reviewing all of our Latin American commitments and Santa Clara looks most questionable."

A stretch of the rose garden was visible through the window, and beyond it the Washington Monument, ghostlike in the morning mist from the Potomac.

"I haven't read Haas's review, Mr. President. I can't know on what basis he would arrive at that opinion."

The President was patient. "The basis, Sam, is that we've been subsidizing the country ever since Hoover—*Hoover!* First it was direct loans and not one penny ever repaid. Year after year of it— right up to the Alliance for Progress—and now direct budget support. A hundred million a year, Sam, and what do we have to show for it?"

"You could make the same case against almost all of our Latin American commitments."

"There's a difference, Sam, and you know it. Who else down there is doing business with Red China?"

"I don't think they have much choice, sir. China will take their copper. We won't. I've told you many times that we ought to relax our import embargo—perhaps even stipulate a percentage of Santa Claran copper in our own defense procurement."

The President forced a smile. "Why don't I take you with me on a campaign swing into copper states like Montana and Utah, and let you try that on for size out there? No, Sam, you'll have to do better than that."

Hood glanced toward the Secretary of State for support, but

Adams, who was studying, intently, the gold eagle atop the Marine Corps flag standard behind the President, did not respond. The ambassador slid his spare six-and-a-half-foot frame forward in his chair.

"I think Secretary Adams would agree with me, sir, that Jorge Luchengo's government deserves a little more time. He's been in there only three years and there have been very visible reforms."

"And I think the Secretary would agree with me, Sam, that we had much sounder reasons for supporting the Novarese regime. It was at least democratic. It had popular support. Your man Luchengo took power by force and holds it by force. And, unlike Luis Novarese, he's not spending a nickel of what we're giving him to go after Jiminez in force. I take it he's still raising hell up there in the mountains?"

"That's correct but the best deterrent to Jiminez is a strong economy—and without this appropriation—"

"Goddammit, Sam, I'm not going to chase the ghosts of Fidel Castro and Che Guevara around Latin America into infinity. The CIA claims that Jiminez has no more than two or three hundred guerrillas, most of them kids. Luchengo ought to be able to handle a ragtag bunch like that."

Hood held his temper. "I have not written a single cable suggesting that Jiminez has the forces to depose Luchengo. I have written, and often, that his sabotage of the mines and the rail line is just as menacing as a direct march on the capital." Hood saw the President glance at his watch. In another minute or two his intercom would ring. "In this office, three years ago, Mr. President, I told you I didn't want this assignment. I had the closest of associations with President Novarese in the OAS and much resistance to serving as ambassador to the regime that had stood him up against a wall."

"You were the right man for it."

"I was not the right man for it if I haven't been able to persuade you in three years that Luchengo—whatever I once thought of him—has been a change for the better down there. And I dispute the statement that he still holds power by force. There were elections last year and he won handily."

"Haas's report—"

Hood was suddenly tired of it. "I must tell you that I strongly resent being brought up here to defend my judgments against a summary on Santa Clara I have never seen, written by a man who has never been there."

"You're too rough on Haas, Sam. I'm confident he had full access to your cables. Adams can confirm that."

The Secretary of State did not like being involved at a point of such direct confrontation. But it was, at least, an opportunity to support Hood and to vent his own resentment of Haas and the entire concept of a "little State Department" within the White House.

"Mr. Haas, of course, had the fullest cooperation of our Latin American desk, Mr. President. But I, like the ambassador, have not seen his recommendations to you. I can't know what weight he has given to our files as against perhaps conflicting intelligence from other sources. I would add that I agree with Mr. Hood's *on-the-scene* evaluation. The department supports the commitment to Santa Clara, if not in the present dollar amount, at least—"

"Sir."

"Yes, Haas."

"May I explain to the ambassador and to the Secretary that on your instructions my review and recommendation were written for your eyes only. I would have had no objection whatever—"

The color rose in Hood's aquiline face, sharpening the contrast with his blue eyes and steel-gray hair. "Perhaps you would like to summarize it for us now then, Haas?"

"The summary, Mr. Ambassador, is that this country—and certainly the Congress—will no longer support the subsidy of a dictatorship that lacks popular support and that trades in war matériel with Red China. Novarese was at least *anti*-Communist. He wouldn't accept a Soviet legation in Ciudad Alarcon. And he did send dollars back to us for arms to fight Jiminez."

Hood had heard it all before—the oversimplifications that serve as conventional wisdom, the catch phrases that might belong in a New York *Daily News* editorial but did not belong here. The ambassador threw up his hands. "That's a total distortion, Mr. President, and if Haas did read my reports, he gave them no credibility whatever. I'll repeat to you now, sir, what I've been reporting for months. If we cancel our support of Luchengo, or even reduce it substantially, the certain consequence is another Bolivia or Cuba. Luchengo will either have to accept greater economic dependence on China or face collapse. Either way, you'll have Jiminez."

"Aren't you assuming the worst, Sam?"

"No, I'm assuming the probable."

The intercom finally rang. "Tell them to wait," the President told his secretary. "We're almost through here."

Hood stood up. "President Luchengo will expect me to call on him tomorrow. The decision's final?"

"It is. Try to appreciate my position, Sam. If I don't cut the budget down to size, the Congress will. And either way the Santa Clara appropriation won't be in it. I could fight for it on the Hill but I would lose—and this isn't a good year for picking scraps you can't win." The President came around his desk and put a hand on Hood's shoulder. "Again, thank you for coming up. And, Sam, I'd like to announce this in my own way and in my own time."

"The west basement entrance?"

"If you don't mind."

Secretary Adams said nothing until they were at the door of Hood's limousine. "I'm sorry that I couldn't be more helpful in there. But appropriations more important than Santa Clara's are also on the line, and I can't afford to pick scraps I can't win either."

"This could have been won," said Hood, "and you will regret that it wasn't."

Hood's last view of the south lawn was one of the Kennedy magnolias marking the corners of the rose garden. He thought of other days when his voice was heard with respect in the White House. But he did not ask the driver to swing into Arlington on the way to the airport. There was no time this morning for the walk up the hill to the graves. The travel specialist at State, on Haas's orders, had him on a very tight flight schedule.

At 4 P.M. the correspondents jammed their way into the clutter of desks and wire service teletype machines in Busby's rabbit warren of an office. Excerpts from the transcript of his briefing:

Q. Have you spoken to the President today?
A. Only briefly.
Q. What did he think of the Harris poll this morning?
*A. I didn't ask him. (Laughter.) I have one short announcement.
I don't think you'll need a release on it. The President met this
morning with Secretary Adams and Ambassador Hood for a routine
review of budget support for Santa Clara, one of a series of reviews
of all foreign aid commitments prior to submission of the budget.*
Q. That's all of it?
A. That's all I have.
Q. Is Santa Clara in or out?
A. You'll know that when we release the budget.
Q. Why didn't the ambassador come out this way?
A. Probably because he had nothing to tell you.
Q. Not even hello?

Sam Hood had once held Haas's position in the White House,
but that was four presidents ago. Then, there was no dictum
against staff fraternization with the correspondents. Hood drank with
them and won their money playing stud poker, and they held a stag
dinner for him at the National Press Club when he left for a desk
in the State Department.

After the briefing, the older hands wrote the only story they
could. In Ciudad Alarcon, President Jorge Luchengo's information
officer woke him from a restless siesta to show him the lead that
had come over the AP wire a minute earlier: "The South American
republic of Santa Clara apparently will be the first victim of administration slashes in foreign aid. The secret nature of Ambassador
Samuel V. Hood's conference with the President today left little
doubt that . . ."

Luchengo read no further.

THE AMBASSADOR spent the night in Guatemala City, the end of the jet run, and caught the only shuttle flight to Ciudad Alarcon the next morning. From the air, the terrain of the Republic of Santa Clara was a diorama of its history. It was a downhill country. Its rivers, riches and revolutions all ran from the mountains to the sea.

To the north were the Andes, an insurmountable barrier to the rain clouds that swept up from the Pacific in spring, fall and winter, releasing their torrents to flood back to the sea through the dry arroyos of summer.

In the lower reaches of the mountains was the copper mining settlement of San Quentin, whose output was Santa Clara's one source of wealth, and it, too, made its way down to the sea on a rail line to the port of Ariella. And because life was poor and hazardous for the miners of San Quentin, its deep pits were the crucible of revolution, whose violence swept south into the foothills and the ancient citadel of their oppression—the capital city of Ciudad Alarcon.

In his Maserati, hidden in the shadows of the white stucco terminal, Johnny Partridge was waiting, as he had every morning for two years. He knew his man would come eventually—probably in the guise of a sportsman with rod or gun cases to try his luck with the wild boar in the arroyos or the black marlin off Ariella. And when he came, Partridge would know him.

He saw the ageless Electra stagger through the hot thermal turbulence above the foothills and plummet toward the landing strip. The pilot hit the brakes and cut the engines the instant the wheels were on the runway. Ten shrieking seconds later, the plane shook to a stop a hundred feet short of a deep barranca. It had been a routine landing and a routine vigil for Partridge. Hood was the only passenger.

From the balcony of the presidential palace, President Jorge Luchengo saw the ambassador's car swing into the embassy court-yard across the plaza. He went back to his desk and rang for his secretary. "When Mr. Hood calls for an appointment, tell him four o'clock."

The plaza of Ciudad Alarcon held all of Santa Clara's history a patriot would want to remember. In its center was the statue of Guillermo Perez—*El Libertador*. On a humid Tuesday morning in 1898, Perez had led a small band of miners down from San Quentin to attack the even smaller garrison of Spanish troops guarding the palace of the viceroy.

The precise oppression that led to the revolution after two cen-turies of Spanish domination is lost in time. The school children of Santa Clara were taught that Perez was a student of the American Revolution—and his first official act was to rename one of the major thoroughfares leading into the plaza the Calle de George Washington. But irreverent historians in the barrios of San Quentin credit their liberation to a more pragmatic cause—government en-forcement of a church ban on Sunday cockfighting, the miners' one day off. But whatever the provocation, casualties were light. A soldier died with a miner's pickax in his head, trying to reach a saber next to his bunk, and an insurrectionist fell from the roof of the palace raising the flag of the new republic.

It was all over by eleven o'clock mass and by that night the viceroy and his guards were aboard a Spanish freighter waiting at Ariella for its cargo of copper. At first there were angry mutterings from Madrid and, after five days of fiesta, Perez took the precaution of mining the railroad bridges and the docks at Ariella against the possibility of an expeditionary force from other Spanish territories in the hemisphere. It never came. Three weeks to the day after the Santa Claran revolution the battleship *Maine* was sunk at Havana and in the war to come Santa Clara was forgotten.

Since Perez, Santa Clara had not been a nation of heroes. Even he was shot in his bed in the eighth month of his presidency by his brother-in-law, the colonel in charge of the palace guard. In the years since, Santa Clara had known thirty-seven governments. But the statue of *El Libertador* still stood in the plaza—the bare peon's foot on the throat of the tyrant, the massive arm thrusting the flag of the First Republic skyward from the haft of a miner's pickax.

Hood's doctorate at Harvard was in international law. A Fulbright scholarship took him to Paris for a year where he met and married the daughter of the first counselor of the American embassy. It was the one impetuous act of his life and the marriage did not survive even the first year of their return to the States and the depressing contrast between the French capital and Champaign-Urbana, where he had taken an associate professorship at the University of Illinois. He left the post after only a year to accept a Guggenheim grant to edit the public papers and letters of Joseph P. Kennedy, former ambassador to the Court of St. James. On his second visit to Hyannis Port, he met the ambassador's oldest son— President-elect John F. Kennedy—and they found more in common than their love of sailing.

Hood was then twenty-five. Now, the photographs on his office wall—all in identical thin black frames with white matting—were the record of the intervening sixteen years. There was the mass oath-taking of the President's staff the morning after the inauguration. Hood was in the back row and the camera had caught him blinking. Next to it on the coarse adobe wall was his first presidential commission: "REPOSING special trust in your Integrity, Prudence, and Ability, I do appoint you Special Counsel to the President, DONE at the City of Washington this twenty-first day of January, in the year of our Lord One Thousand Nine Hundred and Sixty-One, and of the Independence of the United States of America the one hundred and eighty-fifth." Earlier, the press had found only one fact of interest in his appointment—that he was the youngest member of the President's staff.

Hood was in the background, too, in most of the later photographs: with Kennedy at Caracas, Bogotá, Mexico City . . . with Johnson at El Paso, Honolulu, Camranh Bay. Then, after his transfer to

State and career service rank, with Harriman in Paris . . . with Nixon at London, Midway and Bucharest. The photographers had continued to send him prints, but he had given up framing them long before his assignment to Santa Clara. There had been times when he thought of taking them all down, except for the first White House commission and perhaps one or two others. But they were still on the wall—the biography of a man behind the man.

There was little else to ornament the austere white walls except the gift of an elephant tusk from John Kenneth Galbraith, onetime ambassador to India, an Andrew Wyeth original and prints of works by Paul Klee and Pablo O'Higgins.

Hood's office in the embassy was on the third floor and its windows gave on the plaza—an exact replica of thousands of other city squares in Latin America. There was the rusting wrought-iron bandstand in the center; the ornate fountain which had been dry for years; a symmetrical pattern of gravel walkways dividing sere patches of dead grass and a scattering of dusty palms, and iron benches which were the domain of the city's patriarchs in the sunlit hours and of young lovers at night. But if the plaza was succumbing to neglect and the rigors of weather, the American embassy was a model of affluence and immaculateness, from the dress uniforms of the Marine guards at the gate to the pristine white of its Alhambran façade, over which flew an American flag of heroic size.

Hood spent only half an hour on the letter to President Luchengo: "On instructions of my government, I must inform you that the present annual credit to the Republic of Santa Clara will not be continued beyond the current fiscal year. I can assure you that my government has come to this decision reluctantly and after long and intensive studies of its own most urgent priorities. . . ." There was the obligatory paragraph summarizing "my government's long history of assistance to Santa Clara," the sum of direct loans to present and past regimes still unpaid, and the pro forma assurance that "its present decision in no way diminishes my government's treaty obligations to the Republic of Santa Clara with respect to mutual defense and hemispheric progress. . . ." And, finally, "the willingness of my government to review its present decision if future developments may warrant."

The three-story palace, built two centuries earlier for the Spanish viceroy, gave the impression from the street of both solidity and elegance. The stone walls, three feet thick to resist the searing summer heat, were given an annual coat of whitewash to repair the ravages of age and rain. Filigreed balconies ran the length of its two upper stories, and faintly discernible above the main entry were the bas-relief images of the Spanish royal family whose largesse had built this monument to colonialism.

But the first step inside brought one face to face with the fading opulence of the palace. Dominating the foyer was a towering, once white marble fountain, now a blotch of greens and reds from accumulations of algae and rust. The circular lobby was oppressively humid from the warm spray of the fountain and the dank emanations of rubber plants. Murals circling the walls were peeling and their original vivid colors were now faint pastels. The humidity had also taken its toll of three peacocks, wandering limply over the blue and white tile floor.

Hood made his way across the foyer to the deeply worn marble staircase leading to the President's office on the second floor. Foreign Minister Arturo Lara, tense, sparrowlike and in his late forties, was waiting at the head of the stairs.

"The President asks that you wait, Mr. Hood. You would, perhaps, join me in my office?"

"A pleasure." It was a game of mock courtesy they had been playing for all of Hood's three years in Ciudad Alarcon.

Lara's office, three doors down the broad corridor from the President's, was a reflection of his own vanity. On one wall was a huge oil portrait of himself in the pose of a conquistador. Behind his desk was a rank of flagstaffs bearing the ensigns of every government maintaining diplomatic relations with Santa Clara.

Lara shoved a box of cigars across his desk. "A Havana, Mr. Hood?" The little smile. Hood declined. "You have a letter from your government, Mr. Hood?"

"I do."

"May I know what it contains?"

"I'm sorry, Mr. Lara, but I am to deliver it personally to President Luchengo."

The little sigh. "Mr. Hood."

"Mr. Lara."

"We return once more to the question of protocol. Your first relationship is with this ministry. You cannot continue—"

"And once more, Mr. Lara, the letter is for delivery, by hand, to President Luchengo."

"It is over your signature, Mr. Hood?"

"It is."

"Then it was your decision, again, to ignore this ministry. I must insist—"

The buzzer linking Lara's office to Luchengo's broke into his reprimand. "The President will see you now, Mr. Hood. As for our own discussion—"

"We must continue it by all means, Mr. Lara."

Luchengo met the ambassador at the door. He was as tall as Hood and, at sixty-six, still held himself as rigidly as the younger man. There was no gray in his wiry black hair and no creases in the broad, flat planes of his Indian face. The only evidences of the infusion of Spanish blood into his heredity were his gray eyes and long spatulate fingers. They sat facing each other across Luchengo's desk.

"You have a message for me, Mr. Hood?"

The ambassador gave him the letter and let his eyes sweep the office as Luchengo read and reread it slowly, his face revealing nothing. The desk was barren except for a telephone, an intercom console, a pen stand and a square of clear plastic containing a fragment of green stone. It was almost pure copper—a relic of his first major find in the Andes. On the wall to Hood's right was a photograph of Luchengo's graduating class at Colorado A & M (Summer, 1933) and next to it a yellowing photograph of Franklin D. Roosevelt. On the opposite wall were the fading remnants of the first flag of the Santa Claran Republic and, strangely, the official state photograph of Luchengo's predecessor, Luis Novarese.

Luchengo finally laid the letter on his desk. "A scotch and soda, Mr. Hood?"

"I would like one."

Luchengo rang for the drinks. "Your letter presents me with difficult choices. Is there no possibility of changing this decision?"

"I think not."

Luchengo rose from his desk to take the drinks from the Indian girl, uncomfortable in her crisp white smock. *"Salud,* Mr. Hood." He took his own drink to the window opening on the plaza. He had never been at ease behind his desk. It was no place to work. A man could leave a draftsman's table and go to the door of the construction shed and watch the bold lines on the blueprint take form in steel and concrete. Here nothing took form. He had agreed to come down from the mountains and sit behind this desk only because there was no one else.

Luchengo lit his pipe with slow deliberateness. "Do you agree with this letter you have written, Mr. Hood?"

"I do not and I have made my objections known."

"But your government no longer listens to you?"

Hood let it pass. "My government, as you are aware, faces difficult choices of its own. If this decision presents you with a financial crisis, my own President faces a national debt at its absolute constitutional limit. If you are facing Jiminez, we are facing Communist China."

Luchengo came back to his chair. "You are not being candid with me, Mr. Hood. You send us a hundred million dollars a year. That you can no longer afford. But you can afford thirty times that amount every year to maintain—what shall we call it?—your American embassy on the moon?"

Hood took a long sip of his drink.

"No, Mr. Hood, your own embassy *here* is more important. Have you told your President there are no children with empty bellies on the moon and no Communists, either?"

It was, at least, an opening. "My letter, Mr. President, clearly reaffirms my government's mutual defense commitments. If Jiminez—"

"Jiminez! Jiminez is nothing! He exists because certain conditions exist in this country—conditions your government has the resources to help me change. And I am not speaking of tanks or bombers, Mr. Hood."

There was a rebuttal to that. "I can tell you, sir, that, if it were not for Jiminez, I question seriously that our assistance to your regime would have continued even this long."

Luchengo laid his pipe on the desk. "And Jiminez no longer concerns your President?"

"Our CIA reports from Bolivia on his present strength—"

"Your CIA reports, for once, are correct, Mr. Hood. But *why* are they correct? Why do his *compañeros* desert Jiminez? I will shock you, Mr. Hood. But if I had been born a peon; if I had gone into the mines when I was ten and had no juices left for my wife when I was thirty; if I had no hope that nothing, *nothing* would ever change—I would be up there in the mountains with Jiminez, Mr. Hood. Yes!"

His anger left him. "I know why they go to him, and I know why they come back—because I do not waste your dollars chasing chickens in the hills, as Novarese did. I spend them on the chickens I already have. They leave Jiminez because they come down to their women's beds when they can no longer stay away. And they find a little *carne* in the pot with the *frijoles*. They find that a day's work in the mines is now only twelve hours. And they find that there is a doctor in the barrio."

He went back to the window. The plaza was in deep shadow but the distant crests of the Andes were still gleaming with light. "And do you know what they do in the morning, Mr. Hood? They go over to the mines and they tell the foreman they have been in Ariella working on the docks or in the fish sheds. He smiles and puts them back to work—and I have another chicken. You have an English word for that, Mr. Hood."

"Amnesty?"

"Amnesty. It is not a good word in America, is it?"

"No, I am afraid it's not."

"Then perhaps I have been wrong. Should I have gone hunting, Mr. Hood? If I had, would your war correspondents still be here, as they were with Novarese, counting the dead? Would you have had to write this letter, Mr. Hood, if I had an army in the Andes instead of a doctor in the barrios?"

The ambassador had no answer.

"Tomorrow I will have to consult with Han Li-wong."

"I regret that, Mr. President."

"And I regret it too. Good night, Mr. Hood."

"Good night, sir."

At the door, Luchengo laid a hand on the ambassador's arm. "It is a very foolish world, my friend."

"It is that."

Now even the highest peaks were in darkness and Hood found it suddenly cold in the plaza.

T WO YEARS EARLIER, the decision of Jorge Luchengo to trade with the People's Republic of China had brought angry protests from administration critics in Washington and demands for cessation of American assistance. Cartoonist Paul Conrad of the Los Angeles *Times* took note of the controversy with a drawing of a slavering Chinese dragon licking a lollipop. And the symbol he chose for Santa Clara was appropriate—a circumstance for which the regime of 1928 could be held entirely accountable.

In that year Santa Clara fought its first and only external war. A priest had been slain in a worker uprising in Escalante, the state adjoining Santa Clara to the west. Refugees reaching Ciudad Alarcon told of rioting in the streets and the imminent collapse of the government. To the military junta then governing Santa Clara, the opportunity for conquest was clear. It was just as clear five days later that the government and army of Escalante were still firmly in control. What was left of the Santa Claran invasion force fell back to its borders in frantic retreat.

The Treaty of Ariella was signed four months later. It took from Santa Clara all possible invasion approaches to Escalante—almost the entire coastal slope leading to the sea. The capital's only remaining link with its principal seaport, Ariella, was a corridor twenty miles wide. But the rigid lines of the corridor were indifferent to the meandering course of Santa Clara's lifelines—the railroad and the parallel road running from the mines at San Quentin, through Ciudad Alarcon, to the docks at Ariella. Santa Clara was forced to reroute them at points where they intruded on the new boundaries of Escalante. A direct loan from the Hoover administration paid for most of the reconstruction and set in motion the republic's perpetual dependence on the American dollar.

The cartographers dutifully redrew its boundaries—the roughly circular mountain and upland regions and the narrow stem running eighty miles to the sea . . . the Lollipop Republic.

Han Li-wong, Communist China's one representative in Santa Clara, did not have ambassadorial or even consular rank. Luchengo had been firm with Peking that he would barter only for copper, not diplomatic recognition, and Han had to settle for the title of trade envoy and for the indignity of a legation three blocks from the plaza and directly across a narrow street from the city's raucous central market.

His credentials, however, were more formidable than his title of trade envoy. He had been a ranking member of Peking's first trade mission to Cuba. He was in Hanoi, intermittently, until the armistice, and later in Paris, Belgrade, Cairo and the capitals of emerging African states. Wherever trade was a weapon or a provocation in Peking's mounting conflict with Washington and Moscow, the effervescent Mr. Han was on the scene. But his milieu was the market place, not the chancellery. In his long career he had never met a chief of state or even a prime minister until his assignment to Santa Clara. Negotiations with them were left to other, more illustrious representatives of Peking. And Han, privately, held a low opinion of their competence. Unlike himself, most of them were strangers to the Western world—awkward, suspicious proletarians in the ambient salons of diplomacy. Han could forgive them their tactlessness and bluster. Their instructions were not to negotiate but to propagandize, threaten and subvert. What he could not forgive them was their failure to convince Peking of the vulnerability of China's position, and to recognize, as he did, the many opportunities for at least a temporary rapproachement with its antagonists. Han, a doctrinaire Communist, was certain that China would ultimately triumph. But he was also certain that victory—hopefully without war—could not come until China had a nuclear capacity at least approaching that of the two superpowers. Thus the most urgent goal of Chinese diplomacy was to buy the time Peking must have to create that arsenal. If China's diplomats were not blind to the opportunities for prolonging the ultimate confrontation, Han felt, they were patently unsuccessful in moving Peking toward that more opportunistic policy.

Han, like all Chinese of his rank, was never without his little red-bound copy of *Mao's Thought*—as omnipresent a part of his traveling kit as his passport. But he was also a collector of his own aphorisms and one of them was the summation of his long disenchantment with Peking's foreign missions: "The more difficult role of the diplomat is not to reason with foreign governments but with his own." Averell Harriman was his concept of a great diplomat.

Han was sent to Santa Clara because copper, with zinc, is essential to the smelting of brass and because brass is essential to the manufacture of shell casings. He had not been eager to accept another trade mission, and certainly not to a nation as unimportant as Santa Clara, until he was told that he would have additional responsibilities. He would maintain direct, if covert, liaison with the insurrectionist Jiminez and would have full authority to explore broader relations with the Luchengo government. It was this precise contradiction in China's involvement with Santa Clara that Han found most appealing—the opportunity to test his own faith in historical inevitability against the precipitous policy of which Jiminez was the symbol. That and the fact that he now had the tacit rank, if not the portfolio, of a diplomat. He took with him

to Santa Clara a small technical staff, his cook, his shell collection
and his tennis racket.

Han saw President Luchengo the morning after Ambassador Hood's
call, and his vintage Cadillac was waiting for him in the street,
the ridiculous red pennants drooping from their staffs on the front
fenders, when he came down the steps of the palace. His driver
held the door open and they left in a swirl of exhaust fumes on
the one-minute ceremonial drive to his quarters. His session with
Luchengo had not been entirely satisfactory, but his cable to Peking
would be read with more than passing interest.

Luchengo had told Han he was finally willing to review the
maximum tonnage clause of the trade agreement. But that would
require an acceleration of production, for which new equipment
must be bought. To finance it, a payment in advance against the
next quarter's shipments would be necessary.

Han was dubious. He told Luchengo he could recall no precedent
for such an arrangement. His own government—and Han was
apologetic for its pragmatism—would be justified in regarding it as
a request for a direct loan. And that, of course, was without
precedent in the absence of diplomatic recognition or, at least, discussions toward that end.

Luchengo disagreed. There was no possibility of misinterpretation
if Han's cable to his government was specific, and he would
expect it to be. He would also expect the earliest possible response
to his proposal.

On his return to his quarters, Han took a split-leaf philodendron
from his office and put it on the balcony facing the market. Ten
minutes later the son of the dairy merchant brought two liters of
milk to the kitchen door and left with a message summoning Francisco Jiminez to Ciudad Alarcon.

One of the annoyances of Han's tenure in Santa Clara was
the requirement that his own recommendations to Peking must
contain the reaction, if not the endorsement, of Jiminez. And he
had long since lost patience with the revolutionary, whose strategy
was in direct conflict with his own.

Jiminez' reaction to Han went beyond impatience. His early

expectation that a Chinese legation in Ciudad Alarcon would lead to an increase in arms shipments had been only partially met. And he was certain that Han's amiable machinations at the palace were only prolonging his own stay in the Andes. The tone of his relations with Han had become increasingly peremptory and were the subject of another of the Chinese's aphorisms: "Every Don Quixote must have his Sancho Panza. But when Sancho Panza starts to think he is Don Quixote, the crusade is lost."

But if Han thought of him as gauche and inept, Jiminez had a far higher opinion of himself and of his destiny. He had been born in San Quentin, the son of a miner, and had gone into the shafts himself at the age of eleven. At thirteen he had been buried for three days in a cave-in, and was finally taken out of the shaft with the bones of his left leg in splinters.

There was no hospital in San Quentin then and his mother had to straighten and splint the leg. He came out of it a cripple and with a hatred of the oppressors that took him in his late teens to Bolivia to join the tin miners in their strikes against the government, and then, because of his courage under fire and his revolutionary zeal, to Havana in the first days of Castro's rule. There he became a protégé of Che Guevara's and eventually went back to Bolivia with him. He was one of a handful still with Che in the last, desperate days of hunger and flight before Guevara died in ambush. Jiminez found his way back alone across the Andes to San Quentin.

Now in his mid-forties, he had the appearance of a man ten years older. But with his limp, the deep etchings of suffering in his face and his association with Castro and Guevara, he was the idol and leader of the young miners at San Quentin. He had known their poverty and danger. He had been to places where the peons had brought tyrants to their knees—and he had the knowledge and courage to lead them to their own freedom.

In the barrios of San Quentin, he taught them Marxism and guerrilla tactics and, through old friends now in high position in La Paz, a thin stream of weapons and ammunition came across the Andes. The stream had swollen to include more and heavier weapons since the Chinese had come to Santa Clara to supply him from the sea, and the firebrands were quick to accept Jiminez' assurance that the time was approaching to strike their own blow. They left with him for the mountains to begin as Castro had begun in the Sierra Maestras a generation earlier.

Late in the afternoon the son of the dairyman was back at the kitchen door to report that Jiminez was waiting, and Han left for the rendezvous. He had always found the market a distasteful place. The crowds of strident women haggling with merchants; headless chickens hanging over pans that caught the dripping blood; the stench of turning vegetables; the swarms of flies crawling over the meats in open displays—all were affronts to his senses. He hurried through the teeming aisles to the rear of the market, then up a flight of stairs to a musty hallway, where two of Jiminez' guerrillas, barefoot and wearing the coarse white cotton pants and shirts of the upland peasants, were standing guard before the door of a storeroom. They let him enter with surly nods.

Jiminez, also in the garb of a peon, was on his back on a stack of rice sacks, trying to recover the strength lost on the long burro ride south on clandestine trails bordering the highway. Han might have thought he was asleep except for the thin spiral of smoke from his cigar.

Still staring upward, Jiminez finally spoke. "I am here. What do you want?"

Han, five paces away, did not come closer. "I met with Luchengo this morning."

The revolutionary sat up slowly, grimacing as he swung the lame leg to the floor with both hands holding it at the knee. "And what did you learn?" Jiminez was only slightly taller than the squat Han, but unlike the rotund Chinese, there was not a spare ounce of flesh on his almost skeletal frame. His face was thin, dark and brooding and his hair prematurely gray. Han had never seen him smile.

"That the Americans will give Luchengo no more money."

Jiminez was suspicious. "Why would he tell you that?"

"He didn't. But he is now willing to sell more copper to my government. Would he do that if he still had the American dollars? No, Jiminez, the government is desperate. Our time has come."

Jiminez rose unsteadily to his feet. "To do what?"

"To increase his dependence on us, of course. To place him in our debt to the point where he must grant more and more concessions to us."

"*Us?* What have you to do with me—or me with you? Every peso you give Luchengo keeps me away from Ciudad Alarcon that much longer."

Han was patient. "You will never enter Ciudad Alarcon without the arms we give you."

"*Sí, sí!* You give me guns with one hand and pay Luchengo's army with the other. It is you, Han, who betrays me."

"I do what my government tells me."

"No, you are a fat dog. Does your government know you lick the fingers of Luchengo and of your *gran amigo*—the *yanqui* ambassador?" He took a threatening step toward Han, but his leg almost gave way and he fell back against the rice sacks.

Han had long since become immune to Jiminez' tirades. "One of the instructions my government has given me is to ask your advice on matters affecting—how shall I say it?—our *mutual* interests."

"My answer is no. My answer is that the revolution will fail if you support my enemy."

"Then I will include your answer in my report to Peking."

"But you will urge Peking to send Luchengo more pesos?"

"Obviously."

Jiminez again lay down on the sacks, dragging the leg after him. "Do what you will but it will come to nothing. Soon, very soon, there will be no copper at all from San Quentin. You force me to it."

"I would advise you very strongly against—"

"Go!"

The guards heard the shout and threw open the door. Han glanced warily from them to the prostrate figure of their leader, and left. Back in his office, he wrote a cable strongly recommending acceptance of Luchengo's proposal, adding a single sentence to the effect that Jiminez was against it.

Han then rang up Ambassador Hood to confirm their weekly tennis match.

Foreign Minister Arturo Lara's duties at the palace were not demanding and he had frequent opportunities to ride in the afternoon —most often in the upland forest of pine and cypress above Casa Castillo, the ranch home of the widow Constanzia Novarese. That they often met along one of the woodcutters' trails was not an accident.

Lara felt neither guilt nor disloyalty in his role as an informer. If Luchengo had forgotten his debt to the Castillo family, Lara had not. His education, his rise in the civil service, his present position—all came from the patronage of the Castillos. That he could rise no further until there was a change of regimes in Santa Clara did not compel Lara to question his own motives. A higher rank would merely enable him to serve the last of the Castillos more effectively.

A mile below, he saw Constanzia Novarese spur her horse over the stone wall separating the pastures of Casa Castillo from the savannah of the foothills. She kept the palomino stallion at full gallop until they were lost from sight in the first growths of timber. Lara would have to tell her once more that she rode too recklessly. But not today. He would do nothing to diminish the news he brought from the palace.

She dismounted a short distance down the path to water the palomino at a shallow brook, and walked slowly toward Lara— severe and imposing in the black Spanish riding habit.

"I bring you the best of news, señora."

"You always bring me the best of news, Lara, but nothing changes."

Lara was not very useful to her. There were no secrets at the palace and the information he brought her was always available from her cook, who had heard it from a typist in the market, or her stableman, who had heard it from a junior clerk in a cantina. She kept her occasional rendezvous with Lara only to confirm what she already knew or would learn in a day or two, and most of it was unimportant.

"There will be no more dollars from the Americans."

"How do you know this?"

"Mr. Hood told our great leader yesterday. And the American news services confirm it, señora. It is true."

All of her world could be seen from the granite ledge—the road north to San Quentin, Casa Castillo and beyond it to the south the capital, its low skyline luminous in the afternoon light.

"What will happen next, Lara?"

"It is already happening. Luchengo is begging the Chinese for money."

"And will they give it to him?"

"Perhaps. But the end is coming, señora, believe me."

She was no longer brusque with him. "It is good news, Lara. Thank you."

Señora Novarese had buried her husband where he fell, next to the wall in the patio of Casa Castillo. There was a small shrine to his patron saint over the grave, but no other marker except the pockmarks of the bullets in the wall. She had been born to a tradition of violence and vengeance: the workers' uprisings at the Castillo mines and her family's savage reprisals; the recurring military coups, many of them set in motion from Casa Castillo to install more sympathetic regimes; the armies advancing and retreating up the long road in front of her home. And there was always a victor, the grinning savior of the republic who came to the *casa* to pay his respects to Don Castillo. Most of them were fools, alternately posturing and deferring in the presence of her father, the *bandoleras* still slung over their shoulders.

But not Colonel Novarese. He came not to defer but to demand that the don comply with the goals of the new regime the colonel would lead. And that same year the don also had to accede, but more willingly, to his daughter's decision to marry the colonel. It would, after all, be useful to have a Castillo in the palace to protect his interests, which, of course, were also Santa Clara's interests. But he died the fourth year of their marriage without forgiving his daughter for the changes that had come. Novarese's decision to resign his army commission to hold an election for the office he already occupied was insane. It was even more insane to win it by promising land and tax reform. The latter cost Don Castillo a hundred thousand pesos the first year, and his daughter would not enter Casa Castillo again until the morning after his death. She buried him in the family chapel. She buried her husband a year later in the open courtyard where the grave, the shrine and the bullet scars would not let her forget.

Eventually he, too, would rest in the chapel, but not while the assassin Luchengo was still alive.

Señora Novarese spent her days in patient waiting. In the mornings she taught the children of servants at Casa Castillo to read and write in an adobe hut next to the stables. Her father had built the school for her while she was still in her teens—his one concession to his daughter's restlessness. The staff was small now and there weren't many children left, but she kept it going.

In the evenings she saw Ambassador Hood occasionally. He was an old acquaintance from her husband's days in the Organization of American States, her one link with the world beyond Santa Clara—a world she and Novarese had found challenging and compatible. It was unfortunate that Hood was no longer actively sympathetic to her own position, but that, she was certain, could and would change.

She saw much more of Johnny Partridge. She knew what he was and it did not concern her. They had much in common. In their own ways, they were both exiles and they were both fatalists. But most important, he was not a part of all that had taken place. He was blameless—innocent.

T HE POOR, a majority among Ciudad Alarcon's one hundred thousand inhabitants, had no choice but to look up to the rich. From their barrio in the southern section of the city the terrain rose gradually in a series of surface—and social—levels toward the northern limits.

In the slums, where the narrow dirt streets were either dusty or muddy, depending on the season, there was no structure more than one story high, and the shacks gave no protection against either the summer heat or the long, chilling season of rain. Except for vegetable gardens, thriving from night soil, there was little flora. The trees had long since been cut down to fuel the cast-iron outdoor cooking pots.

The asphalt paving began at the northern reaches of the barrio. Here were run-down stores and cantinas, the slightly more habitable homes of their lower-middle-class *propietarios,* a small, shadeless plaza and a soccer field. Still farther north, the homes, the stores and their clientele took on a progressively more respectable appearance as the streets rose toward *el centro*—the downtown section of government buildings, embassies and consulates, the most exclusive shops and the central plaza.

The Santa Clarans and foreigners who spent their days behind desks and cash registers in *el centro* spent their nights on what the poor spoke of as *los pocos collados*—the little hills looking down on Ciudad Alarcon from the north. At even the lowest level of the hills, the *casas* were two stories, with soaring palms and bougainvillaea flaming from the adobe walls guarding their courtyards.

Still higher were the homes of the very wealthy and of the diplomatic corps from the more affluent nations with embassies or consulates in Santa Clara. Ambassador Hood's residence, on a two-acre site behind high walls and wrought-iron gates, was the most impressive. Three stories in height with gleaming white stucco walls and a red tile roof, it was a landmark in the city and a reminder to those below that *los Estados Unidos* was the richest country in the world.

Hood found his residence, with its vast lawns, olympic-size swimming pool, tennis court and staff of twenty gardeners, cooks and housekeepers, a continuing embarrassment. But he knew that it would be a waste of time to propose to his superiors in the State Department that a bachelor ambassador could make do with a smaller villa on one of the lower streets where his subordinates and their families dwelt. Wherever assignments or travel to foreign capitals had taken him in his years in the State Department, the American embassy and the ambassador's residence were—*had* to be —the most opulent.

Han Li-wong, as always, was punctual for his ritual Saturday morning tennis match at Hood's residence—a contest that was both incongruous and inconclusive. Hood had never lost the first set to Han and never won the second, and neither had the energy or the inclination for a third. They were an unlikely pairing: Hood tall and lithe, and Han a head shorter and fifty pounds heavier.

The deep etchings in his face and his graying hair were testaments to Hood's long years of conflict and responsibility, but Han's bland countenance was ageless. He could have been forty or sixty.

This morning, as always, Hood took the first set handily, following his powerful serve to the net and putting Han's return away easily while the Chinese stood smiling haplessly in the backcourt. But a tiring Hood was no match for Han's precise volleys and passing shots in the second set, and they left the court for a shower and lunch.

Han had once tried to draw an analogy between their games and their ideologies. It was a case, he said, of imperialist aggression versus historical inevitability. "You Americans try to cover the whole court. You dash here and there scoring quick points and you exhaust yourselves. The second set must always go to us. We watch and wait and conserve our strength. Then, when you tire, we place our shots very, very carefully."

Hood could not agree. "The more relevant question, Mr. Han, is who will win the third set and match."

On this Saturday, over cold lobster and *salade Niçoise* in the patio, Hood came back to the analogy. There had been a thin edge to his cordiality all morning.

"Today, Mr. Han, I thought we might consider a deciding set after lunch."

Han had been hopeful that the ambassador would not overreact to events of the week, and it was distressing that he had. "But why today, my friend? It can wait a little longer."

"I thought you might sense a slight advantage." It was too abrupt.

"There is no advantage, Mr. Hood. Let us speak frankly. Yes, there have been overtures to my government—overtures that the government of Santa Clara has found necessary in light of—"

"I'm aware of the reasons, Mr. Han."

"But I will tell you that it is nothing that should create difficulties between your government and mine. Or between you and me." His smile was a rebuke.

"I would hope not. But you should know that I have given President Luchengo assurances that our mutual defense commitments are still very much in force. A miscalculation of our intentions would be most unwise."

Han was no longer smiling. "That is of no interest to me."

"But it would be of interest to Jiminez."

"Then I suggest you communicate your threats to him, Mr. Hood, not to me. I accept no responsibility for Jiminez."

"A little more salad, Mr. Han?"

"I think not."

It had not been one of their better mornings.

Even in Johnny Partridge's supercharged Maserati, the eighty-mile run to the sports fishing dock at Ariella took slightly more than two hours. The first fifty miles south of Ciudad Alarcon were a steep, winding descent through a millennia-old canyon cut by the Río Verde, whose headwaters were in the Andes. Thirty miles north of Ariella, the road cut through the last stretch of canyon, known as the Arroyo Seco, and onto a desert plain sloping toward the sea.

If the ancient river had left its deep, tortuous scar on the face of Santa Clara, the pattern of rainfall had left a more gradual but equally dramatic mark on the landscape. From the lush greenness of Ciudad Alarcon, vegetation became scarcer and hardier as the terrain fell off toward the sea. In place of the palms and tropical pines of the capital, the canyons in their final descent had only

scrub oak and coarse bunch grass, and there was no flora at all on
the desert plain except a scattering of yucca and cactus.

But the barren landscape south of the Arroyo Seco took nothing
away from Partridge's anticipation of the day. Constanzia Novarese's
moods were unpredictable. But today she was in high spirits, urging
him to greater speed through the mountain passes and taking the
wheel herself for the final dash to Ariella.

Without her telling him, Partridge knew the reason for her exu-
berance. It was now common knowledge that Luchengo had lost his
American stake. But the politics of Santa Clara were important to
Partridge only to the extent of their effect on the moods of Señora
Novarese. And today was promising.

Partridge was thirty-four and only slightly taller than the señora.
He was compactly built and had the quick, fluid movements of an
athlete. His jaw was square and his intensely dark brown eyes were
characteristic of his Sicilian ancestry. The one incongruity in his
appearance was his sandy blond hair—a throwback to a wandering
forebear from northern Italy.

Partridge's cruiser, the *Mañana,* was waiting alongside the dock,
with the crewman, José, at the stern to help them aboard. Partridge
had bought the boat originally because the sea might be his only
way out of Santa Clara if the time for flight came. But he found
himself spending more and more time aboard it, trolling for the
giant black marlin in deep water or diving for smaller game fish
in the coves. And, very often, Señora Novarese joined him.

Partridge hesitated before following her aboard. "I wonder if we'll
need José today?"

"You will if you're going after marlin, Johnny."

"Then let's not go after marlin. José, you have the day off."

He was an old man whose hair was still dark under the fraying
Dodger cap a fisherman had given him five years earlier. *"Gracias,
señor."* He cast off the lines and stood smiling on the dock as the
cruiser idled to the breakwater and then, with a powerful surge
from both engines, raced along the coast through a gentle ground
swell.

Except at Ariella, the twenty-mile coastline of Santa Clara was
an escarpment of rocky bluffs, broken only by narrow canyons

where streams, dry except in the rainy season, had cut their way to the sea. But at Punta Bunda, across the border of Escalante, there was a natural breakwater and a calm anchorage. Punta Bunda had been a minor shark fishing port until it was ceded to Escalante in the Treaty of Ariella. After the Santa Clarans left, the village had fallen into ruins except for a jetty extending into the bay.

Just outside the reef guarding the harbor, a rooster fish struck Partridge's troll and took off for blue water in a series of shimmering leaps. It was ten minutes before Partridge could bring it alongside on his light tackle. He gave the rod to Señora Novarese while he tried, vainly, to gaff the still struggling fish. Finally, in an explosion of spray, it broke free from the line. Partridge was wet to the skin.

"That's why we bring José along," said the señora, laughing.

"And this is why we leave him behind." Partridge tried to hold her in his arms.

"No, Johnny—please."

"Why not?" He took her by the shoulders.

"Because I don't know what I want." She tried to free herself.

"What—or who?"

It was an old quarrel. "It's not like that with Sam Hood. Why can't you believe that?"

"Because it was like that once, wasn't it?"

"If I tell you no, you won't believe me. If I tell you yes, it can never be like that with us, can it? If you want me to answer—"

"I don't want to know."

Her head was against his chest. "I try, Johnny, I try."

"And I try not to push it. But almost two years. We're a little ridiculous, you know."

"I'm ridiculous. I don't know why you—"

"Why I wait? I don't know either."

"Perhaps you shouldn't wait."

"No chance." His lips swept over the dark sheen of her hair. "No chance."

From the bluff overlooking Punta Bunda, Francisco Jiminez saw the cruiser drifting seaward in the backwash of the breakwater and, far to sea, a Chinese trawler waiting for nightfall to approach the cove. If the American and the Castillo woman did not leave soon, he would have to radio the trawler to delay its landfall. But moments later he saw the *Mañana* turn slowly and retrace its course back to Ariella. Then he led his work force and their pack burros down the rocky cliffside to the village. For more than an hour he sat alone at the head of the jetty, watching his guerrillas splash nude in the surf and, in the fading light, the glint of the setting sun on the superstructure of the approaching trawler.

Santa Clara had many advantages for a man for whom a contract was out and it had been out for Johnny Partridge for two years. The little box from Miami came every month with its greetings from The Brotherhood—a .45-caliber bullet. But whoever they sent would not find it easy. He must come either by air to the capital— and Partridge met the one daily flight—or by air or sea to Ariella. There he would have to pass through customs and the two hundred pesos a month Partridge paid the port city's only inspector to report on tourist arrivals was double his official salary.

Partridge and Ambassador Hood met only when Señora Novarese found it amusing to have them at the same dinner table.

But Hood had a full FBI report on Partridge, alias Giovanni Petracci. He was a member of the Cosa Nostra, but by blood, not choice. He was of the new and elite generation—the sons of capos who did not have to earn their spurs with a gun. In The Brotherhood's massive new complex of legitimate interests, it was necessary to develop a cadre of young Mafiosi who could manage their enterprises from a cover of respectability and social acceptance.

Little was known of Giovanni Petracci's activities except that they were entirely legal. He had been a director or member of the board of three California corporations involved in the construction of shopping plazas, condominiums and a chain of pizza parlors. He had no police record, except for speeding tickets. There were no charges pending against him and no grounds for extradition.

But much more was known of his father's activities. Rico Petracci had come up from the ranks as an enforcer for both Vito Genovese and Albert Anastasia. But he was not of their rank and kept out of the headlines. It was known that he left New York in the late 1950s and nothing more was heard of him for many years until Peter Maas, editor of *The Valachi Papers,* brought the story of the Cosa Nostra up to date in an exposé in *Look* magazine. He identified Petracci, who had changed his name to Partridge, as the capo in command of the Mafia's gambling interests in Las Vegas and Reno. The exposé led to his indictment and conviction for criminal conspiracy, and he was sent to the federal prison at Atlanta, where he died three years later. His widow went back to her native Sicily.

When the Maas exposé broke into print, Mr. and Mrs. Partridge were living in Beverly Hills. They were a quiet couple and their neighbors, themselves frequent visitors to Las Vegas, saw nothing unusual in Mr. Partridge's trips to Nevada. All they could tell the reporters was: "It's impossible to believe. They were such nice people."

Johnny Partridge's degree in business administration from UCLA, his membership at The Factory and his bachelor apartment at Malibu were no longer of much use to him. But he was still of use to the Cosa Nostra, and he was sent to Miami Beach and later to Honolulu to explore real estate investments—the efficient young executive, complete with attaché case and alias.

Partridge went along with the syndicate until his father died in Atlanta, forever immune from reprisals for the sins of his son. But then he withdrew six hundred and fifty thousand dollars from banks in five cities, got his passport at El Paso and caught a jet to Guatemala City.

When the first little box came from Miami, Partridge wrote an uncle, Salvador Petracci, in Cleveland, pleading that his only violation of the blood oath of The Brotherhood had been to leave it. He had taken nothing with him that was not his own.

The word came back that he would be given a hearing. He was to be at the International Hotel in Los Angeles a week later. He was. But when the summons came to appear in a third-floor suite, he took a bellman along to run interference and stood to one side at the door. At the first knock, the door was flung open and the bellman took the shotgun blast. Partridge was already out of range down the hallway before the assassin got off his second shot.

But Partridge had never entirely lost hope that he would return to the States—and with immunity. The old capos like his uncle were dying off and with them the Old World passion for vendetta. The coming leadership was of Partridge's generation—more cautious, more eager for respectability. Eventually they would grant him a hearing, if their elders would not. It was just a case of finding an angle—a proposition that only he could put together—and one they could not refuse.

Partridge had a comfortable suite in El Jacinto, the capital's one first-rate hotel. Early in his exile he had been impatient to leave Santa Clara. But on a rainy afternoon, while exploring the country north of Ciudad Alarcon, his Maserati blew a tire on the road fronting on Casa Castillo, and he met Constanzia Novarese for the first time. He was still anxious to leave Santa Clara—but not alone.

T HE PRESIDENT, as always, got up at six-thirty. He flung aside the heavy drapes in the bedroom on the second floor of the White House and glanced only briefly at the south lawn and, in the near distance, the Washington Monument, glistening in the first rays of the sun in a cloudless sky. Then he sat on the edge of the antique four-poster bed until the sudden brightness brought him to full wakefulness.

On a table within reach of the bed was a complex of telephones and intercom buttons—an electronic mistress that had driven most First Ladies in recent history to occupy an adjoining bedroom. Even in bed an American President can never be more than seconds away from communication with heads of other major governments or the remotest of America's military outposts.

There were three telephones on the table—all manned at the

other end twenty-four hours a day. The first, connected with the regular White House switchboard, was for routine non-security calls. The second was an open line to the White House Communications Agency in the basement of the West Wing. From it, he could speak around the world on lines secure from eavesdropping. The third was a direct two-way line to the headquarters of both the Strategic Air Force and the nation's missile command. If he ever had to use it, it would probably be his last word from the White House before he and other high-ranking government officials and their families were evacuated from Washington.

The third telephone had rung only once—during the administration of John F. Kennedy. He answered it with foreboding. "This is the President." The incredulous voice at the other end said, "I must have the wrong number. I'm trying to reach a French laundry." The mystery of how the call was able to penetrate the supersecret system was never solved, although a White House communications specialist spent more than ten years trying.

The President hit one of the intercom buttons and a minute later a waiter brought a tray of coffee and orange juice, a stack of newspapers and a hand-delivered letter that had come after the President went to bed. It was from National Party Chairman Jim Mallory, urging the President to delay the announcement that he would seek his party's nomination for a second term. The President read it angrily, threw it aside, then glanced at the front pages of the New York *Times,* the Washington *Post* and the Baltimore *Sun.* All three gave prominent play to his address the night before in Philadelphia to the convention of the National Association of Manufacturers. He had cast himself in the role of the budget-cutter—always a ritual performance before the NAM. He had told his audience that there were limitations to what he could accomplish, that seventy per cent of the federal budget was written into law and was untouchable— for example, Social Security, Medicare, veterans' benefits and debt retirement. But the remaining thirty per cent, over which he did have control, had been cut to the marrow. He had taken a long, hard look at foreign aid—particularly to those countries in Latin America and elsewhere that were unwilling to help themselves. And the new budget told such countries loud and clear that there was a limit to America's generosity and patience. That brought the biggest applause of the night.

The President turned next to the editorial pages of the three newspapers. This morning, for a change, there were no cartoons, editorials or columns attacking the administration. He was as sensitive to such criticism as an actor to bad reviews. The only aggravation this morning was the letter from Mallory. The President pressed another button on the intercom and told the White House garage to send a car to Georgetown to pick up the national chairman.

Mallory's private telephone rang a minute later, waking him from a sound sleep. He looked at the bedside clock—six forty-five. It had to be the President. No member of his staff would wake him at such an hour.

"Jim, there's a car on the way over there for you. I'll expect you here in half an hour."

"It's that important?"

"It is."

The President hung up, then buzzed the Secret Service to inform them Mallory was on his way and had clearance to come directly to his suite. The national chairman shaved with a cordless electric razor on the ten-minute ride to the White House and tried to organize his defenses against the harangue he knew was coming.

The preferential primaries across the nation were now over and the President's position was precarious. His name had been on the ballot, but against his wishes, in only two states—Oregon and Nebraska, which automatically include all probable aspirants on the ballot except those who are willing to declare in writing that they are not and will not become candidates. That, of course, the President could not do. Despite a heavy vote in his own party because of concurrent primaries for the House of Representatives and the Senate, thirty-five per cent of the voters withheld their votes from the President. There was unanimity among national commentators that Oregon and Nebraska were indicators either of indifference or of outright disaffection within his own party.

The California primary, a week later, was an even graver portent. There, a youthful faction in his party had qualified its own slate of electors, pledged to support a liberal Negro senator from New York.

The President, unwilling to lose the state's electoral votes by default, had no choice but to ask the governor of California to form a favorite son delegation in opposition. It was obvious to the voters, of course, that the second delegation was a front—that the governor would withdraw after the first convention ballot and support the President.

But there was little interest in the contest. Only sixty-one per cent of the voters cast ballots for the opposing delegations, and the governor's slate won by an embarrassing ratio of only three to two.

But the President had always been lucky in politics and the long series of hard-fought primaries matching contenders in the opposite party had produced a front runner against whom he would have the best chance in November. Harlan Grant, the senior senator from Illinois, had won all of the primaries from Nevada to New York, except in those states where he chose not to oppose a native son. Grant was handsome and articulate, perfectly cast for the politics of the television era in which charisma has become a more significant qualification for the nation's highest office than intellect, commitment or capacity for leadership.

But Grant was also a demagogue, thrust into national prominence by his exhortations against the gains won by black America, against the dangers of the new détente with the Soviet Union and against the President's refusal to crush with force the new Communist regime in Bolivia. He was, contradictorily, an isolationist in domestic policy ("We are two Americas—black and white—and we must accept it") and an adventurist in foreign policy ("Our own survival demands that we destroy the nuclear capability of Communist China before it can destroy us").

Nor had Grant been above exploiting the divisions and hatreds in American life in the wake of the unsatisfactory conclusion, four years earlier, of the war in Southeast Asia.

Jim Mallory knew that primaries, for many millions of voters, are little more than an opportunity to express their prejudices and fears, their resentment of the intrusion of government in their own affairs and the compulsion for a simplistic resolution of the crises they woke up to every day with the morning newspaper.

But Mallory also knew that when it came to the ultimate choice of a President the majority of Americans reverted to a soberer judgment. Harlan Grant might win the nomination of his party. It should, in fact, go to him by virtue of his willingness to enter the primaries and by his long record of victories. But it was most unlikely that he could win in November—even against an incumbent whose early prospects were not encouraging. The President, at least, was a known quantity—and the same anxieties that drove many Americans to support Grant as a token of protest would later impel them to turn away from the unknown and violent changes he might bring.

The car swung through the southwest gate and came to a stop in front of the diplomatic entrance to the White House, where an usher was waiting to escort Mallory to the elevator and to the President's suite. Sitting outside in the corridor was a man holding a black leather valise on his lap. It was known humorously as the "golf bag," but there was nothing amusing in its contents—the code numbers the President would dictate to our nuclear defense and attack forces if he ever had to use the third telephone. The man, or his relief, was never more than steps away from the President—day or night, in the White House or away from it.

The President was dressing when Mallory arrived. "Jim, I think you're playing games with me on my announcement, and I can't say that I like it."

"I'm doing what I think is right for the party."

The President, knotting his tie in front of a wall mirror, turned sharply. "The party? *I'm* the party, and don't you forget it." He gestured to Mallory to follow him across the hall to the family dining room, where coffee and rolls were set out on the table.

"A week ago, Jim, I approved the letter to the A list announcing that I'm running again. I thought it would be in the mail by now. Instead, you send me this letter saying you want to hold off on it. Why the stall?"

"It's not a stall. I just think it's unwise."

"My God, Jim, we're only a couple of months away from the convention."

Mallory took the plunge. "I'm going to level with you whether you like it or not. I just happen to think that it's best for you to be non-political for as long as possible. You took a beating in Oregon, Nebraska and California. Your rating in the polls has never been lower. Very frankly, you couldn't pick a worse time to announce."

The President flushed. "What the hell difference does it make? Everybody knows I'm going again."

"That's exactly the point. Why announce the obvious this early? One, you cut yourself off from a hell of a lot of free TV time. Two, everything you do becomes political instead of governmental. Why set yourself up as a target for Grant sooner than you have to?"

The President was unimpressed. "Christ, he's all over TV now. Maybe I'm the one who ought to be demanding equal time." He studied the national chairman warily. "You know what I think? That you don't want me to announce at all. You want me to go into an open convention."

"That's it exactly."

The President threw his napkin on the table. "That has to be the silliest goddam idea I've ever heard."

Mallory was calm. "No, you should let the party come to you. The way you're looking now, we should create at least the appearance of a choice at the convention—and there's not one chance in a thousand that you would lose it."

"I don't like the odds." The President got up from his chair. "I want that letter in the mail before the end of this week."

"You have the authority to order me to do it, but I still insist—"

The President cut him short. "I also have the authority to hire and fire national chairmen."

That same afternoon the A list—persons who had contributed in four figures or more to the President's last campaign—was fed into computers at the party's national headquarters. The list was in the form of magnetic cards and the data was voluminous: the name, address and commercial or professional association of the contributor; his birthday; the name of his wife; whether the President had ever met him personally and, if he had, if they were on a first-name basis; his history in party politics, and much more.

But the computers were programmed to extract only that information pertinent to this letter, and the computer tapes were then fed into a battery of robotype machines which simultaneously were receiving another tape of the actual draft of the letter.

First one tape and then the other would alternate in activating the robotype, whose speed was four hundred words a minute. The computer tape led off with the name, address and personal salutation. Then the letter tape, by electronic signal, took over:

"I want my closest friends to be the first to know that I have made the decision to seek my party's nomination for a second term. . . . I am determined to follow through on the great initiatives this administration has set in motion. . . . I know I can count on you, as I have in the past, for guidance and assistance."

The electronic duet continued through the entire letter, switching from the basic text to a repetition of the first name of the recipient in three different paragraphs; a reference to the President's concern with the contributor's specific financial interests, and closing with the President's regards for his wife—again with the first name.

There was also a postscript in the President's hand, written by an automatic stylus, expressing the hope that "we can get together the next time I'm in . . ."

One of the letters, to a defense contractor in Omaha, arrived while he was at the office. His wife couldn't believe it was actually a personal letter from the President. She tested the typescript with an eraser, and it did erase. Then she wet a finger and ran it lightly over the President's signature. The ink did smudge.

Her husband was a more important man than she had thought.

JOHNNY PARTRIDGE was just leaving as Sam Hood drove through the massive wooden gates of Casa Castillo and there was only a curt exchange of nods in passing. It was a relief to the ambassador that Constanzia Novarese would spare him another awkward evening with the Mafiosi.

His hours alone with her were important to Hood. There was, of course, the cool dignity of the *casa* itself—the Goyas and early Picassos on the white walls; the contrast of intricate tapestries with the bulk of the roughhewn beams, and the Andes—changing in all lights and weathers—looming through the deep-set arching windows.

Hood always found in this place a sense of timelessness, of sanctuary, that the changes in his relationship with Constanzia Novarese could not alter or diminish. On his first night in Santa Clara three years earlier, Hood had come to Casa Castillo to express his government's sympathies, and his own, over the assassination of her husband and his friend. Hood saw no change in her since their last meeting months earlier at a reception for heads of state at an Inter-American conference in Bogotá. He had always found her strikingly attractive. She was in her early thirties—slim and patrician but with a certain sensuousness in her grace of movement. Her green eyes were set in a full face over high cheekbones and her long hair had a blue-black sheen.

That first evening at Casa Castillo she had been warm and gracious and there was no sign of the depth of her bereavement, even when she took Hood to the fresh grave in the courtyard when it was time for him to leave. He thought her stoicism unnatural and his instincts were borne out two nights later when the telephone rang in his study toward midnight.

Could he come to Casa Castillo at once? She was sorting through her husband's official papers and there were lapses in the chronology with which Hood might be able to help her. The flat tone of her voice and the lateness of the hour were forewarnings to the ambassador of what he might expect on his arrival at the *casa*. The señora was in the library, sitting amid a litter of documents on the floor. She rose unsteadily to greet him and her hand shook in his. He led her to a divan and there swept back the dark cascade of hair half covering her face. She tried to smile but only for an instant, and then she was in his arms, sobbing.

Hood held her for long minutes before he became aware, unbelievingly, of the urgency of her embrace. He tried to move away from her but her face rose from his shoulder to his cheek, and her lips were eager and demanding. Afterward, it would all strike him as insanely improbable—the fierce, wanton coupling and, finally, her flight from the library, only to return a short time later in an austere black dressing gown, her composure absolute, to ask if he could stay for coffee. He did, but neither in the hours of conversation until dawn, nor in the three years since, had there been so much as a word between them to recall that night of desperate loneliness. Hood, however, could never watch her cross a room or observe her quicksilver changes of mood without resummoning the images of that night. If it was also constantly on the verge of the señora's awareness Hood did not know and she gave him no sign.

That their relationship had since become one of cordial formality was due entirely to the ambassador's gradual acceptance of Jorge Luchengo's right to govern. If he had come to Santa Clara as an ally of the señora, he was now the advocate of her husband's assassin.

It was still puzzling to Hood that his welcome at Casa Castillo could survive this defection—and when he was with her he could think of no better word. And, again, she gave him no clue. They spent their evenings together quietly with Bach or Vivaldi or speaking of old friends or new books. And when they did turn, infrequently, to events in Santa Clara, it was with a curious and impersonal detachment. There were no recriminations and no effort to reinvolve him as her partisan.

If Hood found this strange, Señora Novarese did not. Only here, and in her presence, could Hood be fully aware of his tenuous loyalties.

She met him at the door in pearls and a gown of black lace. "You're late, Sam."

"I was held up by the troops on the road. There are reports that Jiminez is on the move tonight."

She put a record on the hi-fi before mixing his whisky and water. They had not been together since his return from Washington and he had been in no mood to call.

"Your trip home must have been a disappointment to you, Sam."

Hood lit a cigarette. "Yes, it was a disappointment to me." And then he went a step further. "But then, you would have to look at it differently, wouldn't you?"

His words hung in the air.

"Do we want to pursue this, Sam?"

The ambassador's three years in Santa Clara had been without crisis. There had been nothing, until his summons to Washington, to disturb the casual pace of his own life and work, or his willingness to accept, without challenge, that first tithe but not the whole of a relationship with this woman. But now he felt the certainty of change. The troop carriers could be heard from the road, their gears whining on the long grade toward San Quentin.

"Yes, I think we should pursue it, Constanzia. I think we've already put it off too long."

She went to the window and threw it open. The trucks were louder now. "What do you think I want, Sam? That? No, I've seen too much of it. Santa Clara has seen too much of it."

"You'll see more of it—and soon." He paused. "What *do* you want?"

"I want Luchengo dead." She said it as calmly as if she were asking him if he would have more ice in his drink.

"That's barbaric. It would solve nothing."

"He's a murderer. I think you execute murderers in your own country, Sam."

"Yes, but because the law, not vengeance, commands it."

She spoke very slowly. "If the murderer of my husband had been a hungry peon from San Quentin, or one of Jiminez' barefoot guerrillas, I would not concern myself with him. But Jorge Luchengo was Luis' friend—*his friend!* That is his crime."

Hood's tone was gentle. "I can't defend Luchengo. But I know that the whole history of this country has been one of violent transition—"

"Yes, but violence against the oppressor. Luis was not that. He was a good man. And he was also your friend."

"Yes, he was my friend. And I came here three years ago determined to—" He paused.

"To avenge him?"

"Perhaps. But I did not find an oppressor, Constanzia. If Luchengo did betray your husband, he did not betray the cause they fought for together."

"And what has become if it? What purpose did Luis' death serve?"

Hood had no answer.

"You judge me too harshly, Sam. If I want Luchengo's life, that is not to say that I am willing to pay for it with the blood of my own people. Jiminez is not the answer."

"But isn't that the choice—Luchengo or Jiminez?"

"It doesn't have to be. Your government could intervene."

"Constanzia, my government is responsible for what's going to happen. It can't create the crisis and then use it as an excuse to depose Luchengo."

"It can't? You're an expert on your country's Latin American policy. You know better than that."

He was unwilling to argue the point. "I left Washington with the impression that my government has very little interest in Santa Clara."

"For the moment, perhaps. But your troops will come—because Santa Clara will be Communist if they don't. Whether it happens through Jiminez or Mr. Han, the result will be the same. But they should come now. It would spare Santa Clara much suffering."

Hood was growing impatient. "Who would we intervene in support *of?* Who would we place in power?"

"Arturo Lara."

"Lara's a fool!"

"A fool, yes. But an anti-Communist who would do your bidding. And it would not be the first time your country's made that choice."

He studied her face for a long moment. "If it did come down to Luchengo or Jiminez, and I think it will, who would you choose?"

"Jiminez, of course. Then you would have to intervene."

"We no longer intervene, Constanzia, with just a battalion of Marines. And from a bomber at ten thousand feet it's very difficult to tell the combatants from the non-combatants. You would want that?"

She went back to the window. The road on which she had seen

troops marching, again and again, was a gleaming scar against the moonlit slope.

"There's a fact of life down here, Sam, that you may not know. Most of the children born in the barrios and the back country die very young. If not at birth, from smallpox, typhoid, hunger. But if a child lives to be five, we say he's bulletproof—that nothing can kill him. We're an old country, Sam—and we're bulletproof."

U NTIL THE MOUNTAIN of copper had been found by the Spanish almost two centuries earlier, there was nothing to distinguish the site of what was now San Quentin from a hundred other canyons in the Andes. A stream, fed alternately by the snow thaw in the mountains and the torrential rains, was an occasional watering place for herdsmen moving sheep from their seasonal pastures. The dull green streaks in the flanks of the mountain were, to them, no more than a curiosity.

A party of Spanish officers, hunting wild boar in the arroyos, found the mountain by accident—and Santa Clara was no longer one of the empire's least important outposts. Change came swiftly. The first labor force sent to San Quentin were inmates of the prison at Ciudad Alarcon. But they could not begin to tap the vast wealth of the mountain and entire families were forced to go north. They built their shacks along the stream, which every year took on a darker cast from the wastes of the smelter. In the early years, they dug shafts into the mountain, following the green lode wherever volcanic upheavals had thrown it, and sent the ingots to Ariella on burros. The workers died young and their sons took their places.

Progress did not come to San Quentin until after Guillermo Perez' war of liberation in 1898. Because he could not operate the mines himself, Perez sold them to the Castillo family, and they

brought the steam shovels from America and built the railroad.
For a time life was better at San Quentin. The shovels could
scoop up as much ore from the open pits in one bite as a team of
miners could extract from the shafts in an entire day. The Castillos
built the first church at San Quentin and an aqueduct to carry
pure water from a diversion of the stream above the discharge of
the smelter.

It was good to work in the open air, to say confession again,
to have pure water for your children to drink. But the wages the
Castillos paid would buy little more than the beans, the flour and,
once a week, the mutton that had been their dole from the Spanish
commissary. The miners saw the mountain grow smaller every year
and the Castillos richer. And from time to time, when they could
find a leader, they went on strike. But that only brought the
troops and the masses for the dead.

They had put their faith in Luis Novarese, who had told them
he would seize the mines from Don Castillo—that they would
belong to the workers. But Novarese had married the daughter of
Castillo and did not keep his promise. Jorge Luchengo had made
the same promise and kept it. But there was little change in their
lives and now there were rumors he could no longer pay them for
their work.

From his sentry post on a hillside above the smelter, the soldier
of the republic saw only desolation—spirals of smoke from the
huddle of shacks lining the river; the mounds of slag, gray in the
moonlight, and the deep, open wounds in the flank of the mountain.
He was afraid. The captain of the guard had told him that
Jiminez might attack tonight and that more troops were on their
way from the capital.

The sentry heard nothing before he felt the point of the knife
at his back and the hand over his mouth. The voice was his
brother's.

"Do nothing foolish, *hermano*. My *amigos* are going down the
hill. You and I will keep each other company."

The guerrillas crept past them into a rocky defile leading down
to the stream and to the supports of the rail bridge over which the
ore was brought from the open pits to the smelter. From where the

brothers sat, they could see the hut in which they had been born and the church in which they had been baptized. They smoked and waited. Finally, a second before they heard the concussion, they saw the bridge glow red from the explosion and crumple burning into the stream.

There were exchanges of gunfire as the guerrillas ran back up the defile and past the sentry post. His brother spoke to the soldier. "Your captain will find it very strange that you are still alive."

The soldier shrugged and followed his brother into the darkness.

JULY

J ORGE LUCHENGO had built the bridge and his engineer's eye told him it would take at least a month to reconstruct it—a month in which there would be no copper for the Chinese ships at Ariella and no pesos in payment for it. He had come to San Quentin before dawn to survey the damage and had found the town sullenly indifferent to the attack.

Only a handful of workers were now in the arroyo, clearing away the smoldering timbers. Hundreds more stood watching on the hillsides, deaf to the shrieks of the siren summoning them to work. On still higher ground was a skirmish line of troops.

Luchengo watched the army jeep splash through the shallow stream and climb the slope toward him. The young captain was tense with anger.

"They will not work, sir. They say if they put the bridge up Jiminez will knock it down again."

"You told them they must work or there will be no pay?"

"They laugh. They say there will be no pay even if they do—that your pockets are empty." The officer was impatient for orders. "The troops are in position, sir. Shall I—"

Luchengo cut him off. "No. They will go back to work when

they're ready—when there's nothing else for them to do." Then he went back into the superintendent's office—a rusting quonset hut—with the blueprints for the bridge he had drawn thirty years earlier.

Jorge Luchengo had been at the head of his class in science and mathematics at the Escuela Técnica in Ciudad Alarcon, and Don Castillo had lent his family the money to send him to America for a higher education. It was not so much a loan as an investment. Young Jorge must study mining and must work at San Quentin on his return.

But at Colorado A & M he saw the American society struggling to alter its own future—a society in which Franklin Delano Roosevelt's Common Man could speak up, without fear, for his just share of the nation's wealth. The phrase "New Deal" was not easily translatable into his own language or milieu, but its achievements were. And when FDR spoke of the greed of the economic royalists, Luchengo saw the face of his own *patrón*.

The first years after his return to San Quentin were both challenging and frustrating. The don would invest, without question, in Luchengo's proposals for increasing production, but was scornful of his radical suggestion that he should reinvest at least a part of his greater profits in higher living standards for the workers.

"You give them the tail and then they will want the head, and after the head the whole cow. No! They eat, they sleep, they feed their *muchachos*. It is enough."

In the early years Luchengo had no ally—until young Colonel Luis Novarese was put in command of the army garrison at San Quentin. The colonel's own sense of the injustices at San Quentin had come slowly—after strikes in which he had sent his troops into the barrios to shoot down the leaders and to force the miners back to the pits at bayonet point. His orders were abhorrent to him. It was the duty of a soldier to defend his country, not to murder his own countrymen.

The colonel and the engineer spent much time together. Warily at first, and then with growing trust, they spoke with passion of what was wrong in San Quentin—wrong in Santa Clara. And the greatest wrong, of course, was that the profits of the mines should flow into the hands of one family while those who dug the riches from the earth were living, and driven, like animals. No, conditions would not change until the Castillos themselves were driven from San Quentin. But there was no incident—no provocation—to arouse Novarese and Luchengo to action until the mountain of slag began to move. For more than half a century the smelter had been discharging its ore waste into an upland valley between the mine and the town. Every year the heap grew higher and more unstable.

But Don Castillo always refused when Luchengo told him he must build earthworks to contain the slag or, at least, stop adding to its bulk by extending the conveyor belts to a new site. No, that would cost too much.

The huge mass, towering over the town, began to move with the first fall rains—slowly, almost imperceptibly. At Luchengo's urging, Don Castillo himself came to observe it, but he saw no danger. It had held for fifty years. It would hold one more.

In defiance of the don, Luchengo gave orders that the miners were to move their families into the old Spanish mine shafts on higher ground. But many would not go and finally the mountain fell, crushing their huts and flinging them into the swollen stream. The toll of dead was sixty, most of them children.

Don Castillo gave the workers a week to bury their dead and to ask penance for their sins that had brought God's wrath. Their mourning gave way first to hopelessness and then to rage. They struck with fire and explosives at every symbol of their repression— the smelter, the conveyors, the giant diesel shovels. Colonel Novarese defied the orders from Ciudad Alarcon to crush the uprising and kept his troops in their barracks while Luchengo went to Casa Castillo to plead with the don for clemency for the workers. The old man struck him in the face, accusing him of conspiracy with the peons.

His debt to his *patrón* now paid in full, Luchengo went back to San Quentin, where he and Novarese had only hours to forge a revolutionary coalition of soldiers and workers. The miners would agree to it only after receiving Luchengo's personal pledge that the new regime would seize the mines from the Castillos.

When the troops came up the road from Ciudad Alarcon to restore order and to punish the rebellious garrison, Luchengo's miners and Novarese's troops were waiting—together. The *federales* fell back before their fury and Don Castillo's puppet president in the capital fled to Mexico City.

Novarese, according to plan, became the thirty-sixth president of the republic because the army was his and because Luchengo had no such ambitions. In the first months of the new regime there was land and tax reform, and Don Castillo built a new school and hospital at San Quentin. At the insistence of the government, he also reduced the working hours at the mines. But the principal commitment of the revolution was not met. Novarese pleaded that the *norteamericanos* would equate nationalization with Communism and would withdraw their financial assistance to the republic. Life *was* better at San Quentin, he argued. The higher taxes Don Castillo was forced to pay were at least a partial redemption of the pledge. Time—he had to have more time. Luchengo heard his explanations, saw the daughter of Don Castillo sitting next to him, and went back to his office in San Quentin dreading what he knew must come.

If the older workers at San Quentin still had faith in Luchengo, the young did not. First in secret gatherings and later openly in the plaza they heard the words of Paco Jiminez. He was one of them but he was no peon. He had been to Bolivia to fight against the oppressors there. He was a disciple of Fidel Castro and of Che Guevara, who had kept *their* promises to the workers. No, there would be no great change in San Quentin with a lackey of the Castillos as superintendent—with a *presidente* who slept with the daughter of Don Castillo.

Luchengo did nothing to silence Jiminez until the first outbreak of violence—an unsuccessful attempt to dynamite the smelter. Minutes before the troops came to arrest him, Jiminez fled into the mountains—and the next morning more than a hundred of the younger miners went to join him.

The superintendent could no longer wait, and he found willing co-conspirators among the generals who saw in Jiminez' growing strength a clear threat that the red flag of Communism would fly over Santa Clara. The coup was swift and bloodless. Troops occupied the palace while Novarese and his wife were airborne from an Inter-American conference at Bogotá. Luchengo was waiting for them at the airport and they were taken to Casa Castillo.

There, Novarese was given a choice. If he would sign a declaration nationalizing the mines, he would continue as president, but with his decisions subject to approval of the junta. If he would not sign . . . But he knew what the alternative would be.

"A stroke of the pen, Luis. I ask nothing more." But Novarese heard Luchengo only distantly. He was looking at his wife and he found in her implacable countenance not the answer he was looking for but the Castillo answer.

Seconds after he heard the volley of shots in the courtyard, Luchengo signed the declaration—his first official act as the thirty-seventh president of the republic.

And now, three years later, he was back at San Quentin—back in his old office. Should he ever have left it? He didn't know. There were no answers to such questions. But there was a bridge to be built.

T HE SECRET could not be kept from China's enemies much longer. In daily overflights, the telescopic cameras aboard the American SR-71 spy planes operating from Thailand's Udorn air base had seen nothing unusual at Lop Nor, the Chinese nuclear complex in the wastelands of Sinkiang Province.

But soon the technicians would begin testing a new rocket engine on underground test mounts and the powerful shock waves—equal to an earthquake registering five on a scale of ten—could not escape early detection by seismologists in the Soviet Union. And it would be a secret no longer that China finally had an intercontinental delivery capacity for its nuclear warheads.

All of the Soviet Union, but only the West Coast of America, would be within its six-thousand-mile range, and it was now necessary, for purposes of nuclear diplomacy, that China obtain a launch site within the Western Hemisphere.

Han Li-wong's assumption that his cable to Peking would be read with more than passing interest was correct. But his second assumption—that his government would grasp at the opportunity to extend its trade with Santa Clara—was not. The response from Peking was brief. Han was to advise Luchengo only that his request was still under consideration and to instruct Jiminez to desist from further attacks on San Quentin that might provoke an American counteraction. Han also was told to expect further instructions from a courier who would be aboard the freighter *Jining* on its next call to Ariella in ten days. Never before in Han's two years in Santa Clara had his government been unwilling to entrust a communication to normal code channels.

That, and the cable itself, told Han that he was no longer his own man—that Peking had lost patience with his efforts to draw Santa Clara more deeply into the Chinese orbit through economic dependence. Yet Han had been certain that his government would agree with his own appraisal—that the American cessation of aid to Luchengo was a clear opportunity for China to expand its Latin American beachhead. The alternative, just as clearly, was the collapse of Luchengo and a victory for Jiminez, which would almost certainly compel American intervention. That, obviously, would not be in China's long-range interests, but it was precisely the course his government had chosen.

A week earlier Han had sent Jiminez a message strongly protesting the attack on the bridge and the disruption of copper shipments. He had even felt safe in advising the revolutionary, "You weaken your own claim on my government's support by such actions." Now Han found it humiliating to have to inform Jiminez that he had won—that China would do nothing, beyond its present commitment, to strengthen the Luchengo regime. In his message to Jiminez he led off with the statement: "On direct orders from my government, you will wage no further attacks on San Quentin that would impede production." Only in the last paragraph did he refer to Peking's rejection of his own recommendation, describing it as "tentative."

Luchengo sent for Han that same afternoon. He was impatient with the delay. "You have been urging me for two years to sell you more copper. I finally agree. But the weeks pass and there is no answer from your government. I find that very strange."

"Such decisions require time."

"Not this much time, Mr. Han—not when the initiative was yours." Luchengo lit his pipe. "You are aware, of course, of the attack on San Quentin last week?"

"I am and I regret it."

"Do you, Mr. Han?" He didn't wait for the answer. "Then you know that I have only the copper now on the docks at Ariella for delivery. There will be no more until we are back in production and that will be at least a month. Would you advise your government?"

"Immediately."

"Will you also advise Peking that I again insist on an early and positive response, both to an increase in shipments and to advance payments. I would draw the most serious conclusions from further delay."

"They would not be justified."

"Please, Mr. Han, let us speak frankly. The withdrawal of American assistance to Santa Clara creates obvious difficulties for me. But your government seems most reluctant to exploit the opportunity. I must ask myself why."

Luchengo raised a hand to cut off Han's objection. "And now Jiminez, for the first time, feels safe in stopping all production at San Quentin. You don't find that curious, Mr. Han?"

"I find it regrettable. My country needs your copper."

"We are speaking frankly, Mr. Han. Jiminez has always had the capacity to interfere with copper shipments from San Quentin— copper for *your* government, Mr. Han. It is quite obvious that he has held back, until now, because there would be no reason for your presence in Santa Clara if I had no copper to sell you."

Han rose heavily from his chair. "I deny that. I will not listen to such accusations."

"Sit down, Mr. Han. You will listen to whatever I tell you. And I will tell you that my suspicions are such that I am sending for Mr. Hood to discuss his government's defense commitments to mine."

Han was shaken. "May I say, in all respect, that you see dragons where there are none?"

"Perhaps. But your government can put my suspicions to rest simply by honoring your past assurances to me. Is that too much to expect?"

Han lied. "No, it is not too much." The attack of nausea hit him on his way back to the legation and he spent the rest of the day in bed.

Cable from Ambassador Hood to Edward O'Farrell, Assistant Secretary of State for Inter-American Affairs:

SITUATION WORSENING HERE. WILL REVIEW WITH LUCHENGO LATER THIS WEEK, AT HIS REQUEST, TERMS OF MUTUAL DEFENSE AGREEMENTS. HIS CONCERN CLEARLY THE RESULT (1) OF JIMINEZ ATTACK ON SAN QUENTIN, SUBJECT OF LAST ADVISORY TO YOU, AND (2) INORDINATE CHINESE DELAY IN RESPONSE FOR STOPGAP ECONOMIC ASSISTANCE. SAN QUENTIN WILL BE OUT OF PRODUCTION A MONTH OR MORE. IF PAYROLL UNMET, MASS DEFECTIONS TO JIMINEZ AND ESCALATION OF ATTACKS CERTAIN. AGREE WITH LUCHENGO'S ANALYSIS THAT CHINESE RELUCTANCE TO EXPAND TRADE AGREEMENTS COULD PRESAGE NEW AND MORE ACTIVE ENCOURAGEMENT TO JIMINEZ. GRAVITY OF SITUATION TO US IMPLICIT IN OUR TREATY OBLIGATIONS TO RESPOND TO EITHER INTERNAL OR EXTERNAL SUBVERSION. AWAIT INSTRUCTIONS.

On receipt of the cable, O'Farrell conferred with the secretary of state, then put in a call to Special Assistant Gene Haas at the White House.

"I must have ten minutes of your time."

Haas glanced at his appointment schedule. "I'm tied up. It can't wait until later in the day?"

"I think not."

"What's the file?"

"Santa Clara."

"We've put that behind us, Mr. Secretary."

"No, I don't think we have, Mr. Haas."

"All right, I'll be waiting for you."

The presidential assistant read Hood's cable grimly. "Do you agree with this assessment of our treaty obligations?"

"I do," said O'Farrell. "We had no more to go on in the Dominican Republic."

"And you're defending our intervention there?"

"I'm defending nothing, Mr. Haas. I'm simply presenting you with a development that both Secretary Adams and I believe should be brought to the President's attention—and immediately. We will both be available at his call."

Haas left to check with the President's appointment secretary and was back in three minutes. "Ten o'clock tomorrow morning. There will be just Adams and yourself?"

"From State, yes. But it would be wise to have someone from Defense and the CIA."

"You think it's all that serious?"

"Don't you?"

Johnny Partridge saw the article in the Latin American edition of *Time,* under the headline: APALACHIN REVISITED.

It was the biggest jolt to The Brotherhood since 1957 when sixty Mafiosi were taken into custody by New York troopers at an underworld summit in the upstate hamlet of Apalachin.

The haul in an FBI raid last week at a plush motel on the Las Vegas Strip was smaller. But for the fourteen Mafia chieftains now free on $100,000 bail each, the junket to Las Vegas may prove far costlier than Apalachin. No material evidence was found in New York and the capos eventually won a reversal of their conviction on charges of conspiring to obstruct justice.

But the payoff in Las Vegas was much bigger—ledgers containing the arithmetic of the Mafia's interstate operations in narcotics, gambling and prostitution. With such evidence, and with the certainty of vigorous Justice Department prosecution in an election year, the federal prison at Atlanta, long-time home of Frank Costello and other top Mafiosi, may host the next—and last—summit of The Brotherhood.

Surprisingly, Partridge's uncle in Cleveland—Salvador Petracci—was not among those seized in Las Vegas, although he was of higher rank than many who were. Yet Partridge felt it would be unsafe to write or call him. The contact, if there were one, would have to be made from that end.

One week after the raid, and the day after Partridge read of it, he got a letter from Salvador Petracci:

"Dear Giovanni, I am planning a trip for friends of mine. They are wondering if they would like it where you are. Could you write me a letter to the name of Sal D'Vidio, General Delivery, Cleveland?"

The answer was on the next day's plane. Partridge wrote his uncle to meet him at the La Siesta Motel in San Ysidro, California, three days later.

T HE PRESIDENT read Gene Haas's briefing for the ten o'clock meeting at breakfast and sent for the special assistant to join him in the Oval Office ten minutes before it was to begin.

"I don't like the looks of this at all. When was Hood up here? Just last month, wasn't it?"

"Yes, sir." Haas felt his collar tightening

"And didn't he tell us this could happen?"

"Not exactly, sir. He agreed with the intelligence reports that Jiminez wasn't much of a threat at that time."

"*At that time,* yes. But he also said that if we cut Luchengo off at the pockets we could expect Jiminez to move—and fast. He was right, wasn't he?"

Haas was silent.

"And if Hood was right, you were wrong. Correct?"

"It wasn't just my recommendation, sir. Adams went along with it."

The President's voice rose. "Adams went along with it because I told him to, and on the basis of your evaluation."

The intercom rang to announce the ten o'clock appointment. "Hold them there a minute." Then to Haas: "I want you to go back to your office and call Senator Breckinridge. Tell him I want him to stay loose on that Santa Claran appropriation. I may have to put it back in, or at least some of it."

"Won't you need me here?"

"If I do I'll send for you."

Ambassador Hood was dressing for dinner with Han Li-wong at the Chinese legation when a messenger from the embassy brought him the reply from O'Farrell:

HIGHEST LEVEL DISCUSSIONS HERE RAISE SERIOUS QUESTION OF OUR TREATY OBLIGATIONS IN LIGHT OF LUCHENGO FAILURE TO UNDERTAKE MAXIMUM MILITARY EFFORT AGAINST JIMINEZ. ADVISE HIM FULL COMMITMENT OF OWN FORCES VITAL CONCOMITANT TO POSSIBLE ACTION BY US AND CONFINE DISCUSSIONS TO THAT POINT. . . . FOR YOUR GUIDANCE ONLY, FOREIGN RELATIONS BUDGET STILL OPEN AND TENTATIVE RECONSIDERATION HERE OF RESTORING SANTA CLARAN BUDGET ASSISTANCE.

Since his trip to Washington, Hood had given much thought to submitting his resignation and not simply because the President's decision was a rejection of his judgment. Through four administrations Hood had gone along with too many decisions with which he disagreed to resign for that reason alone this late in his career.

No, if he did ask the President to relieve him, it would be a ploy—a trump card he could play to force a reversal of the decision. His resignation would add the dimension of crisis to developments in Santa Clara, and that the President would not risk—not this summer. It was more likely he would call Hood to Washington, remind him they had been together a long time, and ask him to stay on the firing line. In exchange, he would take another look at the situation.

The last sentence in O'Farrell's instructions was encouraging and Hood put off for the moment his thought of proffering his resignation. But he could not put off questions that had been recurring to him through most of his public career—and more often in recent years. Would he actually resign? And if he did, would he have the courage to speak out against the policy he could not in good conscience administer or defend?

Hood didn't know. He knew only that presidential appointees, like himself, were bound by an inviolable code: *Don't rock the boat.*

Privately, you may dissent as much as you like before a decision is made. But once it's made, you go along with it. And if you can't do that, then leave the government—but quietly. Hood knew many officials who had gotten out and the ritual was almost always the same—a letter to the President pleading that "urgent personal affairs require my attention" and closing with an encomium to an administration "I have been proud to serve." And the simultaneous release of the President's letter, expressing the "deepest personal regrets" and the hope that "I may continue to call on you for counsel and guidance in the future."

And that would be the end of it. No press conferences or appearances on Face the Nation or Meet the Press to challenge or expose the policy they could not condone.

But most appointees chose to remain and to implement and defend the very decisions they had fought against earlier with the deepest personal conviction. Their rationales were many. They could influence events more effectively within the administration than out of it. They could fault the President on foreign policy but not on civil rights—and one had to look at the total picture. And, certainly, the alternatives if the opposition party took power would be much worse.

But only the political amateurs—the New York lawyers, the Ivy League academicians and the executives on leave from major corporations—had to invoke such rationales. It was always simpler for the President's cronies—veterans of his many political wars. Right or wrong, he was *their* man—and disloyalty to him was unthinkable.

In either case, the code would prevail. Presidential appointees must accept that their allegiance to the man who put them where they are takes precedence over their personal convictions and their right to public protest. Only later, on their return to private life, would they have to face the verdict of their own consciences. Had they been more loyal to the President than to the nation? And if they had left Washington, not quietly, but denouncing the policies which they knew to be fraught with error, what influence might they have had on the history of their time?

Like all Chinese on foreign missions, Han Li-wong had brought his own cook along with him to Santa Clara. In many respects Han was not as distrustful of the Western world as most of his colleagues, but his tolerance of its culture did not include its cuisine. One of his own aphorisms was that "The measure of a civilization is not to be found in its art galleries but in its kitchens." It was written on a dyspeptic morning after a seven-course Lebanese dinner honoring the arrival of a Chinese trade mission to Beirut.

To Han, his own simple diet was a mark of non-indulgence—an assignment of the animal function of nourishment to its proper importance. In contrast, most Westerners he had known—and among them Hood—put an almost decadent emphasis on food. And such food! Fish and fowl whose subtlety was lost in rich wine sauces— vegetables whose character was left in the pot—and the wines, dulling the palate even to the strange flavors that were left.

But Han was not happy with the chef he had brought from China, and the chef was not happy with Santa Clara. In the market across the street from the legation he could find no acceptable substitutes for the staples of his native Canton. Bean sprouts, pea pods and bamboo shoots were alien to this hostile climate.

The rice was of poor quality, the fish too strong and the meats and poultry too sinewy for the rapid braising in light oil that was integral to his art.

Day after day the cook went to the market, hoping that new foods would arrive with the changing seasons. But there was no relief from the hanging clusters of chilis and chorizos and the burlap sacks of corn flour and pinto beans. The new fruits and vegetables that did arrive were frighteningly unfamiliar to the cook, and he always came back to the embassy bearing rice, chicken, pork, shellfish, eggs and the mildest peppers he could find.

Han's entreaties that the cook should at least try to vary the menu, particularly when Hood was his guest, were unavailing. And this evening, as always, dinner at the legation was egg flower soup and a bland mixture of rice, chicken and shrimp.

The legation itself was almost as austere. It was built in the provincial Spanish style with thick adobe walls and small windows—a fortress against both the summer heat and the winter cold. It had once been the home of a merchant who had fled to the suburbs to escape the clamor of the market across the street.

On the lower floor were the kitchen, an airless dining room, sleeping quarters for the small staff and a large parlor, dominated by a huge photograph of Mao, that served as the office for Han's two assistants. They had little to do except coordinate ship arrivals at Ariella with the fluctuating production schedules at San Quentin and arrange for the refueling and reprovisioning of the vessels for the return voyage.

The second floor was Han's domain. It was smaller than the first, set back on all four sides to accommodate a gallery with wrought-iron railings. The only chambers were a bedroom, a bath and Han's study. In this city of tropical verdure, the legation's only plant life was the philodendron in Han's study and the sere remnants of the cook's last effort to raise a vegetable garden in the courtyard.

After dinner Han and his guest, as always, had their thimble cups of rice wine in the study. There, too, Mao was smiling beneficently from the wall. But the photograph was smaller to accommodate the high cases, with glass facings, that held Han's formidable collection of seashells. They came from every sea and ocean in the world—delicate pink murex from the Mediterranean, whose living creature was the ancient source of dyes for the royal purple togas of the Caesars; deceptively lovely cones from Fiji, which could kill a man with the poison in a dart smaller than the stinger of a bee; and a thousand other species, all in the bright or subtle protective colors of the coral reefs which were their habitat.

But Han, like most conchologists, was a specialist in one species. His was *Cypraea,* the cowry, one of the most prestigious of all sea snails. The smaller money cowry, strung on a cord like wampum, had been a form of currency for centuries from the South Seas to Africa. The ovate shell with its labial aperture was a fertility symbol in the primitive areas where it was found; and, decorating the prows of war canoes, a talisman of invincibility.

But because of one specimen in his collection, Han's fascination with *Cypraea* went beyond its practical uses or occult significance to man. His treasure was *Callistocypraea aurantium aurantium Gmelin*—the golden cowry. The hump of the shell and the teeth guarding the labia were bright orange and, in startling contrast, the lower edges and base were a pure white. Han's specimen, almost five inches in length, was extremely valuable. There were probably no more than ten others in museums or private hands of similar size or perfection.

The golden cowry was not kept behind glass with the rest of Han's collection but on his desk, set like a jewel in the recess of a black velvet case. The shell had a sensuous attraction for him and he often took it from its setting to stroke its glistening symmetry with his fingertips. He had bought the shell ten years earlier from a dealer in Hong Kong and since that time his relationship to it had become one that could embrace an almost human affection and could impart to the animal that had made it, from the enzymes of its own body, a perseverance that was analogous to his own experience.

It was a sultry night and the slight stirring of air in the study was damply oppressive. Sitting on opposite sides of the desk, Han and the ambassador were silent for long minutes, sipping the tepid wine and listening to the babble from the street.

The golden cowry was between them, lustrous in the fading light.

They were friends but they were also antagonists and their moods when together often reflected the tide of conflict. For Hood the rivalry was implicit but not personal. He was a professional. He knew that distant events and decisions, over which he might have little control, could determine the success or failure of his mission in Santa Clara. He could present his views to Washington and argue for their acceptance. But win or lose, his continuing role was to try to advance in Santa Clara the self-interests of his own government.

But for Han, new to diplomacy, the conflict was deeply personal. Santa Clara was the world in miniature in which he and Hood— worthy adversaries!—were waging a struggle of conflicting ideologies whose outcome would be a portent of the world to come.

But now, it would appear, the game was to be taken out of their hands, and Han was resentful—more of the possibility of American intervention, which would be decisive, than Peking's rejection of his own judgment, an error he might still be able to reverse. His dark, brooding eyes, magnified by the thick lenses of his glasses, fell on Hood reproachfully.

"I wonder, Mr. Hood, how many more evenings we will have together?"

"Many, I would hope."

"Let us be candid. President Luchengo has told me why you are going to the palace tomorrow."

"Then he must also have told you why he thinks the mutual defense discussions are necessary."

"Yes, but I did not find his reasons very convincing—and I hope that your government will not." He forced a smile. "It would be sad to say good-by to you, my friend. But if there were American troops on the streets of Ciudad Alarcon, I would have to leave, and very quickly."

"Yes, your government probably would recall you, but no more quickly than mine would recall me if the troops were Jiminez'. We can hope it won't come to that."

Han's gaze fell on the cowry. "Our hopes or your armies will change nothing. Events will take their own course."

"You surprise me. I had not thought of you as a pessimist."

"On the contrary, I am an optimist. And I know precisely what the future will be."

Hood shook his head. "There are no historical certainties. History is a series of accidents. And the most we can hope to do is to prolong the ultimate accident."

"Yes, but life will survive even that." Han took the gleaming shell from its case. "Here is the future. Here is the certainty that my culture must survive and that yours will not."

"You hold in your hand, my friend, the shell of a dead creature— one that did not survive."

"Ah! But that merely proves my point. Have I never told you the story of the golden cowry, Mr. Hood, and of this specimen particularly? Here, let me pour you another glass of wine." Hood sat back in his chair.

"Probably no creature in the world has a stronger will to live than the fragile snail that built this shell. To frustrate its natural enemies, it deliberately chooses to inhabit the outside ledges of the coral reefs, where it must endure the constant battering of the seas."

"But again, your specimen did not survive."

"Nor did the native diver who took it. He was torn to death by the razor edges of the coral. This was in his hand when they found his body."

"And the analogy?"

"That my race will risk more, will suffer more, to survive than yours. We will not retreat, as you will, from a hostile or terrifying environment. To the contrary, we choose it because we are more able to survive it than you."

"And the golden cowry is taken only by man?"

"No, most often they are found on the reefs or the beaches after great storms that have torn them loose from the coral. But it is an act of nature, Mr. Hood, not of man."

"There, then, is the flaw in your analogy. Man now controls the most elemental force of nature and can unleash the greatest of all storms. And what will survive that?"

Han was no longer listening. He held the cowry in one hand, caressing its sleek surface with the stubby fingers of the other. His eyes were half shut in rapture and he took no notice of Hood's "Good night."

THE CABLE from the Santa Claran desk of the State Department was on Ambassador Hood's desk the next morning:

PALMER JOYCE AND CREW ARRIVING THERE WITHIN THE WEEK. GOOD LUCK.

In the battle for audience ratings among the news departments of the major television networks, Palmer Joyce was Universal Broadcasting Company's star performer. And he was just that—a performer, not a newsman. His nightly appearances on UBC's news shows and his frequent hour-long special reports drew the network an audience of tens of millions and Joyce an annual income of a hundred and fifty thousand dollars.

Joyce saw himself not as a reporter of the news but as the adversary of those who made it. He was a specialist at asking the antagonistic question whose purpose was not to elicit information but to put himself in direct and often angry conflict with the person he was interviewing. His on-camera donnybrooks with the great and near great had become part of the dismal mythology of a television era in which the brief sensation was more certain to attract an audience than thoughtful, in-depth reporting.

Joyce was held in contempt by his colleagues in Washington because he had no expertise in government or politics and because his own ego and personality always took precedence over the story he was reporting. But to millions of Americans he was a hero—a reporter with guts.

Hood sent for the embassy's press attaché, Carl Reasons, and gave him the cable.

"Joyce is all yours. Keep him away from me unless he absolutely insists on an interview."

"That's easy. I can keep him hopping around for two or three days just looking at projects built with American dollars—the same VIP tour I set up for the congressional committee last year."

Hood shook his head. "That's exactly the wrong way to handle Joyce. There must have been a leak in Washington and he already knows what the story is. You try to lead him around by the nose or brainwash him and we'll end up looking even worse. Just be available if he wants your help—nothing more."

The leak in Washington was in the office of Robert E. Breckinridge, chairman of the Senate Foreign Relations Committee. It had been an error in judgment for Gene Haas to call the senator personally to advise him that he might have to restore all or part of the Santa Claran appropriation to the foreign aid budget. Breckinridge had been in the Senate twenty-three years and it was offensive to him to receive orders from White House underlings instead of the President himself. But beyond the offense to his dignity, Breckinridge was up for re-election and saw dangers to himself if he had to do the President's bidding.

The older generation in his Midwestern constituency was against all foreign aid and the young campus militants were stridently against assistance to the Luchengo dictatorship. Breckinridge had won his own party primary handily by pledging his support for drastic cuts in foreign aid and had even specified Santa Clara as one of the least deserving countries. To reverse his position now would place him in a highly vulnerable position in the fall election.

After the call from Haas, the senator spoke briefly to Bill Groat, his administrative assistant and chief political adviser. They agreed that pressure had to be brought on the White House to quash the Santa Claran appropriation, at least until after the election, and that adverse public opinion was the pressure the President understood best.

That afternoon Groat met Palmer Joyce for a drink at the bar of the National Press Club. He didn't have to tell him much—only that there were rumbles from the White House that the Luchengo government was on the brink of collapse.

That evening Joyce told his audience, "The dominoes are beginning to tumble in Latin America." In his next special report he would "expose still another shocking failure in American foreign policy."

The lights in the presidential palace in Ciudad Alarcon were still burning long after midnight. The crisis President Jorge Luchengo laid before his ministers was obvious—the balance in the treasury was inadequate to finance government operations for more than another month. Luchengo was faintly hopeful that the Chinese might still agree to his proposal for an advance payment against an increase in copper shipments. But until that decision was forthcoming drastic contingency planning was necessary.

To Luchengo, the order of priorities was clear. The payroll of the nation's only basic industry at San Quentin must be met, or the government could anticipate mass defections to Jiminez and, perhaps, the permanent shutdown of the mines. It was his intention to issue a decree the following day ordering a halt to all public works projects and placing the army and all civil servants on half pay for the duration of the crisis. It was, he conceded, only a stopgap solution. But could his ministers propose another way out?

The Minister of the Interior put up strong resistance. The cessation of public works would cause further unemployment and unrest in all parts of the country. An across-the-board reduction in the government payroll was the equitable answer, not preferential treatment for the miners.

General Carlos Silvera-Guzman, the Minister of Defense, agreed. The miners could be driven to the pits at bayonet point, but there was no force that could compel a rebellious army to obey orders. And he reminded Luchengo bluntly that an army revolt had led to his own ascendance to power.

The dispute continued until long after midnight, but the arguments against Luchengo's original plan were unavailing. The decree would be issued the next day.

The only minister who did not take part in the debate and who did not leave the palace with a sense of foreboding was Arturo Lara.

"You can wait no longer, señora. You must speak out now against the decree and against Luchengo."

From their rendezvous on the high mountain trail, Constanzia Novarese saw the capital shimmering in the oppressive summer heat. The day she had been waiting for was approaching, perhaps with dramatic suddenness, but she felt an ominous quality in the air.

"No, Lara, Luchengo will fall—with or without me."

"But he must not fall to Jiminez. That would only bring the Americans, who would keep him in power." Lara argued his case persuasively. There was no imminent danger to Luchengo from Jiminez as long as the mine payroll was met. But the decree was certain to provoke an angry reaction within the army. Troops of the palace guard already had torn the decree from the wall of their barracks and trampled it in the dirt. But Señora Novarese was not convinced.

"If what you tell me is true, the army will act. But there is nothing I can do."

"You will forgive me, señora, but you are wrong. A revolution must have a leader."

"I could not be that."

"If not a leader, then at least a symbol—a symbol of Luchengo's betrayal—a symbol of the changes the revolution would bring."

"No, I have kept to myself at Casa Castillo for three years. I am without influence. I am only the widow of Luis Novarese."

Lara drove home his point. "That, señora, is exactly why you do have influence. Colonel Novarese was of the army, and he has many old friends in positions of high command. Even Silvera-Guzman stands against Luchengo."

The faintest of smiles lit her face. "You are very ambitious, Lara."

"I don't deny it. Yes, I want power. But I also want what you want—vengeance against Luchengo. I have not forgotten, as he has, the patronage and generosity of your father."

Her voice was weary. "What would you have me do?"

"You must write a statement for the radio and the newspaper. Luchengo would not dare suppress it. You must say that you have kept your silence for three years but can keep it no longer. You must say that Luchengo's many failures—and now the blow he has struck at the army—are unlocking the door to Jiminez and Communism. You must go often into Ciudad Alarcon. You must be seen in the streets and in the cathedral."

"In widow's black?" She put a foot in the stirrup and flung herself easily into the saddle, her green eyes smoldering. "I am not a peasant to go mourning in the streets."

"Be angry with me if you like, señora. But there must be an alternative—a *visible* alternative—to Luchengo and to Jiminez. And only you can be that." Lara laid a hand on the pommel of her saddle. "You will not be alone, Constanzia." His words came in a rush. "I have not spoken before out of respect for your sorrow. But I ask you now to look at me not as your servant but as a man. May I dare to—"

Her riding crop came down sharply on his wrist and the palomino shied against Lara, almost driving him from his feet. A moment later the last of the Castillos was spurring the horse recklessly down the steep trail, the peon staring after her.

Johnny Partridge was flying to the States the next morning. The proposition he would present to the representatives of the Cosa Nostra for an extradition-free sanctuary in Santa Clara had only one missing element—a Santa Claran of stature who would front for the operation and whose involvement would protect it both from a possible change in governments at Ciudad Alarcon and from the certain protests that would be heard from Washington.

Constanzia Novarese was the obvious choice. Her position as the widow of a former president gave her immunity from harassment by Luchengo, and Ambassador Hood's relationship with her was a reflection of the respect with which she was still held in official circles in America.

At dinner that night at Casa Castillo, Partridge took the casual approach. He told her he was flying home to try to interest an

American syndicate in his plan to develop Ariella as a major tourist center. There was nothing in his words to arouse her suspicions. On many of their trips to Ariella he had spoken of its similarities to Mazatlán on the Pacific coast of Mexico—the long, curving peninsula creating a natural yacht harbor, the miles of beaches and the abundance of marlin and sailfish within a short run of the sports fishing docks.

The capital investment, however, would be too great for him to handle alone. And there was one major stumbling block to selling the project to the American syndicate. Santa Clara's laws, like those of many Latin American nations, forbade foreign corporations. A citizen of the country must hold at least a fifty per cent interest. But such countries, eager for foreign investment, often were willing to overlook the fact that the local interest was proxy in nature, just as long as the laws of the country were technically met.

"And you want me as your figurehead, Johnny."

"You wouldn't be a figurehead at all. You would have an active voice in the management, and you would come out of it with stock options that would be worth a fortune if the project succeeds."

"I don't need money."

"Perhaps not. But you do need an involvement." His concern was genuine. "You're an important woman in this country. You can't spend the rest of your life in mourning."

Her voice was reproachful. "Have I been that much the grieving widow, Johnny?"

"That was out of line. I'm sorry."

Later, over coffee and brandy, she told him of her conversation with Lara. "If I had no other reason for saying no to you, Johnny, it would be that I haven't the slightest desire to encourage a project that would prolong Luchengo in power—and your plan would do that."

Partridge disagreed. "The early money for Luchengo wouldn't amount to much. The tourist dollars—the big money—would be two or three years away. And if Lara is right, Luchengo will be long gone by then. And in the interim you can accomplish what Lara suggests without starting a blood bath. You'll have position and a base of operations against Luchengo—and all out front and legitimate."

"Legitimate, Johnny?"

"Absolutely. I've never tried to hide my background from you, and I won't lie to you now. I don't deny that there will be certain advantages for my associates in the States—one of them a refuge from prosecution. But the operation itself will be entirely legal from the word 'go.' If it weren't, believe me, I wouldn't try to involve you."

"No, I don't think you would."

He left with her agreement to serve as a director of the Buena Vista Development Corporation.

PALMER JOYCE flew into Ciudad Alarcon on the same plane that would carry Johnny Partridge north. The commentator's entourage was impressive—eight cameramen, assistant cameramen, soundmen and grips. Carl Reasons was waiting with cars to transport them to the El Jacinto Hotel and a truck for their heavy cases of cameras, film, lights, reflectors, sound equipment and cables.

"I'll be here two or three days," Joyce told Reasons, "and I can find my own way around. All I want you to set up is an interview with Hood on my last day."

"I'll try to arrange it," the press attaché replied.

"You'll *try* to arrange it? You will arrange it. Or I'll have to presume His Excellency expects me to come up with questions he won't want to answer."

At that moment Joyce saw Partridge striding toward the ancient Electra.

"I know that man. Who is he?"

"His name's Partridge. He's an American living down here."

It hit Joyce on the way into town in the car. "You were being pretty cute with me back there, Reasons. He might call himself Partridge now but I know him as Petracci. He's a hood. You knew that, didn't you?"

"I know that his passport's in order and that he behaves himself. That's all that interests us."

"Thank you. I'll quote you on that."

Johnny Partridge and the man sent to kill him were both on the scene a day early and for the same reason—to check out San Ysidro and to plan their escape routes from the border town. For Partridge, it was, perhaps, an unnecessary precaution. He was almost certain that Salvador Petracci had written him in good faith. But if he was wrong he was not going to let his uncle set him up for the kill as he had in Los Angeles two years earlier.

But Franco Martinelli, alias Frank Martin, hadn't the slightest doubt that he would be leaving town in a hurry. He didn't like accepting contracts in a town as small as San Ysidro. There was only one fast highway to San Diego, twenty miles to the north, and it would be crawling with police cars in the Sunday traffic. An escape into Mexico would be simpler but months could pass before it would be safe to recross the border after the kill.

Martinelli was sent to San Ysidro by Peter (Papa) Brodaglio, the successor to Partridge's father as the Cosa Nostra chieftain for California and Nevada, and one of the capos under federal indictment resulting from the Las Vegas raid. He had agreed to the border meet with Partridge but only to lure him back to the States. Brodaglio had no confidence in Partridge's Santa Claran proposal and knew that his own chances of escaping prison were slight. But he was determined that his son should inherit his territory. Partridge's return to grace would present the Mafia with a formidable rival to his son and in a territory in which Partridge had already proven himself to be an effective operator. It was too great a danger to Brodaglio's plans and he gave Martinelli orders to kill Partridge, but without informing him that the contract did not have the approval of the hierarchy. An accident would be waiting for the assassin on his return to Los Angeles to remove the one witness to Brodaglio's violation of the Mafia code that a hit on one of its members must have the consent of a majority of the capos.

To avoid American immigration inspection, Partridge flew directly to Tijuana. There he got a room at the Caesar Hotel, then took a cab across the border to San Ysidro. He was just one of the thousands of American tourists who throng to the Mexican border town every weekend. Martinelli had arrived in San Ysidro three hours earlier and his tracks were still fresh. At the private airport on the outskirts of the town, Partridge tried to arrange for a plane and pilot to be standing by for immediate takeoff the following afternoon.

"Sorry," the operator told him, "I can keep only one plane on standby, and it's already taken for tomorrow."

"We might be going in the same direction. Can you tell me who he is and where he's staying?"

"He just gave me the name of Martin—Frank Martin—and laid down a two-hundred-dollar deposit. Said he was going to either L.A. or Vegas. That's all I can tell you."

Franco Martinelli! He was small time—a gun for hire. He didn't belong in the same company with Salvador Petracci. But did Petracci know he was there? That was the question and the answer would be at La Siesta Motel. It would be safe to go there. Martinelli wouldn't hit tonight if he had no way out until the next day. And he wouldn't risk being seen by Partridge.

Yes, the desk clerk had a reservation for a Mr. Sal D'Vidio for the next morning. And there were two others in his party—Mr. Mario Cassavettes and Mr. Philip Hartung. Cassavettes, like Partridge, was the son of a capo and now a specialist in the Cosa Nostra's real estate ventures. But earlier he had been involved in the procurement of prostitutes among show girls in Las Vegas and New York. The assignment was taken away from him when it became known that he was also his recruits' most frequent customer. He also had a reputation as a heavy drinker who owed his mid-echelon position in the Mafia to the influence of his father, who was one of those awaiting trial.

Hartung was the junior partner in Burton, Foster and Hartung, a New York law firm that put together many of The Brotherhood's legitimate investment corporations.

"But you have no reservation for a Mr. Frank Martin?"

"None."

A bellman, lounging at the far end of the desk, overheard the conversation and caught up with Partridge along the pool facing the street.

"Your name Partridge?"

"It could be. Why?"

"There was a Frank Martin in here a couple of hours ago. Said he was a friend of Partridge and gave me ten bucks to let him know when he arrives."

The bellman had a name tag over the lapel pocket of his uniform.

"When are you off duty, George?"

"In twenty minutes, Mr. Partridge. And if you want to raise Martin's ante I'll be in the beer joint across the street."

Partridge and a pitcher of beer were waiting for the bellman in a back booth. He was out of uniform now and wearing a garish Hawaiian sports shirt and blue slacks. It wasn't that hot but his face was glistening with sweat.

"What makes you think I might want to sweeten the pot, George?"

"Easy. The first five Martin gave me was to call him when you got here. The second five was for not letting you know he was asking. I had to figure maybe he was planning a little surprise for you."

"All right, what does fifty dollars buy me?"

"For fifty I don't call your friend. For another fifty I tell you where he's waiting for the call." The sweat was now beginning to stain his sports shirt.

"You're having a big day, George."

"I have to make up for the slow ones."

Partridge slid two fifties across the table.

"He's at the Happy Hours Motel, a couple of blocks down the street toward the border."

"He's there now?"

"He said he would wait for my call."

"George, I don't know how to thank you."

"Easy," said the bellman. "We don't know each other. We never met."

"Then what the hell are you doing at my table drinking my beer?"

"Look, mister, I did you a favor." His glass shook in his hand.

"And you were paid for it. Now crawl back under your rock."

The bellman tried to control his legs on the way to the door, but was half running before he got to it.

Partridge spent another five minutes at the table, then went to the telephone booth in the front of the café. He rang the operator and told her to connect him with the local sheriff's office. While he was waiting, his eye caught a large poster over the bar, advertising a *Gran Corrida de Toros* the next day at the Tijuana bull ring.

The desk sergeant came on the line.

"I'm going to say this once and I'm going to say it fast. There's an ex-con at the Happy Hours by the name of Frank Martin."

"That's a crime?"

"It is if he's carrying a gun and hasn't got a license for it."

"Who is this?"

Partridge hung up, left the café and began walking slowly toward the border. He was in a liquor store across the street from the Happy Hours buying a pack of cigarettes when the sheriff's car drew up in front of the motel.

Two minutes later a deputy came out with Martinelli, his hands manacled behind his back. A second deputy, three steps behind, was carrying the evidence—a shotgun and a .45 automatic.

Partridge took a cab back across the border to the Caesar and told the driver to come in with him. At the ticket stall in the lobby he bought four front-row seats for the *corrida* the next afternoon. The desk clerk gave him an envelope. He put all but one of the tickets in it, wrote the name Sal D'Vidio across the front of the envelope and gave the cab driver ten dollars to deliver it to the desk at La Siesta.

The *gran corrida* began at four in the afternoon and Partridge was the first of his party to arrive. The opening matador had not been a crowd-pleaser and attendants were clearing away a litter of seat cushions and empty bottles from the arena when Partridge saw his uncle, Cassavettes and Hartung moving down the aisle toward him.

Cassavettes had had a bad night, and it was Partridge's guess that he had spent most of it in the cantinas and bordellos of Tijuana. In his early thirties, with a slight physique, he might have been handsome except for the too sensuous, almost feminine mouth, the dark pouches under his eyes and approaching baldness between his temples.

Partridge stood to let Hartung take the far seat in the box, then Cassavettes and Salvador Petracci. At that moment the second bull came out of the chute and was met with another crescendo of howls from the *aficionados*. The animal was small and its horns were short and blunt. But when the *torero* took its initial charge on his knees, there was a scattering of *olés* from the stands.

Petracci was not happy with the arrangements. "I don't like crossing borders, Johnny. And I don't like crowds."

Cassavettes and Hartung were intent on the action in the ring and the blood from the picador's lance was a little too much for the Manhattan lawyer.

"I don't like crowds either, Uncle Salvador. But nobody's likely to put a slug in me in front of five thousand witnesses."

"You think I would be here if there was still a contract on you?"

"I didn't know if you would show—and Franco Martinelli was looking around the hotel for me yesterday."

"You're crazy. He's in Brodaglio's family. Brodaglio agreed to this meet."

Partridge didn't press it. He would let Petracci continue to believe he thought Martinelli was still on the prowl. Petracci didn't press it either. He had set one trap for his nephew in Los Angeles and couldn't blame him for being cautious now.

"I'll check it out, Johnny. If you're right, there'll be a hit but not on you."

The matador had brought the bull directly under their seats, its flanks gleaming red from the wounds of the lance and the *banderillas*. It was a hot, humid afternoon but Hartung felt cold and faint.

"I'm sorry, Mr. Petracci. But if we don't leave, I'm going to be sick."

It was a ten-minute cab ride back to town, where they found a small café off the main street. It was empty except for the bartender and two plump B-girls signaling to servicemen on the street from a front-row window. The four men took a booth in the rear and had beers all around, except Uncle Salvador, who drank only red wine. From the street, they were just another party of bettors from L.A. or San Diego waiting for the parimutuel action to start at the jai-alai fronton.

Cassavettes took over. "Generally, your proposition looks good, Johnny, although the legal aspects bother Hartung a little." He had only three questions of his own. Was Partridge certain the airstrip outside Ariella would take jets?

"The government Electra flies in and out now. We might have to lengthen it—that's all."

And would the present docking facilities accommodate cruise ships?

"They should. I've seen two or three freighters and ore carriers in there at the same time."

Finally, was there an adequate labor pool to staff the hotels, restaurants and other facilities?

"Yes. At least a third of the population is out of work—and that's one of the reasons I think Luchengo will buy the deal."

There were, of course, myriad questions Partridge would not have the expertise to answer: the local availability of heavy construction equipment; meteorological data on the maximum length of the tourist season; the willingness of the Santa Claran government to furnish police, fire and other essential services.

But Cassavettes told Partridge that a project feasibility study organization in Los Angeles was already under contract and would soon be directing specific questions to the appropriate ministries in Ciudad Alarcon.

"With the right answers and a little luck, Johnny, my father and his friends could start moving down there in three or four weeks—and they haven't much more time than that."

One of the B-girls at the window caught Cassavettes' eye and he instinctively ran a hand across his forehead to be certain the longer growth of hair on the sides was covering the bald spot.

Hartung was recovering both his color and his disdain for the three Sicilians sitting with him. There was only one aspect of his involvement with the Mafiosi he did not find distasteful—the large fees they paid him for cloaking their investments with corporate respectability.

"I'm afraid I don't share your optimism, Mr. Cassavettes. I see at least two very serious legal difficulties with this proposal. The first, of course, is the requirement that a Santa Claran national must hold at least a fifty per cent interest. That we can handle with stock options. But I shouldn't have to tell you, Mr. Partridge, that we wouldn't have a prayer in the Santa Claran courts if your proxy tries to play games with us later."

"That won't happen."

"May I finish, Mr. Partridge? We're talking in terms of an eventual outlay of fifty, perhaps sixty, million dollars. Your nominee would have to be absolutely dependable and, I should add, entirely sympathetic to what I might call certain fringe aspects of the project."

"Would you accept the widow of the former President of Santa Clara—a wealthy woman in her own right—a personal friend of the U.S. ambassador?"

Hartung was incredulous. "You can get her?"

"I've got her."

"And she knows what your connections are?"

"She knows."

"May I ask what your relations with her are?"

"Don't push it, Hartung. Just take my word for it. What was your second question?"

"This matter of extradition. Agreed, there's no treaty now but when certain of our—what shall I call them?—when certain of our investors arrive on the scene, a treaty could be agreed to, and very quickly, on demand from Washington. What guarantees can you offer against that?"

"None. But I think it's unlikely. Relations between the States and Santa Clara aren't exactly cordial at the moment. And Luchengo, or whoever's running the country, would have to weigh the project's obvious economic advantages against the static from Washington. The country's broke, Hartung—flat broke. We couldn't put this together if it weren't."

"I still think it's a poor risk."

Cassavettes broke in. "That's what we pay you for, isn't it, Hartung?—to eliminate risks. But if you want out . . ."

"I didn't say that, Mr. Cassavettes."

"I'm no lawyer," said Partridge, "but we ought to be able to throw a clause in the lease contract to the effect that there can be no change in the present rights or status of American citizens down there."

"We'll consider that, Mr. Partridge. Thank you."

Salvador Petracci had not spoken a single word. He was sleepy from the wine and at this hour, at home in Cleveland, he would be napping in the sun alongside his pool. He understood none of this. He had spent fifty of his seventy years as a manipulator of horse books, prostitutes, narcotics and terror. This new world of feasibility studies, stock options and corporations was alien to him and would always be. It was much better in the old days when the Cosa Nostra *was* Our Thing—when the only time you had to sit at the same table with a lawyer was in a courtroom.

Partridge left them in front of the café, went back to the Caesar to check out and was on the eight o'clock plane south. At the same hour Salvador Petracci, waiting for his plane in San Diego, saw a headline on the newsstand: SEIZE MAFIA GUNMAN IN BORDER MOTEL.

He was no longer an old man—a relic of a dying order. There were still orders that only he and his peers could issue—responsibilities only they could accept.

Three days later Mrs. Peter Brodaglio came home from a trip to the Brentwood Country Market and found her husband floating face down in the swimming pool. He had had two prior heart attacks—and the coroner wrote this one off as his last.

Palmer Joyce's success on television was the result of his ability to exploit the frustrations and fears of millions of Americans and to pander to their suspicion that the nation's failure to exorcise its devils was the result of stupidity, appeasement or betrayal in high places.

He was in Santa Clara to document one of his recurring themes—that most of the billions spent on foreign aid go to countries that play a double game with the Communists. To Joyce, the President's decision to abandon Santa Clara was confirmation of still another American failure to buy the loyalty of an ungrateful and cynical regime. And he would permit nothing he saw or heard there to change this preconception.

His first interview was with President Jorge Luchengo and it could not have gone better if Joyce had written the script himself. The commentator had arranged the interview through the Santa Claran embassy in Washington, which had given Luchengo advance notice both of Joyce's reputation for belligerence and of his great influence on American public opinion. His own staff had briefed Luchengo intensively on the questions he might expect and the answers that would be most persuasive in alerting America—and the American President—to the growing crisis in Santa Clara. But he never had a chance to present his case. Joyce took the offensive with the first question and never lost it.

"Isn't it a fact, President Luchengo, that your government is on the verge of collapse?"

They were facing each other across the presidential desk. One camera and a powerful battery of lights were on Luchengo. A second camera, out of sight range of the first, was on Joyce. But the lights behind it were of low intensity because of the soft sun glow striking the newsman's face through the window.

"You put it too extremely, Mr. Joyce. We're having difficulties, yes, but—"

"Would it also be extreme to suggest that you blame your difficulties on the American President's decision to deny you all further economic assistance?"

The lights struck Luchengo's face with almost physical impact. He saw Joyce only as a silhouette. "We're a small country—a poor country. Obviously your assistance was important to us."

"Then you do blame the President?"

"I did not say that. We have been most grateful for your help."

"And that leads to my next question, sir. Exactly how much dollar help have we given your military dictatorship over the past three years?"

"Again, Mr. Joyce, I must object to the form of your question. Mine is not a military regime."

"We can go into that later. But for the moment would you answer my question?"

"The amount is three hundred million dollars."

"And would you say it was a wise investment on the part of my country?"

"I would. We have spent it on schools, roads, hospitals."

"May I ask how much of it you have spent to combat internal Communism?"

"The answer to Communism is to combat the conditions in which Communism can exist."

"And you believe that you've been successful?"

"To a degree, yes."

"To the degree that Communist troops under Paco Jiminez have been able to sabotage your one basic industry?"

The lights were not only blinding but hot. When Luchengo took a handkerchief from his pocket to wipe the perspiration from his face, Joyce gave a signal to the cameraman to zoom in for an extreme closeup.

"You told me a moment ago, sir, that you have taken three hundred million dollars from the American taxpayers and have spent none of it in military action against the Communist Jiminez. At the same time you grant recognition to Communist China. Would it be unfair to suggest that yours is not exactly an anti-Communist regime and it was on that basis that the American President—"

"I am losing patience with you, Mr. Joyce, and with your misstatement of the facts. We do not recognize China. We never have. And as long as I am President we never will."

"Only five or six blocks from where we sit now, Mr. President, is a building with the flag of Red China flying over it. You may not call that recognition—"

"It is a trade legation—nothing more."

"Nothing more? Isn't it copper that you sell to China? And isn't copper a strategic war material?"

Luchengo stood up from his desk. "You have not come here, Mr. Joyce, to ask for my views. And I have no further interest in listening to yours."

"You are breaking off this interview?" Joyce was hopeful that he would. The second camera crew already was maneuvering to catch Luchengo stalking from his office.

"No, not without correcting statements of yours that are unjust to my government and to me."

"I'm listening."

"We do trade with China, yes. But only because your own country's trade barriers give us no other choice. You criticize us but you apparently find no fault with your other allies who trade with Peking—Japan, China, Canada, France, Great Britain . . ."

"You are wrong, sir. I, and most other Americans, are critical of all governments that lend aid and comfort to the war lords of Peking. . . . And how else have I been unjust to you?"

"In your statement that I am a military dictator. You must know that free elections were held here only last year."

"I won't argue whether they were free or not. But how you perpetuate yourself in power, sir, is not the most important question. How you originally came to power is. It was a military coup d'état, was it not?"

"It was. But it also had the support of the workers. My predecessor had not kept faith—"

"Wasn't Luis Novarese more than just your predecessor? Wasn't he also your friend?"

"We were very close."

"And you had him shot to death. Is that correct?"

"Yes." And then he did walk out—slowly, without anger, un-dramatically.

The next day both Han Li-wong and Constanzia Novarese refused Joyce's telephone requests for interviews—Han "because I am a very minor trade official and I have no authority to speak for my superiors," and the widow because she sought the advice of Ambassador Sam Hood.

"Stay away from him, Constanzia. He only wants to play you against Luchengo—the pathetic widow, kneeling by Luis' grave. And I don't think you want to go for that."

Joyce left with one of his crews for San Quentin at midday. The other took a position on the roof of the market across the street from the Chinese legation. The zoom lens caught shadowy glimpses of Han in his office; the Chinese insignia and flags on the old Cadillac in the courtyard and, finally, Han stepping out to the balcony for a breath of air. When he saw the camera on the roof, he impulsively threw his arm across his face and fled back into his office. Joyce would love it.

The crew then drove out the San Quentin road to a height commanding a view of Casa Castillo. They left the car behind and set up the camera, with its extreme telescopic lens, in a concealing growth of brush.

Late in the afternoon the widow came out of the adobe classroom next to the stables—her small band of pupils surrounding her, tugging at her dress. She stood for a moment, the children still with her, watching a servant place fresh flowers on her husband's grave. The cameraman, observing the scene through the range finder, told his assistant: "Honest to Christ, we're up so close I can almost smell the posies."

Joyce was also having a good day in San Quentin. He and his crew were kept waiting fifteen minutes in a steaming office while the officious colonel in charge of the army garrison telephoned Ciudad Alarcon for permission to let them have the run of the town. Joyce would describe it in his special report as forced detention.

Later he was able to contrive further evidence of the police state theme that would dominate the report. He shot footage of workers rebuilding the bridge and of sentinels at their posts on the surrounding hillsides. Skillful intercutting would create the effect of conscript labor.

Poverty, too, must exist in a police state, but that he did not have to fabricate. In the older section of town he shot the decrepit shacks, the hopeless faces of the very old, and children running nude in the streets.

Nor did he forget Jiminez—the tangle of iron rails and wooden girders left by the dynamiting of the bridge, the "Viva Paco!" scrawls on walls and buildings, and the menacing circle of mountains from which the revolutionary—Joyce would tell his audience—must eventually emerge and in force, as Fidel Castro had from the Sierra Maestras.

Through most of the day a swarm of curious San Quentinos—most of them children—had been following Joyce and his crew. There was also a crowd waiting around their camera truck when they came back to load their equipment for the return trip to Ciudad Alarcon. And among them were sympathizers of Paco Jiminez.

The incident began when one of the provocateurs threw a stone at a sentry guarding the barracks door. Within seconds, soldiers were pouring out of the barracks and advancing on the crowd with rifles at the ready position. One of Joyce's photographers was already on the hood of the truck with a hand-held camera and he caught it all: more stones thrown from the crowd, a volley of warning shots from the soldiers and the Santa Clarans retreating, cursing the troops.

The skirmish didn't last more than a minute. But it left in its wake a woman kneeling over a child trampled in the crush, an old man with blood on his face, the colonel with his saber drawn.

The chief photographer had been with the network thirty years. On the road back to Ciudad Alarcon, he spoke to Joyce.

"You know that was staged for our benefit. I've seen it happen more times than I want to remember—Watts, Columbia, Chicago, that march on the Pentagon. Those aren't cameras we're toting around—they're incitements to riot. My God, did you see that kid down in the street?"

Joyce smiled. "Count your blessings, my friend. Count your blessings."

They were old adversaries. In his days at the White House, Sam Hood had made no secret of his contempt for Joyce and his methods. Hood had been before Joyce's camera only once, seven years earlier, after emerging from a Senate hearing at which he had testified in support of reviving the Alliance for Progress. Senators opposing it had given him a rough time and he was in no mood for Joyce's baiting in the corridor outside:

"Mr. Hood, do you actually expect the American people to believe that . . ."

The telecast was live and there was no way to cut off Hood's answer: "What I would like the American people to believe, Mr. Joyce, is that the correspondents for Tass and *Izvestia* are more objective reporters of the Washington scene than you are."

Except for that, the only other direct quote Joyce had ever gotten from Hood was "No comment." The newsman was looking forward to the afternoon interview. This time, as an ambassador, Hood would have to hold still for the questions of a correspondent for a major network.

The interview, at Hood's insistence, was held at a table in the sunny patio of his official residence. Hood had long been aware of Joyce's third-degree lighting techniques. Beyond the patio was the tennis court and swimming pool, to which the children of the embassy staff had an open invitation. Their shouts rang across the lawn.

"Is that yelling going to interfere with you, Joyce?"

"No, let them have their fun. It's good background." When the special report went on the air, Joyce would contrast the American youngsters splashing in the pool with the street urchins of San Quentin, and the opulence of this setting with the poverty of San Quentin's barrios.

They had only a brief conversation while the crew was setting up. "Let's start," Hood said, "with the understanding that I'm not going to comment on the internal affairs of Santa Clara. I will comment on how and where American aid has been spent here and what impact I think it's had."

"I'd rather play it by ear as we go along," Joyce replied.

The crew was ready.

"Mr. Ambassador, I would like your comments on the President's reasons for denying further assistance to a country that is clearly in danger of going Communist."

"Even if your appraisal were correct, I have no authority to speak for the President."

"But you were against the President's decision, weren't you?"

"My views were made known to him, yes."

"That doesn't answer my question."

"Then perhaps you should ask questions that are within my authority to answer."

"Cut!" The whirring of the cameras came to a stop. "I'm down here, Hood, as the representative of a major television network. Do you intend to cooperate with me or not?"

"You're down here, Joyce, to try to document your own simplistic preconceptions of what's happening. I'll answer questions that are proper and relevant to my position here. But I'm not going to play straight man for you."

"All right, let's try again." The cameras began to roll. "I understand, Mr. Ambassador, that there's a Red Chinese trade legation in this capital. Is that correct?"

"Yes, the People's Republic of China has a representative here."

"And I understand, further, that you and this Communist are friends—that he has even been a guest in this residence."

"That's correct."

"And you have given him the run of the place, knowing that all of Red China's foreign emissaries bring with them secret orders for espionage?"

"I have given him the run of that tennis court over there, Mr. Joyce, and all he's ever brought with him was his racket."

The sound man broke into laughter.

"Cut! . . . I'll give you one more chance, Hood. You either answer my questions or I'm going to tell an audience of ten million Americans—who pay your salary, incidentally—that the ambassador to Santa Clara was totally uncooperative with me."

Hood stood up. "If you do, it will probably be the one true statement in your entire report." With that, he strode into the residence.

AUGUST

THE CAPTAIN of the Chinese freighter *Jining* was waiting for Han Li-wong at the head of the gangway and took him to his private quarters behind the bridge. A man in his mid-sixties was standing at one of the ports in the cabin, watching the activity on the dock. He was tall for a Chinese and the second mate's uniform he wore hung loosely on his gaunt frame. He did not turn to face Han until he heard the captain close the hatch and leave.

Han could not place him, although the taut, brooding face was remotely familiar. Nor did the man introduce himself. He took an envelope from his inside coat pocket and gave it to Han. The secret orders, signed by the Minister of War, were brief:

"You will continue as nominal head of the Santa Claran trade delegation. But you will act under the direct orders and authority of the bearer, who will serve as an adviser to the liberation forces of Francisco Jiminez. Hereafter, the principal function of your legation will be that of communications liaison between the bearer and the Ministry of War."

It was inconceivable to Han that he had lost all authority. Why?

Except for the rejection of his proposal for expansion of the trade agreement, his superiors had found no past fault with his actions.

The man was now sitting at the captain's navigation desk, observing Han's dismay. A topographical map of Santa Clara was spread out before him.

"Do you find your orders confusing, comrade?" His voice was low and gentle.

"No, they are very clear."

"But you don't approve?"

"I don't understand the reasons for—"

The smile was gone. "It is not necessary that you understand. It is only necessary that you obey. Your first instructions, Mr. Han, are to inform the port authorities that the *Jining* will be unable to sail for at least a week because of engine repairs. That will arouse no suspicion?"

"None."

"And would it arouse suspicion if I were to reconnoiter the road from here to Ciudad Alarcon almost daily?"

"Not if you were acting as the ship's officer in charge of re-provisioning the *Jining* for the return voyage."

They left the ship a half hour later for Ciudad Alarcon. At the Arroyo Seco thirty miles north of Ariella, where the highway and railroad ran closely parallel through a ravine climbing steeply toward the last rank of rocky foothills, the older Chinese had the driver stop the car. He took the topographical map from his briefcase to compare it with the terrain. And Han suddenly knew where he had seen this man before—in newspaper photographs standing next to Mao Tse-tung on reviewing stands for parades of Chinese rocketry in Peking. He was General Gi You-gin, the ranking missile specialist of the army's construction battalions. He had been the architect of Hanoi's anti-aircraft rocket system in the Vietnamese war; the defense rocket positions along the Ussuri River in Manchuria during the clashes with Soviet forces during the late 1960s and early 1970s, and the short-range missile emplacements still protecting Lop Nor from Russian incursions across the Sinkiang-Uighur border.

General Gi glanced up from his notations on the map. "Now you recognize me?"

"Yes, General."

"And now you understand?"

"Yes . . . I understand."

It had been a quiet morning in the White House. The budget, whose deficit the President had been able to cut from nineteen to eight billion dollars, had gone through Congress three days earlier.

There had, of course, been the ritual outburst—always more clamorous in an election year—from the opposition party in Congress, the opposition press and Harlan Grant, the President's most likely opponent in the November election. The administration's failure to ask for new taxes to balance the budget was election-year opportunism and its certain effect would be a new recession, possible devaluation of the dollar and a further weakening of America's defense capabilities.

The administration's counterattack was also ritual. Percentagewise, it had been the smallest budget increase in a decade; the improving economic outlook would generate new revenues that could more than offset the deficit, and those senators and congressmen who were now most critical of the budget had been the most adamant in resisting budget cuts affecting their own districts.

The President had come out of it with no worse than a draw and he was willing to settle for it. His desk, for the first time in weeks, was clear of staff memos recommending that he hang tough or accept compromises in the joint Senate-House conference on the budget, or suggesting that "only a personal call from you" could persuade a recalcitrant legislator to go along with him.

The President was tired and was looking forward to a long weekend at Camp David when the call came from Secretary of State Sterling Adams.

"I've just had a message from Ambassador Kharlamov. He insists that he must see you at the earliest possible moment."

"He gave no reason why?"

"None."

"All right. Set it up for three this afternoon. You'll be here?"

"Yes, and Kharlamov suggests that we limit it to the three of us."

"You'll work out the cover with him?"

"I already have. He's returning to Moscow the first of the week for routine consultations. We'll just announce that he's coming over to pay his official respects to you before leaving."

The President sent for Press Secretary Busby. "Kharlamov's coming over at three today. He says it's urgent. Have you seen anything on the news wires to suggest what it might be?"

"I'll recheck but I've seen nothing."

"All right, just tell the correspondents he's going back to Moscow in a couple of days and is dropping by to pay his respects."

Back in his office, Busby ran a quick eye over the reams of copy that had come in during the night and morning from the news teletypes of AP, UPI, Reuters and Agence France Presse. There was no hint of a developing crisis. Excerpts from his ten o'clock briefing of the White House correspondents:

Q. You say it's strictly a courtesy call?

A. That's correct.

Q. Then the President will still be going to Camp David tonight?

A. If there's a change of plans, I'll let you know.

Q. Why should a courtesy call from Kharlamov change his plans?

A. Look, if you want to read something more into this, I can't stop you.

The correspondents let it go at that. But, to a man, they got word to their wives not to expect them home for dinner.

Ambassador Alexei Kharlamov's limousine came through the west gate of the White House grounds at five minutes to three and swung to a stop in front of the West Lobby entrance. Waiting for him were Secretary Adams and a host of reporters. Kharlamov, a squat, balding man, smiled and waved for the cameras but was deaf to the questions flung at him from all sides.

Adams led the ambassador across the West Lobby, the press still on their heels, and through a door into the Fish Room at the far end. They were now in President's country, out of bounds for the reporters, and Kharlamov paused to wipe the perspiration from his face and hands. The room was given its name during the administration of Franklin D. Roosevelt because of his penchant for hanging game fish trophies on the wall—a practice later presidents would follow. Kharlamov was no longer grinning. His expression was as cold and forbidding as those of the giant fish hulking over him. From the Fish Room, they went through the appointment secretary's office and then through another door into the Oval Office.

Kharlamov spent forty minutes with the President and afterward they stepped out into the rose garden and the bright sunlight to face the television and still photographers. The correspondents already had the word from the press secretary. "If you want them together at all, it will be just pictures—no questions. Understood?"

The camera session over, Kharlamov and Adams retraced their steps through the White House, and the Secretary of State saw the ambassador to the door of his car.

The President did not fly to Camp David that evening. Instead, he met in the Cabinet Room with his ranking foreign affairs, defense and intelligence advisers. Present were the Secretaries of State, Defense, Army, Navy and Air Force, the chairman of the Joint Chiefs of Staff; the director of the CIA; and foreign affairs specialists on the President's own staff.

The President sat at the center of the long octagonal walnut table. In front of him and all the other officials were yellow legal pads and pencils. There was an easel behind the President and on it a large map of the world.

"You are all aware," he began, "that I met this afternoon with Ambassador Kharlamov. He told me that the Soviet Union now has definite evidence that China has an ICBM."

There was, strangely, little reaction around the table. The President's very decision to call them together at this hour was a portent of grim developments. One or two of them may have thought of the safety of their families or of themselves, but only for the briefest of moments. They were all professionals, chosen not only for their expertise but for their ability to react swiftly, effectively and without emotion to the most perilous exigencies.

Martin Trask, the director of the CIA, was dubious. "We've had Lop Nor under daily surveillance. But neither the SR-71s nor our satellites have shown new or unusual activity."

"No," the President replied, "the Russians have it straight from a defector—a Chinese missile technician who took his training in Moscow. He got across the Uighur border two days ago and told the Russians the whole operation is underground at Lop Nor— missile assembly, engine testing, the works."

Trask was reluctant to concede that the Chinese could conceal an operation of such importance from his own intelligence apparatus. "The defector could have been a Chinese plant, Mr. President. Just the threat that they're close to deploying an ICBM would deter Soviet aggressiveness on their borders."

"No," the President replied, "I told you the evidence is definite. The defector gave the Russians a precise schedule of past engine testing—the day, hour and exact length of burn. And it corresponds exactly with Soviet seismological recordings at times when there was no apparent above-ground activity."

"Perhaps they're still just working on a prototype at this point," said Secretary of the Army Leverett Rhodes.

The President shook his head. "The frequency of the engine tests precludes that. There's no doubt at all—they're in production. But the mystery, gentlemen, is why they don't announce it. In the past, they've always taken the propaganda initiative when they had a major breakthrough. They were ahead of our own and Russian intelligence in announcing their first H-bomb and their shorter-range nuclear rockets."

"Perhaps," said General Mark Courtland, chairman of the Joint Chiefs, "they'll wait until just before they start flight tests, which we would have to spot."

"You're probably right," said the President. "But the Russians think, and I agree, that they will probably announce it then only as a prototype and will try to conceal the fact that they already have twenty or thirty more just like it. To put it very bluntly, they're not looking for propaganda this time. They're looking for launch positions."

Secretary of Defense Burgess Rand spoke next. "Do we have an estimate of its range?"

"Yes, up to six thousand miles. The defector describes it as a counterpart of our Minuteman and with MRV capability."

"That," said Rand, "puts Moscow right under the gun."

"And our own West Coast," said the President. "No, gentlemen, they finally have us in range—if not our silos, at least major population centers."

"I would agree," said Trask, "that the development is alarming. But certainly the threat to the Soviet Union is far greater than to us. They can hit the Soviets' first strike capacity but not ours. My estimate would be that they will do nothing foolish. They'll continue to stockpile to deter Soviet aggression along their border. But I can't see them pulling the trigger until they have a second strike potential. It would be suicide to do otherwise."

"I don't share your confidence," said the President, "that Russia is necessarily their prime target."

"But they would have nothing to gain by attacking non-strategic targets on our West Coast."

Courtland was a step ahead of Trask. "I think the President is suggesting that they may try to find launch sites in this hemisphere, which would bring the entire continental U.S. within range."

"Exactly," said the President. "Now if we can look at this map for a minute"—one of his aides went to the easel with a long pointer—"we find only two locations in this hemisphere which are both under Communist control and within range of all of our silos and SAC bases. The closest, of course, is Cuba. But we can cross that off. Even if we and the Russians weren't Castro's biggest export markets, his break with Peking is final. And he also has a very long memory. That leaves us with only one other possibility— Bolivia." The aide's pointer swung from Cuba to the Latin American nation.

"Bolivia would be doubtful too," said Trask. "We know they're flying conventional weapons and ground-to-air missiles into La Paz, but they have no seaport for moving in the heavy stuff. They would have to dismantle the ICBMs and fly them in one component at a time. That could be done, I suppose, but our agents there should spot it very quickly."

" 'Should' is a chance we're not going to take," the President replied. "I want you to move more agents in there. And I want you to step up our SR-71 and satellite observation."

"It will be done, Mr. President."

"And you will also coordinate our surveillance of Lop Nor with the Russians. There will be no more overlapping flights. I agreed with Kharlamov to both coordination and to a full exchange of intelligence."

"Yes, sir."

Sterling Adams was still studying the map. "May I call your attention, Mr. President, to Santa Clara? It's also within range and Jiminez' last attack was his most damaging in two years. We can't afford to overlook the possibility—"

"I'm slightly ahead of you there, Sterling," said the Chief Executive. "I'm calling Ambassador Hood up for consultations. We may have to prop Luchengo up a little longer. . . . Gentlemen, I don't think there's much more we can accomplish here tonight. But starting tomorrow morning, the top priority for all of you and your departments is a total re-evaluation of our political and military options vis-à-vis China. And I also want an updating of those same options against the certainty that they can't be too far away from an intercontinental strike capacity."

Air Force Secretary James Halverson spoke for the first time. "It impresses me, Mr. President, as it does Trask, that the greater threat at the moment is to the Soviet Union than to us. This removes, I believe, the remotest possibility of Russian intervention if we were to—"

"Jim, I've been over this with you time and time again. We're not going in there. Agreed, you could knock out their production in one strike, and Borichev would probably love us for it. But where would it leave us?"

"It would leave us immune from nuclear attack, at least from China, for another four or five years."

"It would also leave us with a ground war in Asia that would tie us down for a hell of a lot longer than that. Next to it, Vietnam would look like a minor skirmish. If the Russians want to buy that, okay. But they don't and we're not going to either."

"We're just postponing the inevitable."

"Can't you understand, Jim, that we *want* the Russians under the gun in the East? We take the pressure off for them and they'll move twenty or thirty divisions—and their heavy hardware—back to the West. Do you want that with the shape NATO's in right now? And do you also want to give the Russians the first chance they've had in thirty years to put the whole Comintern back together? And, believe me, we attack China and that's exactly what you'll have."

"Sooner or later, Mr. President."

"Then it's going to have to be later. And that's final, Jim."

The President glanced at his watch. "Chairman Borichev is going to break the story at noon tomorrow Russian time. I'm going to address the nation on live TV tomorrow morning at ten. Until then, gentlemen, I will expect all of you to be unavailable for comment." He was looking directly at Halverson.

The advisers left as they had come, through the west basement entrance and the southwest gate, avoiding the correspondents who were milling around the press secretary's office. There was clearly a major news break in the offing and the wire services, networks and newspapers would staff the White House around the clock until the word came.

The official alert had come at six o'clock that evening from Press Secretary Busby. From the transcript of his briefing:

I have two brief announcements and I will have no comment on either of them. First, the President will not be going to Camp David tonight or over the weekend. Second, he will address the nation on live TV and radio tomorrow morning at ten. That's it.

Q. Can you tell us if it involves Kharlamov's visit today?

A. I'm not going beyond what I've already told you.

Q. Can we go off the record for a minute?

A. No.

Q. Can we expect further announcements from here tonight?

A. Not as far as I know.

Q. But you wouldn't advise us to go home?

A. My advice would be to go with what you've got because I'm taking no more questions.

The first Washingtonians, outside of government, who knew that a crisis was developing were the capital bureau chiefs of the four TV-radio networks. They form a committee which decides whether a presidential announcement is of sufficient importance to warrant an interruption of regular network programs.

Busby met with them privately in his office an hour after Kharlamov left the White House. They, too, came and left through the basement—unseen even by the correspondents for their own networks.

The press secretary told them only that it was the desire of the President to address the nation on radio and television the next day on a development of the gravest national importance.

"Will he want prime time?"

"No, the timetable is such that he should go on tomorrow morning. We'd like fifteen minutes at ten o'clock. He'll do it from his office."

"I don't understand your reference to a timetable."

"Keep your eye on the wire tonight and you will."

The chairman of the committee glanced quickly at the other three news executives. They were all in agreement.

"Okay, you've got the time. When can we announce it on the air?"

"I'm briefing the correspondents here at six," Busby said. "You can go with it then."

When the flash that China had an ICBM came from Moscow later that evening, the timetable reference was no longer a mystery. Clearly, the earliest possible response from the President, assuring the nation that it was in no immediate peril, was in order.

Even before the President's emergency session with his highest advisers, speech writers were already at work on the first draft of the address. It was somber and yet reassuring. Although China had made a giant stride forward, the new missile could not reach American shores from the Chinese mainland, and there was little chance that Peking would risk nuclear devastation by attacking those American bases that were within its range.

However, the government was stepping up its surveillance of Bolivia and would respond swiftly and appropriately if there was evidence of an attempt to move the missiles into the one militant bastion of Communism in the Western Hemisphere.

The President said the most imminent danger was to the Soviet Union and, recognizing the joint responsibility to curb the recklessness of Peking, the two governments would pool their intelligence efforts to minimize the danger. The peroration was an appeal for calmness in this grave hour and for a renewal of that spirit of courage and national unity against which no enemy had ever been able to prevail.

The speech writers went over the first draft with the President late that night and he found it generally acceptable.

The full text of Chairman Borichev's announcement came over the diplomatic wires much later. There was no reference to the agreement to coordinate American-Soviet surveillance of China's missile-producing capacity or to a mutual exchange of existing intelligence on the missile center.

The President met with the Secretaries of Defense and State and the Vice President an hour before he was to go on the air. They agreed that if Borichev was unwilling to reveal this precedental agreement it would be impolitic for the President to announce it.

Air Force Secretary Halverson watched the telecast in his office at the Pentagon and his reaction to it was one of disgust. Would the President never understand—until it was too late—that the enemy was *Communism?* And Communists the world over, whatever their temporary differences, had an identical long-range objective: the destruction of the American way of life.

Until the White House had specifically forbidden him to use it, his favorite speech analogy had been that to distinguish between Russian and Chinese Communism is to distinguish between lung cancer and stomach cancer. Both would kill you if you didn't cut them out by the roots before they spread too far. And the implication was clear that America's Air Force was standing by to perform the necessary surgery.

Halverson's reaction to the Chinese missile breakthrough was the more intense because the President had cut two billion dollars from his budget request, and Congress another half billion. It was still up eight billion over the previous year, but his increase had been the smallest, percentage-wise, among all the services.

After the Security Council session, he was convinced—if the President was not—that air and missile strikes against China were a certainty, perhaps within the year. And, by God, if the Air Force was going into action it would be at maximum strength.

Halverson had lost the first round of the budget fight. But Congress would reconvene after the national conventions and he was going back for a supplementary appropriation.

One of his brightest young information officers had come to Halverson weeks before with a plan to apply pressure on both the President and the Congress to leave the Air Force budget intact. The strategy was to flood Washington with powerful friends of the Air Force, who would testify before committees, hold press conferences and collar legislators in their offices.

The technique was not original. All of the services stage their own marches on Washington at budget time. But Halverson's information officer had one new gimmick—the Air Force lobby would have the status of a permanent watchdog committee.

Halverson hadn't gone along with the plan because there was no crisis development to justify it. But now there was. He reread the wire, over his name, that would go out that same afternoon to one hundred of the nation's most prominent aviation executives and former Air Force generals:

I URGE YOU TO ACCEPT APPOINTMENT AS A FOUNDING MEMBER OF THE NATIONAL SECURITY ADVISORY COUNCIL, A VOLUNTEER ORGANIZATION THAT WILL PRESENT IN WASHINGTON AND IN YOUR OWN COMMUNITY THE CASE FOR MAINTAINING OUR AIR FORCE AT AN EFFECTIVE DETERRENT AND COMBAT LEVEL. . . .

He glanced at the list of addressees his staff had drawn up. He knew most of them personally or by reputation, but could not recall Donald Marston, President, Heli-Commuter Corporation, New York, N.Y.

IN HIS WEEK-LONG survey of the terrain between Ciudad Alarcon and Ariella, General Gi You-gin found no potential missile site of greater strategic advantage than his first choice—the heights surrounding the Arroyo Seco thirty miles north of the port city.

It was a natural location for artillery, whose line of fire could control all movement on both the rail line and the highway, and the seizure of such a logical military position by Paco Jiminez should, therefore, arouse no suspicion as to its ultimate purpose.

Even more important, once the artillery emplacements were built, they and their underground support network of tunnels and ammunition bunkers would be quickly convertible to missile launching sites.

Control of the rail line and highway was also vital. It would prevent the government from strengthening its garrison at Ariella and would facilitate rapid delivery of the missiles from the port to the launch site. And Jiminez would move against Ariella at the appropriate time to capture the docks and cranes necessary to off-load the ICBMs and the complex of computers and electronic gear that would direct them to their targets.

Still another advantage was that the Santa Claran government's maintenance yard for both the railroad and the highway was only a mile north of the ravine. On his sweep south, Jiminez could easily seize the bulldozers and other heavy construction equipment necessary to fortify the arroyo.

General Gi sent only one message to Jiminez, through Han's courier, during the entire week of his stay in Santa Clara. And when the *Jining* finally left Ariella, the general was aboard. But the first night at sea, the freighter kept a rendezvous with a Chinese trawler bound for the fishing grounds off Santa Clara.

When the trawler put into Punta Bunda the next night, with its cargo of arms and munitions, Jiminez was on the dock to welcome Gi.

Within days of Johnny Partridge's return to Ciudad Alarcon, the Ministers of Interior and Trade began receiving inquiries from Resort Research, Inc., of Los Angeles "in behalf of a client exploring the possibilities of a major tourist development on the Santa Claran coast." The requests for information were extensive: the average day and night temperatures and humidity at Ariella for all twelve months of the year; the approximate opening and closing dates of the annual migration of marlin and sailfish off the coast; the present availability of competing tourist accommodations; the geologic stability of the ocean front (would it support high-rise construction?); the harbor's capacity for small craft; ad infinitum.

Simultaneously, the Minister of Justice was in receipt of an inquiry from Burton, Foster and Hartung, asking for clarification of Santa Claran statutes involving foreign investment, corporate organization and court precedents to establish the equal standing of foreign investors in litigation with their Santa Claran associates. Phil Hartung, who signed the letter, already had done extensive research on both questions, even before the meeting with Partridge, and knew precisely what the answers would be. Their purpose was to distract attention from his third and most critical question: "Can the Republic of Santa Clara offer inviolable guarantees to our clients that, as party to a lease agreement, the government will respect all present rights of American citizens, either in temporary or permanent residence?"

The inquiries had been brought to President Luchengo's immediate attention and he told his ministers to respond as quickly as possible. But he found it strange that American interests would even consider a Santa Claran investment of such magnitude when the republic was clearly on the brink of economic collapse. Yet he knew that this would also be the most opportune time for American investors to exact the greatest concessions from him. Routinely, Luchengo had copies of the inquiries sent to the economic attaché at the American embassy in Ciudad Alarcon, with a request for information on the reputability of Burton, Foster and Hartung.

Ambassador Sam Hood heard the President's crisis address on short-wave radio and was already preparing a dispatch, warning of Santa Clara's increasing vulnerability to Chinese subversion and intervention, when the cable came instructing him to return to Washington for immediate consultations.

He was met at Dulles International Airport early in the evening by Edward O'Farrell, Assistant Secretary of State for Inter-American Affairs. They were old friends and O'Farrell, who was not often given to optimism, was uncommonly cheerful.

"You'll have twenty minutes with the President tomorrow, Sam, and this time I think you'll win the argument. The prime focus here, of course, is on Bolivia. But I think we've been able to convince the President that Jiminez is a long shot he can't afford to ignore."

Hood caught glimpses of the Potomac through the trees and the white skyline of the Capitol in the distance.

"I wouldn't call Jiminez a long shot at the moment. Luchengo's broke. San Quentin's still shut down. The army's in an ugly mood. It could blow up overnight."

"Then you've got a better case than I thought. Don't pull your punches tomorrow."

Ahead of them, Hood saw the Lee Mansion on the crest of the highest slope in Arlington National Cemetery. They were nearing the interchange at which they would turn left onto the Memorial Bridge and into the District of Columbia.

"Ed, if you're in no hurry, I'd like to run up to the Kennedy graves for a couple of minutes."

O'Farrell understood. He, too, was often drawn back to the graves and for the same reason. A little of himself was also buried there. He and Hood had come into government together in the first days of the New Frontier. They were much younger then and much more hopeful that the world could be changed and that they could help to change it. If a little of themselves was also buried on that slope in Arlington, they both knew that it was not just their youth. That, at least, would have been acceptable. What was not acceptable was that after sixteen years they were now part of the same rigid establishment—defenders of the same conventional wisdom—that they had once known to be the enemy of all change and of all hope for change.

Even at this late hour there were hundreds of other visitors in the queue leading past the graves. It was a half hour before Hood and O'Farrell got back to their car. There had been no word between them for all that time, and Hood didn't break the silence until they were caught in the heavy traffic of the capital.

"No matter what happens tomorrow, Ed, I don't expect to be with the department much longer. You might let the Secretary know."

"Come off it, Sam. I always leave Arlington with the same feeling you have. I ask myself what the hell I'm still doing hanging around. But what else could I be doing that would be more important? So Adams is gutless. Would the guy who takes my place do a better job of propping him up and pushing him in the right direction? And because I can't answer that question, I'm still here. You quit and who takes your place? Haas? He wants it, you know."

Hood shrugged. "I think Haas would be exactly the right man to replace me."

"You're not serious?"

"I am. You and I can rationalize as much as we want. We can try to convince ourselves that even if we can't have it our own way we can at least stop the Haas's from pushing it too far the other way. But the rationale doesn't hold water. They keep old hands like us around, Ed, precisely because we can hold the line where it is right now—because we can give the old policies at least the appearance of continuity and viability. Haas comes out of this a hell of a lot cleaner than we do. He at least believes what he's doing."

"That's too pat, Sam."

"No. Latin America is going to explode in our faces and you know it. And the longer it takes to happen, the worse it's going to be. We still have a slim chance of convincing them down there that we do give a goddam—that we are willing to put some life and heart back into AID and the Alianza. But we won't do it as long as you and I are around to hold what's still left together."

"And Haas?"

"Haas would muck it up in a hurry down there. But he would at least force the issue—would at least compel the President to look realistically at what's happening. And that's more than I've been able to do."

"It would be a hell of a price to pay."

"For Santa Clara, yes. But there's only one way we can go after that—the right way. And I don't delude myself that we would do it even then because it was right. We'd do it because it would be a hell of a lot cheaper in the long run."

O'Farrell said nothing until the car was in front of the Mayflower. "Hold off on the resignation, Sam. Let's wait until we know what happens tomorrow."

"All right, we'll wait." He shook O'Farrell's hand as he got out of the car. "That's what we do best, isn't it?"

There were five of them—the President, Secretary Adams, Ambassador Hood, Special Assistant Gene Haas and Wilson Carew, a Latin American specialist from the CIA. They sat at the conversational unit facing the fireplace in the Oval Office—and the informality was a sign that the President was willing to listen. He was not willing, however, to admit past error.

"If it weren't for this China missile development, Sam, I wouldn't be reviewing the Santa Claran picture at all. Everything that's been happening down there just confirms the decision that we've been wasting our money on Luchengo."

Hood kept his silence.

"I'm taking another look at it," the President continued, "because right now we can't risk adding Santa Clara to Bolivia as a possible launching point. Your man Luchengo isn't much but he's the only holding force against Jiminez, short of moving in there ourselves—and that we're not going to do." He paused to light his first cigar of the day. "Sam, do you see even the slightest possibility that the Chinese could slip missiles in there?"

"Not at the moment, Mr. President. Jiminez' base of operations is in the mountains north of San Quentin, where it would be impossible to bring them in by air."

The President glanced at Carew for confirmation.

"We agree with that, sir. The critical indication would be an effort by Jiminez to move south. And if that were to occur—if he got control of the railroad and the port—we think Santa Clara would even be a much more likely launch site than Bolivia. But none of our intelligence suggests that he's planning such a move, or that he has the troops to carry it off."

Hood spoke up. "At this moment, that appraisal would be correct. But the only control on Jiminez' strength or his aggressiveness is the ability of the central government to resist. And I must tell you very frankly, Mr. President, that the Luchengo regime could fall tomorrow. If it did, the road to Ariella would be wide open."

"In other words, we're back to your favorite subject—money?"

"Yes. Money to keep the army intact—money to keep the mines open. If Luchengo can't do both, nothing will stop Jiminez."

The President turned to Secretary Adams. "Do you agree with all this?"

"I do, yes."

Then to Haas: "The ambassador is presenting exactly the same arguments he did the last time he was up here. You still think he's wrong?"

Haas fumbled with the manila folder on his lap. "My earlier position, Mr. President, was that Luchengo did not have popular support and that his relations with Peking were inimical to our interests. The present crisis there, and his recent efforts to expand trade relations with China, would appear to confirm both judgments."

"That doesn't answer my question."

Haas took a deep breath. "I would agree with the ambassador—but only in light of the Chinese development—that we should strengthen Luchengo and reassert our support of him in language that Peking will understand."

The President studied Hood for a long moment. "All right, Ambassador, you win. But don't expect too much—certainly not the full amount we've been sending Luchengo in the past. Breckinridge and the other hard-liners on the Hill aren't going to like this at all."

"I would hope," Hood replied, "that I can tell Luchengo as soon as possible. It would prevent his having to announce new austerity measures that could only stir up more trouble."

"No, Sam, hold off until I see what I can put together with Breckinridge."

"And if he says no?"

"I'll cross that bridge when I come to it."

The decision, then, was not at all final. "If we're through here, I'd like a private word with you."

"Of course." They went through the secretary's office and into the Cabinet Room.

"I want you to know that I disagree absolutely with your statement out there that Santa Clara merits reconsideration only because of the Chinese development. Even without that, you have no choice but to—"

The President tensed. "Don't tell me what choices I have."

"I can tell you one choice you have—that money or my resignation."

"You wouldn't walk out now and you know it. You're holding down a critical spot and you've been around too long to even consider resigning at a time like this."

"That's exactly it, Mr. President. I have been around too long."

The President took Hood by the arm and led him toward the door. "I know how you feel, Sam. It's been a rough couple of days for me too—and that's why I want the first team with me now."

"I meant what I said."

"Then you have my word for it that I'll do the best I can for you."

Simultaneously, Haas and Carew were having a private conversation in the hallway. "You know, Haas, I was low man on the totem pole in there and I wasn't about to butt heads with Adams and Hood. But there is another possibility we've been kicking around over at the agency."

"And what would that be?"

"A military coup against Luchengo. Let's face it, he's never tried to knock out Jiminez. But there are two or three generals down there who *are* anti-Communist and who would chase the bastard all the way to Bolivia if we gave them the hardware to do it. What's more, they've got the Foreign Minister, Lara, on their side. It *could* be put together."

"Do you think there's time?"

"Jiminez is still up in the boondocks, isn't he? And, as I said inside, we see no signs that he's going to move soon."

"And Lara's the key man?"

"That's the way we read it."

Haas thought for a moment. "I'll be in Mexico City next week for a plenary session of the OAS. Lara will be there too."

Carew grinned. "Then maybe you ought to buy him a couple of drinks."

Haas took the CIA man into his office. "I want you to put all this in memo form and get it to me as soon as you can."

"Now wait a minute. I said we were just kicking it around. It hasn't gotten as far as the director yet and, after today's decision, it may not. I have no authority to—"

"All right, I'm giving you the authority. You have a specific request from the White House for an agency report on the possibilities of encouraging the establishment of a new and more stable regime in Santa Clara. Will that do it?"

"I'll have the memo on your desk before you leave for Mexico City."

J OYCE here. Is your man in town?"

Bill Groat, administrative assistant to Senator Breckinridge, was wary. "Just until six tonight, then he's catching a plane home for a couple of days of speechifying. Why?"

"That lead you gave me on Santa Clara. I've come back with a story you wouldn't believe, my friend, and with this new China crisis it's going to blow the lid off this town."

"What do you want with the senator?"

"I want you to bring him over to the studio at three this afternoon. I'll show him the rough cut, then I want four or five minutes of comment from him as chairman of Foreign Relations."

Groat hesitated. "I don't know. You gave him a rough going over the last time you had him."

"All right, let's put it this way. After he's seen the footage, if he decides he doesn't want to comment, I won't push him. But I guarantee you he will. And, believe me, he'll score a hell of a lot of points at home."

After Breckinridge saw the rough cut, he was eager to go before Joyce's cameras for comment on the tragic consequences of American support of undemocratic regimes. The policy had cost us Bolivia, now menacing our very survival, and might soon cost us Santa Clara. Must we always have to learn the hard way that dictators such as Luchengo, lacking popular support, would always be easy prey to Communism? He spoke, too, of his own long record of opposing appropriations to nations such as Santa Clara. And, finally, he paid tribute to Palmer Joyce for his journalistic enterprise and courage.

When the senator got back to his office, there was a message to call the President. Groat heard only one end of the conversation.

"Mr. President, we took the Santa Claran appropriation out on *your* recommendation. Remember? And, very frankly, the cuts in foreign aid are the best issue I've got going for me at home. I reverse my position now and they'd nail me to the cross. . . . I appreciate that you wouldn't ask if it weren't important. But it's also important that you come back with workable majorities in January. . . . If it's that critical you've got contingency funds available. You don't have to come back to the committee for approval. . . . No. After the elections we can take another look at it. But right now I couldn't raise five votes, even if I went along —and I don't. . . . I'm sorry, too. Good night."

The senator glanced at Groat, who was shoving campaign schedules and speech texts into a briefcase. "Wait until he sees that Joyce special next week. It's going to raise a real stink. I'll give you ten to one right now that he won't dip into that contingency fund for so much as a dollar."

"No bet, Senator."

Ambassador Hood was back in Ciudad Alarcon three days before President Luchengo sent for him. It was market day in the plaza and the squeals of suckling pigs, the squawks of chickens and the strident cries of farm wives could be heard through the open windows of Luchengo's office. He took the ambassador out to the balcony.

"You observe, Mr. Hood, the one constant of life in Santa Clara. Governments come and go. Armies advance and retreat. But Friday is always market day in Ciudad Alarcon. I remember a revolution when I was very young. There was fighting on all the roads. But the farmers and their wives still came to town. This palace was under siege. There were machine guns where we're standing now. But down there in the plaza it was just another market day."

They went back into his office. "I sent for you, Mr. Hood, to advise you that the machine guns may return to that balcony. I may have to declare a state of national emergency within ten days. After that I can't guarantee the security of foreign residents. You should plan now for the possible evacuation of your own personnel and of other Americans here."

Hood was unwilling to believe it. "You're expecting a major attack from Jiminez?"

"No, not immediately."

"Then why?"

"Why? Because under a state of emergency the constitution—and I am a constitutionalist, Mr. Hood—confers on me the extraordinary powers I must have to save this country. In other words, I must become what most of your countrymen already think I am—a dictator."

"It's that critical?"

"It is. In ten days I will no longer be able to pay the army. I will no longer be able to pay the workers at San Quentin. Santa Clara is bankrupt."

"A state of emergency won't change that, sir."

"No, but it will enable me to maintain order and to discourage Jiminez for a while longer. I will have the authority to execute soldiers and officers who conspire to rebel; to imprison workers who refuse to work; and to suspend all rights of free speech and assembly."

Hood was aware that such actions would create a wave of public protest in America that could cause the President to reverse his decision. "Even if you were to invoke your emergency powers, sir, it would only be a question of time until Jiminez moves."

"That's correct. And I couldn't stop him. He would be in Ciudad Alarcon within a week. But the key words were yours—*a question of time*. Time for your country to act in the interests of its own security." He lit his pipe and studied Hood through the spirals of smoke. "Why can't you be candid with me? I know the purpose of your summons to Washington. A schoolboy could look at a map and tell your President that Santa Clara, not Bolivia, is the most probable site for Chinese missiles."

"You're quite right," Hood replied, "and there is very grave concern in Washington."

"But you have no word for me?"

"Not yet."

"Do you think you will have word within the next ten days?"

"Hopefully, yes." Hood had already gone beyond his White House instructions. "But I would hope that if there is a delay in Washington you could postpone the exercise of your emergency powers. It would arouse a public reaction that would place the President in a most difficult position."

There was a sharp edge to Luchengo's voice. "His position will be much more difficult if this government falls and Jiminez is sitting behind this desk. And there isn't much time left, Mr. Hood."

"There are practical limitations on what the President can do."

Luchengo's fist hit the desk. "No! There are only political limitations on what he can do—and you are telling me that you serve a politician, not a statesman. He is the most powerful man in the world and yet he is unwilling to exercise that power for fear of losing it. He will act only when he must—only when events frighten him more than the public opinion polls. It's insane!" He went to the window, intent on the color and clamor of the plaza. "You advise me not to use the power I have because it might displease your President. And yet I must use my power only because he is afraid to use his. You don't find that ironic?"

"I am not here to defend the President. I am here to give you the best advice I can. And I must repeat that there are certain realities you must face."

Luchengo came back to his desk. "No, there is only one reality I must face—Jiminez. And I will not go running into the streets to ask the people if they approve. I will do what I must. Good afternoon, Mr. Hood."

Within an hour Hood sent a cable to the Latin American desk of the State Department, warning of the new development and urging that Secretary Adams advise the President of the risks in further delay. He then sent for the embassy's security officer.

"I assume we have a plan for the emergency evacuation of the American colony here?"

"We do. We can have choppers in here from Albrook Air Force Base at Balboa within five hours. Your residence is the mobilization point." The security officer had his wife and three children with him in Santa Clara. "Is there something I should know?"

"It's no more than a possibility at the moment. But we may be nearing a state of national emergency here. I want you to alert Albrook that we may require those helicopters. Except for that, I don't want one word of this conversation to go beyond that door. Understood?"

"Yes, sir."

The embassy's legal officer caught Hood as he was preparing to leave for the day.

"Just before you went to Washington, I got a request from Luchengo himself to check out a New York law firm that's trying to negotiate a deal for a tourist development down around Ariella."

"Yes?" The ambassador was dining that evening with Constanzia Novarese at Casa Castillo and was impatient to leave.

"I got the answer back from the Justice Department today.

The firm—Burton, Foster and Hartung—has legitimate clients but it's also a front for the Cosa Nostra."

"You haven't told Luchengo yet?"

"No, I think this is one you will want to handle. A couple of weeks ago Johnny Partridge made his first trip out of Santa Clara in more than two years. We've been able to trace him as far as Tijuana, Mexico."

"Go on."

"The FBI has had a tap on the switchboard at Burton, Foster and Hartung ever since that raid on the Mafia summit in Las Vegas. And Philip Hartung, one of the partners, was in San Ysidro, California—just across the line from Tijuana—the same weekend Partridge was up there."

"All right," Hood replied, "I'll handle it tomorrow."

"There's one more thing the FBI got on the phone tap you ought to know. If the deal is put together, one of the principal stockholders will be Constanzia Novarese."

Hood said nothing.

"Here's the file, sir. It's all yours."

"No, there's one last thing I'd like you to do. Call Partridge at his hotel. Tell him I want him in this office at ten tomorrow morning. And tell him to bring his passport with him."

But the appointment was kept much sooner. When the ambassador drove into the courtyard of Casa Castillo that evening Partridge's Maserati was already there.

THE DINNER had been a tense, quiet affair. It was not until coffee and liqueurs in the cool, candlelit patio that Constanzia Novarese broke the pattern of evasive conversation.

"Mr. Partridge tells me that you want to see him at the embassy tomorrow?"

"That's correct," Ambassador Hood replied.

"And he is to bring his passport with him?"

"Yes. But I'd prefer not to go into it tonight."

Partridge had not known that Hood was coming to dinner. And he had told the señora of the call from the embassy only to alert her to a probable difficulty with the project, not to ask for her intervention with the ambassador. But now that it was out in the open, he could no longer suppress his resentment.

"The call from your man was a bluff, Hood. You can't lift my passport as long as I stay clean and you know it."

"Tomorrow, Partridge."

"No, tonight. This involves the señora too. In fact she's probably the only reason you're throwing your weight around."

Hood rose to the implication. "You're suggesting what?"

"Let's not play games," said Partridge. "I don't know what your personal feelings for the señora are and I don't care. What I do know is this. You've left me alone down here for two years—no heat at all. But when you discover that my relationship with the señora involves a little more than a fast highball, you decide it's time to roust me."

"That's a cheap gambit, Partridge. I want your passport because you are no longer clean, as you put it. You've been in direct contact with your Mafia associates in the States, and the evidence is clear that you're trying to arrange a covert operation in this country. That you were able to persuade Señora Novarese to lend an element of respectability to it is quite incidental."

"You're wrong, Hood. This is a straight deal or the señora wouldn't be in it. You have no reason to lean on me."

Hood lit a cigarette. "Just that one trip of yours to the border to confer with your old friends would be grounds for sending you back to insure your availability as a witness at the conspiracy trials."

"You're running another bluff," said Partridge. "You take my passport and I can still stay here as long as I like. You can't extradite me."

"That's true. But the Santa Claran government can deport you as an undesirable alien, and I intend to take the evidence I have to the palace."

"You would do that, Sam?" Señora Novarese's voice was reproachful.

"I must. If I have reason to believe that an American national is engaging in illegal activities here, I have no choice but to inform the palace."

Her voice was low over the sputtering candles. "If you accuse Mr. Partridge of illegal activities, then you also accuse me."

"Not at all. I don't think you fully understand who your associates in this venture will be. There are thirteen leaders of the Mafia Brotherhood awaiting trial in the States and most of them are probably looking for a place to run. No, I question that Mr. Partridge's deal is as legitimate as he would like you or me to believe."

Partridge lost his Sicilian temper. "Legitimate! Have you ever had the guts to take a look at your own brotherhood?"

Hood was tired of the argument. "I don't know where all this is leading us."

"Then let me spell it out for you. You spoke a minute ago of my *covert* operation. How in the hell did you come up with all this information on my deal if it weren't for a little covert wiretapping by the FBI?"

"I'm not at liberty—"

"Of course you're not. But we both know you're pushing me around with evidence that no court in the country would accept as legal. But that doesn't bother you or your brotherhood, does it?"

Hood ground out his cigarette. "I think we can end the evening right here."

"No, you'll hear me out. Covert! What would you call the CIA?"

"Espionage," Hood replied wearily, "is a legitimate function of government."

"You peddle that to the poor bastards who bought it on the beach at the Bay of Pigs."

Hood glanced at Señora Novarese. Her face was pale, intense. Perhaps this confrontation between himself and Partridge had always been inevitable. "If you are trying to equate a criminal organization with the American government, Partridge, I can point

out one significant difference. My brotherhood, as you put it, operates in the national interest—or, at least, in what it believes the
national interest to be. Yours has only one interest, one motive—the
dollar."

"You've got to be kidding," Partridge said. "We're backing the
play of dictators all over the world and we come running to prop
them up every time their own people try to throw them out. Why?
Because they pay off by letting American corporations go right
on bleeding the country dry. You wouldn't call that a dollar motive?"

"Then let me put it another way, Partridge. The government isn't
peddling narcotics or prostitution."

"That's right, Mr. Ambassador. But it is peddling howitzers,
warplanes, tanks—and all over the world. I've never had a hand
in narcotics, but I'll guarantee you they don't kill as fast as a B-29.
And don't try to tell me that prostitution is dirtier than napalm."
The rage left his voice. "I don't buy the rotten side of the Mafia,
Hood. I never have. But you buy the whole bag in your operation.
Why can't you look at it the way it is? Why can't you admit that
your brotherhood and mine will do whatever they think they must
to survive? They'll lie, they'll break the law and they'll hire guns to
do their killing. There's just one difference between you and me."

"I would hope there was at least one," Hood replied.

"The difference is that I know what I am and you don't."

Hood stood to leave. "Good night, señora. It's been an interesting
evening."

She took him to the door. "I'm sorry, Sam. I shouldn't have had
him here tonight. I was wrong to interfere."

"Tonight or tomorrow, it would have been the same."

She laid a hand on his arm. "Was he right? Are you after him
because of me? If you are, Sam, that would be wrong."

"That could be part of it. I do want to protect you in this."

"Nothing more?"

"I don't know . . . I don't know."

On the drive back to his residence, Hood tried to fathom his own
motives. Was it to protect the señora that he was acting against
Partridge? And if it was, what was he protecting her from—a
deeper involvement with the project or with Partridge himself? The

questions only brought him back to what he had told her at the door. He didn't know.

But he did know that the quarrel with Partridge had left him with a realization he could define. He *had* bought the whole bag. And if he could not justify his position against Partridge's bizarre analogies, could he justify it in the sterner trial of his own conscience? The answer to that was no. In one respect, Partridge had been wrong. Hood did know what he was.

He had already come to his decision when the Marine guard swung open the gate to his residence. He would not intervene personally in the Partridge case. He would have the legal officer deliver the Justice Department report to the palace the next morning, but without comment or recommendation.

Jorge Luchengo sent for him the same afternoon. The President was tired but his tone was brusque. "Implicit in this report you have sent me, Mr. Hood, is the recommendation that I should reject this proposal."

"Yes," said Hood. "My government could hardly approve of an arrangement whose clear intent is to furnish an extradition-free refuge to American criminals fleeing prosecution."

Luchengo tensed. "I wouldn't consider this proposal for one minute if your government would honor the commitment you gave to me. You've heard nothing from Washington?"

"Nothing."

"Then I have run out of time, Mr. Hood. Now we will find out whose commitments are the most dependable—your government's or the Mafia's."

"You will regret the decision."

"Perhaps. But I have more cause to fear a Communist army in the Andes than a handful of refugees at Ariella. Good afternoon, Mr. Hood."

Philip Hartung flew into Ciudad Alarcon a week later and was met at the airport by Johnny Partridge, who no longer had reason to conceal his involvement. Partridge had cabled Hartung that President Luchengo was now fully aware of the Cosa Nostra's sponsorship of the project, but the New York lawyer was not pessimistic as they drove toward the plaza.

"The Santa Claran embassy in Washington wouldn't have set up this appointment with Luchengo if his answer was a definite no. He's willing to listen."

Partridge was still doubtful. "On Luchengo's desk right now is a request from the U.S. ambassador for my deportation."

"You're still here, aren't you?"

Hartung had brought with him from the States a large folding case, containing a three-dimensional diorama of the tourist development; a feasibility study showing that the project would attract a minimum of sixteen thousand upper-income American tourists a year, who would contribute in excess of seven million dollars to Santa Clara's economy; a lease contract; and a five-million-dollar check for the first annual payment.

A copy of the actual lease had been sent to the palace from New York three days earlier and Luchengo and his ministers had studied it thoroughly. The lease was for ninety-nine years and would entitle the Buena Vista Development Corporation to develop an area extending three miles along the beach front to the west of Ariella and four miles into the interior.

Hartung met with Luchengo and the Ministers of Tourism, Finance and Interior in the President's office for more than an hour, and his presentation was persuasive.

Construction of the project would employ a thousand Santa Clarans and at least that many more would have permanent employment staffing the hotels, the restaurants and other facilities. The development would furnish Santa Clara, without cost, a more modern airport and new harbor improvements. It would encourage the location in Santa Clara of new American service industries. All this, together with the lease payment and tourist expenditures, should assure the government of a minimum first-year income in excess of eighteen million dollars.

The ministers were enthusiastic. The project would relieve the republic's chronic unemployment and balance of trade deficit and, for the first time in its history, Santa Clara would not be a one-industry country.

Luchengo finally dismissed his ministers.

"You are most convincing, Mr. Hartung, but I must question your good faith. You have kept very important information from us."

"The identity of my clients."

"That and the fact that Señora Novarese will be the principal Santa Claran stockholder. You can't be unaware of her opposition to me and to my government."

"Señora Novarese was chosen, Mr. President, because she is a woman of international reputation, whose name alone will contribute greatly to the success of this venture. We are willing to accept another Santa Claran if you can propose one of equal stature and financial ability to participate. We are completely open on this. As for my clients, I can tell you that apart from past activities, of which neither you nor I would approve, they are now among the largest real estate and resort developers in America. The entire thrust of their activities in recent years has been toward lawful enterprises. They are operating projects even larger than Buena Vista in Florida, Las Vegas, Puerto Rico, Hawaii and in many other places—and there has not been the slightest indication of criminal activity."

Hartung began gathering his papers from the desk—all but the check for five million dollars.

"It strikes me as strange, Mr. Hartung, that your clients would risk this large an investment at a time of great unrest in this country. But perhaps it has an importance to them of which I am unaware."

"Not at all, sir. Your internal politics don't concern us. The lease is binding, even if a change of government were to occur. But even if it weren't, we're convinced that whoever is sitting where you are now would appreciate the economic worth of this development." Hartung had one final point. "The lease, sir, safeguards the present rights of Americans in residence here. We understand, for reasons still unclear to us, that there have been representations to you from the American ambassador concerning John Partridge. You should know that we are counting on him for an important management role."

"No," said Luchengo, "I have heard nothing from the ambassador concerning Mr. Partridge directly. I do, however, have a report from his legal officer on you and your clients in which his name appears."

"His status, then?"

"His status will be exactly the same as the other participants'. If they respect the laws of this country—and Mr. Partridge has—there will be no difficulties. If they don't, I will order their deportation and I want that to be very clear." Luchengo took the pen from his desk set. "I will accept this check, Mr. Hartung, and I will sign this contract. But you must understand that I cannot guarantee the agreement beyond my own tenure in office."

"That's a risk we're willing to accept."

And it was done.

Partridge was waiting in front of the palace, but there was nothing in Hartung's expression to indicate either success or failure as he got into the Maserati.

"Yes or no?" said Partridge.

"Yes."

Partridge found it hard to believe. "I never thought he'd go for it—not after that FBI report and the heat on me from the ambassador."

"You're wrong on that last point. All Luchengo had was the FBI report. If you are on the ambassador's list, he did nothing about it."

When they were only a minute away from the airport, Hartung took an envelope from his inside coat pocket. "Here's a draft for two hundred thousand for early expenses—and you're going to have to move awfully fast at this end. Our friends are standing by for the word. They'll fly into Acapulco in a week and charter a yacht to bring them to Ariella."

"That doesn't give me much time."

"They don't have much time. They're due to surrender on the indictments two weeks from now."

Ambassador Hood heard the news from his legal officer later that afternoon. "Luchengo went for that Mafia deal. He has a check for five million and they have a ninety-nine-year lease."

"All right," said Hood. "You'd better inform the Latin American desk and the Justice Department immediately."

"Will do. Incidentally, Partridge sent his passport over this morning. What do you want me to do with it?"

"Send it back to him," said the ambassador. "If the entire Mafia isn't persona non grata with Luchengo, Partridge isn't likely to be."

The following day Johnny Partridge bought the Hotel Playa del Sol in Ariella for one hundred thousand dollars from the Banco Nacional de Santa Clara.

The Playa and its casino had been built forty years earlier as a gambling mecca for wealthy Americans, but World War II had put an end to its brief affluence and the bank took it over in default of payments. It had been kept alive through the years since by the seasonal trickle of tourists and marlin fishermen, but always at a deficit.

It took the bank's directors all of an hour to agree to sell the hotel for half the asking price, and Partridge and Constanzia Novarese drove to Ariella the same afternoon to prepare it for occupancy by the Mafiosi.

The coastline at Ariella ran east and west and the Playa stood on a peninsula extending from the eastern limits, facing the city and its waterfront across the harbor. On the seaward side of the peninsula was an imposing stretch of beach and the rolling Pacific surf.

At its extreme outer point the peninsula swept upward to a craggy headland on which the Spanish had built a lighthouse at the turn of the century to guide their ore ships into the narrow passage between the land spit and the breakwater. The terrain was strikingly similar to the zodiacal crab—the city forming the body and the peninsula and breakwater the arching claws encircling the harbor.

Partridge knew that the rococo if musty elegance of the hotel would contrast poorly with the comforts the Mafiosi and their wives had left behind. But it would have to serve until the corporation built its first residential units. Señora Novarese took charge of refurbishing the most spacious suites, and three shifts of painters, plasterers and plumbers went to work around the clock.

THE PRESIDENT had one reason for delaying and another for later refusing the emergency appropriation to Santa Clara. But he would not be able to call either of them into evidence in his own defense in the national crisis that was to come.

The first was the hope that Gene Haas's secret conversations with Foreign Minister Arturo Lara in Mexico City would produce an alternative course of action—a military coup d'état against President Luchengo that would bring to power a regime the President could support without political penalty at home.

But Haas came back to Washington with a negative appraisal. Lara, while certain that a coup could succeed, was unwilling to lead it. And he had to admit that no single general in the dissident army—not even Carlos Silvera-Guzman—had the prestige to carry it off without the public support of the widow of former President Luis Novarese. And she, he conceded, was deaf to all entreaties to join the coup.

At that point there was still time for the President to act—and without the advice and consent of Senator Breckinridge and his colleagues. But on the evening of the day he read Haas's report he found another justification for doing nothing—Palmer Joyce's special report on Santa Clara.

It was a national sensation—an indictment of American foreign policy which had an emotional appeal to all elements of the political spectrum from the campus revolutionaries to the troglodyte right. For the former, it gave credence to their propagandistic image of Luchengo—a despot who would stop at nothing to maintain his power. (Witness the slave labor and the army's attack on women and children at San Quentin. Witness the dictator's remorseless admission that he was the murderer of his liberal predecessor.)

For the right wing, it was further evidence that Washington was still blind to the menace of Communism—still wasting millions of American dollars on corrupt regimes which were either unwilling or unable to defend themselves against a clear and present danger. (Witness Luchengo's admission that he was not warring against the Communist Jiminez. Witness his arrogant statement that he was accepting American dollars at the same time he was trading in war matériel with Communist China.)

That the ultraliberals chose to ignore the danger from Jiminez and that the ultraconservatives chose to emphasize it was a testament both to the narrowness of their dogma and to Joyce's skill as a propagandist.

The President saw the special report in his office with Press Secretary Busby and Haas on one of the four TV sets built flush into the wall to the left of his desk. There was one for each of the networks and it was his habit to have a picture on all four at the same time during the overlapping evening news shows, flicking on the sound by remote control only when one of the networks cut to politics or commentators on the Washington scene.

But on this evening the news shows were long since over and the Joyce report held the President's full attention. He spoke to his aides only twice during the hour-long documentary, after Breckinridge's brief appearance ("That bastard!") and after Joyce's announcement that Ambassador Hood had refused to grant an interview. ("Not one damn word from him and he expects me to go out on the limb.")

When it was over the President glanced at Haas. "You might have been right after all. It would be suicide for me to stick my neck out after this." Then to the press secretary: "All hell is going to break loose around here tomorrow and we'd better come up with the right answer."

"The right answer," said Busby, "is that Joyce, as always, is peddling his own line of crap. The show's a total distortion of what's happening down there."

"And you think you ought to tell the press corps that tomorrow?"

"I think I should say what I always say after one of Joyce's blasts—that we never dignify him with a response."

"Do you agree with that, Haas?"

The special assistant was frequently the target of Busby's rancor for leaking stories in support of his own position on decisions still under debate by presidential advisers. Haas had always denied it, but there was no way he could escape a direct conflict with the press secretary now.

"I agree with Busby, Mr. President, that Joyce is distorting the picture somewhat. And I agree with you that Hood might have tried, at least, to set the record straight. But, accurate or not, the report was effective. I think we can expect a flood of wires tonight and tomorrow and, certainly, the opposition on the Hill is going to capitalize on it."

(The telegrams already were pouring into the White House, demanding actions ranging from withdrawal of diplomatic recognition of Santa Clara to military intervention against Luchengo's regime, and more than one speech writer for minority leaders was at work on attacks against the President for delivery from the floor or publication in the Congressional Record the next day.)

"I think Haas is right, Busby," the President said. "We're only a week away from the convention and I'm not going to Los Angeles with this albatross hanging around my neck."

"Mr. President, I've spent three and a half years around here calling Joyce exactly what he is—a liar and a fraud. If I stand up there in the morning—"

"Cool down, Max. I'm not asking you to award him a Pulitzer prize. All you have to do is point out that Luchengo was cut off at the pockets by the Congress—and at *my* request."

"And if Hood turns out to be right—if the Communists do take over down there?"

"There are no signs of that happening. I think Hood is crying wolf."

The President told Haas to stay behind when Busby left. "Has the platform drafting committee gotten around to the Latin American plank yet?"

"It's in fair shape."

"What do you think of it?"

"I have to like it. I'm writing most of it."

"I want a paragraph in there calling for a good hard look at all of our Latin American handouts. You can even cite Santa Clara as one of the reasons for it." The President had an afterthought when the special assistant was halfway to the door. "You might even knock heads with Busby again and let a couple of the columnists know that the Santa Claran reference is in there at my specific request."

From the transcript of the press secretary's morning briefing:

Q. What was the President's reaction to the Joyce special last night? That's my bureau chief's question, not mine. (Laughter.)

A. I've had no reaction.

Q. You were with him when he saw it, weren't you?

A. The administration's position is very clear. Santa Clara is not in the current budget and it was taken out at the President's request.

Q. We hear rumbles on the Hill that he's trying to restore it.

A. I have nothing on that.

Q. Perhaps you would favor us, once again, with your own fearless opinion of Joyce.

A. I would but you might print it. (Laughter.) That was off the record.

The President heard the questions and answers from a small speaker built into his desk and sent for Busby when the briefing was over.

"That wasn't much of a case you made out there."

"I took the questions as they came, sir."

"You didn't have to take that last one."

"They already know what I think."

"What you think isn't important. You're speaking for me. Or have you forgotten that?"

"All right, sir, I'll plant a question for the afternoon briefing and go into it in more depth."

"You do that."

The tennis match was over and again it was a standoff. Ambassador Hood's net attack won the first set, 6–2, and he had Han Li-wong at match point three times before finally succumbing to his back-court volleys in the second set, 10–8. It was the closest Hood had ever come to settling their rivalry without the third set neither was eager to play.

They were in the steam bath of the ambassador's residence, clad only in towels and wreaths of mist.

"You were not in your best form today, Mr. Han. I almost had you."

The Chinese forced a wan smile. "You are too modest, Mr. Hood. My game never changes. You, however, were at top form today."

Hood ran more water from the tap onto the blazing hot stones and new eddies of steam sprang toward the low ceiling. It had been a pleasant morning, his one escape from a tense and frustrating week, and he was grateful to Han for his company. He thought of the last time he had seen Han and of the hypnotic effect on his friend of the golden cowry—the talisman of his faith.

"Perhaps next week, if I'm in even better form, I might prove that that golden cowry of yours is vulnerable after all."

Streams of perspiration were pouring down Han's face from his bald pate, clinging momentarily to the slight stubble on his chin, then dripping onto his rotund belly. "No, today only proves my theory. You had me at match point three times and even with your best effort you were unable to dislodge me from my reef." But he said it with little of his old ebullience.

Later, over a seafood salad in the patio, they sat listening to the splashing and shrieking of the children in the pool.

"You and I are growing old," Han said to the ambassador. "And the world we will leave to them will be more hazardous than our own."

Hood glanced up in surprise. Han's remark was entirely out of character.

"Yes, Ambassador," Han continued, "we both share the guilt." His face swept across the lawn to the riotous scene at the pool. "Perhaps we should stop trying and leave the future to them—to the uncynical."

"I wish there were time," said Hood, "but there isn't."

Hood led the Chinese through the cool corridors of the residence to the front portico, where his driver was waiting. Han paused at the head of the steps, his large, sad eyes intent on Hood's.

"If you do ever win the deciding set," he said, "I will present you with a gift of the golden cowry."

Hood tried to banter away his friend's grimness. "I have a better thought. I'll take you to Washington and you can present it to the Smithsonian. I understand it has an excellent collection."

"I've never seen Washington," said Han and trudged down the steps to his car.

Han Li-wong had spent many weary nights trying to break the code in which General Gi You-gin's messages were brought to the legation by secret courier for transmission to Peking. But if he was unable to penetrate the mystery of the ciphers, their significance was all too clear to him.

In past seasons the Chinese trawlers had come alone to the fishing grounds off Santa Clara. But shortly after General Gi's arrival the flotilla was accompanied by a mother ship whose purpose, ostensibly, was to process and freeze the catch of tuna, permitting the fleet to extend its stay.

Han knew that the larger vessel must have brought with it assault weapons and munitions for the offensive Paco Jiminez would launch to secure the missile site. It lay off the coast ten days, discharging its cargo, via the trawlers, at Punta Bunda under cover of night. When it left, with only a token catch of fish in its holds, it was replaced by an identical ship which kept far to sea.

The patrol craft of Santa Clara's *guardia costa* had not been aware of the switch. But Han, monitoring the fleet's radio frequency, was. And he knew that when the second ship made its move toward Punta Bunda—a maneuver he could verify by the increasing strength of its radio signal—Jiminez and General Gi would also be ready to move.

Han was not the inscrutable Oriental and, from the day of General Gi's arrival, his staff had seen an inexplicable change in him. His brisk attention to the smallest affair of the legation was replaced by a listless indifference—except for his fervid concentration on the code and the radio receiver. His aides, unaware of the source of his anxiety and of his sleepless nights, found Han's apparent languor a welcome change from his former officiousness, and wrote it off to the melancholy that afflicts many Chinese emissaries who have been away too long from the only environment they understand. Even the cook was now safe from his tirades. Han ate his tasteless porridge of rice and shellfish without complaint.

The source of his depression was not entirely the decision of his masters to embark on what he knew to be an insane adventure. Han had been a witness and, at times, a party to Peking's recklessness too long to underestimate its capacity for the futile and the unpredictable. More directly, he saw the decision as one for which he personally was to blame. He had come to Santa Clara with the hope of proving to his government that its policies must not always be immutable—that it could achieve its aims through peaceful and rational initiatives.

But the appearance of General Gi had put an end to that hope and had left Han with a sense of deep personal failure. His machinations had led only to circumstances in which *his* legation had been chosen as the instrument for the latest and, perhaps, last of China's miscalculations.

Han took no comfort from the fact that Ambassador Hood must also share the responsibility. He, too, had seen in Santa Clara the round of the world—and he, too, had been unable to dissuade his masters from error that inevitably invites more fearful error. It was clear to Han that his government and Hood's would order their recall when the storm broke. But he could not conceive of an end to their relationship. There was a bond of good will and respect between them and if that were broken—if the dialogue were to end—all hope would end too. It was the subject of one of his most recent aphorisms:

"The guns speak only when reason is silent."

J OHNNY PARTRIDGE was waiting when the hundred-foot ocean cruiser *Reina del Mar*—home port Acapulco—came alongside the dock at Ariella. The first man off the gangway was Mario Cassavettes.

"It looks great, Johnny—just great! You know what my mother said when she first saw it? She said it looks like the town she came from in Sicily. You know—the warm sun, the blue water, the white buildings and all that. She was like a girl again."

Partridge was only half smiling. "Just as long as she knows it's like Sicily in other ways too."

"Like what?"

"The vendettas. Only here they call them revolutions and they come king-size."

"They all know it," said Cassavettes, "but they took the risk. At least they can bust out of here if they have to and that's more than you can say for the maximum security block at Atlanta."

Partridge had all of the town's available taxis waiting on the wharf—a parade of vintage hulks held together only by countless layers of gaudy paint and the prayers of their drivers to replicas of their patron saints dangling from the rear-view mirrors. Also waiting was a boisterous crowd of barefoot *muchachos,* huckstering swordfish spears and sombreros.

To reach the taxis, the capos and their wives had to run the gamut—the women smiling at the raucous youngsters; their husbands grim, anxious for the safety of four walls. It was ten minutes of bedlam before the caravan finally left for the hotel, with Partridge and Cassavettes leading the way in the Maserati.

"They all came?"

"Every one, Johnny. My parents—the Angelos and Scarpattis

from Vegas—the Marconis and Gianninis from Detroit—the Scudis
from Miami—"

"You can give me a rundown later, Mario. There's just one name
I want now. Who's the capo?"

"My father, Bruno, and I'm his consigliere. You'll deal with him
through me." He saw the anxiety on Partridge's face. "Relax,
Johnny. It's like I told you in Tijuana. You're back in the family."

Partridge wasn't that certain. "All of them, including your father,
agreed to the contract on me, and it was given to Luigi Scudi to
carry out. Did you know I got greetings from him every month
in the mail—a .45 slug? And once his enforcers tried to deliver it
personally."

"Why all the sweat, Johnny? If the proposition is as good as you
said it was—"

"I also said there were risks. I want you to remember that."

Cassavettes said nothing more until they left the main road and
swung right onto the peninsula. "You're not wondering why capos
who ran their own families at home are willing to step down and
let my father run this one?"

"I would have gotten around to asking," said Partridge.

"I'll tell you. Because I bought the deal from you and I had to
sell it to them—and against a hell of a lot of opposition."

"Scudi?"

"Among others. And I was able to sell it only because my
father was backing me all the way. In other words, it's got
Cassavettes written all over it—and if it doesn't work out . . ."

"They'll come looking for you."

"And my father."

"And you'll come looking for me."

"You said it yourself, Johnny. It's a gamble for all of us. You
put the game together and there's no way you can deal yourself
out."

The Maserati drew up in front of the Playa del Sol. Cassavettes'
glance took in the moldering drapes, the weather-beaten façade
and the sere palms clacking in the wind on either side of the
entrance. "It's not exactly the Fontainebleau, is it?"

"No," said Partridge, "but it's the best available."

Around them the convoy of taxis came to a wheezing, back-firing halt and Señora Novarese emerged from the lobby to greet her co-directors of the Buena Vista Development Corporation.

Their total worth was in excess of half a billion dollars. They were the owners of enterprises ranging from casinos to conglomerates, from bordellos to banks. They wore five-hundred-dollar suits and slept in quarter-million-dollar homes. They had powerful influence in the halls of government, and no man spoke to them except with deference and respect.

Yet now they were afraid—victims of the old peasant fears and suspicions they had brought with them from Sicily and Italy in their long-ago youth. Their fear had never been of the law, but of their own kind, and the animal caution born of it was all that had kept them alive in their rise from street killers to Cosa Nostra overlords.

Years before they had become a brotherhood, but it was only an expression of their fear. None of them could forget the old days when the families were constantly at war. All of them had lost sons and brothers in bloody ambushes from Brooklyn to Beverly Hills. And, finally, because their terror was greater than their avarice, they agreed to become brothers—to divide America into fiefdoms of crime—and to try the aggressors in a court from which there was no appeal and the only sentence was death.

But they came to Santa Clara without the protection of their own law and its enforcers and their first glimpse of Ariella was as forbidding as Ellis Island had been a half century earlier.

Within an hour of their arrival at the Playa del Sol, Mario Cassavettes met Partridge in the lobby. "Let's have a drink, Johnny. You're going to need one."

The cantina was off the rear of the lobby, facing a patio and swimming pool, whose surface was green with scum. A black marlin hung over the bar, its skin peeling away to reveal the yellow cotton batting inside. On the walls were scores of fading photographs of anglers standing on the sports fishing docks with their catch, blinking proudly into the sun. The bartender, who had been with the hotel for all of its forty years, took five minutes to mix two highballs.

"The place is a hell of a mess, Johnny. Everybody's screaming at me."

"It's all there is," said Partridge, "and we haven't had much time to clean it up. They'll just have to be patient. We've got crews working."

"That's one of the complaints," said Cassavettes. "They don't want strangers prowling around. My God, Johnny, most of their places at home are like fortresses—walls, guards, electronic alarms."

"Then you'll just have to move them back to the *Reina del Mar* until the place is ready. You are going to keep her here?"

"We have a six-month charter. But we'll hold out at the hotel a while longer. It's at least safer. Now for the other beefs. You've got Scudi in the suite adjoining Angelo. They hate each other's guts."

"I'd forgotten," said Partridge. "Angelo lost his first son to Scudi in the war over the Florida horse books."

"And two nephews," said Cassavettes.

"I'll move Angelo," said Partridge.

"But not next to Marconi. Their wives don't get along."

"All right. What else?"

"This one's closer to home. My father will eat only my mother's cooking."

"We've got a good chef. He ought to be willing to at least try the food."

"No chance. He had a marinara sauce laced with cyanide in a Detroit restaurant thirty years ago and his gut still hurts. No, he trusts my mother, and only my mother, to cook for him. You're going to have to build a kitchenette up in the suite."

"For Christ's sake, Mario, they're going to have to put up with inconveniences for a while. And your father, as capo, ought to be the first to understand that."

Cassavettes swirled the ice in his drink. "I'm just the consigliere. Why don't we go upstairs and you can tell my father how a capo should act?"

At that moment Constanzia Novarese came into the bar, and

the two men stood. She was smiling warmly. "You must think we're poor hosts, Mr. Cassavettes. But we've had very little time."

"Not at all," he said. "I think you've done wonders. Will you join us?"

"Perhaps later," she said. "I'm supervising our first dinner. I want it to be a success."

"Italian?"

"Yes. Antipasto, scampi and spaghetti."

"With a marinara sauce?"

"How did you know?"

Mrs. Cassavettes came down to the kitchen only minutes before dinner and, ignoring the chef's sullen resentment over her invasion of his precinct, made an omelette for her husband.

Señora Novarese had the tables set at a massive picture window facing a seaside promenade. But the arrangement was not to the liking of the capos. They led their wives to tables against the walls, despite the objections of the headwaiter.

When Señora Novarese and Partridge came into the huge dining room and saw them, sitting at remote distances from each other, he laid a restraining hand on her arm.

"Leave them alone. The men won't sit with their backs to an open room—or to each other."

"But why? They have nothing to fear from each other. They're all friends."

"Brothers, yes," said Partridge. "Friends, no."

After dinner Partridge and the señora took a walk out the narrow service road leading to the lighthouse. Near the top of the promontory they paused to watch the last scarlet streaks of the sunset.

"You must have had quite a day, Constanzia. But give it a little time and we'll work it all out."

"No, it's been fascinating. I like the wives. They've been very gracious—not at all demanding."

"And the men?"

"Silent, dominating. Very much like most men here and in all Latin countries."

The dusk was turning to dark when they began walking back.

"Look, Johnny!"

A woman was walking slowly, hesitantly down the incline from the hotel toward the surf. She stood looking to seaward for a long moment. Then another woman, and still another, came after. Finally one of them, and then all of them, took off their shoes and stood ankle deep in the cool froth of the ebbing waves.

Behind them, their husbands were watching from the terrace facing a sea that was not the Mediterranean but was evocative of other times and other places. Now they heard laughter as the women, lifting their black skirts, ventured farther into the gentle curl of the surf.

THERE WAS little the FBI could have done to prevent the flight of the Mafiosi. All were free on bail until their day in court, and all were expert in evading surveillance.

Their most common escape ruse had been to charter a plane to fly them to the Mexican border, where they would cross as tourists—without having to show a passport or a visa—and then board a Mexican airliner for Acapulco. All of them left their homes in cities across the nation on the same day, and by midnight the pattern of exodus was clear to the FBI. It was just as clear that Santa Clara was their eventual destination, and urgent requests were sent to all Latin American nations with reciprocal extradition treaties to watch for them at airline terminals.

But the Mafiosi already were aboard the *Reina del Mar* before the Mexican immigration authorities began screening incoming flights to Acapulco. And the ship was already at Ariella before the American consul at Acapulco was able to trace the check in payment of the charter to a front corporation for the Mafia.

The escape was a headline sensation in the Western world, and Palmer Joyce let out all the stops on his nightly television commentary. "The responsibility for the flight of the archcriminals rests directly with Ambassador Samuel V. Hood. This reporter has first-hand knowledge that Hood was aware, for at least two years, of the presence in Santa Clara of one Giovanni Petracci, alias Johnny Partridge, a known Mafia hoodlum. And yet the ambassador stood by, indifferently, while Petracci was plotting the escape of his partners in crime from American justice."

The only virtue Joyce could ascribe to Hood was consistency. "The ambassador has been just as blind, just as indifferent, to the plotting of Red China's secret agents in Santa Clara, and is, in fact, a personal friend of the ranking Communist spy—a frequent guest in the ambassador's residence there. Unbelievable? Not if you're aware of the ambassador's long career of Communist appeasement in both the White House and the State Department."

Joyce also had a prediction. "Despite the President's reluctance to break with his old cronies, it's doubtful that he can survive the embarrassment of Ambassador Hood much longer in this election year. Look for a new man in Ciudad Alarcon and a new policy that will tolerate neither Communists nor the Cosa Nostra in the very shadows of an American embassy."

The storm at home had only minor repercussions in Santa Clara. Acting on instructions of Secretary of State Sterling Adams, Ambassador Hood had a brief audience with President Luchengo, urging him to return the fugitives to American jurisdiction or face the possibility of reprisals, among them a trade embargo. Luchengo told him curtly that the time for threats was long past and that he would continue to honor his agreement with the Buena Vista Development Corporation as long as its principals continued to honor the laws of the republic.

There was also an accusatory cable from White House Special Assistant Gene Haas, instructing Hood to "clarify the embassy's role in this affair, most particularly its failure to alert the appropriate federal agencies." The ambassador replied:

AN INQUIRY FROM THIS EMBASSY TO THE JUSTICE DEPARTMENT ALMOST A MONTH AGO LED TO THE DISCOVERY OF COSA NOSTRA INVOLVEMENT IN THE BUENA VISTA DEVELOPMENT CORPORATION

AND THE PROBABILITY THAT THOSE UNDER INDICTMENT WERE CON-
TEMPLATING REFUGE HERE. MORE THAN A WEEK AGO THIS EMBASSY
ADVISED BOTH THE LATIN AMERICAN DESK AND THE JUSTICE DE-
PARTMENT THAT PRESIDENT LUCHENGO HAD SIGNED THE BUENA
VISTA CONTRACT. I WOULD THINK THAT NO APPROPRIATE FEDERAL
AGENCY OR OFFICIAL COULD BE UNAWARE (1) OF THE IMPLICATIONS
OF A COSA NOSTRA AGREEMENT WITH A GOVERNMENT WITH WHICH
WE HAVE NO EXTRADITION TREATY; AND (2) OF THE RECENT DETERI-
ORATION OF AMERICAN-SANTA CLARAN RELATIONS WHICH WOULD
HARDLY IMPEL THE LATTER GOVERNMENT TO A SPIRIT OF FRIENDLY
COOPERATION.

Aware that he could accomplish nothing without the cooperation
of the palace, Hood took only token action against the fugitives
at Ariella. His emissary was Bennett Cullers, the American consul
in the port city.

In his twenty years at the consulate, Cullers' duties had fallen into
a deadly and often demeaning routine. There were occasional
queries from American concerns on import and export opportunities
in the port city. At least once or twice a year he would investigate
complaints by the Santa Claran government that American tuna
clippers were poaching in its territorial waters. But his most frequent
chore was to arrange for the release from the city jail of American
sportsmen—always penitent the next morning after underrating
either the potency of the local tequila or the virtue of stray señoritas
on the street after dark.

If Cullers' position was a sinecure, the price he paid for it
was subservience to the succession of ambassadors in Ciudad Alarcon. And his judgment that all of them were inept political appointees did not exclude Sam Hood.

The consul, a respecter of local customs, was having his siesta
when the *Reina del Mar* discharged its passengers in full sight of his
offices facing the waterfront. When he awoke, he saw the ship
alongside the wharf, but it was flying the Mexican ensign, and he
thought nothing more of it until the midnight call from Ambassador
Hood, instructing him to pay a pro forma visit to the Playa del Sol.
Cullers spent a sleepless night and had too much coffee for break-

fast. His hands, clutching his attaché case, were trembling when he found Johnny Partridge having breakfast on the terrace.

"I've been expecting you, Mr. Cullers. Coffee?"

"I don't think we'll have time for that." He found both Partridge's smile and his hospitality disconcerting. "I'm here to check the passports of your guests. If you'll have them all come down to the lobby—"

"I'm afraid I can't do that."

"You have no choice," said Cullers. "They're American citizens and they're under my jurisdiction."

"They're also here with the full knowledge and consent of the Santa Claran government."

"Let's speak plainly, Mr. Partridge. There were certain irregularities incident to their departure from the States. To put it bluntly—illegal flight to escape prosecution."

"And you want them to surrender their passports to you?"

"Exactly."

"And after that?"

"After that it's out of my hands. But you can be certain that our embassy in Ciudad Alarcon will request their deportation as undesirables—a request with which the Santa Claran government will comply."

"Are you a gambling man, Mr. Cullers?"

"I am not."

"If you were, I'd lay you a hundred to one that the Santa Claran government will tell the embassy what I'm going to tell you now—to go to hell."

The consul hid his hands under the table to conceal their shaking. It was unfair of the embassy to place him in this position. The matter was clearly of such importance that Ambassador Hood should handle it directly.

"Your comment will appear in my official report, Mr. Partridge. And I warn you that you place your own status in jeopardy by shielding whoremongers, murderers—"

"I'd be very careful if I were you, Mr. Cullers. You're speaking of the directors of a corporation that has a multimillion-dollar contract with the Santa Claran government—a contract that was signed personally by President Luchengo."

Cullers took refuge behind the specificity of his instructions. "I repeat. I have orders to pick up their passports, and I insist—"

"Don't be an ass, Cullers. None of them could beg, borrow or steal a passport. But they all have one credential for leaving the States that the government can have back with no argument."

The consul didn't understand.

"Criminal indictments."

"That's not very amusing, Mr. Partridge."

"No, I suppose not. But then, you didn't come here looking for laughs, did you?"

THE PRESIDENT and Harlan Grant both won the nomination of their parties on the first ballots of conventions held a week apart in Los Angeles.

Their certain triumphs had been forecast weeks earlier and there was little interest across the country in the dreary rituals of roll call, oratory and counterfeit enthusiasm which have always been the trappings of America's quadrennial celebration of the democratic process.

The only surprise came a week later with publication of Lou Harris' first post-convention poll. Grant was still leading but by only six per cent of the vote, his poorest showing of the summer. It was Harris' opinion that voters were fearful of Grant's hawkishness and were convinced the President would react more cautiously and responsibly in the face of the growing nuclear threat from China.

On the morning the poll came out in the newspapers, the President had breakfast with Jim Mallory.

"I think this ought to be worth four or five million dollars to us, Jim."

The national chairman agreed. "I've already been on the line to A list contributors here in the East. It looks very, very good."

This response from corporate executives, who invest in a presidential candidate as warily as they do in a multimillion-dollar merger or capital improvement, was an indicator just as encouraging as the Harris poll that the odds were moving in favor of the President.

"Hit them good and hard," the President said. "Tell them it's the early money we remember the longest." In his optimism, he felt uncharacteristically warm toward Mallory. "We're going to carry this off, Jim, if we can keep it cool between now and November. The poll is right. I think the Chinese missile development was a plus for us. What's important now is to wrap up the congressional session without losing too many points. Grant and his people will be raising hell with every administration bill that's still pending on the Hill. But I want to be absolutely non-political until Congress goes home on Labor Day. I want to be a working President sticking to his desk while Grant is playing politics."

"I agree with that generally," Mallory replied. "But I think you're going to have to step out front on the civil rights bill for proportional employment of minority workers by federal contractors. It's a definite platform commitment and we've got to have it."

"I thought we were all right on that one."

"We would have been if we could have put it through early in the session. But the Southerners insist they're not going to buy another civil rights bill just before the election."

"All right, you tell them for me that I'll be back in January with a lot more muscle than I've got now and I'll shove an even tougher bill down their throats."

"That won't scare up one vote," said Mallory. "You're going to have to twist arms by telling them they either go along or their states are going to lose federal contracts."

"I won't do it, Jim. There's no way you can keep pressure like that out of the newspapers. Dammit, I've done a hell of a lot for the blacks. But if the goddam cities blow up again this summer—and I'm out front again on civil rights—we could throw this election."

Mallory tried to object. "I think we have to put up a fight, even if we lose. The platform . . ."

The President was very patient with him. "Look, Jim, I've been around a lot longer than you have, and I can tell you that platforms are forgotten by the voters a week after they're written."

"Not this time—and not by the black vote."

"I'll give you another lesson in politics," the President said. "When you go picking berries, you go where they grow the thickest— and they grow a hell of a lot thicker in white suburbs than they do in black ghettos."

The intercom rang. The operator had Air Force General Leonard Moody, the White House military adviser, on the line. The President listened for no more than ten seconds.

"I'll be right down, General. Be in my office." He hung up. "It's Santa Clara," he told Mallory grimly. "Jiminez has finally broken loose."

They were six hundred against five thousand but the Arroyo Seco was in their hands within hours of the initial assault. Yet there was nothing the Santa Claran generals could have done to crush Paco Jiminez' forces unless they had known his objective, and the arroyo had never been of strategic importance in the republic's long history of recurring revolution.

The attacks on the central government had always come from rebellious miners at San Quentin to the north and the objective had always been Ciudad Alarcon. The disposition of federal troops was a reflection of the general staff's certainty that when Jiminez did come out to fight it would be from his mountain refuge above San Quentin.

The government kept a permanent garrison of fifteen hundred in the mining town and a thousand more in defense positions along the road to the capital. Three thousand were held in reserve in Ciudad Alarcon to reinforce the northern brigades and to defend the city in the unlikely event that Jiminez, with his small force and light weapons, was able to penetrate the outer defenses. A token force of five hundred was in Ariella, more as a prideful show of force to foreign visitors than for whatever military purpose they might serve.

It was this deployment and the improbable choice of objectives that guaranteed the success of General Gi You-gin's battle plan, to which Jiminez had given prompt and admiring approval.

Jiminez' own forces were in position two days before the attack. He left only a hundred of his guerrillas in the mountains above San Quentin. His main force of five hundred, moving south from the Andes only by night and along trails far to the west of Ciudad Alarcon, was in bivouac in deep ravines only three miles from the Arroyo Seco. Waiting for them was the huge cache of automatic weapons, mortars and ammunition that had been brought ashore from the Chinese trawlers at Punta Bunda.

Han Li-wong knew hours before the Santa Claran generals that the offensive was imminent. On the preceding afternoon the radio signal from the mother ship lurking offshore gradually began to increase in intensity and Han's direction finder told him its landfall would be Punta Bunda.

The assault began at two o'clock the next morning with a mortar attack on the garrison at San Quentin, and the government's re-action was as swift as it was predictable. President Jorge Luchengo met at the palace with his command staff within an hour of the first alarm from San Quentin. Their decision was to send half of the three thousand troops in the capital to the mining town to reinforce its defenders and with orders, for the first time, to pursue and destroy Jiminez' forces. The small garrison at Ariella would be brought north to the capital as partial replacements.

In the early hours after the first mortar shells fell on the barracks at San Quentin, there was nothing to warn Luchengo or his generals that this might not be just another of Jiminez' hit-and-run forays. The troop train from the capital met with no opposition on the run north and found San Quentin quiet except for the structures still burning around the garrison compound. But once the train was in the town there was a second mortar bombardment and this time the target was the newly rebuilt bridge. It fell flaming into the ravine within minutes. By the time the federal troops were able to traverse the banks of the ravine and the swift currents of the river to pursue the guerrillas, they already were circling the town to destroy key bridges on the road to Ciudad Alarcon. Luchengo's troops were now cut off from rapid deployment to the south.

But the troop train from Ariella to Ciudad Alarcon did not reach its destination. Five miles north of the Arroyo Seco it was blown off the tracks by dynamite charges and most of the survivors of the derailment and explosion were cut down by machine gun fire. Only two hundred of the five hundred soldiers were able to fight their way out and start their retreat back to Ariella. A desperate radio message from their commanding officer was the first indication that the assault on San Quentin had been only a diversion—that Jiminez' prime objective was between the capital and the sea.

But where? Even if Luchengo had known the answer, it was too late. The insurrectionists already had taken the Arroyo Seco, its surrounding heights and the vital construction equipment in the maintenance yards a mile north. The Chinese vessel was already discharging its cargo of artillery and shells at Punta Bunda, and the guns would be in position above the arroyo within a week unless Luchengo was able to mount a successful counterattack.

But that threat was remote. Rapid movement of troops from San Quentin was impossible because of the destruction of the bridges, and Jiminez' sappers also had blown the road and rail spans in the foothills south of Ciudad Alarcon, immobilizing the troops still in the capital.

The only sections of rail line and highway still intact were between the arroyo and Ariella. The invasion route to the port city was open. But that phase of the operation must wait until the missiles were on their way from China. A premature action would be too obvious a clue to General Gi's ultimate intentions.

Through the long night of violence, Jiminez lost only eleven of his troops—all slain in skirmishes at highway bridges north of the capital. The army's fatalities were three hundred and forty.

SEPTEMBER

Except for Consul Bennett Cullers' call at the Playa del Sol, there had been nothing to disturb the Mafiosi's first days in Ariella. The fugitives were stoically indifferent to the furor their escape had aroused at home, and Johnny Partridge saw signs that they might adjust to their exile more rapidly than he had thought possible. The patriarchs began to join their wives on long afternoon walks along the beach, and the second night after their arrival there was a high-stakes poker game in the hotel lounge. But they felt secure only at the Playa, and only after Partridge had made arrangements for crewmen of the *Reina del Mar* to guard the gate at the landward approach to the peninsula and to patrol its shores at night in the cruiser's motor launches.

Partridge and Mario Cassavettes spent the first days touring the corporation's leasehold and working out a timetable for the arrival of surveyors, architects and construction specialists. They were having a late drink in the cantina when the announcer on the government radio cut off the music to report that Paco Jiminez was attacking San Quentin. Cassavettes spoke no Spanish, but the anxiety on Partridge's face was obvious.

"What's happening?"

"The Communists have come out of the hills. They're hitting San Quentin, a mining town up north."

"How far north?"

"More than a hundred miles." Partridge shoved his glass toward the old bartender, whose only reaction to the radio bulletin had been a small yawn.

"You think I should wake up my father?"

"No," said Partridge. "Jiminez makes a pass at San Quentin three or four times a year, but it's always a one-night stand. He runs right back to the hills."

"What if it's different this time?"

"Let's cool it until morning. We'll know more then."

Cassavettes shook off the answer. "I'll repeat the question. *What if it's different this time?*"

Partridge glanced toward the bartender. "I'll tell you what I'll do, Mario. I'll start to panic when he starts to panic." The old man was swaying on his stool. He was asleep.

When Cassavettes left the cantina Partridge shook the bartender awake and sent him home. Then he sat at the bar alone, waiting for the next radio bulletin.

It came at three o'clock in the morning—a terse announcement that Jiminez' forces were sweeping south in an apparent effort to encircle Ciudad Alarcon. But President Jorge Luchengo was confident the army of the republic would destroy Jiminez' forces, which were now cut off from their refuge in the Andes.

Partridge first awoke Constanzia Novarese, who did not try to conceal her excitement over the news. "Finally, Johnny. Finally!"

He was incredulous. "You want this?"

She threw open the twin doors to the balcony and the night wind caught her long hair and gown. "I've been waiting for it—praying for it—for three years."

He went to her, turning her slowly until her face was very close to his. "No, you've put all of that behind you."

"Never, Johnny. Not until Luchengo is dead."

"Then let me tell you this. If Jiminez marches into Ariella, we'll both be dead before Luchengo. You want that?"

She put her cheek next to his. "No, but what will happen will happen. There's nothing I can do."

He drew away from her. "You're wrong. You can stop lighting candles for Jiminez."

Cassavettes had not been able to sleep and was at the door within seconds of Partridge's knock. He had taken off only his jacket and shoulder holster, which were flung over a chair. An ashtray on the nightstand next to the bed was full of butts.

"You look like bad news, Johnny."

Partridge told him of the latest developments. "All we can do now is wait."

"And what the hell do I tell my father—that we're here exactly three days and your whole goddam deal blows up?"

"*Our* deal, Mario. You tell your father there's nothing we can do but wait. There's no place to run."

"I'm waking up my father now. You wait."

Bruno (The Bull) Cassavettes was no more than five and a half feet tall, but his presence was one of brute power and menace. Although he was in his early seventies, his two hundred pounds were still rock hard, and his hair was a bristly black. In his youth he had been known as The Bambino because of his massive head and squat legs. But he became The Bull on a night in Brooklyn when a gunman for a rival family shot him twice in the back as he was paying his check in an Italian restaurant. His gun arm useless, Cassavettes charged his assailant with his battering ram of a head, crashing him into a wall and driving fragments of broken ribs into his lungs. He strangled on his own blood.

In later years the Cosa Nostra put his hard head to use in mediating the conflicts threatening interfamily warfare on the East Coast. He was chosen for the role, not only because he was fair, but because his vengeance against those who defied his decisions was swift and certain.

Johnny Partridge had to wait only five minutes for Mario Cassavettes to return with his father. The old man wore a long black dressing gown, and its resemblance to a judicial robe was not lost on Partridge, who stood to acknowledge his arrival, then sat again on the edge of the bed.

The capo took a chair at a table facing him, an old knife scar gleaming faintly through the dark stubble of his beard. His fierce gaze fell on Partridge for a full minute before he finally spoke. His voice had a high, feminine pitch.

"You will stand."

Partridge got up from the bed. The rituals of the old East Coast families in which a capo had the status of nobility were alien to him.

"Now come closer to me. Your face will tell me if your words lie."

Partridge came to within a stride of the table, looking down on the little man. "I tell it the way it is."

"Then you will tell me why this Jiminez already is pushing us around."

"He's not."

"You mean not yet," said Mario Cassavettes.

Before Partridge could answer, there was a gentle knock on the door, and the younger Cassavettes let his mother into the suite. She was carrying a glass of warm milk for her husband to ease the pain of the cyanide ulcer that always struck him in moments of tension. She left as quickly and as silently as she had come.

The old man drank the milk in one long swallow. "You tell this Jiminez to stay where he is or he will have two wars to fight."

"We have no control over him," said Partridge. "He operates alone."

The capo's voice was strident with rage. "You tell him that where I am capo nobody operates alone!"

Partridge glanced toward Mario Cassavettes for support. "Would you explain to your father that it's not the same here as it is at home? We have no muscle to back up threats against Jiminez. Right now all we can do is watch and wait."

"I'll go halfway with you," said the consigliere. "I agree that we can't put the heat on Jiminez. But I don't agree that we should just sit around."

"What then?"

"We send word to Jiminez, like my father said. But we don't threaten him. We work out an agreement."

"You can't deal with Jiminez," Partridge shot back. "He's a revolutionary—a Communist."

"You've been away from the action too long," Mario Cassavettes replied. "We *are* dealing with the Reds—heroin, hashish, opium. If there's a buck in it for them, they'll listen."

"It might come to that later," said Partridge, "but not now. My God, if Luchengo found out we're playing games with Jiminez, we'd all be on the next plane back to the States."

The argument had its effect on the capo. "Yes, we must always go with the power. But we have to be ready if it moves to Jiminez."

"That's a wise decision, Mr. Cassavettes. Our deal is with the government—with Luchengo—and we should stick to it."

"But only as long as he can protect the territory he sold us," said the capo.

"The odds favor him," said Partridge. "This fighting's nothing new. It's been going on for years, and it's always Jiminez who pulls back."

The capo was a student of the tactics of violence. "This Jiminez, you tell me he always loses, but he always comes back for more. How is that?"

"He hasn't many troops," said Partridge. "He hits and runs. He never fights Luchengo head on."

"Then he's a very smart boy," said the old man. He was a survivor himself of many years of such warfare in his youth when powerful Mafia families had been brought to their knees by the tactics of ambush and attrition. Nor could he forget that the time always came when a man had to reappraise his loyalties according to the tide of battle. "Maybe one of these days it will be Luchengo who runs. Then we go to Jiminez."

"I'd call Jiminez a long shot," said Partridge.

"It's the long shots that break a book." The capo grimaced from a sudden spasm of pain in his stomach. "We will be ready to hedge our bet. Our big action stays with Luchengo, but we'll

buy a couple of win tickets on Jiminez if he starts looking good."
He stood to leave, but Partridge had a final point.

"I hope you understand that we knew when we bought in here
that there were risks—that Luchengo could guarantee us nothing
if he lost power. I made that clear to your son, and he should have
made it clear to you."

"Don't try to lay it on me," said the younger Cassavettes. "I
took your word—"

"No more!" The capo glared at his son. "If there is ever a
hearing—if there is to be punishment—you stand with him, and
I will do nothing to protect you." His glittering eyes swept from
his son to Partridge. "You think we came here because of him—a
man who runs away, who spits on his father's grave? No, we
came because of you, and if you were wrong, your crime is
greater than his."

He went through the door without looking back or closing it
behind him. Partridge also went to the door, but paused to look
back at Mario Cassavettes.

"You're a gutless wonder, Mario."

"No, I just know my father better than you do. He wouldn't
hesitate one second to vote for a hit on me."

"But your cop-out didn't work."

"Not this time, but don't push your luck. I'm the only gun
they've got down here now. If there is a hit, you'll still get it first."

"I'll remember that," said Partridge, and left the door open
behind him. He felt much better.

President Luchengo's staff did not advise the embassies in Ciudad
Alarcon of the hostilities until it became apparent that the initial
attack on San Quentin was only the first action in a general offensive.
The telephone call awoke Ambassador Sam Hood at five in the
morning and within an hour he met with his ranking assistants at
the embassy.

His first cable was to the President's military adviser:

MAJOR REBEL ATTACKS NORTH AND SOUTH OF CIUDAD ALARCON.
HEAVY GOVERNMENT CASUALTIES. ACTIVATING STANDBY EVACUATION
PLANS FOR EMBASSY PERSONNEL AND U. S. NATIONALS.

His second message was to the Air Force command at Balboa in the Panama Canal Zone, requesting that evacuation helicopters be kept on twenty-four-hour alert.

Simultaneously, his staff was calling the more than two hundred American citizens in the capital, advising them of the situation and of plans for their evacuation if they chose to leave the country.

The first incoming call to the embassy, at six forty-five, was from an aide to President Luchengo, asking Hood to come to the palace immediately. He found Luchengo strangely calm, despite his gaunt appearance and the frenzy of activity in his office.

An automatic rifle, lying on his desk amid a jumble of papers and maps, caught Hood's attention.

"We took it from one of their dead," said Luchengo. "It's Chinese—their newest."

On the wall to the left of his desk was a large-scale map of Santa Clara on which were drawn in heavy red and blue crayon a series of arrows and circles indicating, respectively, the movement of insurrectionary and government forces and the points of engagement. Staff officers huddled before it, adding new symbols as messengers arrived from the Ministry of Defense with the latest combat and intelligence reports.

Luchengo told Hood to join him at his desk and had one of his secretaries bring them coffee. "You have your evacuation plans in order, Ambassador?"

"I do. We have helicopters standing by at Balboa."

Luchengo took a long sip of his coffee, his haggard eyes intent on Hood. "I want those helicopters. I want them today."

"I can't do that," Hood said. "I have no authority to call them in except to remove our own people."

"Your people are safe for a time. Come." He led Hood to the map on the wall. The largest of the red circles was drawn at the convergence of the railroad and highway at the Arroyo Seco.

"Jiminez is concentrating his forces here," said Luchengo. "He has blown the bridges between the Arroyo Seco and the capital. His objective, then, is Ariella, not Ciudad Alarcon." They went back to Luchengo's desk and, to his surprise, Hood saw a trace of a smile warm the President's features.

"Jiminez' strategy, if we read it correctly, will result in his certain defeat. We've lost the first skirmishes. But, for the first time, we have him out in the open. He has cut off his own line of retreat to the Andes and, if we can drive him from the arroyo, he must fight on the coastal plains. And there we will destroy him."

"Do you have an estimate of his strength?"

"Not more than five or six hundred," Luchengo replied, "and nothing heavier than mortars. But we must drive him out of his present position before he can secure it."

"And you can't deploy your troops for an attack without an airlift?"

"Exactly, Mr. Hood. Your helicopters and by tonight at the latest." He drank the last of his coffee. "You appreciate, of course, the significance of Jiminez' movement toward Ariella instead of the capital."

"I do," Hood replied, "and I think my government will too." He got up from his chair. "You must prepare map coordinates for both loading and off-loading of troops. I'll alert Balboa and clear a radio frequency for you." Hood paused before turning to the door. "Your planning should minimize the risk of enemy contact with our aircraft."

"You can be certain that it will, Mr. Hood. And I hope that you will be able to minimize the greater risk of delay."

The ambassador's second cable of the morning to the President's military adviser was in his hands two hours after the first:

LUCHENGO CERTAIN JIMINEZ' NEXT OBJECTIVE PORT OF ARIELLA. SIGNIFICANCE CLEAR IN LIGHT OF CHINA MISSILE DEVELOPMENT. LATEST CHINESE INFANTRY WEAPONS IN HANDS OF INSURRECTION-ISTS. LUCHENGO ADVISES JIMINEZ NOW CRITICALLY VULNERABLE TO COUNTERATTACK. URGENTLY REQUESTS HELICOPTER TROOP-CARRIERS TODAY (REPEAT) TODAY FOR OFFENSIVE DEPLOYMENT OF OWN FORCES. OUR RISK OF ENEMY CONTACT MINIMAL. JIMINEZ' STRENGTH NO MORE THAN SIX HUNDRED. HELICOPTERS NOW IN READINESS ALBROOK AIR FORCE BASE PER MY EARLIER EVACUATION ALERT. I ENDORSE LUCHENGO REQUEST FULLY.

ONLY Ambassador Hood's first cable was before the President when he met that same morning in the Cabinet Room with the Secretaries of Defense and State, the chairman of the Joint Chiefs of Staff, the director of the Central Intelligence Agency, his own military adviser and Special Assistant Gene Haas.

The President's first decision of the day was against calling the full National Security Council into emergency session. Hood's cable was merely informative and, although Jiminez' move toward Ariella was disturbing, there was, as yet, no call from Santa Clara for invocation of the mutual defense treaty.

The President began his questioning with CIA Director Martin Trask. "Is there even the slightest evidence, either from our surveillance or the Russians', that the Chinese might be flight-testing the missile at Lop Nor?"

"None at all, Mr. President. But we shouldn't overlook the possibility that the rocket engines could be a larger prototype of the intermediate range propulsion system they've already got. In that case, they might risk flying the big one with only the underground tests we're already monitoring."

"Could they accept a risk like that?"

"They could if they were in a hurry to move, but it would be a gamble."

The next question was to the Secretary of Defense Burgess Rand. "Can you give me a minimal estimate of how long it would take, starting from scratch, to build missile sites down there capable of launching this new one?"

"At least two or three months, Mr. President."

"It didn't take Castro that long back in the sixties," said the President.

"But there are significant differences here. Unlike Castro, Jiminez has an army in the field against him, and if his forces are as weak as we think they are he can't divert too many of his troops to construction work. Furthermore, Castro had Russian technicians to direct the operation and train his launch crews. And there's not the slightest evidence that Chinese specialists are moving into Santa Clara."

The President glanced sharply at Trask. "Just one month ago, when we first found out they had the missile, it was the opinion of the CIA that a move by Jiminez toward Ariella would be a most dangerous sign. Now I'm being told that he may not even have the capability to construct a launch site."

Trask stood his ground. "You're asking us today only for time estimates—not for a reading of Jiminez' intentions. What we're telling you is that the danger isn't imminent. I would like your permission, however, for SR-71 overflights of Jiminez' positions. If there is suspicious activity, we'll spot it early."

"All right. Go ahead."

General Mark Courtland, chairman of the Joint Chiefs of Staff, spoke for the first time. "We don't even know, at this point, that Jiminez will strike toward Ariella. The capital is a much more likely objective, and he's now in a position to hit it from two sides."

It was at this point that Ambassador Hood's second cable was given to the President. He read it to his advisers.

"Well, gentlemen? I think we have a new ball game."

There was a long silence. It was finally broken by the President's military adviser, General Leonard Moody. "What Hood is asking for is direct intervention. The question is whether the situation warrants it. I would want to know a lot more than we do now."

"How much more?" said the President. "If, as Hood says, the Chinese are now arming Jiminez, I think we have to react."

"There's no evidence the weapons came directly from China," his aide replied. "It's much more likely they came from Bolivia."

General Courtland shook his head in disgust. "My God! A disciplined army of at least five thousand against six hundred bare-ass peons, and they're yelling for help the first day."

The President glared at him. "Five minutes ago you were telling me that Ariella wasn't his prime objective."

"I still don't think it is. He has to take the capital or he's no better off than he was in the Andes. If Hood is right—if Jiminez is between Ciudad Alarcon and the sea—he's cut the country in half. He's also cut the capital off from the port and can eventually starve Luchengo out. It's good tactics and it could have nothing to do with missile sites."

"I'm inclined to agree with that," said Rand. "I think we're discussing the remotest of possibilities. I'm not at all convinced that Jiminez would go along with the Chinese on this. He must know that we would intervene at a certain point—that he has everything to lose and nothing to gain."

"You're forgetting Castro," the President replied. "He was willing to take the same chance."

"No. There was a difference, Mr. President. Kennedy had every ICBM in the Soviet Union pointing at him and Castro was counting on that to force his bluff. But China can't back up Jiminez and he knows it."

Secretary of State Adams caught the President's attention with a slight cough. "We do have a mutual defense commitment, Mr. President, and what Luchengo wants is far short of full intervention. If we let him have it, it could save us from a much deeper involvement later. Hood is on the scene and I don't think he would have written such a cable if the circumstances didn't warrant it."

The President spun toward Haas. "I haven't heard from you yet."

The special assistant agreed with everyone. "We should, of course, respect the treaty, but it's invocable only if Luchengo's own forces can no longer resist effectively. And we don't know that to be a fact. We have nothing before us but Hood's cable—and it certainly doesn't amount to a formal request from Luchengo for military assistance. I agree with General Moody that we should know more than we do now."

The President stood up from the conference table. "Thank you all. I'll let you know my decision within an hour."

Minutes after his advisers left the White House, the President was speaking to Senator Breckinridge on the telephone. He read the chairman of the Senate Foreign Relations Committee both of Hood's cables.

"What do you want from me, Mr. President?"

"I want an expression from the Senate—if only from your committee—consenting to whatever action I may find necessary."

The senator had a long memory. "We haven't given the executive a blank check like that since the Gulf of Tonkin resolution—and that was not one of our better moves. No, even if we weren't recessing in two days, you couldn't put it together. You don't need our approval. As Commander-in-Chief, you can do whatever you want."

"Bob."

"Yes?"

"I do need it. The way sentiment's running in this country, I'd be dead if I went in there without the Senate's consent. Christ! Our own platform takes on Luchengo."

"Then you've got at least two good reasons for staying the hell out of there."

There was a cold edge to the President's voice. "I can also stay the hell off the same platforms with you from now to November, and I hear you're not in very good shape."

"That's right. I'm not. But I'd be in worse shape if I went for this resolution. And I can tell you this. If you do intervene down there, you'll need me on the same platform a hell of a lot more than I'll need you."

Haas wrote the cable that was sent to Hood over the signature of the President's military adviser:

DECISION YOUR INTERVENTION REQUEST NEGATIVE (REPEAT) NEGATIVE PENDING FULLER PICTURE OF DEVELOPMENTS AND EVIDENCE LUCHENGO ARMY UNABLE TO DEFEND AGAINST CLEARLY INFERIOR FORCE.

There was no reaction from the White House to wire service reports of the Jiminez offensive until Press Secretary Busby held his afternoon briefing. And, until the President sent for him just an hour before he was to face the correspondents, Busby himself knew no more than the reporters—only that the President had met with his highest military and foreign affairs advisers.

It was the President's intention to play it down. "All you have to tell them, Max, is that we met only because this appears to be Jiminez' biggest move yet—and we're watching it closely. Emphasize that Ciudad Alarcon and our own people there are in no danger. You might add that we have information that Luchengo is mounting an early counterattack."

"That's all?"

"No, but it's all you need to know now."

"You'll have to fill me in sooner or later," said Busby.

"Then it will have to be later."

They had been over this ground many times. "You can't expect me to go out there and field those questions intelligently if I'm kept in the dark."

"You'll know what I want them to know and nothing more," the President replied.

"And that, sir, calls into question both my discretion and my ability to handle myself."

"Max, Max. You wouldn't be here if you weren't the best. But face it. Those two hundred correspondents wouldn't be here either if they weren't the best. And they can't drag something out of you that you don't know."

Excerpts from the transcript of Busby's afternoon briefing:

Q. There was a lot of brass over here this morning. Santa Clara?

A. Yes. We're watching it closely. But the latest word is that the capital is secure and that the government is mounting a counterattack.

Q. No early evacuation of our nationals, then?

A. Not to my knowledge. . . . Now I have one announcement. With the Congress recessing in two days, and the civil rights measure still in committee, the question has come up whether the President should call them back into session. You can quote him as saying that it would be futile in light of Senator Grant's continuing opposition and—

Q. Can we hold off on the politics until we're through with Santa Clara?

A. I thought you were.

Q. No, I think we all have more questions. Secretary Adams will neither confirm nor deny a report that we have a request from the Santa Claran government to intervene. Do we or don't we?

A. I've heard nothing on that.

Q. Would you try to find out for us? (The President heard the question over the speaker in his desk, and sent for Haas.)

A. I'll look into it.

Q. Now, tying into that report is one from UPI in the Canal Zone that we have troop-carrying helicopters on alert status at Balboa. Is that true?

A. Again, I'll look into it.

Q. You don't know?

A. I said I'd look into it.

Q. And how long will that be?

A. Just as long as it takes.

Q. Look, Max, I'm not the only one here up against an A.M. deadline. You're forcing us to speculate and tomorrow you'll raise hell if we're wrong.

At that moment Haas came strolling into the press secretary's office—an apparently casual visitor. But the signal to Busby was clear. He lost little time calling Haas to his side.

"I've got a couple of questions here, Haas, on which you might have fuller information. One, there's a report that Luchengo's calling on us to intervene and, two, that we have choppers on alert at Albrook."

"The answer to the first question is negative," said Haas. "We've had no such request from the Santa Claran government. The answer to the second question is affirmative. But the aircraft are on alert status only to evacuate our embassy staff and other nationals and that may not be necessary."

Haas left before direct questions could be put to him by the correspondents, who finally let Busby read the statement blaming Senator Grant and his minority colleagues for the shelving of the civil rights measure.

All of the correspondents knew that the President heard every word of the more important press briefings in his office, and the older hands knew that Haas's sudden appearance was no accident—that he had come from the Oval Office with information that had been withheld from the press secretary.

Busby had been a rough cross-examiner of White House press secretaries in his own day, and it had been a disappointment to many of his colleagues that he had chosen to walk the other side of the street.

If they were grateful to Haas for filling out their story, they were also resentful of the affront to Busby. It was not just that he was their friend. He was a *newsman*.

AMBASSADOR HOOD had no authority to return to Washington without the consent of the President or the Secretary of State. But his first action after receiving the negative response to his cable was to send another—to the Latin American desk reporting that he was flying to Washington immediately for consultations with the President.

He then telephoned President Luchengo. "I regret that the reply is negative, sir."

But Luchengo's first words were not for him but for a shaken Han Li-wong, who was standing before his desk in the palace. "May I ask you to step outside for a moment?" He was back on the line seconds later. "All right, Mr. Hood. I now formally invoke the mutual defense treaty—and the reply to that cannot be negative."

"I'm afraid it will be," said Hood, "unless you can prove that your own forces are inadequate to—"

Luchengo's voice rose to a shout. "If I could prove that, it would already be too late. If I can attack tonight—tomorrow at the latest—I can end this in one day."

"The decision may be reversible," Hood replied. "I'm flying to Washington immediately."

"That also will be too late, Ambassador. But you may tell your President for me that when he finally intervenes—and he will— it will not be to save my country but his own."

Hood's secretary was waiting for the call to end. "There's no flight north today. They're using the Electra to run troops down to Ariella. The airport's off limits—indefinitely."

Hood got his military attaché, Colonel William Gruver, on the intercom. "I want a helicopter here from Albrook—and fast. I also want an Air Force jet waiting there to fly me to Washington."

Within minutes Gruver rang Hood back. "It's all laid on. The chopper's already on its way. I'll notify the defense command here that it's coming."

The word that an American helicopter had clearance to enter Santa Claran air space did not reach a sergeant leading a reconnaissance patrol outside the city. The aircraft, still at low altitude, came under rifle fire after taking off from the residence with Hood and its crew of three aboard. There was no serious damage to the helicopter, but the radio operator was shot in the leg. His injury was minor and he was able to inform his base of the attack and to receive a message for Hood from his counselor at the embassy.

REPLY YOUR CABLE TO LATIN AMERICAN DESK FOLLOWS. QUOTE PERMISSION DENIED. IMPERATIVE YOU REMAIN ON POST. SIGNED: ADAMS. UNQUOTE.

From Balboa, Hood sent word ahead that his mission was more critical than his presence in Ciudad Alarcon. The news of the attack and the Santa Claran government's prompt admission of responsibility would be flash news by the time Hood got to Andrews Air Force Base just outside Washington.

The automatic rifle had been found in the hands of one of Jiminez' guerrillas slain in a skirmish at one of the road bridges north of Ciudad Alarcon. It was still on Luchengo's desk when Han Li-wong was shown into the office.

"It will not be necessary for you to sit down, Han. I have only one question to ask you." He shoved the rifle toward Han. "Can you explain how this weapon, of Chinese manufacture, was in the possession of forces trying to destroy a regime to which your government professes friendship?"

Han had no ready answer. But the interruption of Hood's telephone call gave him time to think in the outer office. When he came back, Luchengo was not the same man he had left. His icy control had given way to a rage which Han found physically threatening.

"Your answer—now!"

"What can I tell you, Mr. President? I have no knowledge that my government is responsible. This gun could have come from Bolivia or from another country with which we legally trade in arms."

"Is there a difference whether you strike us with your left fist or your right?"

"I have no authority to speak on such matters. I am here only to buy copper."

Luchengo seized the rifle and ejected one of the bullets onto the desk. "Yes, Han—the copper in that shell casing." The interview was over. "You and your staff will leave Santa Clara by the earliest possible transportation. And you will inform your government that its hostile actions toward this republic abrogate all agreements between us."

Han was unable to take the first step toward the door until Luchengo, his face softening almost imperceptibly, rose to his feet and gave the Chinese the smallest tithe of absolution.

"Good-by, Mr. Han."

Newsmen and television cameras were waiting for Ambassador Hood outside the floodlit main gate at Andrews. Assistant Secretary of State Ed O'Farrell was also waiting, but at the ramp where the jet fighter was now taxiing to a stop.

O'Farrell shook Hood's hand. "The Air Force gave out your ETA, Sam, and there's a mob of press at the front gate. I'm to run you out the back way."

"To the White House?"

"No," O'Farrell said, "the President won't see you until nine-thirty tomorrow morning. And, incidentally, he blew sky high when he found out that Adams' cable didn't stop you from coming."

"I didn't expect him to roll out the red carpet," said Hood. "But now that I am here, what can he possibly have on his schedule tonight that's more important?"

"Believe it or not, a cocktail party for congressional leaders and their wives. The session ends tomorrow."

"He can step out for five or ten minutes. That's all the time I want."

"You wouldn't find him very receptive tonight, Sam. Take a look at this." O'Farrell gave the ambassador the final edition of the Washington *Daily News*. There was a picture of Hood on the front page and a glaring headline: LUCHENGO TROOPS FIRE ON U. S. ENVOY'S PLANE: WOUND CREWMAN.

"We had clearance," said Hood. "It was an accident."

"Then let's call it an untimely accident," said O'Farrell. "It gives the President one more excuse to back off."

"Not this time. He'll move or else."

"You'd quit?"

"Yes," said Hood. "But only for openers. If I go, I'll go with a bang, not a whimper."

The car drew up in front of the Dupont Plaza Hotel.

"I'm not at the Mayflower?"

"No, Sam, the press knows you stay there." He saw the look of disgust on Hood's face. "You want company for a little while?"

"They're working you late tonight, Ed."

"No, this is on my own time. Let's have a couple of drinks—maybe dinner."

"Upstairs, of course."

"Of course."

Hood had to smile.

The morning was as cloudy and grim as the ambassador knew the President's temper would be. The guard at the west basement entrance took Hood directly to the Oval Office. The President was alone and did not stand to greet him.

"Your orders were explicit, Ambassador. You were not to abandon your post at a time you yourself describe as critical."

"It's precisely because you reject that definition that I'm here, Mr. President."

"Whatever you want from me, Sam, I can tell you that you're off to a bad start. I hold you personally responsible for the attack on that plane. You had no authority to call it in there." He lit a cigar. "You're pushing me and I don't like it."

"Yes, I am pushing—and hard. I've held still month after month for the rejection of every recommendation I've sent to you—every warning that you were playing into China's hands. But you listen only to Haas and Haas listens only to Harris and Gallup."

"That's enough!"

"No. I'll say what I must because it may be my last chance— and yours. China is going to try to site missiles in Santa Clara. There's no question of it. Jiminez could have taken Ariella the first night. And the only reason he didn't was that it would alert us. If you don't act now—"

The President ground out his cigar. "Yours is a minority opinion, Ambassador. I met this morning with the Secretary of Defense, the chairman of the Joint Chiefs, the director of the CIA—"

"I'm on the scene. I'm laying it out the way it is. They're up here sitting on their duffs, telling you what you want to hear."

"And what would that be?"

"That the situation will hold until after the first Tuesday in November."

The President rang his appointments secretary. "The ambassador is leaving now. He's to go out the basement entrance."

Hood took a paper from his attaché case before rising from his chair. "I have two small formalities to bring to your attention, Mr. President. The first is a demand from Luchengo that we invoke the mutual defense treaty."

"The answer is no."

"May I know why?"

"Because he isn't even bloodied yet. And because the treaty—"

"The second formality is my resignation, Mr. President." He threw the letter on the desk.

"I accept it, effective the day your replacement arrives in Ciudad Alarcon."

Hood had the last word. "If you remember nothing else I've said today, remember this. You're being given lead time John Kennedy never had in Cuba. I warn you. If you don't act now, you're playing politics with World War III."

The President swung in his chair, facing the rose garden window. He did not turn back to his desk until he heard the door close. A guard was waiting in the corridor to escort Hood to the basement entrance, but the ambassador strode past him toward the West Lobby, where the correspondents already were gathering for Press Secretary Busby's ten o'clock briefing.

Busby came out of his office when he heard the sudden clamor of voices in the lobby and was met by one of the senior correspondents. "Hood is willing to go for a press conference. Can we move it into your office? I think we'll want a transcript on this."

There was nothing Busby could do, except to lead Hood into his office and then slip through a private door to the Oval Office to alert the President.

The transcript:

Q. Can you fill us in on the attack on your plane yesterday?

A. We had full clearance. The fire came from a unit that was out of radio contact with the defense command.

Q. Senator Grant says the attack was just one more example of a small pro-Communist country pushing us around.

A. That's ridiculous.

Q. Would it be accurate to say, Mr. Ambassador, that you would not call on the Air Force for transportation if your mission was not highly critical?

A. That's correct. There are aspects of Jiminez' tactics that suggest a risk not only to the security of Santa Clara but to our own.

Q. Would you enlarge on that?

A. It should be obvious that, with the recent detection of China's developing ICBM capacity, a new Communist foothold in this hemisphere could have the gravest significance.

Q. Do you have evidence, Mr. Ambassador, that China is backing Jiminez or that he would accept missiles?

A. No. But I have no evidence to the contrary, either.

Q. But you suspect it?

A. Let me just say that the possibility concerns me.

Q. Does the President share your concern?

A. I can't speak for the President.

Q. From what you've told us, can we presume that you flew here with a request for our immediate intervention to block the possible siting of Chinese missiles in Santa Clara?

A. No comment.

Q. We were told yesterday by Mr. Haas that there has been no request from Santa Clara for our intervention. Was that correct?

A. No comment.

Q. Then you refuse to confirm an official White House announcement?

A. If that's what you want to conclude from a no comment, I can't stop you.

Q. Mr. Ambassador, we all appreciate your coming out here. But you're raising more questions than you're answering. You're leaving us with the impression, one, that the situation in Santa Clara is much more dangerous than the White House will admit and, two, that Mr. Haas may not have been entirely candid with us. Do you want to leave it at that?

A. I have made only one statement here today—that our position and that of the Santa Claran government may be much more critical than we thought.

Q. And you flew to Washington to inform the President of that fact?

A. Obviously.

Q. Were you able to persuade him to accept your view?

A. Again, I think that's a question that should be put to him, not to me.

Q. Just one more question, Ambassador. There were elaborate precautions last night to keep you away from the press. And we were told this morning by Mr. Busby that you would not be

*coming out this way. But here you are. What should we conclude
from that?*

A. That I got lost. (Laughter.)

The President hit the switch to cut off the speaker and spoke
to Busby, who was standing at the side of his desk. "When you
go out there, tell them only that I saw Hood for fifteen minutes
and that he gave me a late report on developments, including a
request from Luchengo for our intervention. And stress that this
was my first knowledge of the request."

"That's all?" said Busby.

"No. Tell them we're considering appropriate action but that
we have no information on Chinese involvement."

"They won't let it go at that, Mr. President. What's at stake
here is White House credibility. Either Hood is misrepresenting the
picture down there or we are."

"Go with what you've got, Max. They're waiting for you."

"All right, but I'll tell you what their story is going to be—that
Hood flew here out of a war zone, and at great personal risk,
to warn you that our intervention was crucial—that you disagreed
with him, and that he went over your head to the press to try
to force you to change your decision. It's his headline and it'll
be a big one."

"It'll be his last headline," said the President.

T HE AIR FORCE pilot had orders to defend the helicopter if
it was brought under fire and two crewmen were manning their
heavy machine guns as the aircraft sped almost at ground level
across the open terrain between the Andes and Ciudad Alarcon,
rose slightly to clear the red rooftops of the city and finally set
down on the lawn of Ambassador Hood's residence.

Ducking under the still whirring rotor blades, the military attaché, Colonel Gruver, met Hood as he came down the ladder. "Ambassador, we have Coca-Cola, American Cash Register and Campbell Soups waiting inside. They want to evacuate now."

"Then start moving them aboard," Hood replied. He heard the low rumble of artillery fire from the south.

"It's from the Arroyo Seco," Gruver told him. "The federal troops went on the attack—if you can call it that—just before dawn. We hear they're taking another mauling."

Hood strode grimly into the residence, where the American businessmen, their families and stacks of luggage were clogging the corridor. The Coca-Cola man stood up abruptly, blocking the ambassador.

"I hold you responsible for this, Hood."

"For what?"

"For the lack of adequate warning—for the fact that we have to fly our wives and children out of here at the last possible moment."

"You're in no danger," said Hood.

"With Jiminez practically on the outskirts of town?"

"That gunfire," Hood replied, "is fifty miles away. But if you're going, go—the helicopter's waiting."

"I warn you, Hood. I have a complete inventory of the plant. When I come back, if there's as much as one typewriter missing, I'll file a claim against—"

"You won't be back," said the ambassador, and broke away toward the staircase leading to his quarters. From behind his barricade of suitcases, the son of the Campbell Soups agent drew a bead on Hood.

"Stop it!" his mother said. "It's no time for games." The thud of distant artillery hung in the air and the boy began to cry.

The critical element was time. Paco Jiminez must be driven from the arroyo before he could fortify it. But even under forced march, the army units at San Quentin—cut off by the blown bridges— would require at least two days to reach the ravine and even longer to move their artillery.

President Luchengo and his generals agreed that they could not wait. They must strike and quickly with their only available force—fifteen hundred troops and three batteries of light artillery that had been flown to Ariella aboard the Electra.

All but five hundred, who would protect the rear of the assault units, were to move north on the highway, whose bridges were still intact, and be ready for action before dawn.

Luchengo was aware of the obvious flaw in his battle plan—that Jiminez would know that the attack could come only from the south and would be ready for it. There was confirmation from the crew of the troop-carrying Electra, which had been observing the frantic shuttling of the bulldozers on the heights above the ravine for a full day, and pinpointing the targets for the army's artillery. All of the defensive positions were being dug on the south face of the ridges.

Yet Luchengo, who had flown to Ariella to join the assault units, was hopeful. He had the advantage of both numbers and fire power. What he did not have was what the Americans could have given him—an airlift of troops to attack Jiminez from the north, where he was defenseless.

The afternoon before the attack, advance patrols from Ariella swept north on the highway, securing the bridges against only token opposition. Behind them came the caravan of troop and artillery transports.

Two hours before sunrise the infantry was in position in barrancas a half mile below the ridges, and the artillery—a mile to their rear and out of range of Jiminez' light mortars—began the bombardment an hour before dawn. The first rounds were on target and Luchengo, from the artillery command post, saw the orange flare of the shells exploding on the heights and then flames towering toward the sky. Within a half hour the entire crest was ablaze and thundering from secondary explosions.

At first light the infantry was to begin moving up the steep slopes, but Luchengo was wary. There was not the slightest sign of life on the heights. Was the position a decoy? Was Jiminez already circling his forces and moving south, as he had at San Quentin? The troops were held in position awaiting reconnaissance from the Electra and from patrols fanning out around the arroyo. But there was no indication of enemy movement and Luchengo gave the order for the infantry to advance.

It came at almost the precise moment General Gi knew it would. From his observation post a half mile to the west of the ravine, he had been watching the shells fall harmlessly into empty gun pits. Jiminez, his guerrillas and weapons were safe in slit trenches three hundred yards to the west of the target zone. Their one activity during the bombardment had been to man electrical detonators to explode gasoline drums and dynamite charges to create the impression that the artillery fire had had deadly effect.

A thin smile lit General Gi's face. His tactic was as old as Korea and Vietnam—straight from Mao's text on guerrilla warfare. Had no one in the Western world read it? Was it conceivable that they could ignore, into infinity, the costly lesson that cannon— yes, and even mass fleets of bombers—were impotent against a mobile force that chose to come out and fight only when it had the advantage of surprise and terrain?

Gi saw the federal troops moving cautiously up the slopes in thin skirmish lines. He would wait until they were almost to the crest, at point-blank range, before calling Jiminez and his gunners from their trenches. And, simultaneously, he would silence the federal artillery. The six cannon brought to Punta Bunda by the Chinese ship were in position below Gi's observation post, hidden from both Luchengo's guns and from aerial observation in a grove of trees. During the long bombardment he had been able to plot the position of the opposing artillery as precisely as the Electra had been able to target the ridge.

Luchengo's first warning came from the crew of the plane, which saw Jiminez' troops throw off the camouflage of brush covering their trenches and run toward their main positions. Seconds later the first Chinese shells fell on an artillery battery only a hundred yards from Luchengo's observation post. He would recall later his first reaction—that it was inconceivable that Jiminez could have weapons of such power. But before the reality could impose itself on him, the next shells struck only fifty yards away and the concussion flung Luchengo and his command staff to the earth with the impact of a massive sledge hammer.

The crew of the Electra saw the muzzle smoke of the Chinese guns and tried to radio their location to the command post. But there was no answer. The radio operator was dead—a sliver of shrapnel in his brain—and the survivors, deaf from the concussion and incapable for long minutes of either awareness or decision, heard nothing.

When there was no return fire, General Gi swung his guns toward the arroyo, and the federal troops fled headlong down the slopes to escape the crossfire of shrapnel and high explosives from the west and the rain of steel from the ridge.

Luchengo's first conscious sensation, a half hour after the almost direct hit on the command post, was of a searing pain that cut through the numbing shellshock like a scalpel. The first face he saw was that of the medic who was removing a wedge of shrapnel from his right shoulder.

Other faces slowly came into focus: two generals, the only survivors of four at the original command post, huddling over a map—a radio operator translating the staccato voice from the Electra into letters and ciphers marking the position of Jiminez' artillery—and the dead, lying in orderly files in a place where all else was disorder.

They were at a new command post, five hundred yards from the first, under a concrete bridge spanning a dry river bed. One of the generals saw Luchengo try to rise to his feet as the medic wound the last turn of bandage into place, and knelt beside his commander-in-chief to report.

The army still had twelve guns in action and was preparing to return the fire of the enemy artillery. Even as he spoke, the earth shook from the first salvos from guns on both sides of the bridge under the protective bluffs of the riverbank.

The reports from the arroyo itself were still fragmentary. But it was apparent that the infantry commanders had lost contact with their units after the panic retreat from the slopes and would not be able to reform them in time to renew the assault for many hours. And even then the attack could not succeed if the enemy's artillery was still in action.

A nod was Luchengo's only response, and for the rest of the day the artillery duel continued. The army lost three guns and General Gi only one. The approaches to the ridge were still in his grasp. At nightfall Luchengo finally saw the hopelessness of his position. The battle for the Arroyo Seco had been lost and he had no choice but to retreat if his army was to have the resources for the ultimate battle. And he gave the order to fall back on Ariella, where he knew it would be fought.

The American embassy had been the scene of calm but intense activity through most of the long afternoon and evening. The communications officer, monitoring the army's short-wave radio traffic, gave Ambassador Hood a running report from the battle scene. When it became clear, early in the afternoon, that Jiminez had won another major success, the ambassador sent for Colonel Gruver.

"Does this look as serious to you as it does to me?"

"Yes, sir. If Luchengo retreats, and I think he must, Jiminez would have a clear shot at the capital."

"You don't think the troops coming down from San Quentin could hold the city?"

"If they were in a mood to fight, yes," the military attaché replied. "But there have already been heavy desertions and we understand many of the companies are at no more than half strength. And it's going to be worse when they hear the reports from the arroyo."

Hood shook his head. "How much time do you think we have?"

"To answer that, I would have to know what Jiminez is going to do next. In his position, I'd counterattack and destroy what's left of the southern army before it got to Ariella. In that event, Ciudad Alarcon ought to be safe for a while longer."

"What if he moves north instead?"

"There's nothing to stop him. He'd be here in two days at the most."

Hood came to his decision. "All right. Let's notify the rest of our nationals to pack up—that we can no longer insure their safety. How many helicopters are available to us?"

"Albrook can lay on eight. We should be able to move everyone out in a day. I take it this includes our own families too?"

"Yes, and all of the non-essential personnel here in the embassy. I'll want just you, the communications staff and the Marines."

"Ambassador?"

"Yes."

"I have a wild hunch I'd like to run past you."

"Let's hear it."

"Jiminez is no Clausewitz but he's no idiot either. He could have had San Quentin or Ariella the first night. He could be knocking on our door right now. But instead he digs in at the arroyo. The question is, why would he throw away all of his chances for a quick win?"

"You tell me, Colonel."

"It didn't add up until today, when we found out he had artillery. And, believe me, that heavy stuff had to come from China. He couldn't have brought it from Bolivia without our CIA agents there spotting it."

"What's your hunch?"

"That Jiminez is going to stay right where he is—and wait."

"Wait for what?"

"Would you believe that new missile the Chinese have got?"

"I'd believe it, Colonel. But Washington wouldn't."

"Shouldn't we at least be on record with it? I can start drafting a cable now."

"We're already on record—and all the way to the White House."

"You've been way ahead of me, Ambassador." There was reproof in Gruver's voice. "I might have been helpful to you, at least at the Pentagon."

"No," said Hood. "The President prefers to believe your disclaimer. What was it?"

The colonel knew when to back off. "That it's nothing more than a wild hunch."

"Yes, that was it."

The ambassador had dinner at his desk. His advisory to the State Department that he was ordering the evacuation had drawn an immediate request from General Leonard Moody for an hour-by-hour report on the progress of the fighting. When the word came at nine o'clock that Luchengo was retreating, Hood wrote his last cable of the day:

LUCHENGO WITHDRAWING TO ARIELLA. HEAVY CASUALTIES. MILITARY ATTACHE AGREES JIMINEZ POSSESSION OF ARTILLERY CONFIRMS CHINESE INTERVENTION TO SECURE POSSIBLE MISSILE SITE.

He took the message to his secretary in the outer office. "Show this to Colonel Gruver before it goes, and tell him I'm leaving for the residence if he wants me."

She stood up from her desk. "We've been told we're being sent home tomorrow."

"Yes," said Hood, "I don't know how much longer it will be safe for you here." He took her arm. "But we'll have time in the morning for good-bys."

"I'm willing to stay, Mr. Hood. We all are." The first tears came.

"I know that and I'm grateful."

She took a call on her intercom. "It's the Marine post at the main gate," she told the ambassador. "Mr. Han is down there. He wants to see you."

"Tell them I'll be right down."

The embassy had been on alert status all day and floodlights cast their harsh illumination over the grounds and surrounding walls. Hood went directly to the gate and the Marine sergeant gestured toward the plaza. Han was sitting on a bench a hundred yards away beneath the statue of Guillermo Perez, *El Libertador*.

The sergeant sensed Hood's intentions. "I don't think you should go over there, sir."

"No, it's all right."

"Then I'll go with you."

"You'll stay on your post, Sergeant."

"Yes, sir." Hood was already on his way across the avenue. The sergeant spoke to the other sentry. "You heard me warn him?"

"I heard you, Sarge."

"Then put it down in the log. I'm not buying myself a court-martial."

I t HAD BEEN a long day for Han Li-wong. His orders from Peking had come only minutes after midnight and they were a rankling disappointment to him.

Han had been confident that his government—if only for propaganda purposes—would instruct him to call on President Luchengo to deny all charges of intervention and to warn him of the grave consequences that could result from his abrogation of the trade agreement and his expulsion of the Chinese legation.

But Han was wrong. His only orders were to destroy all codes and secret files and to accede without objection to Luchengo's demand that he leave by the first available transporation. He was also told to expect further instructions from General Gi You-gin, which he was to obey without question.

Han had been determined to call at the palace one last time to salvage the respect he felt was his due. Luchengo's scornful treatment of him was the more grievous because he felt it was unjust. He could not imagine the circumstances in which Ambassador Hood would suffer the same summary dismissal as he had at the palace. Yet, certainly, he had tried as hard as Hood to avert the present confrontation. And, assuming that he and Hood could fairly be held accountable for the actions of their governments, what was there to choose between American blunders that were an open invitation to Communist aggression in Santa Clara and Chinese opportunism in accepting the invitation?

But his orders gave Han no opportunity to justify himself at the palace—to leave his first diplomatic post with even a semblance of personal dignity. Even his personal safety was in doubt. The government radio, rallying Santa Clarans to the defense of the republic, laid the blame for Jiminez' offensive on Chinese arms and duplicity, and announced the expulsion of Han as the agent of the warmongers of Peking.

Han's staff began burning the legation's secret documents in the courtyard long before dawn. He was on the balcony, watching, when he heard the bass counterpoint of the guns from the Arroyo Seco through the thin crackle of the bonfire.

The Chinese legation was not the only foreign mission in Ciudad Alarcon which had been the scene of night-long activity. When the word had spread that the Americans were evacuating Santa Clara, it was a clear signal to the entire diplomatic community that there would be no intervention by Washington and, without it, no guarantee of safety for the personnel of other embassies and consulates. The diplomatic exodus from Santa Clara would start the following morning in planes under charter to the Organization of American States. And President Luchengo had left orders, before joining his forces at the arroyo, that Han and his staff were to be aboard the first plane to Guatemala City.

Despite the curfew and the danger to himself, Han left the legation late in the evening for a last look at the city as he had known it. The silence of the streets was broken only by the infrequent rumble of an army truck and the thunder from the arroyo. The guns were heard at persistent intervals now in the slow, rhythmic cadence of a death march.

It had not been his conscious intention to call on Ambassador Hood. There was nothing to be said except good-by and that had a finality Han was unwilling to accept. But the dark, descending streets all led to the plaza—to the palace, where he was the enemy, and to the American embassy, where he had a friend.

The sergeant of the Marine guard was insolent and threatening, his rifle at the ready position. But he finally went to the telephone in the sentry box to relay the message to Hood, and now Han saw the ambassador walking toward him through the bright lights encircling the compound and into the deep shadows of the plaza. His face was grim.

"You shouldn't have come here tonight, Mr. Han."

"I'm sorry. I should have known it would be awkward for you." He glanced toward the embassy. The Marine sergeant had left his position at the gate and was standing on the verge of the plaza, observing them intently.

"It's not that at all," said Hood sharply. "It's dangerous on the streets after curfew, and, I would think, particularly dangerous for you."

"I know," said Han, "I've heard the radio. But I came to say good-by. I leave in the morning."

"That soon?"

"Yes, the orders from my government came today."

"Then I'm glad you came, Mr. Han."

They sat down together on the bench under the hulking figure of *El Libertador*—its green patina glowing in the moonlight, breaching even the shadows with the presence of violence.

"You'll be returning to China, of course."

"To a new assignment—yes."

"Whatever it is," Hood replied, "I hope you will have more luck than either of us has had here."

Han glanced at him in surprise. "You can wish me luck."

"Of course." A faint smile lit his face. "For all of your little sermons to me, you are a bit of a heretic, you know. You came here not entirely to promote the faith, but to reform it."

Han put up only token resistance. "No, I may question the means, but not the end."

"The end," said Hood, "can only be the sum of the means. To question one is to question both." They heard the rattle of rifles from a patrol firing at shadows on the outskirts of the city. "You didn't want it to come to that, Mr. Han."

"No," said the Chinese. "Guns solve nothing." He was silent for a long moment. "You accuse me of apostasy, Mr. Hood. But what of yourself?"

"Unlike you, my friend, I have no rigid gospel to question. Yours has dogma, a continuum of vengeful apostles to enforce it, and certain retribution for those who dare to doubt. My faith has no inviolable scripture and its commandments come down from a papacy with a four-year tenure. It takes little courage to defy it, Mr. Han. I can wish you luck because your heresy is far more dangerous than mine."

Han disagreed. "There can be no credit for either of us. There was peace when we came and now there is war. I think we are poor missionaries."

"Perhaps. But we've at least been on the side of the angels." He put a hand on Han's shoulder. "And we won't say good-by—not yet. We still have an old score to settle."

"The third set?"

"Yes."

"But why?" Han spread his hands in a gesture of futility. "If, as you say, there is little moral choice between my faith and yours, docs either of us deserve to win it?"

"One of us—or at least the credos we represent—*must* win it, Mr. Han. One of them is going to prevail, and I would prefer that it be mine."

"But, again, I must ask why. You concede that my faith has doctrine and discipline, and that yours has none—that mine is graven in stone and yours is written in sand."

"But that's just the point," Hood replied. "Mine is capable of reformation precisely because it is not doctrinaire. It can accept new realities and new revelations, and I'm afraid that yours cannot."

"I can't agree," said Han. "In China there is constant re-examination and change."

"Yes, but always toward a more rigid orthodoxy—toward a crueler repression of dissent."

"Please, Mr. Hood. You have had your own inquisitions. You are having them now."

"Agreed. But the dissent continues—and always away from orthodoxy and toward a remission of error. No, Mr. Han, the American faith—however blind or inconsistent—is still the best and, perhaps, the only hope."

"Then our third set becomes academic," said the Chinese. "You are suggesting that you can still influence events and that I cannot."

"I have had no more influence than you," said Hood. "But it's important that we go on trying. If we do—and we must—the time could still come when our third set would prove nothing more cataclysmic than which of us is the better tennis player."

"I would like that," said Han. A faint smile lit his face. "I am an atheist, Mr. Hood—and you?"

"An agnostic, I think."

"And yet we have spoken tonight almost entirely in religious allegories. Why?"

Hood thought for a long moment. "Perhaps because the language of diplomacy, or politics, contains no equivalents for such words as right or wrong—moral or immoral." The ambassador stood. "It's very late, and I'm going to insist on dropping you off at your legation."

"It is late. Thank you."

Hood's car was waiting and it was only a two-minute ride to Han's quarters. Neither of them spoke until the driver swung the door open for the Chinese.

"Good night, Mr. Han."

"I hope you're right—that it is good night, and not good-by." His eyes were huge and intense behind the thick lenses of his glasses.

Hood held out his hand. "Have faith."

The message from General Gi was waiting for Han. He was not to return to China with his staff. On arrival in Caracas he was to take a Lloyd Aereo Boliviana flight to La Paz, where the Communist government would arrange for his covert re-entry into Santa Clara. His new assignment: communications and liaison officer on the staff of General Gi.

In his many years in overseas service, Han had always been able to isolate his own role from the forbidding context of China's world attitudes and policies. As an expert in trade, he saw himself as the antagonist, not the ally, of the militarists in Peking. To Han, the explosive potential of eight hundred million Chinese in the market places of the world was a far more certain instrument of China's ultimate victory than thermonuclear megatonnage. And he could cite precedents in his own career: the gradual estrangement of Japan from the Western nations because of its dependence on China's raw materials and massive buying power; the refusal of many African nations to accept Western armaments and mutual defense treaties written in Western chancelleries, for fear of closing their vital trade channels with Peking.

Han was certain that in time even the superpowers—America and the Soviet Union—must join most of their allies in yielding to the *fact* of China. But the militarists, of whom General Gi was a formidable representative, were just as convinced that time was running out—that a balance of terror, not of trade, was the only deterrent to Western aggression.

Into the early hours of the morning, Han studied his alternatives. To join the staff of General Gi would be to deny both his convictions and his claim to citizenship in a rational world. But he also knew that he could not defy Gi's orders and return to China to plead for a reversal before it was too late. Hood had given him credit for too much courage. He was not a martyr and comrades far more prestigious than he had paid for such dissent with their lives.

Hood! Han also gave thought, but only briefly, to the possibility of asking for political asylum in the West, and he knew he could count on the ambassador's protection. But that, too, would require a degree of courage he did not have, and a renunciation of loyalties he still felt and strongly. If his commitment to the strategies of Communist China was in question, his commitment to Communism was not.

There was, after all, no alternative. He would obey General Gi's order because he could not remove himself from the struggle. Hood himself had said that it was important that they both continue trying. He could join General Gi because his insane enterprise must fail, and its failure would hasten the time when China must accept a more realistic view of its place in the world—his view.

THE ARTILLERY FIRE at the Arroyo Seco awoke Johnny Partridge at five in the morning. The one day of calm between Paco Jiminez' first assaults and the government's counterattacks at the arroyo had been a deceptive sign that this was, after all, just another of the revolutionary's hit-and-run strikes.

Partridge had been in Ariella the previous morning and had seen the survivors of the troop train ambush straggling back into the town. But this evidence of a preliminary defeat for the army was offset by claims on the government radio that Jiminez was now cut off from retreat to the Andes and that federal forces were moving into position to destroy him.

But now the concussion of the guns, only thirty miles away, shook both the walls of the Playa del Sol and Partridge's own hope that the crisis was approaching an end. In the first moment of awareness between sleep and full consciousness, he fumbled for the switch on his bedside radio, but there was nothing but static.

Seconds later he heard frantic voices in the corridor and then an insistent pounding on his door. Mario Cassavettes was clad in his pajamas and robe and had not taken the time to brush his hair. Behind him, Partridge saw four of the elderly women, trying to peer around the consigliere. Down the hall he heard the shrill but authoritative voice of Bruno Cassavettes above the angry clamor of the other capos.

"Come in and shut the door."

"You'd call this just another little skirmish?"

"No," said Partridge, "but that's got to be heavy artillery, and only the government has it. They could be kicking the hell out of Jiminez up there."

"And what if it's going the other way?"

The radio suddenly burst into life with the coda of the Santa Claran national anthem and, a moment later, the voice of an announcer. The battle that would determine the future of the republic was under way. Loyal Santa Clarans would pray for the success of their sons in arms and would remain calm.

Cassavettes stood next to Partridge, waiting for him to translate.

"It was nothing."

"No word on how it's going?"

"Not yet." Partridge nervously lit his first cigarette of the day.

"Losing a little of your cool, Johnny?"

"No. I'm betting that the news, when it comes, will be good."

"And if it isn't?"

"We'll have to fall back on your father's strategy that we go with the power. We can try to contact Jiminez."

"You said he wouldn't listen."

"There's just one chance that he will. Even if he wins today, he's still got a long fight ahead before he can knock out Luchengo. And as long as Luchengo honors his deal with us, the U. S. has one more excuse for not sending troops in to bail him out. At the moment, we're a political asset to Jiminez."

"At the moment. But what happens if he finally does knock out Luchengo?"

"Let's play one hand at a time, Mario. Now why don't you go out there and try to quiet everybody down?"

"What do I tell my father?"

"Just what I've told you. We should know where we stand by tonight."

It took Partridge ten minutes to shower and dress before tapping on the door connecting his suite with Señora Novarese's. She let him in and then took him out to the balcony. In the half darkness to the north, the red glow of the bursting shells could be seen a second before their impact shook the hotel. Partridge put an arm around her shoulder and felt her tremble under the thin robe.

"You're shaking. You shouldn't be out here."

Her eyes were bright with excitement. "It's not the cold." There was another flare in the distance and its answering thunder. "Do you know what this could mean, Johnny?"

"I know. But I wonder if you do."

"Not now." Her head was suddenly against his shoulder, her tense body pressing against his own. "Please, not now."

He ran his fingers through the dark cascade of her hair. "Sorry, I just came to see if you're all right."

"I am. It's a beautiful morning."

He drew away from her. "You can't know what's happening up there, Constanzia."

"I do know." She said it with such certainty that he was afraid she did.

Foreign Minister Arturo Lara spent the morning at the army's communication center in Ciudad Alarcon, concealing his inner elation over the adverse battle reports behind the smoke screen of his Cuban cigars.

But he did not act until the report came that there had been a direct hit on President Jorge Luchengo's command post. He drove immediately to the airport where the Electra was refueling for another series of observation flights. Lara's cabinet rank gave the pilot no choice but to obey the order to fly him directly to Ariella.

Midway in the flight, the word came that President Luchengo had been struck by a shell fragment but was still alive and in command of his forces. But Lara gave only brief thought to aborting his mission. Dead or alive, Luchengo was certain to lose, Lara told himself, and, as a patriot, he must act to save the republic from Jiminez. He had the army driver at the airport take him only as far as the government building in Ariella. And, once the car was out of sight, he caught a taxi to the gates of the Playa del Sol. He was kept waiting while one of the guards rang up Johnny Partridge, who had the sole authority to admit strangers to the hotel.

Partridge was waiting for him on the front steps. "Can you tell me what's happening up there, Señor Lara?"

The Foreign Minister, wearing the uniform of a full colonel, drew himself up to his full height. "I have come from Ciudad Alarcon to report to the señora—and only to her."

"She doesn't know you're here, and she won't until you answer me."

Lara sighed. "It is a black day for the republic, Mr. Partridge—a disaster."

Partridge saw Mario Cassavettes watching them from the cantina. "What do you want with the señora?"

"That is not your affair."

"Do you want to see her or don't you?"

"I do, and I will tell her that her place is not here with you. She is a Castillo and her people call to her."

"Does Luchengo know you're here?"

Lara lost a little of his military bearing. "Please, Mr. Partridge, if you will let her know I am waiting."

Partridge went to the telephone at the desk and was back in half a minute. "Go on up. She's on the second floor—Suite B. And, Lara, when you come down, keep right on marching until you're out that gate. Speak to no one."

A second after the elevator doors shut behind Lara, Mario Cassavettes was on his way across the lobby.

"Who was the brass, Johnny?"

"Lara, but he's not army—just the Foreign Minister."

"Just the Foreign Minister? You sound as if that doesn't amount to much."

"Down here it doesn't. He's a flunky."

"But he knows more than we do."

"No, he came down from the capital. He hasn't been to the front."

"Then what's he doing here?"

"He's an old friend of Señora Novarese's."

"And he just came by for a little chat?"

"You could put it that way."

"Or I could put it another way—that you're a liar, that you're holding out on me."

"Now why would I do that, Mario? It's like your father said. You and I are in this together, remember?"

The glass pendants on the huge chandelier over the lobby chimed from the sonic impact of another round of artillery.

"If there's bad news, Mario, I'll want you to be the first to know." He was smiling. Cassavettes wasn't.

Even before she saw him, Constanzia Novarese knew that Arturo Lara's presence was a confirmation of her own intuition. If he was an opportunist, he was a cautious one. And he would not have come—the risk to himself was great—if he did not believe Jorge Luchengo's position was critical.

She heard his report at a table on the balcony over glasses of Dubonnet and only Lara's account of heavy government casualties struck briefly at her elation.

"Santa Clarans have died for worse causes. At least good may come of this," she said.

Lara did not fully share her appraisal. "Santa Clara gains nothing, señora, if we permit one tyranny to replace another. Jiminez has won a grand victory, but it must be his last."

"Be patient, Lara. Your day will come. You will be *el presidente*. But only when Luchengo is dead."

"Then it will be too late, señora." There was an imploring tone in his voice. "You want only Luchengo's life, and I understand that. But if he dies by Jiminez' hand, Santa Clara could die with him."

"And you, my friend, what do you want?"

"I want him to be driven from power by the Americans—not the Communists. And trust me, your vengeance is mine. He will not survive."

"I know what you want of me, but again I must tell you that I can do nothing."

"But you can, señora! Ambassador Hood is begging his government to send troops. But it will refuse as long as Luchengo is in the palace. The Americans call him a dictator, a murderer. They will come only if there is a coup—a new regime—and the generals, señora, will follow only you."

Señora Novarese wasn't convinced. "You believe that because you want to believe it—because it serves your ambition. But the army would not turn against Luchengo now. It will stand with him against Jiminez."

"Señora, the generals blame Luchengo for this disaster. They blame him for not destroying Jiminez long ago, as your husband would have done. And they will turn against him if there is an assurance that the Americans will help us."

"But you have no such assurance."

"Your name is that assurance—your call to the people to rise against Luchengo and to unite against Jiminez. You have great and powerful friends in Washington."

"You are most persuasive, Lara." She stood to signal the end of their conversation. "But you must believe that the Americans will act—and in time. Jiminez will not spare Luchengo, and the Americans will not spare Jiminez. Then we will both have what we want."

"And if the Americans don't come?"

"Ambassador Hood has told me that they will—that they will not permit a Communist regime."

"Ambassador Hood is in disfavor. He does not speak for his government."

"And you, do you speak for the generals? Does even one of them know you've come to me?"

"But they are with their troops, señora. There has been no opportunity to—" He caught himself as he saw her glance fix on his trim, spotless uniform.

"Yes," she said, "they are with their troops—and that's where they should be."

Johnny Partridge had held the taxi to return Lara to Ariella. He stood watching on the steps of the Playa until the Foreign Minister was safely through the gate, and then went upstairs.

He listened grimly as Señora Novarese told him of the debacle at the arroyo and of Lara's proposal that she launch a coup against Luchengo.

"I hope you told him no."

"I did."

"Then that's the first good news of the day." He took both of her hands. "We may have to check out of here in a hurry—perhaps tonight. If Mario Cassavettes asks you questions, you know nothing. Lara is just an old friend and he wouldn't have left the capital if there was a crisis."

"Johnny?"

"Yes?" He was impatient to leave.

"Where would we go?"

"Up the coast to Escalante. I'll have the boat ready if we need it."

She took a step away from him. "If you go, you will go without me. My place is here."

"You may have no choice but to run."

"Jiminez wouldn't dare—"

"But the Cassavettes' would."

She didn't believe him.

Mario Cassavettes was waiting for Partridge in the lobby. "You ready to level with me now?"

"It was just what I said it was—a friendly little visit. But if you're that uptight, Mario, I'll run into town and try to find out what's happening."

"You do that. But the señora stays here."

Partridge fought back the anger that would expose his hand. "I'll be back, Mario. Don't worry."

"Who's worrying? You might run out on us, Johnny, but you won't run out on her. And the guards at the gate have a standing order. The señora is never to leave the hotel grounds, with or without you."

"She won't like that."

"I suppose not. But do her a favor. Tell her what will happen if she tries."

Partridge shook his head in mock reproval. "You wouldn't shoot a lady, Mario."

"Don't try me."

P RESIDENT JORGE LUCHENGO led his retreating army into Ariella at nightfall, through somber crowds lining the sidewalks, to the bivouac area around the ocean-front airport. After the predawn communiqué that a climactic battle was in progress, there had been no further announcements on the government radio. But the soldiers, haggard with exhaustion and shock, their heads snapping with every jounce of the troop carriers over the cobbles, were mute evidence of defeat.

On their arrival at the bivouac, cookfires were blazing in the dark, and medicos and burial parties stood by to receive the casualties. The women of Ariella, whose sons, lovers and husbands had been at the front, also were waiting. But for those who found their men among the living, there was only brief joy, because they knew this might be only the first of many vigils they would keep. For those who found their men dead or dying in the long rows of litters, there was anguish. But for them, at least, the lonely terror of waiting was over.

President Luchengo, his right arm immobile in a sling, and his tunic flung over his shoulders, spent an hour in the command tent, approving orders for the defense of Ariella, before boarding the Electra, which had been on standby to return him to the capital.

Foreign Minister Arturo Lara, who had been forced to wait at the airstrip all afternoon and evening, was dreading a possible confrontation with Luchengo on the flight north. He did not delude himself that the President was unaware of his loyalty to Señora Novarese, and that his presence in Ariella would arouse suspicion.

The only excuse he could invent was that he had flown to the port to submit to his commander-in-chief a draft cable to the Organization of American States demanding military assistance. He wrote the draft that afternoon in the sweltering concrete structure serving the airport as both a control tower and fueling station. That it should already have been sent from Ciudad Alarcon as a formality safely within his own small authority was the one flaw in his stratagem he would find difficult to explain. But it was better than nothing.

On boarding the plane with his chief of staff and other generals, Luchengo saw Lara sitting alone in the tail section, but gave him only an impassive glance. Minutes later, when the plane was nearing the arroyo, Luchengo left his forward seat for the flight deck to observe the activity below.

The darkness was broken only by the dull glow of lights on

earth movers digging the emplacements for the cannon now moving up to the crest. Surveillance from the air and radio reports to the plane from federal forces guarding the approaches to Ariella and Ciudad Alarcon were not entirely discouraging. Jiminez obviously was strengthening an already formidable position, but he was not taking advantage of his clear opportunities to resume the offensive.

When Lara saw Luchengo return to his seat, he took the cable forward. "I thought you should see this as soon as possible, sir. If you think the situation warrants, it can go off tonight."

The President read only the first paragraph. "You waste my time, Lara. I should not be reading this, but the answer to it, although I know what it will be." The only sign of the throbbing pain in his shoulder was a slight flexing of his jaw muscles.

"An appeal to the OAS would expose to our allies the magnitude of Jiminez' success," said Lara. "I would not act without your approval in a matter of such importance."

"It is of no importance at all," Luchengo replied. "The answer will be no—that this is an internal affair in which the OAS has no obligation to act."

"But it is not. The cable cites evidence of Chinese involvement and the danger not only to Santa Clara but to—"

Luchengo shook his head wearily. "The answer will still be no. Our brave sister republics will act only if the Americans order them to, and the Americans will do nothing until the knife is at their own throat."

"Your instructions, Mr. President?"

"Send it. It can do no harm, and it will be on the record to haunt our allies when their own time comes."

The plane was banking steeply on its final landing approach. With his one free hand, the President had difficulty buckling his seat belt, and Lara bent over to help him. Their faces were only inches apart. "If you found Señora Novarese safe and well, Lara, Ambassador Hood would be glad to know."

Luchengo and his retreating army had been at the outskirts of the city when Johnny Partridge left the Playa del Sol for the

marina earlier that evening. It was time to set his escape plan in
motion by moving the *Mañana* to the cove below the lighthouse.
But his boatman, José, was not aboard the cruiser or in his shack
on the pier, and Partridge went to the nearest of the cantina-
bordellos along the waterfront. In response to his inquiry and a
five-peso note, the bartender sent him upstairs. Through a half-
open door, Partridge found his man spread nude across the bed,
muttering in his sleep. The prostitute, wearing a thin slip, stood
at the window, staring dully into the street. The only light in the
room came from a candle in a niche holding a figurine of her
patron saint. Her one reaction to Partridge's presence was to fling
a sheet over her client.

Partridge tried vainly to shake José back to consciousness, then
spoke to the woman.

"Cafe, por favor—muy caliente." She put on a robe and went
for the coffee. When she came back, Partridge had José sitting
precariously on the side of the bed, struggling to dress himself. He
was a frail man, but he had shown Partridge surprising reserves of
strength in combat with giant marlin thrashing at the end of a gaff.

José had no apologies for his condition. "This is a night, *patrón,*
when *hombres* who are too old to fight should be drunk—should
have a woman." He spoke to the prostitute. "Am I not a man?"

"Sí, mucho hombre."

The first army units were entering the narrow street as Partridge
and José left the bordello, and they had to wait in the Maserati
for the convoy to pass. President Luchengo was in the lead vehicle,
but there were no *vivas* from the sullen crowds. Partridge glanced
at his companion and saw in his thin, dark face an expression of
pure malevolence.

When the street was finally clear they drove to the marina and
spent an hour topping off the water and diesel tanks, and changing
the oil. Finally they cast off the mooring lines and crept out into
the harbor, without running lights. A half mile away, they saw the
cutter from the *Reina del Mar* patrolling off the Playa del Sol.
Twice its searchlight swept toward them, but they found cover
behind the higher hulls of other craft in the bay.

Once outside the breakwater, it was only a short run around the tip of the peninsula to a cove on the seaward side of the lighthouse. The wooden jetty was old and crumbling, but the mooring had compensating advantages. The cove was hidden from sea patrols by a high outthrust of rocks and from observers on the cliff above by a dense tangle of cactus clinging to the precipitous headland. A steep path, cut into the rock, led up to the lighthouse.

After securing the cruiser to a buoy off the end of the jetty, the two men slid the dinghy over the stern, and José took the oars for the mile-long row back to the marina. Partridge gave him a drink from a bottle of whisky he had taken from the cruiser's stores, then had one himself.

"No questions, José?"

"It is very simple. You are afraid. You think you will have to run like a mackerel from a shark. But you are wrong, *patrón*. Jiminez is no shark. You will be safe."

"And the señora?"

José let the oars trail in the water and took another drink. "She is a good woman, and she is the enemy of Luchengo. We will not harm her."

"We?" He studied José incredulously. "You're not for Jiminez?"

"I'm for the people, señor. The people—Jiminez—is it not the same?"

Suddenly they saw the cutter, not more than fifty yards away, and an instant later were caught in the glare of its probing light. The patrol craft's idling engine burst into full life and it bore down swiftly on the dinghy.

Two crewmen with automatic carbines were in the bow, but they broke into smiles when they saw their quarry. Partridge and José were on the floorboards of the dinghy, wrestling for possession of the bottle. José finally rose unsteadily to his feet, threw a wild punch at Partridge and fell over the side. The bottle and both oars went with him.

A laughing seaman on the cutter held José's head above water until Partridge could hand-paddle the dinghy toward him and drag him back aboard. Another of the Mexican sailors took the dinghy's bow line and, at reckless speed, the cutter began towing the smaller craft toward the marina.

Twenty yards off the mooring slips, the cutter swung into a sharp turn and let go of the tow line, careening the dinghy into a piling and splintering its bow. But both Partridge and José had time to scramble onto the slip before the boat went under.

José ran to the head of the dock, bellowing curses at the cutter, now returning to its patrol station off the hotel. A moment later he felt Partridge's arm around his shoulder and saw that he was smiling.

"You need to dry off and we both need a drink, José."

The fisherman slept in a board shack adjoining a ship chandlery on one of the docks. His quarters were a litter of fishing gear, coils of line, cans of paint and other supplies for maintenance of Partridge's cruiser.

The American stood in the open doorway with a bottle of tequila while José changed into dry dungarees and shirt. Across the bay the Playa del Sol stood like a fortress below the white tower of the lighthouse and the intermittent glow of its powerful beam.

José took the bottle from his hand. "I was wrong, *patrón*. It is not Jiminez you fear most. It is your own *amigos* over there."

"Yes. It will be my life and the señora's if I can't guarantee that they will be safe here—and there may be only one way I can do that." He took a long drag on his cigarette, then gave it to José. "I may want to send a message to Jiminez in the next day or two. If I gave it to you—"

"It would reach him, señor."

An hour after Johnny Partridge had left the hotel Mario Cassavettes heard of the army's defeat at Arroyo Seco from the captain of the *Reina del Mar,* who came to the hotel to ask for permission to move the ship from the dock to an offshore anchorage, where it would be safer if the city came under artillery barrage. Cassavettes told him no—that the vessel must remain where it was to re-embark its passengers if the city came under attack. The captain agreed but only after an assurance that the Mafiosi and their wives already were preparing for a swift departure.

It was almost midnight when Partridge got back to the hotel, and when he saw the lights still burning in the cantina he knew where to find Cassavettes.

The *consigliere* was alone at the bar, a row of empty beer bottles in front of him. "You've been gone one hell of a long time. You must have a lot to tell me." He slid a beer down the copper bar.

The cordial gesture did not deceive Partridge. He knew he was playing into a pat hand. "Which do you want first—the good news or the bad?"

"Let's start off with the bad."

"Luchengo took a clobbering today. He came running back to Ariella with what's left of his army."

Cassavettes studied the label on his bottle. "That is bad."

"There's more. Luchengo probably can't stop Jiminez if he decides to take a crack at Ariella."

Cassavettes swung slowly to face Partridge, two bar stools away. "It didn't take you all night to find that out. I knew it hours ago, and my father knows it now. He's not happy, Johnny, and he told me to tell you that."

"Then the good news might cheer him up a little. I've found a contact—a direct contact with Jiminez."

Cassavettes was on his feet. "Then let's move—now!"

"No," said Partridge, "we'll watch the action a little longer. There's still time."

"You'd better be right, friend. You're betting your life on it."

"And yours, Mario."

OCTOBER

AMBASSADOR Sam Hood sent two cables to Washington the morning after the rout of the federal army at the Arroyo Seco. The first was to Edward O'Farrell, Assistant Secretary of State for Inter-American Affairs:

FOREIGN MINISTER LARA ADVISES ME HIS GOVERNMENT TODAY APPEALING TO OAS FOR MILITARY ASSISTANCE. RECOMMEND WE INITIATE CALL FOR EMERGENCY SESSION AND FOR AFFIRMATIVE RESPONSE. NEW SOPHISTICATION JIMINEZ TACTICS AND WEAPONS CONFIRMS EARLIER EVIDENCE CHINESE INTERVENTION. EVACUATION AMERICAN NATIONALS AND NON-ESSENTIAL EMBASSY PERSONNEL NEARLY COMPLETE.

The second cable was to the President:

REQUEST EARLIEST APPOINTMENT MY SUCCESSOR. URGENT YOU HAVE NEW APPRAISAL SANTA CLARAN CRISIS FROM ENVOY IN WHOM YOU REPOSE FULL CONFIDENCE.

Hood had spent the night at the embassy, overseeing the evacuation and the shipment of top secret files. He took time only for an hour's rest and a shower and shave before returning to his desk. The call from Arturo Lara came at exactly nine o'clock.

The Foreign Minister was uncharacteristically deferential. He told Hood of the appeal to the OAS without even a hint of censure, although both were aware that it was a direct consequence of the ambassador's failure to convince his own government of the increasing gravity of the situation. Lara had not had many opportunities to deal with Hood, and it was unlike him to let this one pass without asserting either his new importance or his old officiousness. Nor was his surprising request for a personal interview with Hood an imperious summons to the palace. Lara was willing to come to the embassy at the ambassador's convenience.

Hood's breakfast dishes were still on his desk when Lara was shown into the office a half hour later.

"Shall I send for more coffee, Mr. Lara?"

"Thank you, but I have very little time." His eyes swept the spacious office, pausing only at the photographs of Hood with American presidents of the past sixteen years.

"Most impressive, Mr. Hood."

"I believe this is the first time you've been in my office."

"It is. But today we can forgo the restraints of protocol. This is not an official visit. I come as a . . ." He couldn't find the word.

"As a friend?" Hood's tone was mocking.

"To bring you word of a friend. It will reassure you to know that I spent an hour with Señora Novarese yesterday and found her safe—at least for the moment."

His emphasis on the last phrase—a hint of the more important matter on the Foreign Minister's agenda—was not lost on Hood.

"Thank you. Your report confirms information I already have from our consulate in Ariella. But it was considerate of you to come, and you may trust my discretion."

"Discretion?"

"President Luchengo will not hear of your meeting with the señora from me."

"But he already knows. In fact, it was at his suggestion that I am here now." He was no longer smiling. "But there is another matter involving Señora Novarese which I must ask you to hold in the strictest confidence."

"And the President also knows of this?"

"To the contrary, it would be most dangerous for the señora if he had even a suspicion of what I'm going to tell you."

The ambassador was scornful. "Dangerous for her or for you?"

Lara shot forward in his chair. "For all Santa Clarans who are watching their country die and who know that only a new leader can save it."

"We won't go on with this, Mr. Lara."

"But we will. It concerns your own responsibilities as ambassador."

"I'm the best judge of my responsibilities, and I assure you they don't require me to be party to your conspiracies—or your disloyalty."

The Foreign Minister stood his ground. "Disloyalty? Is it not a fact that you oppose your own President?"

"Very often, yes. But there's rather a clear distinction between opposition and treason."

"In your country, yes. But here the distinction is irrelevant. Mine, unhappily, is a violent society. For the ambitious man—and, yes, I confess to ambition—disloyalty, even treason, are historically acceptable ways to advance politically. I would remind you of the circumstances under which Luchengo himself took power."

Hood shook his head in disgust. "And I would remind you that Santa Clara was not at war. But had it been, Luchengo would have been at the front with Luis Novarese, not at the rear abetting the enemy. You're a pathetic little man, and you won't survive your ambitions. You won't even live out the day if I report this conversation to President Luchengo."

Lara lit a cigar. "But you won't, because you would also be condemning the señora. No, I think I can speak to you quite freely, and I repeat that it would be to your official advantage to listen."

"I don't have to listen, Lara. I know exactly why you're here—

to ask what the reaction of my government would be if you can persuade the señora to lead a coup against Luchengo."

The Foreign Minister studied an ascending smoke ring. "And what would that reaction be?"

"I don't know," said Hood, "but I can tell you what my recommendation to Washington would be—that you are incompetent to replace Luchengo."

"Your opinion of me is unimportant," Lara replied. "What is important is that Santa Clara will certainly go Communist unless America intervenes. It's no secret that you also believe this but that your government won't listen to you."

Hood said nothing.

"It is also no secret that your country will do nothing to help us as long as Luchengo is in power—that his very name is a symbol of oppression and—"

"But you are certain we would intervene in support of Señora Novarese?"

"I am, and if the generals could be given that assurance, they would rise against Luchengo tomorrow."

"And you're proposing to me that I ask my government for that assurance—that I conspire actively with you?"

"Why, Mr. Hood, do you insist on reducing this to personal vindictiveness? It is not a question of conspiracy. It is a question of replacing an impotent and unpopular regime with one deserving of American support. And with that support, I assure you we can destroy Jiminez and his Chinese allies, who would not be here were it not for Luchengo's stupidity."

The ambassador's patience was running short. "The generals know what you are, and not one of them would follow you."

"But they would follow the señora."

"Perhaps. But I question very seriously that she has even been in contact with the generals. You're bluffing, Lara. You have nothing going for you at all unless you can walk out of this office with a commitment from me that I will support your proposal to my government—and that I won't do."

The Foreign Minister had a final gambit. "Then your concern for the señora is not as great as I thought it was. There will be a coup against Luchengo, with or without you, and she will lead it because she will have no choice. She is a patriot, and she will answer the call when it comes. And if it comes too late, when the battle against Jiminez is already lost, her fate and that of Santa Clara will be on your conscience."

Hood rose from his desk. "I'd like one straight answer from you. Did the señora send you to me? Does she know you're presuming to speak for her?"

Lara had nothing more to lose. "Yes. She has told me there is one condition under which she would agree to oppose Luchengo—a commitment of American support—*your* commitment, Mr. Hood."

Hood put through a call to Colonel Gruver, who was directing the airlift of evacuees from the residence. "Hold the next helicopter for me. It'll be detouring to Ariella and inform Cullers at the consulate that I want to see Señora Novarese at two this afternoon."

He faced the shaken Foreign Minister. "Yes, Lara, I'm going to find out if you're lying to me and I think you are. But if you're not, I'm going to tell her that I will advise Washington to reject your proposal to me."

The ambassador stood and Lara rose slowly from his own chair. "What concerns you most—a coup against Luchengo, or the danger to the señora's life if she agrees to lead it?"

"Frankly, you concern me most," said Hood. "Too much history —and most of it bloody—has been written by fools."

"I am a patriot." He said it without much fervor.

"No," Hood replied, "one of Jiminez' peons, lying dead in the arroyo, is more of a patriot than you. He might have been ignorant and misled, but he at least had the courage to stand up and die for his vision of what this country ought to be."

"He was an animal," said Lara. "His vision was no larger than his belly. He died for Jiminez' promise of more *frijoles*."

"Yes, but what are you willing to die for, Lara?"

The Foreign Minister left without answering.

Except for construction battalions working on mortar and machine gun pits around its perimeter, the airstrip at Ariella was quiet. There had been no indication of further assaults by Paco Jiminez for almost a full day, and many of the soldiers in bivouac had been given leave to visit their families in the port city. Combat units that had not borne the full brunt of the attack at Arroyo Seco were moving northward to reinforce defensive positions along the highway and other possible routes of attack on Ariella.

The American helicopter was on the ground for only as long as it took Ambassador Hood to debark and dash clear of the turbulent eddies of dust from the rotors. Consul Bennett Cullers was waiting with a car, and Hood shook his hand perfunctorily.

"You were able to arrange an appointment with Señora Novarese?"

"I don't know, sir."

"You don't know?"

"They wouldn't connect me with her at the hotel. Mr. Partridge took the call. You should know there are rumors that she's virtually a prisoner at the Playa del Sol. She hasn't been seen in the city, and there are guards night and day around—"

Hood broke in impatiently. "What did Partridge say?"

"Simply that he would tell Señora Novarese that you were coming. But whether he will or not is another question."

"You told him I'd be waiting at the consulate at two?"

"I did."

At two-thirty, from Cullers' office, Hood put in a call to the Playa del Sol. It was taken by Johnny Partridge, who had been expecting it.

"Partridge?"

"Yes."

"Did you give Señora Novarese my message?"

"I did."

"Then why isn't she here?"

Partridge knew that Mario Cassavettes had a tap on the switchboard and was probably listening. "She decided it wouldn't be wise to leave the hotel until the town cools down."

"Then I'll come out there. Tell her to expect me in ten minutes."

"I wouldn't do that, Hood." Partridge and the ambassador both heard Cassavettes' sudden cigarette cough through a handkerchief muffling the receiver.

"Are you telling me that it's not safe for me to come there?"

"Don't push it, Hood. I can't go into it now, but there are very good reasons you should stay away from the señora."

The ambassador fought back his temper. "Then put her on the line. I'd prefer to hear them from her."

"I can't do that."

"Then I'll tell you and the third party on the line that I will be coming through that gate in ten minutes and don't try to stop me."

"The guards have orders to let no one through."

Hood spoke slowly. "I'm the American ambassador here, and it's urgent that I speak to the señora. If you try to use force to stop me from carrying out my official duties, I'll go directly to President Luchengo, and I think we both know what his reaction will be."

There was a long pause. "Stay on the line a minute, Hood." Partridge put the ambassador on hold. "We don't have much choice, Mario. We stop him at the gate, and we'll have federal troops crawling all over the place."

"What the hell does he want?"

"It can't involve us—at least not directly."

"All right, I'll tell my dad he's going to be playing host to an ambassador. But he won't see the humor in it."

"You tell all of them to stay the hell in their rooms until Hood leaves." He hit the hold switch.

"I'll tell her you're on your way, Hood."

"I thought you would."

AMBASSADOR SAM HOOD's cable recommending support of the Santa Claran appeal for OAS intervention was on Assistant Secretary of State Edward O'Farrell's desk when he got back from lunch. He read it quickly, then glanced at the routing instructions. It was for his attention only.

He rang Secretary of State Adams on the direct line to his desk. "May I see you immediately?"

"Is it urgent, Ed? I'm just leaving. I've had a call from the President in New York. He wants me to catch the two o'clock shuttle up there."

"Then I'll ride over to National with you, Mr. Secretary."

Adams read the message as the limousine was inching off the ramp from the underground garage into the flow of traffic. "Is the President aware of this, Ed?"

"Not yet."

"Then maybe you'd better fly up with me. We should try for a decision today."

The car sped through light traffic, past the Washington Monument and toward Memorial Bridge.

"I don't have to tell you, Ed, that there's very little chance the other member states will go along. Luchengo hasn't been what you could call an aggressive anti-Communist, and they'll fall back on the old ploy that it's an internal affair."

"That won't wash this time," said O'Farrell. "Their decision to evacuate their own embassy personnel puts them on record as conceding the gravity of the situation."

"We flew most of our people out too," Adams replied. "But I can tell you right now we're not going to find the President very receptive to Hood's opinions."

Although the driver could hear nothing through the soundproof glass separating him from his passengers, the Secretary cast his voice a decibel lower. "The reason he gave for wanting to see me— and I quote him—was to settle this Sam Hood affair once and for all."

"I don't like the sound of that."

"I don't either, but it gives us a little guidance on how far we should push in supporting Hood on the OAS."

O'Farrell had always found it difficult to conceal his disgust with Adams' deference to the President. "This might be just the time, then, to back Hood as strongly as we can. If we don't support Sam's judgment in this case we won't be in much of a position to argue against his recall."

The car left the bridge and swung left onto the off-ramp leading to the airport. "We'll go as far as we can, Ed, but we have to be realistic. The OAS won't go along with intervention, and we both know it. You can't chop forty per cent out of their appropriations, as we did at this session, and still expect them to sit up and bark when we whistle."

"It's much more than that, Mr. Secretary. Those demagogic speeches Haas is writing for the President are an affront to every friend we still have down there. They can accept the budget cuts. They knew they had to come sooner or later. What they can't accept is the President calling them undeserving welfare cases."

The limousine went through the VIP gate, stopping only thirty yards from the waiting jet. They still had five minutes before boarding time. Adams was beginning to regret that O'Farrell was going with him.

"Again, Ed, you have to be realistic. Perhaps the President has gone too far in his criticism. But it is an election year and the mood of the country is strongly against foreign aid. The President can't follow Hood's recommendation without admitting that he's been wrong all along on Santa Clara—and we can't expect him to do that."

"And how long, Mr. Secretary, can we expect Sam Hood to take one slap in the face after another? If you had stood behind him in the past, we wouldn't be facing a decision on intervention now."

Adams took a handkerchief from an inside coat pocket and began polishing his glasses. "I'll overlook that. I know Hood is a friend of yours. But I want it understood that I'm taking you up there with me to support my position, not to antagonize the President."

"What is your position?"

"That we should, of course, support Hood. I'll recommend to the President that an emergency session might be advisable."

"*Might* be advisable?"

"Just that."

"Mr. Secretary, I think you should know that I spent an evening with Hood the last time he was up."

"I recall his last visit," said Adams. "It was in defiance of my

orders that he stay at his post. I also recall his heroics in com-
mandeering an Air Force plane and his impromptu little press
conference at the White House."

"That's exactly what I'm leading up to," said O'Farrell. "Hood
won't hold still for much more, and if the President recalls him,
he won't take it lying down."

"There's not much he could do, is there?"

"To quote him, he could go out with a bang, not a whimper."

"Hood attack the President? That's ridiculous. He's *State*."

At that moment they saw the passenger agent signal to them
from the boarding ramp and left the car. Seconds after they were
airborne, climbing steeply over the Potomac, Adams glanced
warily at O'Farrell.

"You really don't think he would?"

"I do."

Under the wingtip, the Secretary of State saw the broad reach
of the muddy river stretching toward Mount Vernon, and thought
how comforting it would be if the epoch of the thirty-ninth presidency
was now as safely and as illustriously a part of the national
archives as the first.

The President had flown into New York the night before from a
campaign tour of three Western states and the front-page headline
in the New York *Times,* which he read over breakfast in his suite
at the Waldorf Towers, was an accurate summation of the junket:
THIN, HOSTILE CROWDS MAR PRESIDENT'S FAR WEST TOUR.

There had been no more than two hundred party faithful waiting
at the airport in Los Angeles, and the motorcade through the
downtown district drew a lunch-hour crowd of only fifty thousand.
Harlan Grant had had a hundred thousand only a week earlier.
Black pickets demanding a Justice Department investigation of
police brutality met the President at the entrance to the Biltmore
Hotel. And footage of the jeering crowd—and the President's sullen
reaction—was on all four of the major television networks that
night. His address at Town Hall, pledging revenue sharing grants
to the cities for environmental projects, was lost in the shuffle.

It was no better in San Francisco that night and Portland and

Seattle the next day. Only the demonstrators were out in force, and the live confrontation was a more dramatic TV story than the flat rhetoric of his speeches.

It was nine o'clock, and the President still had an hour before leaving the hotel for the dedication of a sea water desalinization plant at Far Rockaway. He would address a convention of the National Urban League in the Waldorf at noon, then go to a filming session at a private television studio in midtown. He was to do ten one-minute spots covering the full range of major policy differences between himself and Senator Grant. In the last ten days of the campaign they would appear at least once on all of the more than a thousand television stations across the nation.

He was scanning the other morning newspapers, whose page-one reports were as dismal as the *Times'*, when Gene Haas, a member of his traveling party, brought him the morning mail pouch from the White House. It had been flown to Manhattan by Air Force jet. Such delivery of papers requiring his signature or immediate action was routine, even if he was half a world away from the Oval Office.

Ambassador Hood's cable urging the prompt appointment of his successor was on the top of the stack. He read it with a growl, then glanced at his military adviser's overnight status report on the world's hot spots. There was only one paragraph on Santa Clara:

"No significant military developments. Jiminez apparently consolidating present position. No evidence missile site preparation."

The paragraph on the People's Republic of China was just as terse:

"Minor clashes Sinkiang border with Soviet patrols. Soviet seismic surveillance for further missile testing and aerial surveillance for missile transport toward seaports confirms our own: negative."

The President then read his schedule for the day. He would have two hours of free time at the hotel after returning from the TV studio at four o'clock and before leaving at six for a hundred-dollar-a-plate dinner in Philadelphia.

On the stand next to his bed was a telephone with a direct line to Washington. He picked up the phone and asked for Secretary of State Adams.

Six hours later Secretary Adams and Assistant Secretary O'Farrell strode through the Fiftieth Street entrance to the Towers. Two Secret Service agents on guard at the special elevator leading to the Presidential Suite, another two outside the elevator on the thirtieth floor, and still another outside the President's door, all knew Adams and O'Farrell by sight, and they were shown into the suite without delay.

The President was in the sitting room with Haas and Busby. They were at a divan, reviewing the text of a speech on ethics in government he was to deliver the next morning to a graduate seminar in political science at the University of Pennsylvania. The Chief Executive acknowledged Adams and O'Farrell with a nod, then shoved the speech into Busby's hands.

"I won't read it. It's even worse than the junk you gave me for the West Coast. There's not one applause line in it—not one quotable shot at Grant." Then he caught himself. Adams and O'Farrell were among his closest advisers in Washington, but they were intruders now. "Gentlemen, can you wait for me in the other room? I won't be long."

On a signal from the President, Haas led them into the huge bedroom and to chairs at the window looking out toward the East River. He came back in time to hear the President warn Busby: "If you can't whip this speech operation into line, Max, I'll find someone who can. I could do a hell of a lot better ad libbing."

Busby held his temper. "It was agreed very early that you were going to take the high road—that you were going to speak to issues and let Grant pander to the rednecks. If you want to change that strategy now—if you want a shouting match with Grant—"

"You're a former newspaperman, Max. You find me one paragraph in that speech that's worth quoting. All it says is that I'm against corruption in government and that I'm going to appoint a commission—my God, another commission!—to draft a code of ethics. It's worth just five seconds on network TV, and they'll give Grant twenty calling me a Communist appeaser. Look, Max, I don't like it and you don't like it, but politics is a brawl—two guys slugging it out in the middle of the street. Grant's in there throwing punches, and what am I doing?"

"You're conducting yourself like a President, not a public brawler, and that's the image the voter will remember."

"Tell that to Harry Truman. He didn't do too badly giving 'em hell. No, Max, I want some guts in this speech. I want that crowd off its ass and on its feet."

"It's not that kind of an audience," Busby replied. "Most of them are with you, but they'd resent a strictly political approach."

"Then why the hell am I going there?"

"You put it on the schedule yourself. You said you were sick and tired of the heckling at every campus you've gone to—that it was important to have one good campus audience. And this is it. They won't carry you out on their shoulders, but they'll treat you with respect." Busby stood up wearily. "Besides, it's not your big event for the A.M. news cycle. You have a motorcade first through downtown Philadelphia with the governor, and the advance people say it looks great."

"They said that in L.A. too," the President shot back, "and there were more cops in the escort than there were people on the sidewalks." His eye fell on Haas, who had said nothing. "What do you think of this speech, Gene?"

"Max is right," said the special assistant. "It is an appropriate theme for this audience. But I do think we can hype it up a little."

"Then why don't you take a stab at it, Gene? You're the only one around here who has the touch."

Busby was furious. "You gave me standing orders weeks ago to run every speech past Haas for clearance. He saw this one this morning and found nothing wrong with it."

"That was before I had the advantage of the President's thinking," said Haas.

J OHNNY PARTRIDGE also had taken the earlier call from Bennett Cullers at the desk in the lobby. A second after the consul hung up, he spoke. "You on the line, Mario?"

"Always," said Cassavettes.

"I think we should let her go to the consulate. Hood will be suspicious if we don't."

"Better he should be suspicious than my father."

Partridge was insistent. "Hood will go to Luchengo."

"Let him. There's no love lost between Luchengo and the woman."

"That's right. But there's also nothing in our contract that gives you the right to hold a Santa Claran citizen as a hostage. And I can guarantee you Luchengo won't like it."

"Can you also guarantee me that she'll come back—that she won't ask Hood for his protection?"

"I'd make book on it."

"No takers, Partridge. Hood might be suspicious if she doesn't show, but at least she won't have a chance to tell him that we may be switching our action to Jiminez."

"She doesn't know that."

"Don't tell me you've been holding out on the lady." Cassavettes didn't wait for a reply. "No more argument. Just come up with a story that Hood will buy."

"No way," said Partridge. "They've been friends too long for him to believe she doesn't want to see him."

"I know and that's why she's not going to see him."

Partridge found Señora Novarese in the kitchen, checking out the week's menu with the chef. He took her outside to the patio off the cantina and told her of Cullers' call and Cassavettes' orders.

"No one—no one!—tells me what I can and cannot do. Sam must

have had an important reason for coming, and I am going to the consulate."

"I wouldn't try to stop you, Constanzia, but they can, and will." From the patio, they saw the sentries lounging at the gate fifty yards down the road. Partridge tried to calm her. "It might not be important at all. There was a report on the radio this morning that the Americans are moving out. Maybe Hood just wants to say good-by."

Her voice was sharp with defiance. "And you don't think that's important? It is to me, whether you like it or not." She faced him. "I should never have become a part of all this, Johnny. It's not at all what you said it would be."

"You're right," he said. "But how could I have known it would blow up like this?"

She put a hand on his arm. "You couldn't. But now that it has, we must leave while we still can." Suddenly she tensed and withdrew her hand. Turning, Partridge saw Mario Cassavettes at the bar, raising his glass to them and smiling. Her voice was a whisper.

"The *alcalde* in Ariella is an old friend of my family's. I can send him word through one of the staff. He will come with the *policía.*"

"No," said Partridge. "Cassavettes would find us before they would. We wouldn't have a chance."

"What chance do we have now?"

"Just one—that the situation will change. There's been no action for more than a day now. Jiminez may have had it."

"No, Johnny, Lara thinks it's only the beginning."

Partridge shook his head. "Lara *hopes* it's only the beginning." He glanced back toward the cantina. Cassavettes was still watching, still smiling. "I've made arrangements of my own. We can run if we have to, but please give it a little more time."

Her face was grave. "If you ran again, they'd never stop looking for you, would they?"

"Never—and they'd find me."

"You know I don't want that, Johnny." A flight of gulls swept low over the patio, their wings flashing in the sunlight. "We'll wait. But Sam Hood will force the issue. He won't take no for an answer."

"I know. Now all I have to do is convince Cassavettes of that."

Two hours later Partridge rang Señora Novarese in her suite. "You were right, Constanzia. Hood wouldn't take no for an answer. He's on his way out here now."

"There will be no trouble?"

"No, it's all right."

She went to the balcony and stood waiting until she saw the car from the consulate pass through the gate, without slowing, and brake to a stop in front of the hotel. Hood paused before starting up the steps and saw the señora wave from the balcony. He also saw the stirring of drapes from windows at which the Mafiosi were watching. Only Partridge was in the cavernous lobby.

"Mr. Ambassador."

"Partridge."

"She's waiting for you—second floor front."

"Thank you. And, Partridge, I may want a word with you when I come down."

"I'm not going anywhere."

"That's what I understand."

Señora Novarese was waiting at the open door. She held a hand out to him, and its trembling belied the cool formality of the gesture. She said nothing until the door was shut behind them and then she was in his arms, her cheek hard against his.

"You can't know how good it is to see you, Sam."

"And it's good to hear you say it. I was given the impression you didn't want to see me." He held her at arm's distance. "What's happening here—Partridge intercepting your calls, guards at the gate?"

She broke away from him. "It's nothing—a misunderstanding. Johnny had no objection to your coming."

"But he's no longer in control here, is he?"

The señora led him to a divan before a low table on which were glasses and liqueurs. "I'm perfectly safe here."

"Are you? I hear you can't even leave the hotel."

She gave him a curaçao. "You didn't hear that in Ciudad Alarcon. You had another reason for coming here."

"Yes, but that can wait. If you're being held here against your—"

"Please, Sam, no more of this."

The ambassador sank back into the cushions wearily. "Lara came to see me this morning. He said you had agreed to lead an army revolt against Luchengo if I could promise you the support of my government. Was he lying?"

"We did discuss Luchengo, yes."

"That's no answer. Did you commit yourself to him or didn't you?"

She took a long time answering. She had little respect for Lara, but he was, at least, her ally—if a self-serving one—against Luchengo. The ambassador was not.

"No, he misunderstood." She saw the relief in Hood's face. "That pleases you, doesn't it?"

"That you're not a party to Lara's little games—that you didn't use our friendship to try to involve me in a conspiracy against a government I'm presumably here to serve? Yes, that pleases me."

"But it pleases you more that there will be no challenge to Luchengo—for the moment, at least." Her face was hard, defiant. "I may not always say no to Lara. If I felt that a coup could succeed—and that it would save this country—I wouldn't hesitate."

The ambassador took a long sip of his curaçao. "But it hasn't come to that, has it? And if it did, you couldn't accomplish much if you don't even have the freedom to leave this hotel."

The señora went to the window and drew the drapes against the hot light of the sun, now low in the western sky. She did not rejoin Hood on the divan but took a chair facing him across the low table.

"You told Lara no, didn't you—even before you spoke to me."

"I told him if he was representing you—if the coup was, in fact, that far along—I would forward his proposition to Washington. I also told him I would oppose it."

"Even if I were involved?"

"Yes. And I would be acting in your best interests, Constanzia. The coup would divide and weaken the army. Only Jiminez would benefit, and I don't think you want that."

She stood, confronting him. "You accuse Lara of dirty little games—of trying to use me to compromise you."

"I think it's obvious."

"It's just as obvious that you came here to use me—to dissuade me from joining Lara. No, Sam, you have no objection to compromising yourself—to meddling in this country's affairs—but only if it serves Luchengo."

"It's in your best interests too."

"I don't believe that."

Hood got up from the divan and went to her. "That doesn't leave us very much, does it?"

"Did we ever have very much?" She took a step toward the door. "Good-by, Sam. Go back to Ciudad Alarcon—to Luchengo. Your place is at his side, not mine. And nothing will ever change that."

The ambassador shook his head. "You're wrong. I've quit, Constanzia. I'm leaving Santa Clara just as soon as my replacement arrives."

The señora was incredulous. "Why?"

"Because, regardless of what you think, I have no power to influence events here. A new man might." Hood forced a grim smile. "He might even be on your side."

She took his hand. "Then it is good-by?"

"It doesn't have to be—not if you come with me. We can put all of this behind us."

"It's too late, Sam." Her voice broke, and the tears came. "I can't leave."

He held her close. "You have no choice. Jiminez is going to win. I'm certain of it. And you will be no safer from his firing squad than Luchengo will be." She said nothing, and he held her away from him. "It's not Jiminez you're afraid of, is it?"

"Don't interfere, Sam. Please."

"You're leaving here with me now for the consulate. After that you can decide what you want to do."

"No."

"*Could* you leave here? Would they let you?"

"Please, Sam. Go now."

His voice was harsh. "Then it's Partridge, isn't it? It's Partridge you can't leave."

He had given her a way out, and she took it. "Yes, it is Johnny." But she couldn't look into his face.

"Then I'm sorry for you." And he left.

The ambassador took the stairway to the lobby, where Partridge was waiting. "You still want a word with me?"

"I certainly do."

"Not here," said Partridge, and he led the way out the entrance, past Hood's waiting car, to the promenade facing the sea. The sun was now a red ball on the horizon.

"I hear in town that you're in more than a little difficulty here, Partridge."

"Do you?"

"A tap on your telephone—guards at the gate—your killer friends watching us now from their windows."

"What's your point, Hood?"

"That I don't give a damn if they gun you down in the next five minutes. But I do care what happens to the señora, and she apparently won't leave without you."

"So?"

"You're still an American. You're still under my jurisdiction. I'll be back tomorrow to take you to the consulate for interrogation—and when we leave, she comes with us."

"No deal," said Partridge. "Once you have me in custody, what's to stop you from hustling me back to the States?"

"You have my word that I won't."

"Your word against ten to life for conspiracy? No, thank you." He lit a cigarette. "Leave it alone, or you'll be responsible for what happens to her, not me."

"Then you admit she is in danger?"

"Only from you, Hood. Only if you keep pushing." He took a long drag. "You had your chance to walk out of here with her, and nobody would have tried to stop you. But she told you no, didn't she? Now why don't you be a good loser? Just climb in your car and—"

Hood took a menacing step toward him. "I've only begun to push. I can reach Luchengo within the hour."

"And you'll tell him the señora's being held a prisoner and he'll send in troops. Right?"

"Exactly."

The ambassador began walking toward his car. Partridge was two steps behind. Together, they saw the drapes part and the señora step out onto the balcony.

Partridge spoke almost in a whisper. "You going to Luchengo?"

"I may."

"Then wave to her, Hood. Wave good-by."

Sterling Adams and Edward O'Farrell stood as the President came into his bedroom and took a chair facing them across a low coffee table. A chill October dusk already was settling over the city and only the faintest murmur of traffic could be heard through the soundproof windows.

Adams had taken Ambassador Hood's cable urging support for an emergency session of the OAS from his attaché case, and now he gave it to the President. "This could be relevant to a discussion of Hood's status."

The President read it, then threw it on the table. "It certainly is relevant. There's nothing in today's intelligence reports to back him up. It's just one more example, Sterling, of Hood's refusal to accept what he knows our Santa Claran policy to be. I'll come right to the point. I want you to find an interim replacement for Hood—a career officer who will do what he's told. After the election, of course, I'll appoint a man of my own."

"You will excuse me, sir," said O'Farrell, "but after the election we may not even have a mission in Santa Clara. We have only a skeleton staff there now."

"That's right," replied the President, "but only because we took Hood's word for it that the collapse of the government was imminent. And he was wrong, just as he's been wrong all summer and fall."

Adams took a deep breath. "In all fairness, Mr. President, I think the situation down there is still too fluid to arrive at such a judgment. Hood may be a little overzealous in pressing his case, but—"

The President cut him off. "Sterling, there's nothing—absolutely nothing—from either the CIA or our overflights to support Hood's reports that Jiminez has Luchengo on the run, or that he's preparing missile sites for the Chinese."

"Hood has been advising us only of probabilities," said Adams, "and events could still prove him right. I feel very strongly that it would be premature to dismiss him."

"I'm not firing him," said the President. "He's quit. He wrote out his resignation the last time he was up—and this morning I got a cable from him insisting that I rush through the appointment of his successor."

O'Farrell was the first to recover from his surprise. "Hood has had one rebuff after another, Mr. President, and what it amounts to is a verdict of no confidence. And not only in him, sir, but in me. I've agreed with most of Hood's recommendations, but Haas has given no more credence to my advice than he has to Hood's."

The President would hear no more of it. It was nothing more than departmental resentment of the "little State Department" in the White House.

"I, not Haas, determine what credence is to be given to your opinions and to Hood's—and I will tell you that I have consistently found those of the CIA and the Joint Chiefs to be more credible and, to date, more accurate."

Adams gave his subordinate no time to answer. "I think you're digressing, Ed, and the President's time is at a premium." He tidied the stack of papers he had taken from his attaché case. "Actually, Mr. President, one decision could resolve both of the questions before us. I, for one, think the situation down there is too volatile to entrust to a new man, and I'm certain Hood would stay on if we went along with his recommendation on the OAS. It can do no harm—the member states are unlikely to go for intervention, at least at this point in time—and it could have certain advantages. To date, all of Luchengo's appeals have been directly to us—for money and for intervention under our separate mutual defense treaty. If we turn it over to the OAS, there's at least a dispersion of responsibility."

"Hood is asking for much more than that," said the President. "He's asking us to take a position before the OAS that totally contradicts our present policy—that concedes a hemispheric crisis that simply doesn't exist. The answer is no. I'm not going to put us on record as favoring intervention, and I'm not going to strong-arm the OAS into it either. The situation doesn't warrant it. The country wouldn't stand for it."

"May I speak frankly, Mr. President?"

Adams tried to stop O'Farrell. "I think the President's position is clear, Ed."

"To you but not to him," said the President. "What do you want to say, O'Farrell?"

"I agree with you that the country wouldn't stand for intervention. But I think you have to change that. I think you have to prepare the country for the very real possibility that we may have to go into Santa Clara—and soon."

"Do you?"

"I do. I think your speeches have to place more emphasis on what is very convincing evidence of Chinese involvement in Santa Clara."

The President was losing all patience with the Assistant Secretary. "Why not go all the way? Why not hail Luchengo as a libertarian, fighting alone against the Communist menace? Of course, we'd have to wash a little of the blood off him and forget that the Reds are there at his invitation."

"The Luchengo regime—whatever you may think of it—is all that stands between us and another Bolivia—or worse. To discredit him, and you have been doing that, is to lock yourself into a position that could be dangerous to the country and to your own chances of—" He had gone too far, and he knew it.

"To my own chances of what?" The President was livid.

"I say this, sir, only because I would prefer to serve under you rather than Senator Grant. I believe the advice you're receiving is more political than pragmatic—more responsive to the mood in this country than to the realities in Santa Clara. And I think it could cost you the election if Hood's forecast of developments is correct, as I think it is."

The President's voice was heavy with scorn. "What you propose, then, is that I commit this country to a war in Latin America to insure my own re-election."

"No, sir. I'm proposing that an appropriate response now would destroy Jiminez and discourage the Chinese from further encroachment."

The President spoke directly to the Secretary of State. "Is it a fact, or isn't it, that Luchengo still outnumbers Jiminez at least four or five to one?"

"Yes, that would be accurate."

"Have you evidence that you could take before the UN, or even the OAS, that would confirm Hood's claims of significant Chinese intervention?"

"There is evidence, sir, that Jiminez has late-model Chinese automatic weapons and artillery."

"Yes, but isn't it far more likely they came from Bolivia?"

"They could have, sir."

"Now let me ask you this. You receive, as I do, a daily report on our overflights of Jiminez' position. Is there the slightest sign that he's preparing to site missiles?"

"It may be too early. He's held the position only days."

"But, as of now, nothing?"

"That's correct."

"Finally, you receive, as I do, a daily collation of our intelligence reports and those of the Russians on Lop Nor. Do they even remotely point to the possibility that the Reds arc moving or even preparing to move the missiles toward shipping points on the coast?"

"No."

"And you still have confidence in Hood? You still think I should accept his suspicions and reject the far more convincing evidence that he's dead wrong?"

O'Farrell spoke up. "I recall, Mr. President, that we also had daily reconnaissance of Cuba, but Castro was able to conceal both sites and missiles until he was only weeks away from launch stage."

"I suspect," said the President, "that our surveillance is a little more effective now than it was then."

"Just as their techniques for concealment would be," O'Farrell replied.

Adams cut off further wrangling. "Your instructions on the OAS, Mr. President?"

"We'll abstain on the basis that evidence of a threat to hemispheric security is still lacking. You're quite certain, Sterling, that the majority will be against intervention?"

"Quite certain."

"Now, on Hood's replacement."

"That poses certain difficulties," said Adams.

"It poses no difficulties at all," the President replied. "He wants out, and I want him out."

Adams took the leap. "Sam might not go quietly. You'll recall that he flew up here last time against my orders."

"And held a press conference that put me on the spot."

"Exactly. I think you ought to weigh very carefully what Sam might do without portfolio—free of all restraints."

The President shook his head. "I've known Sam for years. He's a team player. He won't rock the boat, not four weeks before—" He caught himself. "But even if he did take me on, what harm could he do? If there's one issue on which the campus red-hots and Grant's superpatriots agree, it's that we're not going to repeat the insanity of supporting the Thieus, the Kys and the Luchengos. If he wants to attack me for not rushing troops into Santa Clara, it will be a plus for me."

"Perhaps not," said Adams. "Hood has many friends among the Washington correspondents. They'll give him a big play. And if he should be right—if the Chinese should try to move missiles in there—"

"But you don't seriously think they will."

Adams spread his hands. "I don't know. Other intelligence might appear to contradict him now, but in the past Hood has always been an extremely reliable observer. Certainly it can do no harm to keep him there another month."

The President stood to end the conference. "Thank you for coming up, Sterling. Perhaps you're right. Perhaps we should keep him there a while longer, if only as the devil's advocate." He put an arm around Adams' shoulder and led him to the door. O'Farrell brought up the rear. "Cable Sam," said the President. "Tell him we're moving on his replacement, but it's going to take a little more time."

S INCE the President's crisis announcement two months earlier that China was on the verge of mass-producing an intercontinental-range ballistic missile, joint American-Soviet surveillance of the nuclear test center at Lop Nor had come up with a discovery of major significance.

The Chinese were moving the vast complex from Sinkiang Province, adjoining the Soviet Union, to a new location in the Himalayan state of Tibet, near the border of India. The transfer came as no surprise. Lop Nor was much too vulnerable both to Soviet missiles and to attack by the forty divisions of Red Army infantry and armor along the Sinkiang boundary.

In his report to the President, the director of the Central Intelligence Agency was optimistic on two points. The move from Lop Nor should delay fight-testing of the ICBM until at least the first of the year, and the proximity of the nuclear center to the Indian border would worsen the already tenuous relations between Peking and New Delhi.

Aerial observation of the Tibetan site, however, would almost certainly involve violations of India's air space, for which the CIA would have to have presidential approval. It was given promptly by the Chief Executive and without consultation with the neutralist government of India.

In the intelligence reports from Bolivia and Santa Clara, the President also found grounds for believing that a nuclear confrontation with China was far from imminent.

CIA agents in La Paz and their horde of informants could unearth no information to suggest that the Communist government was preparing to site the missiles of their Chinese ally. Nor did orbital satellites and overflights by the Blackbird—the SR-71 spy plane—produce photographic evidence of launch site construction.

It was the same story in Santa Clara—except for the alarms of Ambassador Hood.

In its surveillance of enemy nations such as China and Bolivia, which had a formidable defense of surface-to-air missiles, the Blackbird flew at evasive altitudes up to seventy thousand feet. Even at that extreme range, however, and at speeds up to two thousand miles an hour, its sensitive cameras could produce images of amazing clarity.

The Arroyo Seco had no defenses against overflights and high-altitude photo reconnaissance of it was known among the CIA pilots as the milk run. But General Gi You-gin, even if he had had the appropriate weapons, would not have tried to drive them off. He knew that their cameras were recording ground activity that would give the CIA absolutely no basis for suspicion and would, to the contrary, persuade the photo analysts that the arroyo was a conventional artillery defensive position and nothing more.

There were, of course, daily changes in the topography of the arroyo. The artillery emplacements, dug hastily by bulldozers within hours of the original assault, were now being reinforced with steel and concrete. There were also new excavations for subsurface storage of fuel and ammunition and for billeting of the guerrilla force.

On the steep slope facing south toward Ariella, where most of the federal casualties had fallen the first day of battle, a zigzag road was being cut to link the heights with the highway and rail line in the narrow gorge.

Day after day the eight telescopic cameras in the Blackbird's belly turrets examined every square yard of the rebel position.

After exposure, the film was fed into automatic developing equipment aboard the plane and the reels were parachuted to a drop zone in the Canal Zone where a supersonic courier plane was waiting to fly them to Washington. Within hours of the overflight the footage was in the hands of specialists at the National Photographic Interpretation Center. They first examined the general terrain of the arroyo to determine if the new construction was assuming the pattern of all known launching sites—depots for storage of the missiles and their transporters, bombproof shelters for storage of nuclear warheads, computer fire control centers and trackage for delivery of the weapons to the launching pads. But they found nothing suspicious, even on the infra-red footage which could penetrate camouflage.

The photo interpreters next examined the film from the SR-71's extreme telephoto cameras, whose resolving power was such that enlargements could clearly define the faces of rebels working in the arroyo. From this footage they were able to calibrate the diameter of electric wires crisscrossing the position and declare flatly that there were no cables—above ground, at least—that could carry the voltage to operate the computer fire controls for even a short-range missile. The analysts gave special attention to the gun emplacements, which could be convertible into launching pads. But it was their opinion, after stereoscopic examination of the concrete foundations, that they were too shallow to support the thunderous recoil of an ICBM firing.

And thus, routinely, the report of the Interpretation Center to the Committee on Overhead Reconnaissance, the Defense Intelligence Agency and the President's military adviser, was always the same. There was no evidence of missile base construction at the Arroyo Seco.

The President had other intelligence reports that were equally reassuring. It would be impossible to move ICBMs to Chinese seaports from either Lop Nor or the new complex in Tibet without detection by Soviet, Japanese or Nationalist Chinese agents within China. And, just as significant, there had been no movement of Chinese missile technicians from the test centers. In 1962 the Russians had sent hundreds of specialists to Cuba to man Castro's

IRBMs and their defensive ring of surface-to-air missiles. China was sending none and Paco Jiminez could not fire even the simplest of rockets without their expertise.

The only prominent Chinese nuclear artillerist who had not been seen publicly in recent weeks was General Gi You-gin, but it was the consensus of intelligence reports that he was in charge of constructing the new test center in Tibet, as he had been at Lop Nor.

How was it possible for the intelligence community to misread its own evidence—to be absolutely certain that there was no early possibility of a Chinese nuclear presence in the Western Hemisphere when that threat of holocaust was only two weeks away?

There were two errors. The first was the Western world's refusal to acknowledge its own long and costly failure to fathom the intentions of Communist China, or its capacity for accepting the unacceptable risk. The examples were written in history—the decision of Peking to send its armies into North Korea, defying America to unleash its nuclear weapons when it had no retaliatory potential of its own; to provoke border warfare with the Soviet Union when it had only a short-range missile capacity whose launch would invite its own total destruction, and its continuing aggressions against India, whose security both America and the Soviet Union were bound by their own self-interests to defend.

The precedents for suicidal risk were there, but they were ignored. And out of this error grew the second—the assumption that China, now that it was developing its own nuclear arsenal, would bide its time until it could achieve a balance of terror with its powerful enemies. Such a balance would require both a mass stockpile of intercontinental missiles and an anti-ballistic defense of a sophistication that would insure a second strike capacity.

The experts were confident that China had neither ICBMs in such quantity nor an ABM defense, and that until it did, it would not present the superpowers with an early threat to their own security—and certainly not from Latin America, where it could have no conceivable objective commensurate with the risk.

If there was in Washington a gradual diminution of the crisis atmosphere since the joint U.S.-Soviet announcement of China's ICBM two months earlier, it was understandable in light of such calculations. If the President felt that he could now concentrate on his re-election, confident that he would have ample warning of the deployment of Chinese missiles in the Western Hemisphere, that, too, was understandable.

It was to prove fateful, however, that an interview with James McManus of Westinghouse Broadcasting, on the plane returning the presidential party from the electioneering swing into New England, would place the Chief Executive solidly on record as denying the imminence of a nuclear confrontation with the People's Republic of China.

McManus, like most of the correspondents accompanying the President, had found little hard news to report. But at the same hour the Chief Executive was motorcading through downtown Boston, Senator Grant had told an audience in Houston that the White House was deliberately down-playing "China's giant step forward in the thermonuclear arms race. It might be good politics," continued Grant, "to conceal this new and ominous threat to our security from the voters. But history will judge whether my opponent has the right to place his own ambitions above the security of the nation."

A half hour before the plane was to land at Andrews Air Force Base outside Washington, McManus took a seat beside Max Busby.

"Let's face it, Max. None of us has an A.M story, at least nothing your man will like. Boston was the mixture as before—nothing in his speeches worth picking up."

Busby was tired. "He had a good crowd for the motorcade— much better than on the West Coast. He's picking up. It's starting to roll now."

"You're wrong, Max. The trip was a disaster." McManus shoved a late edition of the Boston *Globe* into Busby's hands. "Grant made the front page with that Houston speech today. I'd like your man to give me an answer to it."

"No exclusives, Jim. You know that."

"All right, no exclusive. Let all of us have him for a couple of minutes. He ought to reply to Grant on this."

"I'm not going to subject him to an off-the-cuff press conference. He's worn out, Jim, just like the rest of us."

At that moment the President came aft from the first-class section to glance at the news teletypes, huddled among mimeograph machines and a battery of typewriters in the staff news center in the back of the plane. He overheard Busby's last comment.

"Worn out? Never. What is it you want, Jim?"

The other correspondents began gathering around. "Senator Grant charged in Houston today that—"

"I know. I saw the story and it's irresponsible."

Busby tried to cut it off. "Mr. President, you might want to wait until you've seen Grant's full text."

McManus already had his tape recorder rolling and was holding his microphone toward the President. "Could we have just a brief comment now?"

"Of course." He saw the television crews moving into position. "Let me know when you're all ready."

"We're ready, sir."

"I think it's clear, from Senator Grant's comments today, that he's trying to create an atmosphere of panic in this country. As a member of the Foreign Relations Committee he has free access to intelligence reports that show, beyond all doubt, that China has no present capability whatever of waging nuclear warfare against this country. But he chooses not to look at the reports because he knows they would deny him what he believes is an effective issue against me."

McManus got in the first question. "You say no *present* capability, Mr. President. Could you give us an estimate of when China might have an operational ICBM they could deploy against us?"

"Certainly not next week or next month, as Grant claims—or even in the foreseeable future. First they have to flight-test it. Then they've got to stockpile it. Then they've got to find a point in this hemisphere to launch it. And I can tell you unequivocally that none of this could escape our surveillance."

The President's old adversary, Palmer Joyce, who had no interest in a rebuttal to his own nightly pitch that only Harlan Grant could save the republic, spoke up from the back of the circle of correspondents.

"In other words, Mr. President, you're calling the senator a liar?"

"I'm saying nothing of the kind, Joyce. I'm saying that the senator owes it to himself and to the country to determine what the facts are."

"And the facts, as you put them, are that we have nothing to fear, now or in the foreseeable future, from Red China."

"In the area of a nuclear confrontation, yes. That's exactly what I'm saying."

H AN LI-WONG's Bolivian guides had taken him from La Paz through the Andes to the northern border of Santa Clara, where he was met by two of Paco Jiminez' *mestizos* for the final passage to the Arroyo Seco. To avoid army patrols covering possible attack approaches to Ciudad Alarcon, they were able to travel only by night through the canyons to the west of the capital.

But, for Han, the bivouacs at first light were a merciful surcease from the cruel chafing of the wooden saddle on his burro and the chill mountain winds knifing through the fabric of the same black suit he had worn on his departure from Santa Clara.

Despite his anxieties over his new assignment, it was with relief, on the eighth night, that he heard the challenge from one of Jiminez' guard units in a rocky defile leading up to the rebel stronghold.

Han was taken directly to the bunker a half mile west of the main position which had been General Gi's command post during the repulse of the federal attack and was now his working and living quarters. He was left alone in the darkness to haul his two large suitcases down the earthen steps into the underground shelter. The only light, and that from the stars, was through a long

observation slit in one wall, affording a view of Jiminez' fortifications to the left and, to the right, of the highway and railroad,
snaking through the gorge toward Ariella.

On the opposite wall was a wooden table, bare except for a
draftsman's table and a field telephone. Against the wall opposite
the entrance were two cots, one with garments hung on pegs at
its head and Gi's steamer trunk at its foot. Han sat wearily on
the other. But seconds later he heard an approaching vehicle and
footsteps descending the stairs. Han rose unsteadily to face General
Gi and Paco Jiminez. Both were wearing the brown and green
camouflage uniform of the guerrillas.

Gi's voice was taut with annoyance. "Eight days from La Paz,
comrade?"

Han tried to force himself into a posture of attention. "There
were many patrols. We could ride only by night."

Jiminez slid into the chair at the table, massaging the pain from
his atrophied leg. "It does not surprise me that he is late. It
surprises me only that he has come at all."

Gi had been listening to Jiminez' tirades against Han for days
and now he spoke sharply to the trade attaché. "I would not have
brought you here if I had known of Jiminez' distrust of you."

"But he has no grounds to distrust me."

Gi went to the aperture in the wall, observing the zigzag scar
of the new road into the arroyo. "Jiminez accuses you of subverting
his revolution."

"I deny it," said Han. "It is I who have had to restrain him
from acts that would destroy our objective."

"He also accuses you of collaboration with the enemy."

"Again, I deny it. My relations with President Luchengo have
always had but one purpose—to force *him* into collaboration with
us."

"And what of the *yanqui* ambassador?" Jiminez rose snarling
from his chair, balancing himself with one hand on the table. "Is
Hood not also the enemy? And is he not your *gran amigo?*"

Han, wavering on his feet, felt the perspiration breaking out on
his temples. "Ambassador Hood has been most useful to me."

"I am told," said Gi, "that he was the last man you saw before you left Ciudad Alarcon—that you went to his embassy."

"But only to deceive him into believing that I was returning to Peking." Han knew it was a poor answer. "You must believe me. I have been most discreet."

Jiminez took a threatening step toward him. *"Espía!"*

Han stood his ground. "I am no spy, and if you think I am, you are a fool."

General Gi took command. "I will hear no more. Han is here. He is indispensable to me, and there is no time to replace him. You will accept him, Jiminez, as you accept me."

"Accept a *traidor?* Never. For every day this man has been in Santa Clara, conspiring against me, I have buried another of my *compañeros.*"

"And you will bury your revolution, comrade, if your suspicions delay by as much as one day—one hour!—the work I have come to do." He began to unbutton his tunic. "It is late. There is nothing more to be said."

Jiminez' wasted leg trembled uncontrollably and he clutched at the chair for support. "I, too, am a *general.* But you send me away like a peon."

"There can be only one leader here," Gi replied coldly. "You can be a general again when I am gone. It will not be long."

Jiminez left without another word, dragging his withered leg up the stairs. But Han and Gi heard him slap, then curse, the drowsing driver who was waiting to return him to the main position.

The general sat on the edge of his cot, unlaced his boots, then stood to slide out of his pants before stretching himself out on the thin mattress. "You are not above suspicion, Han. And at the proper time I will present Jiminez' charges against you to Peking. You are guilty, at least, of failing to inform me earlier of your hostility to Jiminez. You have made my task much more difficult."

Han took off only his shoes and coat before collapsing on his own cot. He made no reply but lay awake for many minutes listening to Gi's sonorous breathing. But the general was not asleep. Han heard him stir and turn to face him across the narrow distance between their cots.

"I have no reason to question your loyalty, Han. I dismiss his complaints against you as a resentment of your past authority over him—just as he resents mine now. Good night."

Han slept fitfully. His bedding was damp with perspiration when General Gi shook him awake at dawn.

Rank had no privileges at the Arroyo Seco. The general and Han had to share outdoor latrines and wash troughs with the guerrillas and also their breakfast of black coffee, bread and salt pork in the open-air mess area.

Gi saw the distaste on Han's face as they stood in line waiting for the cooks to pile the food on their metal trays. The gaunt face of the old soldier broke into a smile.

"You frown at a feast like this, comrade? There were weeks in the field in Vietnam when a handful of rice was a day's ration—a water snake a delicacy. And in Laos and Cambodia, where the American bombers and the enemy's flame-throwers left only ashes, we often had only the flesh of dogs. But then, you are not a soldier, are you?"

Han was able to down only a crust of the dry bread and half a tin cup of the acrid coffee. From where they were eating, on bags of concrete near one of the gun positions, he could see the blue glint of the ocean to the south. Around them the day's work was already beginning. A bulldozer, far below them, was raising clouds of dust on the new road and a gang of soldiers, working with heavy blocks and tackle, were removing one of the heavy guns from its concrete emplacement. At intervals, patrol parties left to reconnoiter the terrain around the arroyo.

Before returning to their own quarters, General Gi took Han to the small commissary, where he was issued boots, a camouflage uniform and an automatic carbine with clips of ammunition. He was a ludicrous figure walking toward the command post—the clothing issue under one arm and the gun over his other shoulder, as if on parade march.

Again the general was smiling. "Do you know how to use that weapon?"

"I can learn to use it," said Han defiantly.

"May Mao save us if the time ever comes when you must," said Gi. And, aware of the guerrillas grinning and pointing at Han, he took the carbine away from him.

In the dugout Gi gave Han his instructions. He was to be responsible for all radio traffic and for the analysis of intelligence reports from Jiminez' operatives throughout the country. He was also to maintain an inventory of all Chinese supplies arriving at the arroyo, via Punta Bunda, and to issue them to Jiminez only on the approval of the general.

"Have you questions, comrade?"

"Yes." Han glanced around the barren quarters. "The radio equipment? The codes? The records?"

Gi took Han to the foot of the stairs leading into the bunker and shoved aside a section of the raised wooden flooring. Another series of steps, a continuation of the first, led deeper into the cliffside. The general flicked on a light and below them Han saw the glint on a steel door, with a combination lock.

The general spun the dial quickly through five settings and flung open the door. This chamber had concrete walls, floor and ceiling and was garishly bright under the fluorescent lighting.

The radio equipment was on desks along the left wall, and, next to it, a tape recorder. Han glanced questioningly at Gi.

"Two of us cannot guard the frequencies night and day. It records all incoming traffic automatically. If the message is of the highest urgency, it activates an alarm in our quarters."

"It also records our own transmissions?"

"Yes." He glanced warily at Han. "A necessary concession to Jiminez' suspicions."

"You will have no cause to doubt my loyalty."

"Then it won't offend you that I have taken precautions to insure it."

Han saw a gleaming metallic cabinet on the opposite wall. Its face was a complex of dials, switches and computer reels. Thick cables led upward from it into conduits through the ceiling.

"That will not concern you," said Gi. "You are to come no closer to it than you are now."

The general saw Han's eyes widen as he took an involuntary step backward.

"You know what it is, of course?"

"A computer," said Han.

"No," said Gi, "it is much more than that. It is the trigger, comrade—the trigger."

Han had little to do his first day at the Arroyo Seco. He spent the morning in the concrete fire control center with the code books, reviewing all of the incoming and outgoing radio messages since Gi's arrival at the site.

The general's first transmissions were reports on the federal attack on the position and the victory of the rebel forces under his control. There was no word of congratulation in Peking's reply— only a query as to whether the retreat of Luchengo's army south to Ariella, instead of north toward the capital, would affect "the October 18 deadline for seizure of the port city." General Gi replied that the objective would be taken on schedule.

Most of the other transmissions from Gi were routine acknowledgments of the delivery of supplies ranging from infantry weapons to sky search radar.

The knowledge that October 18 was only a week away left Han with no appetite for lunch, and he did not quit the fire control center until late in the afternoon. He glanced at the computer on leaving and felt chill in the hot, almost airless chamber. Han shut the steel door behind him, spinning the tumblers in the combination lock to secure it. Gi had not given him the combination for opening the door.

Han had been in the upper bunker only seconds when he heard the wail of a siren. Through the aperture in the wall he saw General Gi and a crew of workers hurriedly throw a tarpaulin over a cement mixer at the emplacement from which the heavy gun had been taken that morning. Other rebels at the main position were looking skyward. Then, high and to the south, Han saw a dark speck—the Blackbird on one of its two daily overflights.

After the first flurry of action to conceal the cement mixer, there was no apparent confusion or anxiety. Only General Gi took cover, walking briskly toward an underground shelter on whose roof a radar scanner was slowly revolving.

The SR-71 was over and past the site within two minutes of its first detection on the radar. The CIA pilot, through the telescopic range finder controlling the plane's cameras, had seen nothing out of the ordinary except the work on one of the gun sites. But his cameras had seen much more.

That evening General Gi and Han took their food trays to a promontory overlooking the ravine. The dinner was not much more appetizing than breakfast—chunks of stringy beef and peppers in an oily red sauce. To the south they saw the faint halation of lights above Ariella and, at intervals, the piercing beam of the lighthouse.

"You have read the dispatches, Han?"

"Yes, sir."

"Then you know we will be in Ariella in a week."

Han said nothing.

"You have no curiosity, comrade—no interest in why we are here?"

"I know who you are and there could only be one reason why you were sent."

"And do you disapprove?"

"No," said Han. "I accept the wisdom of my superiors, but—"

"Go on," Gi persisted.

"I think we could have won our objectives in Santa Clara without war."

"Perhaps," said the general. "But you must know that Santa Clara is only the first objective. We are planning beyond—to the conquest of all of South and Central America—and your bartering would not bring us that. And I can tell you that there will be no war." There was the rasp of a chuckle in his throat. "Do you think we would risk war with the Americans with an ally like Jiminez?"

"But Peking has chosen to support him as against—"

"As against you and your tactics? No, Han. We have chosen only a *situation,* and we could not have found a more favorable one. A revolutionary force already in existence—a weak central government whose allies are cowardly and dishonorable."

"You misjudge the Americans," said Han. "They will not permit missiles in Santa Clara. They will react as they did against Cuba."

"Ah," said the general, "but you overlook the element of surprise. Ours will be operational, within range of their great cities, before the Americans even suspect. It is a far different situation than in Cuba where the weapons were not yet ready. No, we will present them with a *fait accompli*. And what will they do? Direct their own missiles against an innocent population—against one of their own allies?"

"More likely bombers," said Han. "The arroyo is a small target, far from both Ciudad Alarcon and Ariella."

"And risk a retaliatory strike by us if they do? I think not."

Han stared into the darkness for a long moment. "And what do we gain? A poor country of little importance."

"Of great importance," Gi replied. "We will have a port on the Pacific. We will have an ally with common boundaries with Bolivia and that will leave only Brazil before we have cut the hemisphere in half. But that is only secondary. More important, we will have, for the first time, an effective nuclear deterrent against further American intervention in Asia. It was just such a deterrent, Han, that kept the Americans from interfering with the Soviets in Czechoslovakia and Hungary—that forced them to accept the Soviet role in the Mideast. When the gun is at your own head, you do not act rashly."

Han shook his head. "The risks are very great."

The general stood. "But if the prize is a free hand in all of Southeast Asia, in India and perhaps even farther to the west, the risk is worth taking."

"And you think the Soviets will stand by and do nothing?"

"It will not displease the Soviets," said Gi, "if America must face nuclear devastation from a new direction. Their present peaceful relations are those of two warriors, each of whom is afraid to raise his sword first." He paused. "But I grant you one point. The Soviets will not stand by for long when our intentions in Asia are clear. But by that time we will be ready for them too."

THE REPORT from the National Photographic Interpretation Center to the director of the Central Intelligence Agency on the over-flights of the Arroyo Seco was the first to bear the classification: URGENT.

"Latest reconnaissance reveals 105-mm. gun taken from its mount. New concrete layer, nine inches in depth, over old slab. This adequate to absorb recoil of much heavier weapon, including ICBM."

CIA Director Martin Trask was on his way to the White House minutes after receiving the report and found the President in grim spirits. His next appointment was with his political high command— a response to the Lou Harris poll that morning that had him still trailing Harlan Grant by four points.

The President read the report from the Interpretation Center. "You think it's all that important?"

"It could be," Trask replied. "You don't need a foundation that thick to fire a 105 or even artillery of much larger caliber—and that, Jiminez hasn't got."

"And he hasn't got missiles either," said the President.

"That's correct."

"Then how do you equate this report with our intelligence from China that there's been no flight-testing—that whatever they've got isn't even operational?"

"I'm calling this to your attention only because it's the first suspicious activity we've seen at the arroyo. My hunch is that they're preparing to site surface-to-air missiles. Jiminez can't know how we'll react to his next offensive. If he thinks we're likely to go with air strikes, SAMs would be his best bet, and they would be available to him from Bolivia."

The President sat back in his chair. "What do you recommend?"

"I think we ought to send the SR-71s in at much lower altitudes. Jiminez' radar is picking us up two to three minutes out, and that still gives them time to conceal whatever they're doing. If we came in very low, we'd be under their radar scan and on top of them before they knew it. And, frankly, I'd like a much closer look."

The President had doubts. "I don't want an incident down there. I don't want Jiminez *or* Luchengo knocking one of them down."

"There would be no chance of that—not at their speed," said Trask.

"All right. You have approval. But I want Sam Hood to clear it with Luchengo first. It won't take more than a day or two."

"Thank you, Mr. President. We might just find something interesting."

"I hope to hell you don't," said the Chief Executive.

There were four of them waiting in the President's private dining room—National Chairman Jim Mallory, Press Secretary Max Busby, Special Assistant Gene Haas and National Finance Chairman Braden Wyatt, a former governor of New Jersey. To a man, they were not looking forward to the next hour. Their candidate had clearly lost his early momentum, and the only question was how to close the gap in the short time left.

All of them, except Haas, had disagreed from the beginning with the strategy laid down by the President. But it would not serve their purpose to push that point too far. If they did, his predictable reaction would be to accuse them of incompetence in following his guidelines. And if the conference took that tack, Mallory, Busby and Wyatt would be denied the decision they knew was essential— an eleventh-hour change in over-all strategy.

Unknown both to the President and to Haas, the three had had lunch together that same day in Wyatt's suite at the Mayflower to coordinate their tactics. Busby knew that Mallory had a short fuse and would be the most likely to confront the President directly. His last words to the national chairman at the hotel were, "Stay cool, no matter how rough a time he gives you. We ought to be willing to take a little abuse to win our point."

"I'll do my best, Max. But if he won't listen to reason, we've got nothing to lose by scaring hell out of him."

"Maybe you've got nothing to lose," said Busby, smiling. "But I've got a commitment from him to head up the VSIA if we're back in January."

The President gave them only a cursory nod as he took his chair at the dining table, on which a coffee service had been set. On the surface, his manner was calm.

"We're turning into the home stretch, gentlemen, and we're going to have to decide here and now how we're going to pull it out. The key, obviously, is the voters who still can't decide between Grant and me. The question is, how do we pull them off the fence on our side?"

"I have an opinion on that," said Mallory. "I think they're voters who are finding it hard to buy Grant's extremism. I think they're actually looking for a reason to come over to you. We just haven't given them that reason."

The President spread his hands. "I don't know what more I can do, Jim. I'm on the move six days a week. I've been in forty-five states. And I think I'm speaking to the issues. Grant is only going through the motions. Three or four speeches a week, all before friendly audiences, and the rest of the time he spends in TV studios."

Busby glanced up from his doodling on a yellow legal pad. "But it seems to be working for him. On paid TV he avoids confrontation and he's able to put his points across."

"I know what you're leading up to, Max," said the President, "and I'm not going to buy it. I'm not going to pull a Nixon and hide away in a TV station with guards at the door to keep out all but my own claque. I've been in politics longer than all of you, and I can tell you that the people still want to shake the candidate's hand. They still want color, movement, excitement—not the pablum Grant is trying to force down their throats through the boob-box."

"It worked once for Nixon," said Wyatt quietly, "and I think Grant is smart in going the same route. And you should know, sir, that his ad agency is hounding the networks twenty-four hours a

day trying to buy more time. I would estimate he has at least another six million dollars to spend."

The President glanced up. "What's our budget for the last three
weeks?"

"Half that and today's poll isn't going to help me one bit with
fund raising."

Haas spoke for the first time. "I think I would agree with
the President that the poll shouldn't scare us into a last-minute
change of tactics. If we pull the President off the road and concentrate on TV, the media is going to accuse us of hitting the
panic button."

"It's not panic," said Mallory sharply, "to respond to the clear
evidence that Grant is holding his lead. What the hell are we all
doing here today if it's not to admit that fact and react to it?"

"The poll doesn't frighten me that much," Haas replied. "You
said yourself that the don't-knows are leaning our way."

"I said they *want* to lean our way," Mallory shot back, "and
I'll tell you straight out that those speeches you're writing aren't
giving them much of a shove."

"Please, gentlemen, let's try to stay on the track," said the
President.

"I think we are on the track, sir," said Busby. "You've been
speaking at least twice a day, and most of the time you've had
hostile audiences. And the media has been ignoring their content
and playing up the demonstrators. Last week alone, the police had
to move against the crowds three times and, believe me, it looks
ugly on TV."

The President disagreed. "You couldn't be more wrong. Every
time the campus radicals shout me down—every time a black
raises his fist to me—it's more votes for me in white suburbia."

"I have to go along with Busby," said Mallory. "The people
are sick of violence—of contempt for authority. It frightens them
to turn on the news shows night after night and see that they live
in a country where even the President isn't safe from the mobs."

"But they're also aware that I have the guts to stand up and
face the mob and that Grant hasn't."

"No," said Mallory, "what they're aware of when they watch

your shouting matches with the crowd is that you came into office four years ago with a commitment to restore law and order, and that you haven't done it."

The President exploded. "I've been running my ass off all over this country since Labor Day while you've been sitting on yours over at national headquarters. Don't tell me what the people are thinking. I'm on the firing line and I know. You're not."

"I can't run a campaign from an airplane," replied Mallory.

"And I'm not convinced you can run one from behind a desk, either. You want to know what's wrong, Mallory? I'll tell you. I'm facing hostile crowds because your organization hasn't been able to turn our own people out. Even when Grant does expose himself, he outdraws me. He's got better staff, better paid media, better billboards." The President glanced angrily at Wyatt. "And he's raising a hell of a lot more money."

The long silence around the table was finally broken by Busby. "I think we would all agree, sir, that the principal burden has fallen on you, and that's one of the reasons we ought to try to come to a decision here today. I think you're right. We should have better advancing. We should shake up the staff. And we should have better media—and more of it."

"I told you I'm not going the Nixon route, Max, and that's final."

"We're not suggesting that," said Mallory. "What we are suggesting is a new balance between personal appearances and TV. We should at least try to match Grant's TV budget."

"Wyatt says we don't have the money," said the President dourly.

Mallory sensed that the President was finally giving a little ground. "We can save at least half a million by cutting back on your travel schedule."

"You're still way short."

Wyatt spoke up. "I can raise it if I can guarantee the contributors that it's all going into television."

Haas didn't like the way it was going. "And keep him off the road entirely?"

"No," said Mallory, "but we should cancel all but his important engagements. We'll have to have at least three or four days of his time just to shoot the TV spots. As a rule of thumb, we should reduce the schedule to conventions, major fund raisers and commitments to other candidates, but none below the level of senators and governors."

"In other words," said the President, "no blacks, no students—nothing but friendly audiences?"

"It just happens to work out that way," said Mallory. "But apart from that, TV is the only way you're going to influence voters who can still go either way. They don't go to rallies. They don't read our literature. They don't respond to door-to-door canvassing. The only way you're going to reach them is in the privacy of their own homes."

"Do you agree with that, Max?"

"I do, sir."

"And you, Braden?"

"One hundred per cent."

"Haas?"

"I think we should try to do both—beef up the media budget and keep you on the road."

"No, I can't do both. We're running out of time."

Busby had the clinching argument. "You've already been to forty-five states, sir. You've already stood up to the demonstrators. The case can be made right now that you've taken your case to the people and Grant hasn't. Now you're ready for a new phase—a summing up—a direct appeal to millions of voters at a time to measure your campaign against Grant's."

"I like that," said the President. "A summing up. I might even say that a man who hasn't the courage to face up to his own countrymen wouldn't have the courage to face up to the grave challenges of the presidency."

"That's good," said Mallory. "Very good. It could be our theme—'A time for courage.'"

In a moment the concept—the entire change in strategy—had become the President's, not theirs, and Mallory, Busby and Wyatt knew they had won.

"All right. When can you have the new schedule on my desk, Jim?"

"Tomorrow morning."

"And the money, Braden?"

"We'll have it, and I think we can even shove the ante up a little."

The President stood. "Gentlemen, I think we might have won an election here today."

ACTIVITIES at the American embassy had all but come to a standstill since the evacuation of most of its personnel and other American nationals in Ciudad Alarcon.

Ambassador Sam Hood sent daily reports to the Latin American desk on the republic's declining economy and civilian morale. Food and fuel supplies in the capital were running dangerously low since its isolation from Ariella. Many thousands were without work because of the closing of American and other foreign commercial enterprises and the shutdown of the mines at San Quentin, where there had been a civilian raid on the army commissary in which seven miners were slain. There had also been looting of markets in Ciudad Alarcon and food raids on farmers near the city.

Hood's recommendation to Washington was that only a massive American airlift of critical supplies would enable the Luchengo regime to halt the spreading disorder. The answer from Secretary Adams did not surprise him. He was told that Luchengo had the forces to drive Paco Jiminez from the Arroyo Seco and lift the blockade of the city. If he saw no urgent necessity for doing this, he could not legitimately appeal for American assistance, which would, of course, be tantamount to interference in Santa Clara's internal political affairs. There was still no hard evidence, Adams wrote, that "the workers' revolution, whatever its Communist origins, is presently receiving external support that would justify our intervention."

Hood was fighting a lost cause and knew it. In his years in the

State Department he had always been an unremitting opponent of American recognition of Latin military juntas and American assistance to them in the face of popular uprisings. That the crisis in Santa Clara was not at all comparable must have been clear to Secretary Adams, but Hood knew the pressures from the White House were far stronger than he could apply, and did not press the point.

Nor did he raise objections to another message from Adams urging him "to remain on post for however long it may require to select your successor—a decision, I can assure you, to which the President attaches the greatest importance." Hood read it, correctly, as a signal that he should not expect early relief. But because of Constanzia Novarese's confinement at the Playa del Sol, he was no longer impatient to leave or to surrender the authority with which he might be able to compel her release.

Colonel William Gruver, the military attaché, also sent daily cables to his superiors in the Pentagon, reporting on the continuing hiatus in the fighting and the deterioration in army morale at all levels. Defections to Jiminez were increasing and there had been small, abortive garrison uprisings in both the capital and San Quentin. Gruver was not critical of the army's lack of offensive initiative. It was his appraisal that ground force assaults against the Arroyo Seco would have little chance of success—that only air strikes could dislodge Jiminez from "the very strong position he now holds. I believe it would be in our own best interests to review the central government's recent request for such assistance from us."

The reply from the Pentagon was a reprimand. His responsibility was to report, not to recommend, and certainly not in areas involving such sensitive questions of policy. Gruver did not press his point either. He still had eight years before reaching retirement age, and he had no desire to spend them behind an obscure desk in the Pentagon.

Secretary Adams' cable to Hood, instructing him to obtain permission from President Luchengo for low-level flights of the SR-71s over Santa Claran territory, came late one afternoon. The ambassador read it with mounting irritation. The Secretary clearly was applying "the need to know" rule, under which sensitive information is kept from all but the highest and most involved echelons of government. And Hood obviously was not in that select circle. Adams was emphatic that the ambassador should reassure Luchengo that the request was entirely routine—that its purpose was to enable the spy planes to evade early radar detection. Hood didn't believe it, and he knew Luchengo wouldn't either.

He had not seen Luchengo since the battle at the arroyo and was shaken by the change in his appearance. The face, always gaunt, was now almost skeletal. His eyes, over the deep hollows in his cheeks, had an unnatural glitter. His arm was still in a sling, and he rose weakly to greet Hood, who was unable to conceal his shock.

"It is nothing, my friend—a small wound that refuses to heal."

"You are driving yourself too hard."

"Ah, you agree with the doctors. They recommend a long rest. And when I tell them the wound afflicting this country is graver than mine—perhaps mortal, Mr. Hood?—they go away shaking their heads." His hand fell limply to the desk. "No, it is necessary to maintain at least the appearance of authority. Or, to be more honest with you, the certainty of punishment for those who would weaken our resistance to Jiminez. Since my defeat at the arroyo, more soldiers have died before my own firing squads for desertion or insubordination than have been slain by Jiminez' patrols. And tomorrow, three civilians will be shot for the monstrous crime of stealing a pig from a farmer to feed their children."

"You are at war," said Hood. "You have no choice but to enforce—"

"I have become what most of your countrymen have always thought I was—a dictator who governs by terror." He did not want to go on with it. "This request from your government—what is it?"

Hood told him, and Luchengo was suddenly tense. "But there must be more. What have your planes found at the arroyo?"

"To my knowledge, nothing."

"Please, I have a long memory. And I recall that President Kennedy did not order low-level flights over Cuba until there was almost certain evidence that Castro was building missile sites."

"Your own pilots have seen nothing."

"They wouldn't know what to look for," replied Luchengo, "and they wouldn't know what it was if they saw it."

"I'm sorry, Mr. President, I know no more than you do. But I can assure you of this. If the SR-71s do find evidence that Jiminez is preparing for missiles, my government will not hesitate to react."

"As it has to your own warnings that Jiminez is fighting with Chinese weapons? As it has to my requests both to Washington and to the OAS for military support?"

"There is a difference," said Hood.

"Yes, and we both know what the difference is. Your government has ignored and will continue to ignore every treaty it has with Santa Clara until its own security is in danger. Then, and only then, will it act." His voice grew weak. "But if there are no missiles—nothing to frighten your President—he will do nothing. Do you deny it?"

"I can't deny it. But later he will have greater freedom of action."

"*After* the election?" Luchengo shook his head. "I am coming to believe, my friend, that a dictatorship may be a more honorable form of government than your own. The dictator, at least, can act without fear or deceit—without concern for his own ambitions. And whether he is a good man or a bad man, he is a *leader*. But your President"—he spat out the word like a profanity—"dares to lead, to take a wise but unpopular position, only in his first year or two in office. Then he prays, like a guilty supplicant, that the people will forgive or forget his sins." The tirade over, his voice became a hoarse whisper.

Hood tried to spare him further agitation. "I can wait for your decision, sir."

"My decision is yes. Your planes can fly as low over Santa Clara as they like, and I will advise the army to that effect. It can do no harm and, at most, it might deter Jiminez for a time by creating the impression that your government still has a slight interest in the fate of Santa Clara."

"The flights can accomplish more than that. Surveillance will be much more effective."

"Even if it is—even if it confirms what we both believe to be Jiminez' intentions—it will be too late. You may save yourselves, but you will not save Santa Clara."

Hood stood to leave.

"A moment longer, Mr. Ambassador. I have a question to ask of you. In recent days you have been in contact with both Arturo Lara and Señora Novarese. Is that correct?"

"I was in contact with the señora, yes."

"But Lara came to you?"

"I think you already know that."

"I do," said Luchengo, "and I also know why. But I have no desire to embarrass you and I will not ask you to betray your confidences."

"And I must ask that you not misjudge me."

"You have always had my trust, and you have it now. I intend to ask only a hypothetical question. I spoke earlier of the reputation I have in your country—a reputation that will become more abhorrent when the latest measures I have taken become known to your press. My question is this, Mr. Hood. If there were a change in government in Santa Clara—a regime your President might find it popular to support—is there even a remote possibility that he would?"

"I think the question is academic," Hood replied. "The generals would not follow Lara."

"You misunderstand me, Mr. Hood. The new government would come on my initiative, not Lara's."

The ambassador was incredulous. "You would resign?"

"I would consider it, if I had the assurance that your government would respond, and swiftly, in support of what we may call a more democratic regime."

Hood was cautious. "You told me you were aware of the purpose of Lara's call at my embassy?"

"He could have had but one purpose—to ask if your government would support him—or, more precisely, Señora Novarese—in a coup against me."

"You must believe that Señora Novarese is not a party to his conspiracy," said Hood.

Luchengo shook his head impatiently. "I do, but you are not answering my question. Obviously you would not encourage Lara. He is a fool—a traitor—and he still lives only because he can prove useful to me."

"As a contact with the señora?"

"Exactly. And the proposal I present to you now would not compromise you or what I know to be your regard for me. You would not be asking your government to subvert mine or to recognize a regime that has taken power by force."

Hood's face was grim. "I can't believe you would step aside in favor of Lara."

"I would step aside in favor of *el diablo* himself if it would bring your Air Force. If Jiminez is not driven from the arroyo— if the blockade against the capital is not broken—the people and then the army will rise against me. In Santa Clara food is politics, and a leader who cannot feed his people does not deserve to lead."

"But *Lara?*"

"Lara is nothing. Señora Novarese would assign him no more important a position in her government than I have in mine." He studied Hood's face. "The señora and I were once friends— colleagues—and I have respect for her, just as I had respect for her husband. But I did what had to be done. And I know what you will tell me next—that she has sworn to avenge Luis. So be it."

A chill swept over the ambassador. "You are asking me to sign your death warrant."

"No, my friend. My life is Santa Clara, and I am asking you to save it."

LUCHENGO AUTHORIZES LOW-LEVEL PHOTOGRAPHIC RECONNAISSANCE ARROYO SECO. ADVISES ME CIVILIAN AND MILITARY UPRISINGS AGAINST HIM MAY BE IMMINENT AND THAT HE CONSIDERING RESIGNATION IN FAVOR OF CONSTANZIA NOVARESE IF CHANGE IN REGIMES WOULD ALTER OUR PRESENT POLICY OF NON-INTERVENTION. I REQUEST PERMISSION TO CONSULT WITH YOU PERSONALLY.

Sterling Adams read the cable impatiently. Would Hood never understand that the President was determined not to interfere in

Santa Claran affairs? The ambassador was behaving very strangely. If a popular revolt against Luchengo was imminent, Hood, in the past, had always fought against American military assistance to the repressive government in power. But now, apparently, he was taking exactly the opposite position. Adams could justify himself absolutely. Hadn't he stood with Hood against the President when the question was one of financial assistance to an ally whose economic stability was important to the cohesion of the anti-Communist bloc in South America? And he had gone ever further. He had agreed with Hood that Chinese involvement in Santa Clara was a possibility the President should not ignore. And only days earlier he had argued against the President's decision to replace Hood.

What more could the ambassador expect of him? Events had proven Hood wrong. If Luchengo was in peril, it was the result of his unwillingness to commit his own military forces against Jiminez. And now Hood's last proposal. Was he being merely perverse? Or had he lost all objectivity? Whatever Hood's personal reasons for defiance of a policy that was now clearly set, he could no longer expect Adams to be the lightning rod for the President's annoyance.

Secretary Adams sent to the White House, by messenger, a copy of the ambassador's cable, together with his own memorandum stating that he did not believe a change of administrations in Santa Clara should "substantively affect our present policy on non-involvement in what has patently become a popular movement against President Luchengo."

Two hours later he had a call from Special Assistant Gene Haas. "The President wants you to thank Hood for his prompt action on the overflights. But he agrees with you that a new government put together by Luchengo—even if he's out of it—wouldn't change our position. Tell Hood that, and tell him, further, that under no circumstances is he to return for consultations. I'm sending you copies of newspaper articles and radio transcripts from La Paz on the execution of civilians and other repressions in Santa Clara. Cable them to Hood too—just in case he hasn't heard."

Hidden from the radar at the Arroyo Seco by the high bluffs along the coast, the SR-71 came in low from the sea at six hundred miles an hour. Once over the coastal plain, the CIA pilot held his altitude at five hundred feet and was already within camera range before the radar operator saw the spy plane on his scope.

General Gi You-gin and Han Li-wong, walking to breakfast from their command quarters, heard the air raid siren and the roar of the SR-71's jets in the same split second. Han, watching the black projectile hurtling toward him, felt only panic. But General Gi identified the aircraft instantly and threw a concealing arm across his face. But it was too late.

Six hours later, technicians at the Central Intelligence Agency in Virginia had no difficulty identifying Han. They had scores of pictures of him, shot covertly by CIA operatives and American embassy personnel in Paris, Belgrade, Cairo, Hanoi, Ciudad Alarcon and African capitals—a file that could serve as a pictorial history of his long career. But there was nothing in the files on the taller Oriental with Han, and the duty officer at the center immediately sent full-face enlargements of his photograph to the State Department with a request that Russian assistance be sought in identifying him.

The President was weekending at Camp David when the call came from CIA Director Martin Trask asking for an immediate appointment. The Chief Executive sent for Press Secretary Maxwell Busby.

"Trask is on his way up here by helicopter, Max, and I don't want the press around when he lands."

"What now? Santa Clara?"

The question was ignored. "How many reporters are out there?"

"None, just three or four pool photographers. You were going to hit a golf ball around this afternoon. They're waiting for that."

"Tell them I've changed my mind."

"Shouldn't you give them something for the A.M. editions?" Busby persisted. "They've been here all day."

It wouldn't be a bad picture at that, the President thought—the cheerful candidate relaxing on the links, confident of victory. "All right, I'll go out and do it now, then hustle them back down to Thurmont."

Camp David stands on the heights of the Catoctin Mountains in Maryland, only a half-hour helicopter flight from Washington. The old two-story, brown-shingled residence—commanding a spectacular view of the Catoctins and the forests on their foothills—is in the center of a sprawling Navy compound.

Two hundred yards from the residence is a complex of buildings serving the President and his guests and the Navy staff—a communications center, a gymnasium and bowling alley, stables built during the Kennedy years, and quarters for the service personnel. Adjoining the compound is a helicopter pad, with a fire engine constantly standing by when the President is due to arrive or depart.

Behind the residence itself is a single golf fairway, but with tees and greens at both ends that make it a two-hole course. The photographers caught the President, wearing slacks and sports shirt, lofting an iron shot onto the green and holing out his putt. He left the green, grinning. "That was a birdie, and don't forget it in your captions."

Coming back, he had a bogie and agreed to replay a putt for the cameras, wincing in mock anguish as it ran past the hole.

"That's it," Busby told the newsmen, and led them toward a Navy car that was waiting to transport them to their motels in Thurmont, a small town at the base of the mountain.

One was suspicious. "Why the rush act, Max?"

"Because if you're around I've got to be around—and I haven't had a clear afternoon in the last month."

"You're sure there'll be nothing else today?"

"Just a chopper bringing up mail and situation reports."

One of the most difficult aspects of Busby's position—and that of his predecessors who had come from the working press—was the concealment of important information from their former colleagues. If they did not actually lie to the press, they often did withhold the truth—and they had had to learn to live with the distinction.

The saving phrase in Busby's last answer was "situation report." That, of course, was what Trask would be bringing. That Busby had not told the press that it must be of the highest urgency, or the director of the CIA would not be flying up personally to deliver it, was no more than a routine deception and one he could justify on the limitless grounds of national security.

From the patio in the rear of the residence, where the President was sipping a tall bourbon and water, he saw the Air Force helicopter settle on its pad at the compound. Trask was driven the short distance in a Navy staff car.

"Thank you for coming up, Martin. It would have been rather difficult to explain if I had cut the weekend short to fly back to Washington."

"I understand that, sir."

The President sent for another drink for himself and a vodka and tonic for the CIA director. They took chairs at a wicker table. Around them, the Catoctins were a rampart against the world. The Chief Executive was reluctant to break the euphoria he always felt at Camp David—the sense of escape from decision and crisis that had been common to presidents since Franklin Delano Roosevelt, who gave it its original name—Shangri-la.

But Trask came directly to the point of his mission. He took two photographic prints from his attaché case and laid them in front of the President. "Our first low-level photographs—shot early today. And our first evidence that there are Chinese advisers with Jiminez." He saw the President's face blanch. "This first man is known as Han Li-wong."

The name was familiar to the President. "Isn't he the one Palmer Joyce said was a friend of Sam Hood's?"

"The same, and his presence at the arroyo could be significant, although he has no military background whatever. He's strictly a trade envoy—Europe, Africa, Cuba, a brief stint in Hanoi and two years in Santa Clara. I think we have to conclude that he's with Jiminez to ramrod shipments of military supplies from China and/or Bolivia."

"Didn't Hood inform us that Luchengo had thrown Han out—that he was returning to Peking?"

"He did, and we know that he got as far as Guatemala City. We had nothing more on him after that—until now."

"And the other one—who is he?"

"We don't know. But we should have the answer very soon. In line with your orders to coordinate our intelligence with the Soviets, I've had State give the picture to their embassy for radio transmission to Moscow." Trask drew a long breath. "I do have a suspicion who he might be."

"Let's hear it."

"We've had fairly good intelligence out of China on their missile specialists. Peking keeps them out front all the time—on reviewing stands at parades, in the newspapers and on the radio. Their pitch is that China is already a nuclear power—that they have nothing to fear from us or the Soviets—and here's the first team to prove it."

"Go ahead."

"There's only one we've lost track of—a General Gi You-gin. Our presumption has been that he's in charge of the new missile center they're building near the Indian border, which wouldn't give him much time for propaganda."

"This Gi—how would you rank him in their table of organization?"

"With Werner von Braun in ours."

The President glanced past Trask, watching the evening shadows ascend the Catoctins, invading the bright mosaic of autumn reds, yellows and golds on their sunlit crests.

"But if it isn't Gi," he said, "if he turns out to be no more important than Han—"

"It would still amount to a Chinese presence in Santa Clara and one to which we would have to respond. But it's ticklish. This evidence contradicts all our claims up to this point that the revolution is an internal affair which absolves us of our treaty obligations. And if this man is Gi, we've really been caught with our pants down."

The President was reluctant to accept the possibility. "But, goddammit, where are the missiles? How could they possibly move them eight thousand miles across the Pacific without our detecting it?"

"I don't know. I don't know. But if Gi is in Santa Clara, they must *think* they have a way."

The President took a long drink of his bourbon. It was acrid to the taste. "When do you expect to hear from Moscow?"

"Momentarily. Gi had his training in the Soviet Union. It won't take them long to identify him—if it is him."

"Then why don't you stay for dinner, Martin? We'll wait together."

"Of course."

The call from CIA headquarters came an hour later. The President, watching the director's face, knew all he had to know even before the brief conversation came to an end.

"Gi?"

"Himself."

The President came to a quick decision. "We will move quickly— very quickly—over the next day or two. I'll return tonight and we'll call in Adams and the service secretaries in the morning."

Minutes later the Air Force helicopter was on its way back to Washington with Trask. The President went immediately to his study and spent the next twenty minutes on the scramble telephone. His words were an incoherent jumble over the line but were heard distinctly through an electronic descrambler in Washington—first by Secretary of Defense Burgess Rand and then by Secretary of State Sterling Adams.

Rand was told by the President to instruct the Secretary of the Navy to prepare a plan for a sea blockade of Santa Clara and to alert the service secretaries to an emergency session to be held at nine in the morning.

The Secretary of Defense had questions. "I take it we'll be looking for missiles?"

"For all war contraband that could reach Jiminez."

"You understand, Mr. President, that it will require certain legalities—a declaration of interdiction from you, for instance?"

"I do. But we're not at that point yet."

"How soon would it be put in effect?"

"Perhaps late tomorrow."

"Then I suggest we ought to start deploying major fleet units toward the area tonight."

"Yes. But you're to pass them off as maneuvers—nothing more."

"We're lucky in that respect. We already have light cruiser and destroyer anti-submarine exercises under way between Pearl Harbor and the Canal Zone."

"Good," said the Commander-in-Chief. "Let's hope our luck holds."

Secretary Adams was told to prepare a draft statement, for issuance by the President, accusing the People's Republic of China of a new and hostile provocation in the Western Hemisphere. It was to cite incontrovertible evidence of the presence of Chinese military advisers with the revolutionary forces in Santa Clara. It was to emphasize that the American government had exercised restraint in interfering in the internal affairs of Santa Clara but could not ignore this new danger to hemispheric security. It was to demand that China either withdraw its advisers and desist from further military assistance to the Communist insurrectionists or face swift and appropriate counteraction by America and by its allies in the Organization of American States.

Adams was taken aback. "That's rather strong, Mr. President. But, of course, I don't know what your evidence is. I can be up there in an hour and a half."

"No. I'll want you at the White House at nine in the morning. We can go over the draft then."

"May I suggest a change or two now?"

"You may."

"First, we have not been describing Jiminez as a Communist. To the contrary, our position has been that the uprising is a popular revolt."

"All right, take out that reference. What else?"

"You speak of *further* military assistance. We've never given public credence to Hood's reports that Jiminez has Chinese weapons. That also would amount to an admission we would find it difficult to explain."

"Delete that one too. Just limit it to military advisers. Is that all?"

"Yes. There's nothing more you can tell me now?"

"Nothing you shouldn't be able to read between the lines."

When the President came out of his study, Busby was waiting. "I thought you might want me, sir."

"I do, Max. You had better contact the press that's with us and tell them I'm going back to Washington early tomorrow morning to confer with Adams and the military."

"Just that?"

"Just that."

"Can you cue me in on it?"

"At the proper time, Max—at the proper time."

"And when will that be?"

"When I hand you the announcement you're going to issue."

"Mr. President, either I have your confidence or I don't."

"And I've told you a hundred times that what you don't know the press can't drag out of you."

Within an hour of Busby's alert to the correspondents the news was flowing out across the nation that the President was summoning his top military and diplomatic advisers to the White House for a crisis conference, probably involving Communist China.

THE PRESIDENT was the last to enter the Cabinet Room and found his advisers huddling around a large easel on which were photographs of Han Li-wong, General Gi You-gin and the new work on the gun sites at the Arroyo Seco.

All quickly took their places around the massive rectangular table, waiting for the President to present their options in America's first potential nuclear crisis since 1962. On his instructions, Martin Trask had already given the others a briefing on the backgrounds of the two Chinese and the implications of the construction at the arroyo.

"Gentlemen," said the President, "I first want you to know the actions I am planning today. One of them is a quarantine of the sea approaches to Santa Clara. The other is what amounts to an ultimatum to China. We'll hear first from Rand and Wright, then from Adams."

Defense Secretary Burgess Rand and Navy Secretary Boyd Wright had met at the Pentagon for an hour before leaving for the White House together, and Rand had found serious flaws in Wright's initial planning.

The President glanced at Rand, who said nothing, then at Wright, who knew he would have to carry the ball alone.

"The plan—subject to your approval, of course, Mr. President— is for air and fleet units to track and maintain a plot on all east-bound ships of Communist registry in the Pacific."

"But excluding the Russians," said the President.

"If that's your wish."

The President fought back his impatience. Was there a single man in the Pentagon who did not still regard the Soviet Union as the principal enemy even after years of increasing rapport? "It is my wish. Will you continue, please?"

"We would take no action against such ships," Wright continued, "until it was determined that they were on a course for the west coast of South America and only then when they cross an arc extending one thousand miles offshore."

"What form of action?" said the President.

"First, an order to lay to for inspection of their cargo. If they ignore it, a warning that we will sink them unless they either submit to inspection or alter course to clear the coast by five hundred miles."

Secretary Adams couldn't believe what he was hearing. "Mr. President, I have to object to this plan. Apart from its clear illegality without a declaration of interdiction from you, its effect would be to interfere with entirely legitimate trade that Communist nations are conducting with Costa Rica, Panama, Colombia, Ecuador, Peru and Chile. I don't think we can do this without the prior consent of those governments, and they certainly won't give it to us."

This had been one of Rand's arguments against the plan and Wright knew that it was time to retreat. "What I am presenting is the maximum—the most effective effort—we could undertake to seal off Ariella. It's only a starting point, from which we can—"

"I thought my instructions to the Secretary of Defense were specific, Wright—that we were to have a plan that could be put into effect as early as today."

"We haven't cut the orders to the fleet yet, Mr. President."

"I'm glad to hear that. Rand, you certainly don't endorse this proposal?"

The Secretary of Defense was unwilling to abandon Wright entirely. "I think, if the intelligence we have is correct, we may yet have to go to the actions Boyd suggests. But at the moment I agree with Adams that they're too much, too soon. I personally would recommend—"

Secretary of the Air Force James Halverson could no longer keep his silence. "If I may interrupt, Mr. President, I think we're going at this ass backwards—that we're repeating Kennedy's error."

"And what was that?" The President's tone was almost scornful.

"Delay, Mr. President, delay. Kennedy let days go by fumbling around for a decision while Castro was actually siting missiles against us. Then, when he finally did act, he gave the assignment to the Navy." The word was like a curse. "And the country, unnecessarily, had to sweat out two or three days of terror. If Kennedy had hit the Cuban sites, as he should have—"

The President broke in sharply. "You're sounding more and more like Curt LeMay every day, and if Kennedy had taken his advice, none of us might be sitting around this table now. In addition to that, Halverson, your parallel is hardly relevant. Jiminez has no missiles."

The comparison with General LeMay did not offend Halverson. "I won't argue history with you, Mr. President. But I insist that you can't risk the possibility that even one ICBM could slip through a blockade. I remind you that Khrushchev was able to sneak his missiles into Cuba under the noses of the entire Atlantic fleet. It took a pilot, sir, to locate them on the ground."

Wright bridled. "But the blockade was one hundred per cent effective."

"Yes, after the Navy was told what to look for and where." Halverson glanced back at the President. "It is my recommendation that we avoid another long-drawn-out confrontation—that we bomb the Arroyo Seco. We have a treaty that justifies it. We have a formal request for air intervention from the Santa Claran government that justifies it."

"That," said the President, "is the last option we will examine."

"When you do," Halverson shot back, "you will find that the Air Force plan will be more specific and certainly more immediately operational than the proposal you've just heard."

"I'm certain it will be," the Chief Executive replied. "Can we have your thinking, Rand?"

"Yes, I think we should narrow the area of search and possible interception. I would suggest an arc no more than two hundred miles off Ariella."

"That doesn't give us much margin for error," said the President. "Two hundred miles can't be more than one day's cruising time for a freighter."

"I believe it's on the safe side," Rand replied. "You want to remember there are no longer Chinese or other Communist ships calling at Ariella. In fact, there's practically no activity there at all. If a vessel should approach our screen, the odds are very much against its being a hostile. We'll have at least forty fast ships on the line, including the carrier *JFK*. Nothing is likely to slip through."

The President turned to Secretary Adams. "Would that satisfy your objections?"

"Yes. But before you issue your announcement, we should have President Luchengo's approval, and I'm certain he'll give it. I also think there should be a prior alert to the OAS and a request to the secretariat for an emergency session, possibly tomorrow."

"You'll have time," said the President. "With the delay we've run into this morning, I doubt that we could have the ships on the line before tomorrow."

"Yes, sir."

Adams then read the draft of the statement the President would issue. Only Halverson had an objection. "It's too soft. We ought to lay it right on the line and tell them we'll regard just one missile on one ship bound for this hemisphere as an act of war."

The President didn't comment, and the conference broke up with a request that his advisers keep themselves immediately available for further consultations.

Adams hung behind. "I had a call from the Soviet embassy early this morning. They're naturally quite anxious to know what we're going to do."

"There's no reason to keep them in the dark," the President said. "But when you speak to Ambassador Kharlamov, indicate to him very clearly that I consider the possible consequences even more serious for the Soviet Union than they are for us. Tell him they're under the gun right now and we're not, and that I would expect Chairman Borichev's full cooperation with us."

"Kharlamov will understand that without my telling him," Adams said. "I'll also inform the OAS, of course."

"Of course."

Adams stuck a cigarette in his long ivory holder. "I hope you will appreciate, Mr. President, that this crisis will come very much as a shock to the nation and to our friends in the OAS. As I told you last night, the drastic actions you're planning are in contradiction to all of our recent policy declarations on Santa Clara. The political consequences for you will be most damaging."

"Sterling, what choice do I have? If there have been misjudgments in the past, we certainly can't afford them now."

"I agree," said Adams, "that the blockade should go into effect. But we should also try to salvage as much credibility as possible."

"What are you suggesting?"

"That we ask Luchengo to take the initiative. I can cable Sam Hood within the hour. He can present to the palace our evidence on General Gi and on the new construction at the arroyo. With a little prodding from Hood, it's very likely Luchengo himself would ask for a blockade."

The President was gaining a whole new respect for Adams. "In other words, we would be responding to an appeal from an ally?"

"Exactly."

"I like it," said the President. "But can it be done before tomorrow?"

"We should have the answer back within hours, and I'm certain it will be affirmative. Luchengo is in no position to refuse whatever assistance we indicate is available to him."

"All right, go ahead. I can hold off on my announcement until tonight." At the door the President put a hand on Adams' shoulder. "You know, Sterling, I think this is the first time you've ever come to me with political advice. You ought to do it more often."

The Secretary of State felt uncomfortable. "I don't think of it as political advice, sir. I just happen to believe that questions of such gravity don't belong in the political arena. And I don't doubt that Senator Grant would try to exploit our vulnerability fully and, probably, irresponsibly. And that would be dangerous not only to you, sir, but to the national consensus we ought to have for this decision."

The President was smiling. "'All right, Sterling, have it your way."

An hour later Adams' message was in Ambassador Hood's hands.

FIRST LOW-LEVEL SR-71 FLIGHT REVEALS PRESENCE ARROYO SECO GENERAL GI YOU-GIN, TOP-RANKING CHINESE MISSILE SPECIALIST, AND HAN LI-WONG. ALSO REVEALS NEW CONSTRUCTION POTENTIALLY CONVERTIBLE TO MISSILE SITES. ADVISE LUCHENGO IMMEDIATELY. INDICATE OUR READINESS TO RESPOND APPROPRIATELY SHORT OF DIRECT MILITARY ACTION AGAINST JIMINEZ. SEA BLOCKADE TO INTERCEPT POSSIBLE MISSILE SHIPMENTS AN OPTION WE WOULD CONSIDER.

Press Secretary Busby met with the White House correspondents at two o'clock that afternoon. Excerpts from the transcript:

I have a brief announcement that you can attribute to me.
Q. Why not the President?

A. He'll have an announcement later in the day. Until then, you'll have to go with this. I'll run through it quickly. There'll be copies ready for all of you on your way out. "The President met this morning with his highest military and diplomatic advisers to review what may be a serious development affecting the security of the Republic of Santa Clara. This government is now in contact with President Luchengo to determine if the situation warrants our assistance under our defense commitments both to Santa Clara and to the Organization of American States."

Q. That's all?

A. For now, yes.

Q. Can we conclude from this that Jiminez is planning another offensive—one that could bring down the Luchengo regime?

A. I have nothing on that. Why don't you go with what you've got?

Q. You haven't told us much—only that there's a crisis down there that might require our intervention.

A. That's right on the nose.

Q. Look, Max, the recent line from the White House, State and Defense is that the fighting down there is an internal affair and that we're keeping hands off. The President himself has been highly critical of the Luchengo government. Why the sudden switch?

A. The statement I gave you speaks for itself. There's been a new and serious development.

Q. Would it be off target to speculate that we have evidence that the Santa Claran revolution is no longer an internal affair— that we have proof of Bolivian intervention?

A. I'm not going into that.

Q. Chinese intervention, then?

A. No comment.

Q. Max, whatever's going on down there has obviously caught the administration off guard. Yesterday the President was playing golf. Today he's got a full-blown crisis on his hand. I don't imagine Senator Grant is going to settle for what you've told us.

A. I've told you the President will have a statement later in the day. Now can we wrap this up?

Q. One more question. The administration has been saying no to every request from Luchengo for military assistance. And now, overnight, we're apparently ready to move in and fast. That suggests to me that our own security is now at stake. Have we evidence of Chinese missiles down there?

A. We do not.

Q. Have we evidence that they are building sites—that they may try to move them in down there?

A. I have no comment on that.

Q. On the flight down here from Boston just last week, the President said unequivocally that China had no present or foreseeable capability of deploying ICBMs against us and accused Grant of playing panic politics for suggesting that they might. Does the President still stand by that statement?

A. No comment.

Q. Max, can we please go off the record?

A. No. You're going to have to wait for the President's statement.

The bulletin from James McManus, correspondent for Westinghouse Broadcasting, was on the air to millions of Americans within minutes:

"A White House spokesman would neither confirm nor deny today that the nation is on the brink of a nuclear confrontation with Communist China, but there were alarming indications in Washington that Peking may have chosen the small South American republic of Santa Clara from which to launch an attack on the continental United States. Presidential Press Secretary Maxwell Busby told correspondents there are presently no missiles in Santa Clara but would not respond to direct questioning as to whether launch sites are being built or whether missiles are now in transit from China. The President will issue a statement later today that most observers believe may be a repeat of John F. Kennedy's dramatic disclosure in 1962 that nuclear war could be imminent."

Columnist Joseph Alsop wrote a substitute column for the next day. The opening paragraphs:

"The White House announcement today that we face a crisis in Santa Clara amounts to one of the most incredible credibility gaps in our recent history. The President and those close to him have been insisting for weeks that rebel Francisco Jiminez' military actions to unseat the regime of President Jorge Luchengo were an inevitable result of the central government's repressive policies.

"The President's own campaign speeches have maligned President Luchengo, and have had the effect of creating a growing sympathy in this country for the Jiminez revolt. Whatever the President may tell the nation, the very fact that he is now considering the commitment of American forces to the support of the Luchengo regime is a switch in policy this correspondent finds as incredible as it is suspicious. It also raises the grave question of whether the President—still trailing Senator Grant in the polls—has withheld information from the public that could be damaging to his already tenuous hopes of re-election. . . ."

AMBASSADOR HOOD'S call to President Luchengo was taken by Foreign Minister Arturo Lara.

"I regret that the President cannot receive you. He is in the military hospital—*gangrena.*"

"It is most urgent that I speak to him."

"But it is quite impossible. He is under heavy sedation."

"Are you refusing me access to him?"

"I am following the surgeon general's orders. No one is to disturb him except on matters of the greatest military importance."

"The decision I must have from him fits that description exactly," Hood shot back. "I'm on my way over."

Hood strode swiftly across the plaza, a single Marine guard accompanying him. A cooling late afternoon breeze was stirring the trees in the plaza. But the lobby of the palace was humid from the spray of the fountain and stank from decaying algae in its pool. It was too much even for the peacocks, which had left their perches on the fountain and were wandering forlornly around the marble floor.

Hood and his guard cut directly through the lobby and across the parade ground toward the army barracks and hospital at the far end of the compound. Lara was waiting at the entrance to the hospital.

"You have no objection to my joining you?" said Lara.

"I do," Hood replied, "but I have no time to argue."

The ambassador told the Marine to wait outside and the two army sentries guarding the entrance immediately began to mock the trimness of his uniform, flicking small clouds of dust from their jackets and rubbing their sleeves over lusterless buttons.

Two doctors were standing at the foot of Luchengo's bed in the small room, lit only by a harsh overhead fluorescent light. But the thick adobe walls and the small slit serving as a window gave at least a degree of relief from the searing heat.

When Luchengo saw Hood and Lara at the door, he dismissed the doctors with a wave of his hand, and they left shaking their heads.

"Buenas tardes, Mr. Hood, and thank you for rescuing me." He signed to the nurse sitting at his side to crank the bed to an angle from which he could face Hood. His face was ashen with pain.

"If I were a private in the army," he said, "they would cut this off." He glanced impatiently at his right arm, purpled from the bruises of many injections. "But because I am the commander-in-chief, I must endure my pain and their fear."

"I would take their advice," said Hood. The nurse brought two chairs and Hood and Lara sat facing each other across the bed.

"I apparently have no choice. I can't order them to take my arm—or can I, Lara?"

The Foreign Minister spread his hands. "I think they should do whatever they must to restore your ability to lead us."

"Restore it, Lara?" There was a faint smile on his face. "If there are those who think I have lost it, or who think it can be taken from me, tell them I need only one hand to sign an order of execution."

"We all pray for your recovery, sir."

"Do you?" Luchengo swung his head slowly to Hood. "And

what is the message you can't entrust to my most loyal Minister of Foreign Affairs?"

Hood gave him the sheaf of photographs from his attaché case, and Luchengo studied them carefully. "Ah, your old friend Han, Mr. Hood. And who is the man with him?"

"General Gi You-gin, a Chinese missile expert. The third picture—"

"Shows what could be construction of missile launching sites. Am I correct?"

"You are, sir."

Luchengo fell back on the bed, staring vacantly past Hood toward the window and the green treetops in the plaza, visible above the palace. Then he shut his eyes, alone with his pain. A minute went by, then another.

Lara spoke almost in a whisper. "I told you, Mr. Hood, that he is in no condition—"

"What do you want of me, Ambassador?" Luchengo's voice had all of its old command.

"It is the opinion of my government that this evidence of Chinese involvement justifies our own intervention."

"It comes rather late, my friend, but it pleases me. You are ready, then, to destroy Jiminez' position at the arroyo?"

"We think it more important at this point to prevent the delivery of the missiles and, simultaneously, the further delivery of arms to Jiminez."

Luchengo shook his head impatiently. "You are playing the old game with me. Your President's one concern is for your own security. You will stop the missiles because they threaten you. But I would still be left with Jiminez."

"But could Jiminez continue the revolution without further assistance from the Chinese?"

Luchengo's voice was weaker now. "He could, and would. The people have no food. The army has no will. Jiminez will win because he exists—because he is an alternative to the misery that plagues this country." He was shaken by a new spasm of pain in his arm. "My doctors and your President are guilty of the same insanity. If they amputate this arm, they save me. If your bombers remove Jiminez, they save this country. But no! They look for cures that involve no risk to themselves. And it is too late, too late." The outburst left him spent.

Hood rose to his feet. "My instructions are to ask if you will request formally that we impose a sea and aerial blockade to prevent further—"

"*I must ask?* Please, you would do it with or without my approval."

There was a stir in the corridor and Hood saw Defense Minister Carlos Silvera-Guzman and a retinue of army officers at the door. Silvera-Guzman held back the others and came to the President's bedside alone.

"A development of the greatest urgency, sir." He glared suspiciously at Hood.

"We have no secrets from the ambassador," said Luchengo. "What is it now?"

"Our forward positions on the approaches to Ariella are under attack."

Luchengo rose to a half-sitting position. "In force?"

"Yes, a mortar barrage began twenty minutes ago. Our units at the first bridges south of the arroyo are withdrawing."

"General, I will be flying to Ariella within an hour. I will take personal command."

Silvera-Guzman and Lara exchanged a quick glance. "But it is impossible, sir," said Lara. "The doctors will never permit—"

Luchengo's voice was steady. "Within an hour. Is that understood?" Lara and Silvera-Guzman left together.

Luchengo, struggling to swing his legs over the side of the bed, glared at Hood. "You're waiting for an answer?"

"I am."

"Then tell your President he may do whatever he likes. It is no longer important."

After the shock of learning that the offensive toward Ariella was now under way, Ambassador Hood's first thought had been of Constanzia Novarese.

"I have a favor to ask of you. I have a staff of twelve at the embassy. If we could fly to the coast with you—"

"Of course, Mr. Hood. I think you should be a witness to"—his features lost their harshness—"to whatever happens."

It was eight o'clock in Washington, and darkness already had fallen. On the lawn outside the West Wing of the White House, the television cameras had been in place for hours, and a small dais had been set up for the jumble of microphones.

Press Secretary Maxwell Busby found the glare of the lights almost blinding. "I have a statement from the President to read to you. There will be no further statements from here tonight, and I will take no questions on this one. Here it is:

"'American overflights of the key defensive position held by revolutionary forces in Santa Clara reveal the presence there of potential missile sites, now under construction, and the presence of at least one ranking Chinese missile technician. There are, however, no missiles on site; nor, to our knowledge, has there been delivery of even one to the revolutionary army.

"'This evidence was given today to President Jorge Luchengo of Santa Clara, whose response was an urgent request to this government to take whatever action necessary to intercept missiles and other war contraband that may be en route to Santa Clara from the People's Republic of China.

"'Accordingly, and under instructions of the President, American air and sea units are at this hour moving into position to impose a quarantine on the sea approaches to Santa Clara's only port city —Ariella.

"'This action was taken after consultation with the Soviet Union and with our allies in the Organization of American States.

"'The President regards the actions of the People's Republic of China as a deliberate and dangerous provocation, which will be met by whatever actions on our part may become necessary. Under the charter of the Organization of American States, and in compliance with separate mutual defense treaties between this government and other OAS member states, including Santa Clara, our responsibilities are clear and will be met.

"'At the request of our ambassador to the United Nations, an emergency session of the Security Council will be convened tomorrow, at which he will present the evidence of Chinese intervention on this continent and its implicit peril to world peace.

" 'The President will meet tomorrow morning with the Joint Chiefs of Staff and other advisers to discuss further responses that the situation may require.' "

T HE MORNING Francisco Jiminez and the bulk of his forces left the Arroyo Seco for the drive on Ariella, General Gi You-gin gave Han Li-wong orders to move his cot into the communications and fire control center below their bunker and to maintain an around-the-clock radio watch.

He was given two new frequencies to guard—one for Jiminez' forward command post and another General Gi did not identify beyond telling Han that the code name Cetus would always precede its transmissions. Han could find no Chinese vessel of that name in his international code book, but he had little time to ponder the mystery. Only hours after Jiminez' move from the arroyo, the rebel leader was on the air with reports of federal troops retreating, with only light resistance, from their advance positions.

After each transmission Han rang General Gi in his quarters in the upper bunker on the field telephone, but the general's response was always a laconic "Thank you. No word from Cetus yet?"

"None."

It was almost midnight when the bulletin came over the Santa Claran government radio that American naval units were moving into position to blockade the coast. Midway through the report Han heard his own call signal crackling over one of the receivers in Morse code, then, "Cetus calling. . . . Cetus calling."

Han gave the signal to proceed, then took the message: "32.10 South, 75.20 West." There was nothing more.

Gi was asleep but Han had to wait only seconds for the general to answer the telephone. "I have a message from Cetus—a position report."

"I'm coming down," said the general. He was still stuffing his shirt into the pants of his uniform when he came into the control center and glanced quickly at the message form. "But that can't be correct. They're too far south. Please play the tape back for me."

Han reversed the tape recorder monitoring all incoming and outgoing transmissions to the point where the message began, but Gi's own reading was the same as Han's: "32.10 South, 75.20 West."

The general struck Han's desk with his fist. "Transmit this immediately: 'Your present speed inadequate. Timing of your arrival Ariella crucial.'"

Han sent the message and minutes later Cetus replied: "Encountering heavy seas. Have twice taken evasive action to avoid challenge by Chilean naval units. Proceeding at all possible speed but announcement U. S. action will require further course change eastward to avoid interception."

"U. S. action?" Gi glanced questioningly at Han.

"It came over Radio Santa Clara just minutes ago. The Americans are blockading the coast. They have evidence—"

"I know what evidence they have. Did they identify me by name?"

"No. They spoke only of missile technicians."

"The blockade—did they say how far offshore?"

"Two hundred miles."

A smile lit Gi's face for the first time. "Then Mao is still watching over us, comrade."

When the general left, Han went to the large chart of South America on the wall. The position given by Cetus was approximately a hundred miles off the north central coast of Chile. He then went back to his international code books to search foreign registries for a ship by the name of Cetus but could find none. He next began scouring through the codes for Cetus' radio frequency and finally found it under two vessels of Chinese registry—whaling factory ships operating in the Antarctic. The frequencies were for communications between the factory ships and their smaller whale catchers.

Han was angry with himself for overlooking his most obvious reference source. His English dictionary would have told him that cetus was the Latin word for whale.

He lay awake the rest of the night, his anxiety deepening as Radio Santa Clara gave new bulletins on the crisis which could bring devastation to his homeland. Shortly before dawn he heard that American Ambassador Samuel V. Hood and the staff of his embassy were now operating from the American consulate in Ariella, and that President Luchengo was also in the city to assume personal command of the army.

Jorge Luchengo sent for Ambassador Hood as the Electra was banking sharply for its final approach to Ariella. Hood took a scat facing the President, who was under sedation and had difficulty focusing on the ambassador's face.

"I would like, Mr. Hood, for you to contact Señora Novarese immediately after our arrival. If the situation here is as critical as I expect it to be, I may call on her to join my government, or, if she refuses, to ask her to form a new one."

"I'm afraid it would serve no point," the ambassador replied. "My government gave you no hope at all that it would intervene— even if you were to step down."

"That's no longer a factor," said Luchengo. "I would call on the señora only because she might be able to accomplish what I have not—rally the people to stand fast against Jiminez. I don't expect American assistance beyond the blockade. Santa Clara must now decide its own destiny."

"I will speak to her," said Hood.

"Thank you. But it will be most important that we maintain close communications. You will headquarter at your consulate here?"

"Yes, and I have my communications section with me. We'll be on a twenty-four-hour alert. And you?"

"I'll be at the front, of course."

"Do you think that's wise? Apart from your wound, I would think you would be more in control from defense headquarters."

"I do not intend to *defend* Ariella, Mr. Hood. I intend to attack."

The shrieking of the tires on the runway cut their conversation short and Hood, grabbing at seats to support himself, made his way back to the rear section of the plane, where his staff was observing the scene outside with amazement.

A full company of troops was drawn up in dress parade in front of the concrete control tower, and aging General Jesus Obregon, commanding the defense of Ariella, was in the forefront, at rigid attention, waiting to greet the President.

Luchengo's reaction on leaving the plane was one not of amazement but of cold fury. He strode past the general without acknowledging his salute and into the temporary army headquarters in a small office under the control tower.

General Carlos Silvera-Guzman, two steps behind the President, did return the salute, then spoke in a low voice to Obregon.

"Are you mad? We are in retreat, and you hold troops here?"

"But I have had no orders to commit my full strength to—"

"You can expect them within the next minute," said Silvera-Guzman.

The battle maps on the wall of the headquarters told a story of impending disaster. Jimenez' force had swept fifteen miles down the desert slope toward Ariella and was now the same distance from the port. General Obregon's orders to his commanders had been to fight a delaying action until he was able to reinforce a defense line on the northern perimeter of the city.

Luchengo's first question of Obregon was how many troops he had at his disposal.

"Two thousand actives, sir—no more."

"You had more than four thousand when I gave you command," Luchengo replied. "How can an army that is running from the enemy suffer such casualties?"

Obregon held back his anger. "Our casualties have been light. We have fought, and effectively, where we could. But the final battle will be fought here and on a broader front where Jiminez cannot attack in force without risking encirclement."

Luchengo's face was white with fury. "I repeat my question. Where is the rest of your command?"

"Where all soldiers go when they are not paid, when their families are hungry, when they have no respect for the government that orders them to die."

Luchengo was swaying on his feet. "You can't have had that many desertions—not if you can waste troops at dress parade for a commander-in-chief for whom they—and apparently you— have no respect."

"I am holding them here," Obregon shot back, "because to send them to the front in small units is to invite even more desertions. Yes, my President, we have a prisoner army that will go into battle with the guns of their officers at their backs."

Luchengo braced himself with one hand against a desk. "You are an old man, and you have lost heart for war. I relieve you of this command. Silvera-Guzman will replace you."

Obregon glanced at his successor. "He will have no more success than I—not as long as it is you who gives the orders. You say I no longer have the courage to fight. It is you who are without courage. For three years Silvera-Guzman, I—yes, all of us—have been urging you to destroy Jiminez. But no! We were told to stay in our barracks—that you would tame his peons with promises. And now that it's too late you haven't the *cajones* to—"

"I will hear no more," said Luchengo quietly. "Go back to your family, Jesus. Live a long life."

Two hours later all but a small detachment of troops had left the bivouac at the airstrip and were on their way north to take up positions where the long gorge from the arroyo spread out onto open terrain north of the city.

It was Silvera-Guzman's judgment, as it had been Obregon's, that Jiminez would have to fight on this central front if he were to protect both the railroad to his rear and his own line of retreat.

Luchengo gave his approval to this deployment, with instructions that the troops were not to entrench themselves in defensive positions but were to prepare for the offensive. The key objective was destruction of the last railroad and highway bridge, which Jiminez would reach early the next morning at his present rate of advance.

General Gi left the Arroyo Seco late that afternoon for a conference with Jiminez, whose command post was in a small shack in a switching yard fifteen miles to the south.

The rebel leader was jubilant. "Tomorrow we take the last bridge.

Your rail line to the arroyo will be open and secure. And that fulfills my last commitment to you. Then I am in command and I will be in Ariella tomorrow night."

"No," said Gi, "you will not advance beyond the last bridge. You must coordinate your capture of Ariella with the arrival of my ships, and there have been delays."

Jiminez took a long drink of *pulque* from the bottle on the crude wooden table at which they were sitting.

"Delays? That is your concern, not mine. You gave me five days to take Ariella, and I will take it in five days." He limped to the door, gazing into the bright sunlight, his back to Gi. "Your missiles are nothing to me. I have already paid too high a price for them—waiting, waiting, waiting in the arroyo while Ariella was sitting like a fat chicken on the nest, asking me to wring its neck. No, I will advance."

Gi's voice was calm. "And how do you propose to advance? Through an army that outnumbers you at least four to one?"

The rebel leader came back to the table and unfolded a crumpled battle map that was in a pocket of his fatigue jacket on the back of a chair.

"I also have radio communications. I also know the *federales* are moving up to block me." He jabbed at the point on the map where the gorge debouched onto the plain. "But to prevent me from flanking them, they must dig in on a front of at least five miles. I will cut through their center like a knife through butter."

General Gi disagreed. "And if they do not dig in—if they attack before you can break out?"

Jiminez shook his head. "They will not attack in terrain that favors me."

"You are wrong. Luchengo didn't fly to Ariella to decorate Obregon for his timidity. There will be a change in tactics—and you must change yours to meet it." Gi put a finger on the last bridge. "Here you have all the advantage. You can conceal your artillery and Luchengo's will be on open ground. You can hold this position indefinitely with half of your force."

Jiminez was listening. "And what do I do with the rest of my troops?"

"You move them out tonight toward the west, toward the sea—

and with no weapons heavier than mortars. They will have excellent cover in the ravines running down to the beaches."

"And then?"

"You wring the chicken's neck, of course. When my ships are one day out, you attack Luchengo's front with your artillery, and when he retreats on Ariella—and he will—he will find your western force moving into the city ahead of him. His army will collapse with your guns at his rear and Ariella a death trap ahead of him."

Jiminez took another drink of the *pulque*. "I do not like to divide my troops."

"If you are to honor your pledge to me to keep the rail line open, you have no choice."

Jiminez was still uncertain. "My tactics now are successful. It is very late to change them just because your ships—"

Gi stared at him impassively. "But this has always been the plan. It would be the plan even if the ships were not late."

Jiminez gave voice to his resentment. "But you wait until now to tell me? Why?"

"Because it was not necessary for you to know until now."

H AN LI-WONG had a new position report from Cetus when General Gi You-gin got back to the arroyo early in the evening. The whalers were now more than a hundred and fifty miles farther north and on a course that would parallel Chile's fifty-mile offshore limit.

The general heard the report without comment. For him, Paco Jiminez' challenge to his authority was a potentially greater risk to the success of his plan than Cetus' delay. He spread his long frame on Han's cot, studying his subordinate at the radio desk.

"Why is it, Han, that Latins are such poor Communists? Why are they driven only by ego—by self-glory?"

Han was in no mood for a Marxist lecture. "I haven't given it much thought."

"Perhaps you should have, Han. Over the past two years you might have been able to convert Jiminez into a more obedient ally."

Han's answer to the rebuke was a shrug of his shoulders.

"I have a theory," said Gi. "Could it be this decadent climate? Does the sun—the humidity—burn and drain the resolution out of a man? I think harsher climates produce more dependable Communists. I think a certain hedonism—a weakness of flesh—must exist in a climate where the woman ages too quickly and the man is afraid to lose even one night of her youth. Could that be true?"

If Han was to be drawn into the dialogue, he was determined to disagree. "No, I think there are much more pragmatic reasons. We indoctrinate our young in the schools. We teach them Marxism with their alphabet. Here there are no schools, except for the children of those who oppose us. We have had leaders such as Mao, whose words are the gospel, and whose presence is the god of our revolution. Here there are only the priests, who are the allies of the imperialists."

Gi swung his legs off the cot to face Han. "You describe Mao as a god—his words as gospel? Those are not the words of a Communist."

"I speak only in analogies," said Han.

The general frowned. "I accept none of what you have said. It is too facile an explanation for the lack of militancy in the proletariat, and it is no explanation at all for the weakness of their leaders. Castro was an atheist—a man of education—and yet a defector to the West. And Guevara—also an atheist and a doctor. What sent him to Bolivia but jealousy of Castro? No, Han, it is pride—ego."

"But Bolivia is our ally and Guevara died for that revolution."

"But that's exactly the point," said Gi. "He came too soon and against the will of the Bolivian Communists. His death was foolish and vain. But for Guevara, Bolivia would have been Communist years earlier. Jiminez was a follower of Guevara's, and he, too, thinks only of himself. He accepts us only because he cannot prevail without our expertise, our weapons."

Han could no longer restrain himself. "Nor can we prevail without him now that our tactics have become those of violence and terror."

Gi was on his feet. "You question our tactics?"

Han, beyond the point of no return, felt a strange calmness. "I have always questioned our tactics—here, in Korea, in Indochina, in Sinkiang. They have led us to one defeat after another, and now they will lead us to annihilation. My own tactics would have brought Santa Clara under our control and without this madness, this—"

Gi took a threatening step toward him. "You are a fool, Han. What is more important—your bartering in copper or the opportunity to seize all of South America?" He shook his head unbelievingly. "China places you in a position where your name can live in history, where you can become a hero of the world revolution, and you speak of your own tactics. Are you another Jiminez, full of pride and disrespect for authority?"

Han was silent for a long moment—angry with himself for the outburst that could cost him not only his life but his last opportunity to influence events. But was Gi beyond appeasement?

"Yes, I confess to pride—but in my ministry and what it has been able to accomplish in many neutral nations—just as soldiers must feel pride in their accomplishments. But I am not a soldier, and I must also confess to fear. I am not a brave man, General, but neither am I disrespectful of those I serve."

There was a slight softening of Gi's features. "You have left me no choice, Han. I must report this to Peking, and, at the proper time, I must testify against you."

"I understand."

"But I will also testify that you have borne important responsibilities, effectively, and that you spoke as you have under great strain."

"Thank you."

Gi paused at the door. "You have had no sleep. I can relieve you here tonight, if you wish."

"No. You need your rest more than I, General."

In the upper bunker, Gi lay awake on his cot. He had seen it happen many times before—able comrades bending but not cracking under pressure. But to admit to fear or error when their own lives or careers were at stake—that was courage. Han would be all right, and Gi took a small degree of pride in the knowledge that his own harsh, swift response to his subordinate's first show of weakness had had the proper shock effect.

In the control center Han quickly found the call signal for the American consulate in Ariella and sent the following message, attention Ambassor Hood: "Informational. Chilean authorities report suspicious vessels fifty miles offshore between latitudes 33 and 34 North."

He signed it: "Hancock, Navy Intelligence. Panama."

Han then reversed the tape monitor. The next incoming or outgoing message would automatically erase the transmission to Hood.

Mario Cassavettes' first word that Jiminez was moving on Ariella came from the bartender at the Playa del Sol. He told the consigliere that it would be his last day at work—that he had two brothers with the federal army and that he could not risk falling into Jiminez' hands.

"But you will be safe, señor. Your American Navy is coming to Ariella."

Cassavettes found Johnny Partridge behind the desk in the lobby, arguing with other staff who were also determined to flee from Jiminez' advance.

Cassavettes' voice had an ominous edge. "I'd like a word with you—privately." They went to the far corner of the lobby. "When did you first know, Partridge?"

"That Jiminez was on the march?"

"We can start with that."

"It came over the radio this morning. But there's still no word on how the fighting's going."

"And when did you first know the American fleet was coming?"

"That came over during the night. But don't start panicking. It's a blockade, like the one off Cuba. They won't be coming closer than two hundred miles."

"And what the hell do we do? Just sit?"

"No," said Partridge. "I've given the alert to the skipper of the *Reina del Mar*. We can be on our way on an hour's notice."

"On our way where, for Christ's sake?"

"A good question," said Partridge, "and I don't have the answer."

"You'd better come up with it, Partridge, because if we have no safe place to land, you and the señora won't be going with us."

Cassavettes left to report to his father and Partridge went back to the anxious employees at the desk. But again there was an interruption—a telephone call from Ambassador Hood.

"I want you to tell Señora Novarese that I'll be over there within the hour."

"I wouldn't advise it," said Partridge. "I couldn't guarantee your safety or hers."

"You won't have to. I'll bring a Marine escort with me."

"You do," replied Partridge, "and you'll have to shoot your way past the guards at the gate."

There was a long pause. "Is this line secure?"

"For the moment." Partridge knew that Cassavettes would be with his father, and that the red light signaling incoming and outgoing calls was on the telephone in the consigliere's suite.

"I'll go along with you," said Hood, "if the situation is all that desperate out there. But would you please give the señora a message? I'll call back later for her answer."

"Make it fast."

"Depending on events over the next twenty-four or forty-eight hours, Luchengo may call on her to join his government to mobilize the country for a stand against Jiminez."

"She wouldn't go for that. She hates his guts. She's rooting for Jiminez to win."

"If she won't join Luchengo, he would be willing to step down in her favor."

"It looks that bad?"

"It does—and she could be the difference. Partridge?"

"Yes."

"Where do you stand on this?"

"Let's face it, Hood, my deal is blown, but good. All I want now is to move her out of here—alive. What she wants to do after that is up to her."

"Can you bring her out?"

"Yes, I think I have a way."

"If I can help—"

"I'll let you know."

Partridge saw Cassavettes emerge from the elevator and hung up.

For Constanzia Novarese, her first willingness to involve herself in the Buena Vista project—to escape from the seclusion of Casa Castillo—had become a misjudgment of such proportions that she could not now conceive of having agreed to it.

She had at least been a recluse by choice at Casa Castillo, but here there were guards and the sullen hostility of the Mafiosi— and even of their wives—to remind her that she was a prisoner.

Yet she did not blame Partridge. He could not have known that events would develop as they had, and he, certainly, was in even greater danger. She was only the hostage. Only if they tried to escape together would her own life be in peril.

Her first excitement at the successes of Paco Jiminez, portending the end of the Luchengo regime, was also lost. Alone, as she most often was, she came to the gradual awareness that more was at stake than Luchengo's life—that Santa Clara could die with him. She thought often of Arturo Lara's proposal that she head a coup against Luchengo but felt no remorse for rejecting it. She felt that it was already too late—that perhaps the one role left to her was to stand as a force, even as an expatriate, against the repressions she was certain Jiminez would bring.

But the one constant on which she did not yield to either regret or doubt was that Jorge Luchengo must die for Luis' murder. It was just and inevitable, by whatever hand he fell.

Her answer to Partridge when he gave her Hood's message was

no. "I could never ally myself with Luchengo. It would betray all I believe. Nor would I replace him. Lara and the generals will do that when the time comes." She was lying on a chaise on her balcony overlooking the sea. "I'm terribly afraid, Johnny—not only for us but for Santa Clara."

Partridge sat at the foot of the chaise, the breeze tousling his blond hair. "There's nothing you could have done to change it." He took her hand. "I'll tell Hood."

She tried to smile. "How much more time have we, Johnny?"

"Hood told me the next day or two will decide. But we'll be all right. If the army can't stop Jiminez, I've made arrangements to move our *guests*"—it was his turn to smile—"to the *Reina del Mar*. That will leave just the guards to contend with—"

"And Mario Cassavettes?"

"And Mario Cassavettes."

There was a knock on the door. It was the consigliere. "The red light was on. I thought we had an understanding that I was to monitor all your calls."

"It wasn't important. Just Hood wanting to pay another social call on the señora. She doesn't want to see him."

"You could have told him that without checking it out with her."

Cassavettes was listening in when Partridge made his call to the consulate.

"I spoke to the señora, Mr. Ambassador. She says no."

Partridge's terseness told Hood that the line was no longer secure. "Thank you."

T HE MUMPS can be both painful and embarrassing for a man of fifty-five and for Donald Marston they had also come at a most inopportune time. Bedridden in his apartment on New York's

Central Park West, he had had to cancel both a meeting of the board of directors of the Heli-Commuter Corporation, of which he was president, and his plans to attend a session of Air Force Secretary James Halverson's National Security Advisory Council the next day at the Pentagon.

It was particularly distressing to Marston that he could not go to Washington. Since his appointment to Halverson's civilian lobby for a larger Air Force budget, he had been one of its most militant members. An Air Force colonel in the Korean war, he still held both his reserve commission and his conviction that politicians, including the President, should leave the wars to the generals. It was still galling to him to think that America had been denied total victory in Korea because Truman would not let MacArthur cross the Yalu, and that Eisenhower, Kennedy, Johnson and Nixon had all hamstrung the military in Vietnam when one nuclear strike on Hanoi could have put an end in one day to the drawn-out fighting and the war-ending concessions to the Communists at the Paris negotiations.

Marston, a bristling little man with opaque blue eyes, still sporting a GI crew cut from his military days, was a zealous supporter of Harlan Grant and the chairman of the senator's New York state election committee. Here was one politician who would listen to the generals. Secretary Halverson was aware of Marston's involvement with Grant but let him stay on the council on the grounds that it was a bipartisan organization.

On this October morning the aircraft executive was still glooming over his inability to attend the next day's session when the call came from his doctor that his mumps were finally beyond the stage of contagion and he was free to resume his normal routine. He quickly rang up his secretary and told her to have his private Falcon jet ready for takeoff from the Butler Aviation Terminal at LaGuardia at nine the following morning. The NSAC sessions began an hour and a half later. He would have time to spare.

Jorge Luchengo had been supervising deployment of his troops north of Ariella, and it took Sam Hood almost an hour to reach him by radio-telephone.

The President took the news of the señora's refusal calmly. "I question that her decision is final, Mr. Hood. I will surrender myself to her, if necessary, and to that she will respond."

"If it comes to that," Hood replied, "I have a request—that you permit me to be present."

"Of course."

Hood spent the late afternoon and early evening with Consul Bennett Cullers, working out plans for evacuation of the remaining American diplomatic personnel and the Marine detachment in the event Paco Jiminez' capture of Ariella became imminent.

It was agreed that the airstrip probably would be under attack and it would be unwise to call in rescue helicopters. Instead, Cullers would arrange for the charter of one of the shrimp trawlers, which would be met at sea by one of the blockading destroyers. Approval of the plan, under which the warships would approach within ten miles of the coast for the rendezvous, was given by the headquarters of Commander-in-Chief Pacific, Honolulu, late in the evening.

Hood was preparing for bed when the telephone rang. It was the duty radio officer. "I have a strange one for you, Mr. Ambassador."

"Strange?"

"Yes. Could you come down here?"

Hood went to the radio center in his robe and quickly read the message. "This seems rather specific to me. Why do you question it?"

"First, it should have been sent in code and it wasn't," said the radioman. "Second, the signal was much too strong to have come from Panama. I would estimate the transmitter to be no more than twenty or thirty miles away. And, finally, I ran a quick check with naval intelligence at the Canal Zone. They have no one by the name of Hancock."

Hancock. The message was stranger than the radioman could have known.

"Take this cable down and transmit it immediately—first to CINCPAC, then to the Joint Reconnaissance Center at the Pentagon.

" 'Have reliable information suspicious vessels approaching Ariella. Last known position 50 miles off Chilean coast between 33 and 34 north.' "

The radioman glanced up from his message pad. "Reliable information, sir?"

"I said to transmit it immediately. Please do that."

Defense Secretary Burgess Rand woke the President at two in the morning. He knew, even before he heard the Secretary's voice, that the news had to be bad at this hour of the night.

"I think we've found what we're looking for, Mr. President. Two Chinese vessels—both of a size that could transport ICBMs— are already inside the blockade line."

"*Inside* the line?"

"They're whaling factory ships in the twenty-thousand-ton class. They must have come up from the Antarctic whaling grounds at South Shetland Island. Our line of interception doesn't extend that far south."

"You're certain they're Chinese?"

"We have to presume they are. A photo reconnaissance carrier squadron caught up with them an hour ago off the coast of Chile. They're sailing under blackout conditions and would not acknowledge a radio request for identification."

The President's voice was hoarse with apprehension. "What action did the planes take beyond that?"

"None, except to order them to heave to."

"And they didn't?"

"No, they changed course, heading north and east into Chilean territorial waters. Destroyers are on their way now at flank speed and should intercept at first light. The question now, Mr. President, is what action we take if they resist boarding and inspection?"

"Slow down, Burgess, slow down. How far out from Ariella are they?"

"Estimating their best speed at twelve knots, two days at least."

"Then we have time. Do they appear to have armament?"

"No."

"All right. Advise CINCPAC to have our surface units maintain visual contact but to take no hostile action, even if they continue to refuse inspection, until further orders. But stay on the line a minute longer. I want Adams in on this too."

The President rang the White House operator. "Will you have Secretary Adams rung in on this call?"

Ten seconds later the Secretary of State, still half asleep, was on the line.

"This is the President, Sterling. We have two ships, apparently Chinese, running for cover toward Chile. Do we have to have approval from Santiago to pursue them into Chilean territorial waters?"

"It's my recollection, sir, that the OAS agreements designate the entire South American area as a common defense zone."

"In other words, we can act independently?"

"If we believe our hemisphere security is in jeopardy, yes."

"While you're with us, Sterling," said Rand, "you might want to know that we can thank your department for the first alert on this. It came from Ambassador Hood."

The President was incredulous. "Hood? What was his source?"

"We don't know," said Rand, "but he was right on the money."

Adams spoke. "It might be wise, Mr. President, to fly him back here. If we do commit what would clearly be an act of war against China, we're going to have to put together the strongest possible case for the UN and for the OAS."

"Let's do it," said the President. "I'll call the National Security Council into session at eleven in the morning, and we should have Hood there too. Burgess, can you lay on the transportation that fast?"

"Yes. I'll relieve one of the photo recon planes now on station over the ships and send it to Ariella to pick Hood up. We can switch him to a supersonic fighter at Albrook. But, Mr. President, there's information we must have before Hood's arrival—the source of his information. Without it, we can't prepare a credible case for whatever action we may have to take. Kennedy had U-2 photos of the missiles in Cuba. We have to have equally strong evidence to back us up."

"In my cable to Hood calling him back, I'll ask him to radio it ahead," said Adams.

"Good," said the President. "You'd better leave the line now, Burgess. You've got a hell of a lot of work to do. Sterling, stay on a minute longer. I want you to alert Hood to his flight. Then call Ambassador Kharlamov. He's back from Moscow, isn't he?"

"Yes."

"Tell him I may be placing a call on the hot line to Chairman Borichev between noon and one o'clock our time tomorrow, and that I would be most appreciative if he would be standing by to receive it."

A GRAY RAIN, driven by heavy gusts of wind from the Atlantic, swept over Andrews Air Force Base as the jet came to a whining halt near the limousine where Assistant Secretary of State Ed O'Farrell was waiting for Ambassador Hood.

There was a brief delay as the ground crew put the debarking ladder in place and Adams saw his friend descend it with faltering steps.

"You look like hell, Sam. A rough flight?"

"Turbulence all the way up—and no sleep. But I'll be all right."

A crewman, carrying Hood's attaché case and overnight bag, was a step behind them as they got into the car.

"The White House," O'Farrell told the driver.

"What's all the rush, Ed? We've got over an hour before the meeting, and I could use a fast shower and breakfast."

"I'm afraid not. The President wants you to update him before the session."

Hood fell wearily against the black leather uprest. "Update him or promise not to rock the boat. My God, Ed, he can't believe I wouldn't stay in line at a time like this!"

"Slow down, Sam, that's not it at all. He can't go before the NSC this morning or on national TV tonight without knowing the source of your information. Why didn't you answer Adams' cable?"

"Between you and me, Ed, I couldn't. My source was Han Li-wong."

"Gi's man? That's incredible!"

"Not if you know Han. He's never bought the hard line."

"But to betray—"

"Han wouldn't look at it that way, and I don't either. He could have had but one motive—to stop this before we turn China into a cinder."

"You're going to have to tell the President, Sam."

"I know. But I'm also going to insist that we protect Han."

"He won't give you an argument on that. We have at least forty ships and two hundred aircraft patrolling the coast, and how do we find out that the Chinese already have broken the blockade? Would you believe a friendly call from a Chinese to his buddy, the American ambassador? What a hell of a story for Senator Grant if it ever got out!"

"It won't," said Hood.

"The town's still a sieve, Sam."

"But only you and the President will know. You wouldn't leak it and he wouldn't dare."

Hood studied the bleak Maryland landscape. "I take it there's no chance of the missiles reaching Ariella?"

"None whatever," said O'Farrell. "The only question is whether we can grab one for purposes of evidence."

"But no plans to move against Jiminez?"

"None."

"I'm going to push the President as hard as I can on that this morning, Ed. He'll never have a better excuse to move."

"You'll be wasting your time," said O'Farrell. "I can tell you right now what his thinking is—that he'll stop the missiles and he'll come out of it looking tough and decisive. But afterward, with the election coming up, he's not going to send troops down there to have their asses shot off in the boondocks. And he has history working for him—another land war in terrain that favors the enemy and in a country that isn't worth a nickel to us."

"That's insane," said Hood.

"I don't know that I agree. The odds are that intervention would be damaging to him politically when the missile threat is over. Remember that Kennedy didn't go into Cuba—and the public was behind that decision."

"The situations aren't comparable. We wouldn't be moving in to destroy a de facto government but to preserve one with which we have explicit treaty commitments."

"The distinction's a little too fine," replied O'Farrell. "Look at it this way. Intervention *could* insure Grant's election. And that wild bastard could have us at war with China and God knows who else a week after his inauguration."

The rain was lighter now and Hood saw the dim outline of the Capitol dome. "Washington never changes, does it, Ed? There's always a perfectly rational reason for doing what we know is wrong because the alternative might be worse. Perhaps we deserve the alternative. It might bring us face to face with what we are, and if we could live with that, there's not much we couldn't survive."

"A noble sentiment," said O'Farrell, "but it won't happen that way. We'll go right on doing the thing we can, not the thing we should."

"Always the lesser evil?"

"Exactly. Can you think of a more viable morality?"

Two Secret Service agents were at the west basement entrance to escort Hood and O'Farrell directly to the Oval Office. Secretary of State Adams and Special Assistant Gene Haas were with the President at the conversational unit, facing the blazing fireplace, reviewing the draft of the Chief Executive's address to the nation that evening.

The President stood to shake the ambassador's hand. "Sam, I don't know how to tell you how much I and the nation owe you." He broke into a knowing smile. "I was right, you know?"

"Right, sir?"

"Yes, for keeping an old pro like you on the front lines where you belong."

Adams also came forward to take Hood's hand. But Haas, scrawling on the speech text, gave him only a cursory nod as they all took their places on the divans around the low table.

"Let me bring you up to date, Sam," said the President. "We've been able to keep a tight security lid on this since last night. And, hopefully, by the time I go on the air tonight the ships will either be under escort to Pearl Harbor or on the bottom, if they resist. I won't take up our time now with the Security Council agenda. You'll be sitting in with us, of course. But there's one missing link, Sam. How in the hell did you find out? And why didn't you answer Adams' request for that information?"

"Frankly, I didn't want to entrust it to normal channels. I didn't want to risk exposing a source that can be of continuing value to us."

"That's commendable, but you can speak freely now."

"I'd prefer, Mr. President, to reveal it to you privately."

"Sam, for Christ's sake!"

Haas stood abruptly. "If the ambassador prefers, I can leave."

"Sit down, Haas. I think the ambassador will accept my assurance that whatever he tells us—"

O'Farrell also stood. "We're running short of time, Mr. President. I have no objection to stepping outside."

Adams took his cue from his subordinate. "Nor I."

"All right, gentlemen. Wait in my secretary's office."

Five minutes later the buzzer rang on his secretary's desk, and she told them to return to the Oval Office. The President and Hood were standing at the fireplace.

"I agree with Hood," said the President, "that his source warrants the highest confidentiality. We will attribute our first position report on the ships simply to intelligence operations."

"Mr. President?"

"Yes, Haas."

"The media won't accept that. They'll want specifics. Can't we attribute it to satellite observation or intelligence ship interception of their radio communications?"

"We could, but there would be at least ten thousand space and Navy personnel who would know it was a lie. No, we'll stick to what I told you. If they press us for specifics, we'll refuse comment on the grounds that it would compromise our intelligence security. That's it. Now, if we have nothing more—"

"Mr. President," said Hood, "you appear to have the missile threat in hand. But there's still the question of Santa Clara. Luchengo is suffering mass desertions from the army and increasing disaffection on his general staff. It's my opinion that Jiminez is going to win if we don't act, and I think his willingness to accept the missiles would justify immediate military assistance to Santa Clara."

The President thought for a moment. "I'll go part way with you, Sam. I'll announce tonight that we're now considering intervention. That ought to put a little more backbone in Luchengo's generals and a little more fight in his troops."

"I think we're beyond that point," said Hood. "Nothing short of an actual military presence there can save Luchengo."

"Why don't we take one crisis at a time, Sam?" The President glanced at his watch. "Let's go, gentlemen."

The Chief Executive in the lead, they strode across the Oval Office, through the secretary's office and into the Cabinet Room.

The principals at the long table and their aides, sitting along all four walls, immediately rose to their feet.

It was a brisk, cloudy morning in New York when Donald Marston's chauffeur edged into the cross-town traffic toward the Triborough Bridge and LaGuardia Field. The aircraft executive, leafing through the New York *Times,* frowned at the headline: PRESIDENT'S TV BLITZ CUTTING INTO GRANT'S LEAD. Nor was the news more encouraging on the financial pages. Heli-Commuter Corporation was down a point on the New York exchange in a nervous market reflecting uncertainty over the outcome of the election.

Traffic was heavy on the approaches to the Triborough and an impatient Marston was ten minutes late arriving at the airport, where his pilot had word portending a further delay. "They've got heavy rain and poor visibility down in Washington, Mr. Marston. The tower may put us in a hold pattern."

He was right. The Falcon spent twenty minutes in the hold circle over the Atlantic before it was finally given landing clearance. It was already ten-thirty, time for the NSAC session to begin, when the plane taxied up to the private terminal at National Airport. Marston ran through the rain to the cab stand.

"The River Entrance of the Pentagon—and fast," he told the driver.

There was still another delay at the Pentagon. The guard told Marston he had no civilian admission list for a conference with the Secretary of the Air Force that morning.

"Will you please put me on the line with the Secretary's office?" said Marston. They went inside the guard post and seconds later Marston was speaking to the receptionist. "This is Donald Marston. I was to attend today's Security Council meeting with Secretary Halverson."

There was a pause. "That meeting's at the White House, Mr. Marston. You're certain the secretary expects you?"

"He sent me a wire asking me to come."

"All right, Mr. Marston. I'll leave word at the southwest gate of the White House that Secretary Halverson wants you to be present."

The cab which had brought Marston to the Pentagon was waiting for another fare at the river entrance. "The White House," said Marston.

"And fast," the surly driver shot back."

"There's a five-dollar tip in it for you if you're there within fifteen minutes," said Marston, smiling. The White House! What did Halverson have up his sleeve this morning? A personal briefing for the NSAC by the President? Whatever it was, Marston was thankful he wouldn't miss out on this one.

But the guard at the southwest gate did not have his name on the list. "I just left the Pentagon," said Marston. "The Air Force Secretary's office was to call ahead with my clearance."

"Okay," said the guard, lifting the barrier. "Go to the west basement entrance. They would have a more up-to-date list than I've got."

The car eased up to the White House and Marston paid his fare and the tip. Inside the entrance he was met by another guard. "My name's Marston. I'm due at the council session."

"Yes, sir. We just got a call from Secretary Halverson's office. The usher here will take you up to the Cabinet Room."

The Cabinet Room!

The usher took him into a small elevator, up one floor and down a corridor past four Secret Service agents. Marston had never been in the White House before and could not have known he was outside the President's office.

The usher led him into an office where Mrs. Betty Duffy, the President's executive secretary, was sitting behind her desk.

"This is Mr. Marston," said the usher. "He's here at Secretary Halverson's request."

"Just a moment," she replied. "General Moody will have to take him inside." She spoke briefly into her intercom and seconds later the military adviser to the President came through a side door.

"Follow me," he told Marston. "The session's just starting. Take the first free chair you see along the wall."

J UST AS Donald Marston was entering the Cabinet Room, the lights went out, and the beam of a projector struck a screen on the far wall. On it were the words: TOP SECRET. It took Marston only seconds to orient himself in the darkness, and he took a chair near the door, partially hidden by the projector.

"Gentlemen, the report you will now be given is without question the most sensitive you have yet heard as members of the Security Council. The words on the screen—top secret—mean exactly that, and neither you nor the staff members you have brought with you may subsequently discuss what you will see and hear, except with those also in attendance today."

Marston was unable to recognize the silhouette of the speaker, who was standing next to the projectionist. But whoever the official was, Jim Halverson was putting on a hell of a show—and at the White House!

"All right, we'll look at the first slide."

The picture, lit by aerial flares, was of two squat ships, plowing in line through heavy head seas.

"This first contact, by fleet aerial recon units, was made approximately twelve hours ago off the Chilean coast. Their position was approximately five hundred nautical miles south of Ariella—their speed twelve knots."

Marston felt a growing uneasiness. On either side of him men were jotting notes on yellow legal pads. He glanced toward the central table and was finally able to identify one face—that of Air Force Secretary James Halverson. But he was a third of the way down the table, and obviously not presiding.

"Next slide, please."

The photograph, at masthead level, was of the lead ship.

"You will observe that they carry no flags—bear no identification numbers. Nor would they respond to our demand that they identify themselves by radio. But they are, without question, Chinese factory whalers last seen on the fishing grounds off South Shetland Island ten days ago. You will observe that there are no missile crates above their decks. Next slide."

This photograph was taken from directly astern of the trailing ship.

"What appears to be a large hatch occupying most of the stern is actually a ramp, which they can lower to accept whale carcasses from the killer ships which accompany them. When the ramp is in position below the water line the stern becomes a slipway through which they winch the carcasses to strip and process them in a large below-decks area. We suspect most strongly that when we board the ships—and we intend to—we'll find ICBMs."

Marston heard Halverson's voice. "And if they refuse to let us board?"

"I'll leave that question for the President to answer."

The President!

Marston suddenly knew where he was—and why. He had told both the girl at the Air Force Secretary's office and the guards at the White House that he was to attend a Security Council session with Halverson. But how was it conceivable that he could breach the security of the nation's highest-level crisis council?

What Marston did not know was that Security Council sessions of this size were held only at times of momentous crisis; that only rarely did top-ranking staff accompany its members, and that none of the aides sitting with him along the wall could identify all of his counterparts in the vast bureaucracy that is Washington. Nor could one expect the President, the Cabinet members or the Joint Chiefs of Staff to question the presence of one man among forty.

Only Halverson would know, and Marston decided to slip through the door—and fast. He took a firm grip on his briefcase and was halfway to his feet when the lights came on again. He had no option but to slump back into his chair behind the projector.

The man on his right gave him a quick nod. "I'm Carew—CIA."

"Marston—Air Force."

"It's really hit the fan, hasn't it?"

Before Marston could answer, the President, occupying a black leather chair taller than the others, spoke from his position midway down the table.

"Are there questions for Mr. Trask?"

"Just one," said Army Secretary Leverett Rhodes. "Have we been able to determine the number of missiles likely to be aboard?"

"We have no specific data on the ships you've seen," said the CIA director. "But they're similar in length and beam to a Japanese whaler on which we do have intelligence. Our best guess is that each ship could carry components for six ICBMs."

There were no further questions of Trask.

"Now, let's go on to your question, Halverson," said the President. "If the ships resist boarding, it is our intention to disable them and take them under escort to Pearl Harbor."

"Why not order them to stop now and blow them out of the water if they don't?"

"Two reasons," said the President. "First, despite their refusal to identify themselves, we can't be absolutely certain they have missiles aboard. And the second is that if we do sink them in deep water it could be days—weeks—before salvage crews could haul the missiles up. We wouldn't have much of a case for the UN, would we?"

"It looks to me," Halverson replied, "as if the fox is already in the chicken coop. From the position report Trask gave us, the Navy blockade already has been broken. I'd like to know how."

Secretary of the Navy Boyd Wright bristled. "May I answer that question, Mr. President?"

"Of course."

"Trask's report was that the vessels left the Antarctic ten days ago. Obviously, they were already inside the two-hundred-mile limit before the blockade was in effect."

Halverson wasn't going to let the Navy off that easily. "But you've certainly been flying recon missions since. I don't understand how they could be two days out of Ariella before you knew it."

Wright found himself on the defensive. "For obvious reasons, we haven't spread our air screen that far south. The logical concentration is on the western approaches—the most direct sea lanes from China."

"Are you telling us," said Halverson, "that the first sighting was not by your aircraft?"

The President broke in sharply. "We won't prolong this. I don't think it serves a useful purpose. We've found the ships and we've found them in time. Full disclosure of how we did it would endanger an intelligence operation that can be of vital and continuing use to us."

Halverson sat back in his chair scowling.

"If we can proceed," said the President, "I want you to know the actions—military and diplomatic—that I intend to put into effect. We've set the blockade line on a perimeter two hundred miles from Ariella; and, in compliance with our declaration of interdiction, we will not attempt to board until they reach that line."

"A point of clarification, Mr. President."

"What is it, General?"

"If they should turn back before reaching the line," said Mark Courtland, chairman of the Joint Chiefs of Staff, "how do we prove they're carrying ICBMs?"

"We're ready for that contingency," the President replied. "They're fishing vessels, remember, and the evasive action they've taken moves them into Chile's territorial waters. Under international law, the Chileans have the right to board them for inspection. And Allende has agreed to do it, with our assistance, if necessary. No, gentlemen, there's not the slightest chance that they can either land the missiles at Ariella or return them to China.

"The question is—how will the Chinese react to our seizure of the ships? Our own West Coast is in range of the ICBMs we must presume are already operational on the Chinese mainland. In addition, they could hit our bases in the Far East with both their intercontinental and intermediate range missiles. I think it's inconceivable that they would launch against us, but we're going to take every possible action to deter it. They're going to be told, in language they will understand, that even one launching will result in the retaliatory devastation of China within one hour. I intend to speak to Chairman Borichev on the hot line this morning. I anticipate full Soviet cooperation in moving its own air and naval nuclear forces, in company with our own, into more forward positions against China. Halverson?"

"Yes, sir!"

"I want you to order up a general SAC alert at two o'clock today. I want every available plane either in the air or in first-stage readiness. But I don't want them over China's air space unless, and until, I order it."

"Yes, sir."

"And, Halverson, they're not to violate Soviet air space either. Is that understood?"

"Yes, sir."

"Now for you, Wright." The Navy Secretary shot forward in his seat. "Your Far East Polaris flotilla and nuclear strike carriers also go on alert at two. I assume Air Force and Navy planning on target priorities is in full readiness. What is it you call it?"

"Operation Sunset," said Boyd.

"All right, I think you should both issue the alerts from here now." He turned to one of his White House military advisers. "Will you take them down to the Situation Room, please?"

On his way toward the door, Halverson saw Marston for the first time. His instant reaction was that it couldn't be he—not here! Then he remembered his own hastily canceled meeting of the

National Security Advisory Council at the Pentagon, and shot a second look at Marston. There was no mistaking the bristly gray crew cut and the pale blue eyes. Was such an incredible foul-up possible? Had one of his aides sent Marston here? Halverson took little comfort from the fact that if Marston's presence were discovered the greater blame would fall on White House security than on him.

Marston, shaken by Halverson's glance, heard only vaguely the words of Army Secretary Rhodes.

"Mr. President, what is your planning beyond the seizure of the missiles and precautions against a Chinese strike in Asia?"

"There are no missiles on site in Santa Clara," the President replied. "I believe the actions already under way effectively protect our security."

"Our immediate security," said Rhodes. "But we're still facing what now appears to be the probability of an Jiminez victory in Santa Clara, and the possibility of a future attempt to intrude missiles."

"I agree," said the President, "and we plan to take that question to the OAS."

"I doubt that Luchengo can hold out that long, sir. I think we ought to move now—paratroops behind Jiminez' position, Army and/or Marine units to Ariella, and air strikes on the missile sites at Arroyo Seco."

Most of the old hands around the table were recalling that the identical advice had been given to John F. Kennedy many years earlier, but he had chosen to limit his actions against Cuba to the blockade.

"No, Rhodes. For the time being, we will restrict our responses to those most likely to win support in the UN and least likely to endanger Soviet cooperation with us." He shoved his chair back. "I don't think there's much more we can do now. Obviously, I will expect you all to be available around the clock for further sessions of the council."

"Before we adjourn, Mr. President, there is one question I think we ought to pursue a little further."

"Yes, General Courtland."

"It's inconceivable to me that we've been caught with our pants down, as we have. We were very late spotting the missile sites and almost too late spotting the ships. This suggests to me a serious breakdown in our intelligence. As just one example, we at the Joint Chiefs had no information that Jiminez was capable of mounting his present offensive to seize the missile-landing facilities at Ariella. To the contrary, we were led to believe that he had no such capacity. What the hell's the CIA been doing down there?"

"I'll take that question, if I may, Mr. President," said CIA Director Trask. "We've been running daily overflights of the arroyo and we were onto General Gi's presence and the conversion of the gun emplacements to missile sites almost immediately. Our estimates of Jiminez' strength are and have been extremely accurate."

"Then perhaps you can tell us," said Courtland, "why he's consistently able to bloody up an army many times larger than his own?"

"On that point alone," said Trask, "I'll concede that our intelligence has been faulty. We've had to depend on Ambassador Hood and his military attaché for estimates of the federal army's effectiveness and morale."

"Then, with all respect to the ambassador," Courtland replied, "his estimates have been poor, to say the least."

All eyes were on Hood, whose own were fixed on the note pad in front of him. He made no response.

"The post-mortems can come at another time," said the President. "Gentlemen, we stand adjourned."

THE MEMBERS of the National Security Council and their aides left the Cabinet Room through a door that led directly into the main corridor of the West Wing. Donald Marston thought it wise to lag behind. He would attract less attention and when Secretary

Halverson came looking for him, as he certainly would, he would have an opportunity to explain his presence.

Through the open door by which the President had left, Marston heard the Chief Executive ask Mrs. Duffy to leave him alone with Hood.

Then, a moment later, "Sam, I really appreciate your taking the heat in there without firing back. God knows you gave us more than adequate warning of Jiminez' capabilities—even the probability that he would site missiles. You can't know how much I regret not listening to you."

"It's all right," Hood replied. "With what could happen in the next hour—the next minute—the question of which of us was right or wrong isn't very important."

Marston bent closer toward the door.

"No, Sam, you deserve better—a hell of a lot better. And when this is all over, you name what you want and it's yours."

"I'm sorry, Mr. President, but I think we both know that our policy differences are and will continue to be irreconcilable. I'll return to Santa Clara and remain there as long as I can be useful. But if it becomes necessary for me to evacuate the mission, I want you to act on my resignation."

"I can't change your mind?"

"No."

"Sam, we've been friends a long time and it's important to me that you understand my position. You once accused me of playing politics with World War III. But I couldn't conceive then—and I can't conceive now—of turning this country over to a neo-fascist like Grant. And I thought there was time to put the election behind us before playing into his hands with another foreign military involvement. I was wrong but I can't change that now, can I?"

"No," Hood replied, "just as I can't change my feeling that I've been in government too long—implementing policies I disagree with too strongly."

"All right, Sam, if that's what you want. You go back down there and if you have to close up shop, you have my word that I'll accept your resignation, but with extreme regret."

"Thank you, Mr. President."

Marston heard a rap on the inner door leading into the Oval Office. It was Mrs. Duffy. "I'm sorry to interrupt, Mr. President, but they want you in the Situation Room. Chairman Borichev is waiting to take your call."

Seconds later, Ambassador Hood strode past Marston and out the far door of the Cabinet Room. The interloper no longer felt anxiety over his intrusion. To the contrary, he was grateful that coincidence had put him in a position to alter the course of history. If Hood's accusations were true—and the President had agreed that they were—Harlan Grant had an issue that would win the election.

Marston could not reveal the deliberations of the Security Council. That would be going too far, and he was, after all, a reserve colonel in the Air Force. But the President's confrontation with Hood was another matter. Marston had been an unwitting witness to it, and Trask's opening strictures against disclosure could not apply. Just as obviously, Marston must now avoid Halverson, who would certainly demand of him a pledge to deny that he was even present.

But Marston and Halverson met at the door. "What the hell are you doing here?"

"I flew down for your meeting at the Pentagon, Mr. Secretary. They told me to join you here."

"Well, you start hauling ass right now." The Air Force Secretary began shoving him down the hall. "You weren't here—you heard nothing. Is that understood?"

"Is what understood?" Defense Secretary Rand was blocking their way. "Who is this man?"

"I was to have met him at the Pentagon," said Halverson. "He was told I was here. I don't think we can blame him for what is clearly a failure of White House security."

"That doesn't answer my question. Who is this man?"

"My name is Marston. I'm with Halverson's National Security Advisory Council. There was no intent on my part to—"

Rand cut him off. "You've held military rank?"

"Yes, sir. I was a full colonel—Air Force—in Korea. I now hold that rank in the reserve."

Rand glanced sharply at Halverson. "As of this moment, Mr. Secretary, you will order this man back on active duty—subject to the code of military secrecy and all other Articles of War. You have no objections, have you, *Colonel* Marston?"

"None at all, sir. I've always stood ready when my country was in danger. And from what I heard here today—"

"You heard nothing here today." Rand's voice was crisp with anger.

"Come along with me," said Halverson. "We'll cut your orders immediately."

But in the limousine returning them to the Pentagon, Marston was no longer the meek subordinate officer. "I didn't want to embarrass you back there," he told Halverson, "and I certainly didn't want to attract attention to myself by asserting my rights to Rand. But I can't possibly report for duty before tomorrow morning. My God, I'm running a hundred-million-dollar-a-year corporation. You can at least give me a day to tie up the loose ends."

The limousine was now on Memorial Bridge, nearing the point where it could either continue on to the Pentagon or turn left to National Airport.

"I don't know," said Halverson. "You're hotter than a firecracker. Rand would raise hell."

"It's a question," said Marston quietly, "of whether you trust my loyalty or not. I have my own jet waiting at National—and I assure you, I'll report in the morning."

"You wouldn't be on my council," said the Secretary of the Air Force, "if I didn't trust you." He slid open the soundproof glass separating them from the driver. "We'll drop Mr. Marston off at National."

The president of Heli-Commuter Corporation went directly to his Falcon jet. "Rev it up," he told the pilot, "and ask for immediate takeoff clearance from the tower."

"Sir, we'll have to wait for a break in commercial traffic."

"Not if you tell them you're speaking for Colonel Marston, acting on personal orders from Air Force Secretary Halverson."

Marston then ran to the bank of public telephones in the terminal. He was still panting when he heard the switchboard operator: "Grant for President Headquarters."

"This is Donald Marston, New York chairman for Senator Grant. I must contact him immediately."

"I'm sorry, Mr. Marston, He's not in the city."

"Where the hell is he?"

Her voice was icy. "I'll transfer you to scheduling."

The secretary there told him it would be impossible to reach the senator by telephone. He was on a tour of supermarket centers in suburban Chicago and would be out of touch until his arrival at O'Hare Airport for a flight to Seattle.

"What's his takeoff time?" Marston demanded.

"Three o'clock."

"Now you listen to this, young woman, and you listen good. Call O'Hare and get word to the crew of the senator's plane that Donald Marston is on his way there—that I have information that will win this election for the senator. The message is to be given to the senator the minute he steps on the plane. He's not to take off until I arrive."

"I can't guarantee you they'll hold the plane," she answered.

"Well, I can guarantee you that you'll be looking for another job if they don't."

"I'll do my best, Mr. Marston."

Even in times of comparative calm on the international scene, the Situation Room in the basement of the West Wing has a perpetual air of crisis. The intelligence and communications center for the White House is operational around the clock and is the domain of the special assistant to the President for national security affairs.

On the wall facing the entrance is a huge map of the world on which the advance and retreat of small markers representing armies, navies and air forces reduce world crises to the simplicity of a child's war game.

The Cuban missile blockade and the Bay of Pigs, wars in Southeast Asia, Africa and the Middle East, the border conflicts between Russia and China—all ran their course over the map, itself a changing, mobile record of the birth of new nations and the new sovereignty of territories won and lost.

Spread now, off the coast of South America, were a host of

markers representing American fleet units on the blockade line, and approaching them, the Chinese vessels. Across the Pacific, over the bulk of China and Russia, were markers indicating the deployment of their missiles and military forces.

On the same wall was a chart listing all heads of state in the world and their whereabouts in the event the President had to contact one of them urgently. The day before the chart had Chairman Borichev at his dacha on the Black Sea. Now he was back at the Kremlin.

In the center of the room, under the glare of overhead fluorescent lights, was a long conference table. Pencils, pads and water carafes were already laid out.

Adjoining the main room is a smaller one containing a battery of teletype machines, chattering night and day with reports from the Foreign Broadcast Intercept Service, which monitors all radio broadcasts in both hostile and friendly nations and transmits an almost simultaneous translation of important announcements. Through the night and morning Peking had broadcast nothing on the blockade or the challenge to its ships.

Next to the FBIS machines are other teleprinters for receiving and transmitting both routine and highly secret diplomatic cables to or from the President.

But one teleprinter stands alone at the far end of the communications section in a vaultlike, unshatterable glass cubicle. It is tied into, and can immediately activate, another teleprinter in the depths of the Pentagon—the hot line to Moscow.

The President, Secretary of State Adams, his department's ranking Russian translator and a stenotypist were waiting at the conference table when Secretary of Defense Rand hurried through the door.

"I'm sorry, Mr. President. Halverson held me up a minute or two."

Then began the frustrating ritual of the hot line, belying the myth that it is a means of instantaneous communication between the leaders of the two most powerful nations on earth.

First, the President and his advisers had to settle on the tenor and content of his first words to Borichev, with the stenotypist recording the conversation. It was read back, there were amendments and additions, and the stenotypist finally ran it off on a typewriter for final approval. Finally, it was given to the translator. Neither the President nor Borichev would risk communication in his own language for fear of faulty translation at the other end. Finally, the message was given to the operator of the hot line for transmission to Moscow.

There, Borichev and his advisers read the President's words and, after more long minutes of discussion, typing and translation, the answer was on its way to Washington. It would continue at this slow pace, back and forth between the two capitals, until the "conversation" was over.

The transcript:

THE PRESIDENT: *I deeply appreciate, Chairman Borichev, your willingness to interrupt your vacation to accept this call, but I can assure you it is of the highest importance. As you are aware, units of the American fleet have been patrolling off the coast of Santa Clara to intercept possible delivery of long-range missiles to insurrectionary forces in that republic which are known to be in alliance with the People's Republic of China. Approximately thirteen hours ago, two vessels, unquestionably of Chinese registry and capable of transporting such missiles, took evasive action immediately following detection by our naval aircraft off the coast of Chile. It is our intention to board the vessels, by force if necessary, and escort them to the nearest American naval base if they are found to be carrying war contraband. Clearly, our early interception of the vessels removes all possibility of imminent danger to my own country. But neither you nor I, Chairman Borichev, can presently anticipate the reaction of the People's Republic of China. We must assume, on the basis of Peking's reckless actions along your own common borders, that an attack on Russian or American targets within range of its present nuclear installations is a possibility that you and I cannot responsibly ignore. I would hope, as a continuation of our past mutual efforts to safeguard world peace, that you will join me both in warning Peking of the possible consequences of its present actions and in deploying our* common forces to present the greatest possible deterrent to a miscalculation by Peking that would pose a far greater threat to your own country than to mine.

CHAIRMAN BORICHEV: *I share with you, Mr. President, the deepest concern over the developments you report. But I must advise you of the continuing efforts of the USSR and the People's Republic of China to resolve their differences. The actions you propose to me would effectively destroy all such negotiations and would place me in a most difficult position with other members of the Socialist bloc who are hopeful of an early rapprochement between Peking and Moscow. I am willing, however, to weigh that consideration against your willingness to permit Soviet forces to operate in the Western Hemisphere, and to review with you, at the earliest possible time, the status of the Monroe Doctrine and other ancient and artificial barriers against the Soviet Union's rightful interests in both hemispheres.*

THE PRESIDENT: *I regret the inexactitude of my early recommendations to you. I do not require, nor am I proposing, the presence of Soviet military forces in this hemisphere. Rather, I recommend an Asian deployment on your part, which, in common with our own, would present Peking with the certainty of massive retaliation in the event of nuclear attack against you or against the West Coast of America or our bases in the Far East. I hope you would agree that a decision on our mutual responsibilities in this crisis is urgent.*

CHAIRMAN BORICHEV: *I must refer, Mr. President, to your earlier statements that a greater danger presently exists to my own country than to yours. I can assure you the Soviet Union has more than an adequate defensive and offensive capability to deter attack from whatever quarter, and the willingness of the People's Republic of China—despite its past errors—to negotiate our narrow range of differences is an affirmation of the respect for that capability. I must, therefore, decline proposals that I take hostile and provocative action against a nation whose future is clearly bound with my own.*

THE PRESIDENT: *I regret your decision, Chairman Borichev. But I do not share your confidence in Peking's good faith. Our own joint reconnaissance of China's nuclear launch positions and its present long-range capability can leave little doubt that their first target priorities are in the Soviet Union. You must bear the responsibility for the possible consequences for your own people, just as I must bear them for mine. I must advise you, therefore, that I intend to mobilize, fully, my nation's strike forces in the Far Pacific, and to respond appropriately to further indications of Chinese aggressiveness. I also give you my assurance that the presence of this force in sectors you would normally regard as within your sphere of influence will present no threat to your own security.*

At this juncture, there was a thirty-five-minute delay in the Soviet response.

CHAIRMAN BORICHEV: *I must protest the actions you contemplate. The Soviet Union cannot and will not tolerate the presence of such a force in areas we regard as vital to our defense. Again, I am appreciative of the difficulties you face, and I agree that it is in our mutual interest to resolve them without serious incident. In that connection, it is most coincidental that we are at this time preparing to engage in air and naval exercises from the port of Vladivostok, and that Soviet nuclear divisions are in movement toward Sinkiang border to relieve the present garrisons. Under normal circumstances, we would not announce such routine deployments. But if it would deter you from the actions you plan, and satisfy you that adequate Soviet forces would be in position to counter the improbable developments you conceive, such an announcement will be forthcoming.*

THE PRESIDENT: *Your proposal is acceptable, and I commend you for it. I believe it is most important, however, that you coordinate your maneuvers with our own to avoid the possibility of incident. Within the next two hours, our military attaché in Moscow will deliver to your chief of staff our plans for fleet and air deployment.*

CHAIRMAN BORICHEV: *That would be most useful. Thank you.*

Senator Harlan Grant would not have kept the Boeing 747 and more than two hundred news correspondents and staff members waiting on the ground at O'Hare if Donald Marston had been merely his New York state chairman. But the aircraft executive was also an effective fund raiser among his associates and a heavy contributor himself, and no candidate ruffles his checkbook partisans.

But the half-hour delay before Marston's arrival in his private Falcon jet would prove only a minor disruption of Grant's schedule. There were diminishing head winds between Chicago and the West Coast, and the pilot could still reach Seattle in time for an airport rally.

Nor did the delay disrupt the work of Grant's staff or the deadlines of the correspondents aboard.

The advent of the jumbo jet had revolutionized political campaigning. The candidate was no longer isolated from the staff of his central headquarters. It flew with him, and was instantly responsive to his demands. The entire twin-deck forward section of the 747 was "candidate's country," with a bedroom suite for Grant and offices for his principal advisers on the upper deck.

On the forward lower deck were smaller offices for his speech writers and publicists and their secretaries; a soundproof compartment for the news tickers of the principal wire services; television sets to monitor network news broadcasts; a mimeograph section for producing speech texts, schedules and news releases, and a switchboard for radio-telephone communication.

The after section of the plane, also broken up into small compartments, was the domain of the correspondents. There, too, rank had its privileges. Reporters and commentators for the major newspapers, news services and TV and radio networks had offices along the port and starboard bulkheads. The others wrote their copy at open desks between the two aisles. But all could communicate instantly with their audiences or their editors on the ground.

Through satellite relay, the electronic reporters could be cut into live news shows, even while flying at thirty-five thousand feet and six hundred miles an hour. Print media reporters could file their stories by radio-telephone if they were pushing a deadline, or via Western Union, which had a staff of operators on duty in the aftermost compartment.

The only rows of conventional seats still left in place after the conversion of the 747 were just forward of Western Union and were for the cameramen and soundmen accompanying the TV correspondents.

Palmer Joyce, whose nightly commentary could not have been more pro-Grant if the senator had paid for the time, was standing at the bar near the open boarding hatch with his first martini of the afternoon when he saw Marston, one of his commercial sponsors, dash up the ramp toward him.

"Don, what the hell brings you to Chicago?" Then he put two and two together. "It's you they've been holding the plane for, right?"

"Right, and I've got a story that's going to blow this election wide open."

"Then let's have it. I'm on the air in three hours."

"Sorry, Joyce. This is one the candidate will want to break himself."

"But you're going on to Seattle with us?"

"I am."

"Then we'll have time for a background interview later. I promise not to use it until after the senator lets fly. Okay?

"If it's all right with Grant, certainly."

The 747 was already trundling toward the runway when Marston was taken up the spiral staircase and into the presence of Senator Grant, who was conferring with advisers in the lounge adjoining his suite.

"Welcome aboard, Don. If you can wait just a minute, we're wrapping up a little strategy conference on how I ought to react to Santa Clara. Most of my staff thinks I ought to play the statesman and declare a moratorium on politics until the Chinese pull back. What's your opinion?"

"I have more than an opinion," said Marston. "I have information that will dictate what your decision should be."

"All right, let's hear it."

"Can we speak privately?"

"Of course." He took Marston into his suite, shed his shoes and coat and spread out on the bed. Marston took a chair by a small bar built into the bulkhead. "Help yourself to a drink, Don."

The 747 was thundering down the runway and neither man spoke until they felt it lift clear. It took Marston only five triumphant minutes to describe the events of the morning, but Grant's reaction was not at all what he thought it would be.

"You've put yourself and me in a very dangerous position. The second you knew where you were, you should have left. No one's ever going to believe that you weren't a plant—that you weren't there with my connivance and knowledge."

"Only Halverson and Rand know I was there—and they're not going to admit it."

"If I use what you've given me," said Grant, "the whole country's going to know it."

Marston couldn't believe what he was hearing. "You're not going to use it?"

Grant slid his legs over the side of the bed and sat up. "Certainly not now, and perhaps not at all. If the crisis passes, I'll take another look at it."

"And what if it hangs fire right up to election day?"

"Then I won't use it. I want very much to be President, but there's a point beyond which I won't go. What you're suggesting is that I turn this into a self-serving political issue at a time when tens of millions of Americans are wondering whether they're going to wake up alive tomorrow morning. We're heading for the West Coast—Seattle, Portland, San Francisco, Los Angeles, San Diego. Most of them are prime military targets, and all of them are vulnerable to attack from the Chinese mainland. You expect me to go out there and spread panic and create for the Reds an appearance of national disunity that might cause them to pull the trigger. No, I don't want to win at that price!"

Marston took another straight shot of bourbon. "I've given you evidence that the President has been playing politics with the survival of this country. In my book that adds up to treason."

The senator tried to placate him. "Right or wrong, he's the only President we've got—and I'm going to stand behind him until it's over. I spoke to him twenty minutes ago, pledging support of the actions he's already taken and those he's going to announce to-night."

"Then you've had it," said Marston. "The people are a goddam flock of sheep. They'll rally around the sonofabitch just like you, and the clobbering you'll take on election day will finish you in national politics." He shook his head in disgust. "And I thought you had the guts to go all the way."

The senator let his anger pass. "I may still go all the way. We've still got two weeks to go. If we're out of it by then, an inquiry by the Senate Foreign Relations Committee into our lack of preparedness would be fully in order. But I'll be frank with you, Don. I can't build a convincing case on what you've told me."

"I was there! I heard every word."

"That's just it. Who's going to accept my New York chairman, one of my biggest contributors, a sponsor of Palmer Joyce, as a credible hearsay witness? You have no corroboration of what you heard between the President and Hood—none at all. We could subpoena Hood, but he would automatically claim immunity from answering questions affecting the national security. No, if we go at all, we'll have to find another way. I have friends in the State Department. One of them might just come up with a copy of Hood's dossier of alerts to the President."

"That's it, then," said Marston, smiling. "With that documentation and my testimony—"

"No," said Grant, "I wouldn't want your testimony. It would lead right to me. Believe me, Don, I'm grateful to you. And if we win I'll guarantee you that Heli-Commuter will always be given a fair shake in Air Force procurement. But I must ask you to stay out of this. Will you do that?"

"I don't agree that you should wait," said Marston, "and I don't believe I'm quite the leper you think I am. But you're the candidate. I'll go along with whatever you think is best."

They shook hands on it and Marston left. The Secret Service agent guarding the door between the two sections of the plane had a message for him that Palmer Joyce would like to have a drink with him.

The executive went to the bar in the aft compartment and found the commentator for Universal Broadcasting standing alone— always the pariah among his own colleagues.

"How did it go up there, Don? Did he buy it?"

Marston said nothing until the stewardness put a bourbon in front of him. "You can forget what I told you earlier. There is no story."

Joyce gave him a skeptical grin. "Grant put a muzzle on you, right? You know, I'm going to look more than a little foolish if my own sponsor comes up with a blockbuster and I'm shut out."

"I told you there is no story."

"That's not what you told me when you came aboard. Whatever it is, if it's solid and Grant hasn't got the balls to use it, I have."

There was a flurry of motion near them as other reporters left the bar to congregate around a battery of four television sets—one for each network—hung over the entrance to the Western Union office.

"It's the President," said Joyce. "I have a monitor in my office. Why don't we go in and hear him try to explain this one away?"

The President spoke from the Oval Office for only ten minutes, first showing photographs of the Chinese vessels and charts fixing their position relative to the American blockade line. We would have the cooperation of the Chilean navy in intercepting the ships, he said, and whatever action had to be taken to accomplish it would be in accord with international law. Because there was no chance the ships could penetrate the blockade, the only danger of attack would be from the Chinese mainland.

The West Coast, of course, would be in range of such an attack, but he had taken actions that would substantively reduce that possibility. He had spoken to Chairman Borichev on the hot line and had his assurance of "tactical assistance" in dissuading Peking from precipitate action. Our own nuclear defense—ABM sites both on the mainland and on Hawaii and Formosa—were on alert. Our nuclear strike force was in position, and this combination of deterrents, the President was certain, would compel China to recognize the grave and certain consequences of aggressive action.

But he must caution his fellow Americans that the crisis could persist for days or even weeks. No one could predict how, when or where the Chinese might react to this first challenge to their status as a nuclear power. He was hopeful that the Soviet Union and other responsible socialist states could prevail on Peking to abandon its hostile course.

If not, the rulers of China must understand that the President would not hesitate to employ whatever retaliatory or preventive measures might become necessary, including military action against the revolutionary forces in Santa Clara to insure that the country would never again become a sanctuary for nuclear attack against other nations in the Western Hemisphere.

It was, obviously, no time for partisanship or division. For himself, he would immediately cease all political activity, and he was deeply grateful to Senator Grant for his statesmanlike commitment to remove the crisis from the arena of partisanship.

Finally, it was a fateful hour in our national life, but the President was confident that the courage, the resolve and the prayers of his fellow Americans would prevail, as they always had in the past.

Joyce shut off the set. "What crap! He's running ahead or no worse than even with Grant and he declares a cease-fire on politics. You watch. Even if the Reds yell uncle tomorrow, he'll keep this percolating on the front burner right up to the election. You heard it, Don. Days or weeks, he said."

"I heard it," said Marston. "What I didn't hear is that he knew weeks ago that the Chinese were going to move in missiles, but tried to sweep it under the rug until after the election."

"You can prove that?"

"I can."

"Why wouldn't Grant buy it?"

"Like the President said, our man's suddenly become a goddam statesman!"

Joyce got up from his desk and shut the door. "Why don't you tell me what you know?"

"I can't. I gave Grant my word."

"Look, Don, I've been around politicians a hell of a lot longer than you have. And I can tell you there's not one of them who would stop a blast at his opponent—no matter how rough— as long as his own fingerprints weren't on it. Obviously, Grant can't go with this one himself. But at the right time, I can, and, believe me, he'll thank us for it."

"The right time?"

"After the Commies pull back, I couldn't sell my own network on it until then."

Marston was wavering. "I'm too close to Grant. His fingerprints would still be on it."

"Not if you told the truth—that you went to him with the story and he told you he wouldn't touch it." Joyce's attaché case was on his desk. He edged a finger against the lock button, activating the tape recorder inside.

"I don't know, Palmer. Grant said he might go for a Senate investigation if the situation cools off."

"No way! One, the President has a majority on the Foreign Relations Committee, and they'd never go for a hearing. Two, he won't let it cool off before the election." Joyce had a final trump card. "You said the President was guilty of concealing a clear and present danger to this country just to perpetuate himself in office. That's treason. What are you, Don, if you have knowledge of treason and remain silent? You're an accessory to it. You're an accessory to four more years of treason, appeasement, betrayal."

"When would you go on the air with it?"

"After the immediate crisis is over, and that shouldn't be more than a week. I promise you, I won't go with it until we both agree that the time is right."

"There's one complication," said Marston. "Because of what I

know, they're railroading me back into active service in the Air
Force tomorrow to shut me up."

"That's great. You'll have just that much more credibility. Now
why don't you start at the top?"

"I was at the National Security Council session this morning
and—"

"*You were where?*"

L ATE IN the evening Johnny Partridge and Mario Cassavettes
heard the President's address over the short-wave radio in the
cantina of the Playa del Sol. Outside a rising wind, presaging
rain, was rippling the surface of the swimming pool, and sea
birds had taken refuge in the patio. When the broadcast was
over, Cassavettes ran a nervous hand through his thinning hair.

"That's all she wrote, old buddy. First Jiminez, now the U. S.
Marines. The only question is, who catches up with us first."

"It's not that hairy," Partridge replied. "The President said he
might intervene. But if he hasn't by now, my hunch is he never
will."

"Your hunches haven't exactly been paying off."

"Then the law of averages favors my next one—that we can
buy off Jiminez."

"My father's plan—that we switch our bets if Jiminez starts to
look like a winner? It took you a long time to come around."

"I like to watch the odds right up until post time," said Partridge,
"and that's where we're at now. I have a contact with Jiminez.
I'll start it moving tonight."

"Don't you think we ought to clear this with my father?"

"Clear what? We're just switching bets, not throwing in new
money. I'll send word to Jiminez that if he takes Ariella we'll

recognize him as top man and bankroll him in the same amount we're giving Luchengo."

"Do you think he'll buy it?"

"Why not? The country's bankrupt."

"How long before we'll know?"

"Jiminez isn't too far north of us. A messenger ought to be able to sneak up and back by noon tomorrow at the latest."

"I'll tell my father. And, Johnny, if this doesn't work I'm going to rip up more than losing tickets."

"I got that message a long time ago, Mario."

The rain came suddenly, sheeting against the high windows looking on the pool. The wind, stronger now, sent the aluminum deck chairs skittering across the patio.

Torrents of black water ran a foot deep on the highway into town and Partridge fought the steering wheel to keep the gale from blasting the Maserati off the pavements.

José was in his shack on the pier, oiling and cleaning the fishing gear off the *Mañana* and stowing it in a wooden locker. He saw his employer's look of surprise.

"I think it will be a long time before we go fishing again, señor. *Pulque?*"

They sat together at the table, listening to the thin walls shuddering in the wind and the din of rain on the tin roof. They took turns drinking straight from the bottle.

"*Muy dolorosa, señor.* Today, the *federales* shoot the son of my sister as a deserter. A *niño,* seventeen, comes home to his mother, to his own bed, because he knows he is fighting on the wrong side." He raised the bottle to Partridge. "*Viva Jiminez!*"

"I'm sorry," said Partridge. "If I can help—"

"What can you do, señor? What can I do? *Muerto es muerto.*"

He went to a window, watching the white crests of breakers surging over the breakwater in the intermittent gleam from the lighthouse.

"I think you have come to me, señor, because you know, like my *sobrino,* that your faith has been in the wrong man."

"That's right and I want to send a message to Jiminez—tonight. You can arrange it?"

"Your *amigos* at the hotel, they will help Jiminez—they will pay him for his *protección?*"

"Yes."

"Then it will be done."

"You have a man?"

"My sister has many sons."

Partridge took an envelope from his inside coat pocket. "How will I know when you have the answer?"

"Come, I will show you." He flung open the door against the violence of the storm. Outside the shack was a wooden gallows before which tourists once had their pictures taken with marlin. A line of blue pennants was whipping under the crossbeam. "When the answer comes, señor, I will take down the *banderas*."

From her balcony Constanzia Novarese saw Partridge's returning Maserati sweep past the guard post and stop in front of the hotel. She was waiting at her door as he came down the corridor.

"Johnny!"

She shut the door behind him. Her face was glowing. "You have heard? The Americans are coming."

"I wouldn't count on that," he said. "It was nothing more than a warning that they might." José's *pulque* was still bitter in his mouth, and he took a glass of water from the carafe on the nightstand by her bed. "I can't figure you out at all. If the U. S. sent troops, they'd just put Luchengo back in the saddle, stronger than he's ever been. Or are we both switching sides?"

She didn't understand.

"You know why I drove into town tonight? To arrange a contact with Jiminez—to pay him off if he'll leave this operation alone." She was standing between him and her bed lamp and he saw the silhouette of her willowy figure through her filmy robe. The certainty that tonight, as always, she would deny him—that the possibility would not even occur to her—was galling.

"No *olés*, sēnora? I thought you'd be happy to hear that we're doing business with Jiminez."

She swung slowly toward him. "If you think it's wrong, why are you doing it?"

"To buy us a little more time by making the Cassavettes think the deal can still be held together. But, whatever happens, my conscience isn't hurting. I'm still an American, you know, and unlike the Cassavettes, I draw the line at climbing into bed with the Commies. Even if Jiminez buys the proposition, there's no way the money could be here in time to help him against Luchengo."

She held out a hand to him. "You're still an American, Johnny, and I'm still a Santa Claran. Yes, I did want Jiminez to destroy Luchengo, but only because I thought it would bring the Americans. I saw little difference between the murderer Luchengo and the Communist Jiminez. But if the Americans are not coming—if the Communists take over Santa Clara—I know that their crimes would be as great as Luchengo's. The missiles they are sending could have brought devastation to my country."

Partridge lit a cigarette. "You can't have it both ways. It's going to be one or the other."

"But I don't have to choose, do I?"

"But if you had to choose?"

Ambassador Hood had once put the same question to her.

"It is in the hands of God," she said.

"Not entirely. You could always join Lara's plot to upset Luchengo, do with him what you want, and still come out of it looking like Joan of Arc."

She faced him angrily. "I might do that!"

"I wouldn't advise it," he said. "Your chances of leaving this hotel alive—"

"My chances or yours?"

"Look, baby, I can come and go as I please. You're the only reason I'm hanging around." His glance fell to the fullness of her breasts. "But why the hell I am, I don't know."

"Nor do I when you act like this. Good night, Johnny."

He knew he had gone too far. "We're up against more than just the Cassavettes, Constanzia. You're a Castillo. Your name has to be right under Luchengo's on Jiminez' list. We're both going to be on the run. Do me one small favor?"

"Yes?"

"Promise me that when we go, we go together. We'll both have a better chance that way."

She took a step toward him, her eyes moist. "You're a poor liar. The *Mañana* is waiting. You could have left a long time ago. You could leave now."

"And run out on the lady?" He took her in his arms. "You are that, you know."

Her lips were soft against his cheek. "Be patient with me."

He held her away from him, smiling. "Why not? Here we are, in lovely, romantic Ariella—the Riviera of the Americas—with nothing on our hands but time."

In the morning there were only torn black remnants of cloud in the sky to mark the passing of the storm. The sun, burning cruelly in the clear air, raised a mist from the puddles in the forecourt of the hotel. When Partridge went down for breakfast he saw that the blue pennants were still flying on the pier. But an hour later, after his third cup of coffee, they were gone and he drove into the port.

But there was no answer at all. José simply gave him back the envelope. "Jiminez is not in the arroyo, señor."

"But he must be. That's where the battle's shaping up, isn't it?"

José continued to apply light, deft strokes of spar varnish to the fishing rods off the *Mañana,* which he had strung by their tips from the eave of the shack.

"The *niño* went there. He has many *amigos* with Jiminez. They would not lie to him."

"Then where is he?"

José put down his brush. "You have been a good *patrón,* señor. But you are also a *yanqui.*"

"Why would I give Jiminez money if I were against him?"

"But you also gave Luchengo money to defeat Jiminez. No, señor, I will tell you nothing more."

"All right, José, all right. I don't *want* to know where Jiminez is. But that message must reach him. My life—the señora's—could depend on it."

"It will reach him, but tonight—very late. I will take it myself."

He refused Partridge's offer of a cigarette. "The signal will be the same—the *banderas.*"

Partridge drove back to the hotel, where Mario Cassavettes, a Bloody Mary in his hand, was waiting at the front entrance. "Yes or no?"

"My man couldn't locate Jiminez. He'll try again tonight. Don't panic, Mario. Jiminez will go for it."

"Not if our message never reaches him."

"Why don't you have another drink? You worry too much."

Partridge spent the long afternoon by the hotel pool, watching the pier. Shortly before sunset he saw José carry two red cans of gasoline from the shack, lock the door and descend a gangway to where his own outboard skiff was tied up alongside the dock. His course took him directly toward the opening in the breakwater, then north along the coast toward Punta Bunda.

The Marine guard at the American consulate in Ariella told Partridge that Ambassador Hood was not there but was due to arrive from the airstrip momentarily. Consul Bennett Cullers had driven out to meet him.

"I'd like to wait for the ambassador inside, if I may."

"You're an American citizen?"

Partridge gave him his passport.

"Malibu? Man, that's where it's at! When I was at Pendleton, I'd run up there, spread myself out on the beach, and before you knew it, I'd be throwing down drinks with a chick in her fancy pad with the ocean running right up under the place. And the next morning—"

The Marine saw Cullers' car approaching and drew himself smartly to attention. His lips barely moving, he told Partridge: "Catch me on the way out. Man, I got stories you won't believe!"

The consulate was directly on the street, and Partridge was waiting at the door of the car as Hood got out. "I'd like to speak to you, Hood. It's important."

The ambassador didn't try to conceal his anxiety. "The señora? She's—"

"She's okay."

Consul Cullers glared at him. "Perhaps events have changed Mr. Partridge's attitude and he now wants the protection of his government. I wonder if he deserves it, Mr. Ambassador?"

Hood shot a sharp glance at his subordinate. "I'll handle this, Cullers."

Hood had a large bedroom on the second floor with a sweeping view of the harbor. He was spent after his frustrating morning at the White House and the long flight from Washington, and gestured to Partridge to take the chair facing him across a small writing desk.

"Was Cullers right? Are you and your friends beginning to think you might have a better chance in the American courts than with Jiminez?"

"No, we could do business with Jiminez just as we did with Luchengo."

"Then what do you want?" The ambassador's voice had an impatient edge.

"What we both want—to keep Luchengo in power."

"And to protect your arrangement with him?"

"That's part of it," said Partridge.

"The larger part of it, I would think."

"Look, Hood, I didn't come here to argue. And if you care whether Constanzia walks out of the hotel over there alive, you'll listen to me."

"You said she was all right."

"For the moment. But what happens if Jiminez takes Ariella?"

"You said you could do business with him."

"*I* could. But she's a Castillo, remember?"

"The last time I spoke to you, you were quite confident you could evacuate her safely—that you wouldn't need my help."

"I may not have to move her out at all—not if Luchengo can stop Jiminez short of Ariella—and with my information, he can do it."

Hood sat up in his chair. "What do you know?"

"I tried to send a message to Jiminez last night."

"You want Luchengo to know that?"

"No, but I do want him to know that Jiminez isn't below the arroyo."

"Of course he is. There's been intermittent action up there for days."

"Will you hear me out, Hood? My contact didn't find Jiminez, but he did find out where he is. He's delivering the message tonight."

"Go ahead."

"He left just before dark—but by sea, toward Punta Bunda."

Hood went to the window. Across the bay, the Playa del Sol was a dark hulk on the peninsula. "Jiminez would be with his main force. If you're right, Partridge, the federal army is totally out of position to defend against an attack down the coast."

"I'm right, and you're wasting time. Luchengo should start moving a reconnaissance in force up there."

The ambassador left for the consulate's radio office, and was back in five minutes. "We should know by morning. He's sending patrols out tonight from his reserves at the airport."

"You didn't name me as the source of the information?"

"Obviously not. I don't think Luchengo would place much credence in information from an associate of the señora's. And, of course, I won't tell her either. She could hardly approve of what you've done."

Partridge stood to leave. "The last time you spoke to her the choice was between Jiminez and Luchengo—and there was only one way she could go. Now it's between the Chinese Reds and Luchengo. And she's more of a patriot than you think she is."

Hood took him to the door. "She will always regard Luchengo as her enemy."

"That's right," said Partridge, "but now he's got company. Good night, Ambassador."

"Good night, Partridge—and thank you." A smile lit his gaunt face. "You told me once—rather angrily, I recall—that you couldn't accept much of what the Mafia is willing to do to perpetuate itself. Tonight I believe you. It's a little difficult to stop being an American, isn't it?"

THE FIRST REACTION of the People's Republic of China came twelve hours after the President's warning of American-Soviet cooperation to deter Peking from nuclear aggression. It came, as is most often the case in Communist countries, not directly from its head of state but in the form of an announcement from a government propaganda arm.

The New China News Agency, in a statement broadcast over Radio Peking, charged that "the enemies of the People's Republic are fabricating a crisis in the Western Hemisphere to justify the execution of plans, long in preparation, for the annihilation of China. The clumsy, desperate pretext they have chosen for the mass disposition of hostile forces against us is proof of this intention. The Chinese vessels off the coast of South America, which our enemies intend to seize, carry neither offensive nor defensive weapons, and are in international waters. To interfere with them would be an act of piracy and the American imperialists and their craven Soviet ally must bear full responsibility before the world for the dangerous consequences of their actions."

The translation came over the teletype of the Foreign Broadcast Intercept Service in the Situation Room of the White House, and the duty officer had it taken immediately to the President, who was breakfasting in the East Wing with Secretary of Defense Burgess Rand, Secretary of State Sterling Adams and CIA Director Martin Trask.

The Chief Executive read the brief announcement aloud. "This strikes me as very mild."

"And predictable," said Rand. "They're being cautious."

"Up to this point, yes," the President agreed. "But what happens when we actually try to board? Frankly, I don't like the sound of what Trask has told us."

During the night there had been reports from Soviet observers along the Sinkiang border of redeployment of mobile Chinese missile units away from sites on which the Russians had exact targeting information, and of intensive Chinese aerial reconnaissance along the border.

Trask had also told the President that American spy satellites and SR-71 pilots were reporting the movement of both naval and army units away from major ports and population centers.

"The great danger," the President continued, "is that they might actually believe we would launch a preventive attack."

"There's always that risk," said Trask. "But I wouldn't read too much into their redeployments. I think they're just as much a propaganda response as this first broadcast."

"I don't know that I agree," said Adams. "This is the first time they've had to face joint American-Soviet action. We're pushing them very hard. And we have to measure the deterrent effect of what we're doing against the possibility that they believe we do intend to attack."

"If they do go off the deep end," said Rand, "we're ready for it." His words hung in the air ominously.

"No," said the President. "We took the hard line because we had no choice and I wouldn't countermand a single order I've given. But we're not going to push the Chinese into a corner where they think—even wrongly—that the only way out is war. We have to leave them an option, a very clear option, short of that."

"I think we all agree," said the Secretary of Defense. "But right now the situation is frozen hard."

"Not necessarily," the President replied. "What time today will the Chilean navy try to board?"

"They're waiting for us to move support forces into position to back them up," said Rand. "I would estimate three o'clock this afternoon."

"And we take our case to the UN at eleven this morning?"

"That's correct," said Adams.

"All right, that gives us time. Sterling, you'll contact our ambassador. Tell him I want him to emphasize very strongly before the Security Council that we have no intention of intensifying the

crisis—that we have taken the actions we have to defend ourselves against what we believe to be a belligerent intervention in
this hemisphere. China can prove its own good faith and its
respect for international law by permitting the Chilean government
to inspect ships that are clearly within her territorial waters. If
there are no nuclear weapons aboard, as the Chinese claim, we
will permit them to go on their way. We will, however, continue
to maintain both the blockade and our alert forces in the Far East
until we have clear evidence that they are dismantling the missile
sites in Santa Clara and withdrawing their technicians."

"I agree entirely," said Adams.

"I don't," said Rand. "If the missiles are aboard, and we
know they are, the Chinese will never permit inspection. We're
right back where we are now."

"That's right," the President replied. "But at least we've told the
Chinese that we're holding back—that an attack is not imminent
—that they still have time to look for a face-saving way out."

"If those ships are carrying ICBMs," said Rand, "I don't know
what that way out would be."

"I don't either," said the President, "but let's hope to God they
find one. I don't want to go down in history as the man who
began World War III."

The blame clearly fell on General Gi You-gin. He had no doubts,
nor had Peking, that his failure to disguise the missile emplacements
adequately and the discovery of his own presence at the Arroyo
Seco were responsible for both the failure of the operation and
the crisis that was enveloping and could destroy his homeland.

Han Li-wong gave the general a running summary of the American broadcasts: the identification of the missile sites and themselves;
the blockade; the discovery of Cetus and the massing of American
and Soviet forces around China.

Gi heard it all without once betraying his own emotions. But on
the night Han told him of the President's address, warning that
American forces might be sent to Santa Clara, the general put a
reassuring arm on his subordinate's shoulder.

"You are afraid we will be left here—that we are forgotten?"

Han was afraid of just that. "We have had no message from Peking in days."

"It will come, Han, and it will order us home."

It came the next morning. Gi was to join the revolutionary command, assist in the military operations against the federal forces and, after victory, the general and Han were to return to China by way of Bolivia.

Since his message to Ambassador Hood, and the events it had set in motion, Han's single regret had been over the consequences for General Gi. He tried to convince himself that Gi would survive whatever punishment was awaiting him—that their leaders would be mad to sacrifice his expertise. Han clung to that hope, just as he did to his own rationale that his message to Hood would have an enduring and constructive effect on the future of his homeland and of Communism. He was confident the crisis would pass—that the war clique in Peking would yield to the formidable array of American-Soviet power. And the frustration of its adventurism in Santa Clara was a small price for China to pay if it bought more years for rational negotiation with its adversaries.

Han took their orders to General Gi in the upper bunker. He read them impassively, then went to the aperture in the wall, his glance sweeping across the complex of fortifications and missile sites he had built. In contrast to the frenzy of activity only days before, the only personnel left, other than Han and himself, were a score of guerrillas manning guns on the northern perimeter against the unlikely possibility of an attack from Ciudad Alarcon. Han had grown to like the man—to perceive the almost paternal gentleness behind his austere rigidity.

Gi had known, since the first American contact with the whalers, that his mission was hopeless—that he must now wait upon events that would eventually take him back to Peking, to a court-martial and to his death.

His voice was calm. "We must not blame ourselves or regret what appears to be our failure, Comrade Han, for history will prove that it was not a failure. We have told the world that we have pride in our new strength—that we are willing to take great risks to assert that strength. It is a warning that our enemies cannot ignore—a warning that we will demand our rightful place and that they must eventually accept it."

Han said nothing.

"You do not agree, comrade?"

"I agree only that you should not blame yourself, General, nor should our leaders blame you."

"Ah, but they must, and it is right that they should. Had I been able to land my missiles and to place them in firing position, the Americans would have been forced to yield to us."

Han disagreed. "They are stronger than we and they will strike if they believe themselves in peril."

Gi lit his pipe and studied Han through the swirls of smoke. "Where were you born, comrade?"

"In Shanghai."

"To a mercantile family?"

"Yes."

"I was born a peasant," said Gi, "in the province of Tsinghai in the Himalayas. I will tell you a story to prove that you are wrong. When I was very young a tiger came to the fields near our village. We never saw the tiger—only his tracks—and at night we heard him prowling in the darkness.

"First it was the women who were afraid—for their children and for their sons and husbands working in the fields. And they built fires at night in front of the huts and struck gongs in the temple to keep the tiger away. Then, after many days of seeing the tracks move closer and closer to the village and hearing the tiger thrash his way through the brush, the men also became afraid. And one day the elders of our village met and came to the decision that we must move away—to another valley where we would be out of danger. And we did, leaving behind our huts and our crops. You see, Han, it was not important that we never saw the tiger—that he did us no harm. What was important was that he was there—that he could harm us—and we ran away."

"Why," said Han, "did you not arm yourselves and hunt the tiger down and kill him?"

"Because we knew the tiger was not afraid to die—and we were."

"Has China become that," said Han, "a tiger in the night?"

"A hundred tigers, comrade. And our enemies build their fires and strike their gongs. But in the end they will run before us."

Gi and Han spent the early afternoon packing their gear. Guides were to arrive late in the evening to take them to Jiminez' new position near the coast. Shortly before they were to leave, the general set time charges of explosives in the underground communications and computer fire control bunker, then built a bonfire outside the upper bunker to destroy his blueprints of the missile site and other incriminating documents.

It was already dark and they were three miles away, climbing a ridge, when they heard the blast and, turning, saw a massive tower of flames rising from the heights above the Arroyo Seco. Gi, his leathery face red in the glare, stood watching until there was nothing left but smoke and soaring embers.

Two hours later and four miles from Jiminez' bivouac in a network of coastal canyons, they had to take cover from federal patrols that were moving along the high coastal escarpment to investigate a report that rebel forces might be in the area.

THERE WAS no visible panic, even on the West Coast where thermonuclear horror could strike within the next hour—the next moment. Children went to school, their fathers to work, their mothers to the supermarket. There would be an exodus of tens of thousands from Los Angeles over the coming weekend—football fans fleeing to motels in Las Vegas to thwart the television blackout of a sold-out game between the league-leading Rams and the San Diego Chargers.

Americans had been living with crises too long not to believe that this latest would prove still another false alarm. Berlin, Korea, Cuba, the Mideast, Vietnam, a host of smaller but potentially explosive international incidents, and the riot and arson of the revolution of the young blacks and whites at home—all had left Americans with a deepening cynicism. And because there was nothing they could do to stop a madman in China from pressing a button, they were determined—after their first "Oh, my God, not again!" reaction—not to let it depress them too much.

Nor did the Santa Claran crisis have a visible effect on politics. The long years of crisis had taught Americans that the President, whatever his party or pre-election declarations, had little power over exterior events. There were in the world massive and sinister forces that had a momentum of their own that no one man— perhaps no one nation—could retard.

If Senator Harlan Grant could find no grounds for criticizing the President's decision to move America, once more, to the brink, who else should fault him?

The Lou Harris poll, a week before the President's crisis address, had given him a small but growing lead over Grant. Harris was in print the morning after the President's address with a comment that Americans, traditionally, support their leadership in times of external crisis, and he was certain his next poll would show an even larger point spread favoring the Chief Executive.

Excerpts from radio transmissions from the aircraft carrier *John F. Kennedy,* flagship of the American blockade fleet, to Commander-in-Chief, Pacific, Pearl Harbor:

"Air reconnaissance reports at 1312 local time that Chinese vessels are altering course to 195 degrees; speed twelve knots. Present course and speed will clear Chilean territorial waters prior to our 1500 support rendezvous with Chilean intercept squadron."

"Commander Chilean forces advises at 1358 that he has no authority to intercept or board hostiles beyond his own territorial limits. Will withdraw his destroyers when hostiles enter international waters. My command will pursue and remain close aboard, but will take no further action pending receipt of new orders."

"1612: Hostiles now in international waters, flying ensign of People's Republic of China. Chilean command, which continues to refuse pursuit, now patrolling international line. Can expect hostiles to disperse under cover of night. Repeat request for new orders."

Excerpts from a broadcast over Radio Peking:

"Two Chinese ships, engaging in routine exploration for new whaling grounds off the coast of South America, are now returning to their home port of Foochow after completing their mission.

"Their departure, on schedule, from that area removes the artificial pretext for present aggressive actions against the People's Republic of China by the ruling military clique in Washington and the betrayers of the socialist revolution in Moscow.

"We may now judge whether the American President spoke with truthfulness or deceit in his declaration of today that his government desires a peaceful resolution of the crisis he himself has thrust upon the world. He has drawn tight the knot of war, and only he can untie it.

"Let there be no doubt that the People's Republic of China will respond with fury to further provocations against its ships at sea or against its homeland."

The transcript of a news conference by Secretary of Defense Burgess Rand at the Pentagon two hours later:

Shortly after six o'clock our time this evening, the missile-carrying ships off the coast of Chile changed course and are now, apparently, returning home. Almost simultaneously, there was a statement from Peking that the government of China considers the departure of its vessels as being in full compliance with the terms for resolving the crisis that our ambassador set forth today before the United Nations.

As most of you know, I have just come from a session of the National Security Council at the White House and, at the request of the President, will clarify our position with respect to the new developments. It is the position of this government that China's decision to withdraw its vessels is a meaningless gesture. It not only fails to meet our insistence that the vessels permit a third-party inspection by Chilean naval units but is a patent attempt to avoid such inspection.

The Chinese vessels are, at the present time, beyond the territorial waters of Chile and, thus, beyond that government's jurisdiction. The inspection, therefore, must and will be undertaken by our own fleet units in the area. I will tell you, further, that our intercepting units are now in close contact with the Chinese vessels but are under orders not to interfere with them until ten tomorrow morning to give the Chinese government adequate time to communicate new instructions to their ships.

In order that the Chinese government cannot misjudge our intentions, we have made contact through neutral channels with their embassy in Warsaw. We insist only that the ships submit to inspection without resistance—and there is no reason they should not if, as the Chinese government claims, they are not carrying offensive weapons. If inspection proves this claim to be correct, we will permit the vessels to proceed without further interference. If this claim proves to be false, we intend to place crews aboard and escort them to Pearl Harbor. We intend, further, in cooperation with the Soviet Union, to continue our intensive deployment of nuclear strike forces in the Far East until we have a clear and substantive indication that this is but a single act of provocation, and that further covert operations threatening the security of this country and of the Soviet Union are not also under way.

Let me add, in closing, that the President spoke to Chairman Borichev an hour ago and the actions we contemplate have his full support. Now, are there questions?

Q. Mr. Secretary, there can be no doubt that Chile would be operating within international law by boarding the ships in its own waters. What is our legal basis for intercepting them in international waters?

A. Our commitments to the Organization of American States and our mutual defense treaties with many of its members, including Santa Clara, not only justify but require that we act to defend the hemisphere against hostile intrusion. This would include not only the present blockade to prevent such intrusion but the right to seize vessels attempting it.

Q. Would we find the precedent for this action in our open seas inspection of Russian missile ships bound for Cuba in 1962?

A. I don't think it would be helpful at the present moment to draw that parallel.

Q. As I understand your statement, Mr. Secretary, the President is hopeful that the Chinese will submit to inspection. What evidence is there that they will?

A. Let me say this. Although the Chinese response today was unacceptable, it still indicates a desire on their part to avoid a direct confrontation. We don't know how much further they're willing to go. But we would expect, of course, that they will recognize the firmness of our position and the consequences to themselves if they do not. Now, if that's all, gentlemen . . .

Q. Mr. Secretary, is it a correct interpretation of your statement that we intend to use whatever force necessary to board those ships?

A. If it comes to that, yes.

Q. What happens if the Chinese scuttle the ships? I don't know how much water there is out there, but I would imagine it's beyond salvage depth.

A. That's a contingency we're considering. For now, I would say that the act of scuttling would confirm, beyond all doubt, that the ships are carrying missiles.

Q. One final question, Mr. Secretary. We've had no word from either the White House or you on Peking's military reaction, or lack of it, to the massing of U.S.-Soviet nuclear forces around China's borders. We certainly must know by now whether they're mobilizing or not.

A. I can say only that there have been redeployments of major military units. What they might portend we don't know. They could be purely defensive.

Q. Or offensive?

A. I won't be drawn into such speculation, and it would be both inaccurate and irresponsible to read that into my last answer. Good night.

The first skirmish in the battle of Ariella was fought shortly before dawn when one of the federal search patrols, nearing the border of Escalante, was brought under fire by Francisco Jiminez' advance units.

The brief fire-fight in a moonscape of volcanic rock on the coastal cliff was indecisive, and the lieutenant in charge of the patrol withdrew to radio a report of the action to the headquarters of Commanding General Carlos Silvera-Guzman in Ariella.

Within an hour army reserves at the airport and mobile units on the northern defensive perimeter below the Arroyo Seco had orders to move into position to counter the new threat. The coastal plain was ideal maneuvering ground and, from their observation point on the highest escarpment above the sea, General Gi You-gin and Jiminez saw in the clear morning light the giant swirls of dust marking the advance of the federal troop carriers and artillery.

Jiminez was furious with Gi. "Your *gran estrategia!* They outnumber us. They outgun us. And I have only half my *compañeros* to face them on open ground."

Gi let his binoculars fall to his chest. "Ah, but they have also had to divide their forces. You will order your troops in the arroyo to strike south now."

"That will not save us here. Look at them come!" The first trucks and mobile guns could now be seen three miles away, dashing headlong over the desert.

"Let them come," said Gi. "When they near the ravines and the high ground we stand on now, they must stop. They cannot know how many we are. We will sting them with patrols and mortar fire—and we will wait." He gauged Jiminez' sullen expression correctly. "When the attack comes from the north—when Ariella is under siege—Luchengo will withdraw many of his troops and guns from this position to defend the city. Then we will move from here, and I promise you, *General* Jiminez, that you will lead the victory march into Ariella."

"I want no glory for myself—only for the revolution."

"Of course, of course. The orders for the attack—you will please issue them now."

"*Sí.*"

Gi strode down the shallow incline to the cover of a narrow barranca where Han Li-wong had set up his portable radio equipment. Han was rechecking a message against one of his code books. His face paled.

"You have a message, Han?"

"Yes, from Peking to Cetus."

Gi read it slowly and gave it back to Han with a shrug. "It was the only possible decision," he said. Then he went back up the slope. The advancing *federales* had come to a halt a mile away from the first of the ravines to position their guns. Gi glanced to seaward. It was a cool morning, and clouds of fog were fuming up from the sea. In an hour or more the mist would envelop the heights where he stood. The weather could not be more unfavorable for an artillery attack on his position. Mao was smiling on him once again.

A̲ᴛ ᴇxᴀᴄᴛʟʏ ten o'clock four destroyers, led by the U.S.S. *Winner,* swept close aboard the two whalers and ran up the international flag hoist: "Heave to for boarding." Seconds later a series of pennants broke from the yardarm of the leading Chinese ship: "I am in international waters."

Two miles away the signal was clearly visible from the bridge of the flagship *John F. Kennedy,* and its commander told the *Winner* by radio-telephone: "I am launching helicopters. When they are in position, repeat your first hoist. If they refuse to stop engines within two minutes, fire across the bows of the lead vessel."

A flight of four helicopters left the deck of the carrier and sped at low level over the long, steep Pacific swells, cresting with whitecaps. When they were hovering over the whalers the *Winner* again ran up its signal to heave to. But this time there was no response from the Chinese, and two minutes later a four-inch shell from the *Winner* burst in a steaming geyser fifty yards ahead of the first ship.

Within an instant, a series of underwater explosions shook both of the whalers, and they began to careen wildly out of control. Simultaneously, radiomen aboard the Navy ships and on freighters and shore stations thousands of miles away heard the Chinese transmit their call letters, then the message: "We are foundering after attack by American warships in international waters."

The four destroyers tried to move alongside the whalers for boarding but could not because of their erratic maneuvering and the turbulent seas.

The *JFK* sent the following message to the destroyers: "Open fire on rudder and propulsion gear. I am launching fighters to strafe and clear topside areas." And to the circling helicopters: "Prepare to drop salvage parties when vessels have lost maneuverability and decks are clear of hostile personnel."

Within minutes the destroyers had shot away the rudders and screws of the enemy ships and the fighters, zooming in at masthead level, had left their decks and superstructure a tangle of smoking steel. Both ships were now low in the water from the gaping holes their own demolition charges had ripped in their hulls below the water line.

It was the decision of the flag officer aboard the carrier that one of the vessels, already beginning to sink by the stern, was unsalvageable, and the helicopters were told to lower the damage control parties aboard the remaining ship.

There was no sign of life on the whaler until the helicopters were in range, and then they came under small-caliber machine gun fire from the bridge of the ship. One, its rotor mechanism jammed by a burst of bullets, fluttered into the sea, but a destroyer was alongside a minute later to hoist its crew to safety.

The fighter planes came back to the attack, their rockets turning the ship's bridge into an inferno. Again the helicopters swung into position above the ship, now listing heavily in the trough of the swells.

The first Americans to drop the five feet onto the deck were scuba divers with underwater torches, whose instructions were to secure all watertight doors in the hold to limit the flooding to compartments where the demolition charges had torn holes in the hull. Even in the murky darkness and against the torrent of inrushing seas, they were able to accomplish their mission in a quarter of an hour. When the first of the divers was back on deck, clenching his hands over his head to signal success, the *JFK* radioed the *Winner* to commence boarding.

The destroyer's executive and engineering officers were the first to reach the deck of the Chinese ship, clambering up a ladder held by grapnels which had been flung over the gunwales. Behind them came a party of seamen with automatic rifles slung over their shoulders.

The deck was silent except for the hiss of steam from hot metal, and, overhead, the whine of jets in their landing pattern around the *JFK*. The executive officer went forward to reconnoiter the smoking ruins of the bridge and the crew's quarters. The engineer led the second party down a ladder under the bridge to the massive hold.

A half hour before the confrontation at sea the President was driven to the National Military Command Center in the E Ring of the Pentagon. It was, on a much more extensive scale, similar to his own Situation Room in the basement of the White House. On one wall was a massive glassine chart of the world, showing the exact disposition and state of readiness of our own military forces and those of both hostile and friendly nations. Luminous white blips, moving almost imperceptibly, traced the movements of American nuclear submarines, Strategic Air Command bombers and spy satellites. Red blips gave the teams of seventeen officers manning the center twenty-four hours a day the same information on the movements of enemy war units. In another section of the NMCC specialists were constantly testing the communications lines to all American defense commands and monitoring the world-wide military radio traffic of other major countries. The officer in charge was always an Army general or a four-star admiral. Also present, around the clock, were observers from the White House and the State Department.

It was from this center—if the President gave the order—that the commands would go forth to plunge the nation into war. On this day he was taken first by the admiral in charge to a smaller glassine chart covering only mainland China and peripheral areas in the Far East. On it were hundreds of red and white blips marking Chinese dispositions and those of American and Soviet forces.

The President spoke to the admiral. "Nothing in their maneuvers that should cause us concern?"

"Not yet, sir. We're keeping our distance, and they're keeping theirs. Their strategy, apparently, is to keep their own mobile missile launchers on the move to confuse the Russians, and to pull back their other forces from our most likely first strike targets. But we can, of course, pinpoint their permanent launch sites. They could launch, at most, one salvo before we knock them out."

"And how many do you estimate could penetrate our ABM screen?"

"Four or five, sir—no more. Nothing that could delay or minimize our retaliatory ability. No cause for concern there."

"I doubt if civilians on the West Coast would share your opinion, Admiral."

"No, sir. But I thought you were asking for a military judgment."

"Are you ready with the *John F. Kennedy* now?"

"Yes. Secretaries Adams and Rand are already standing by." He led the President into a dimly lit cubicle and to a chair facing a television monitor. Adams and Rand stood to greet him.

"No action yet?"

"No," said Rand. "It's fifteen minutes before we board."

In addition to the television set, there were also two speakers relaying the voice communications of the boarding party and the carrier. For long minutes the President, the two Cabinet members and the admiral sat watching the clear color picture from the *JFK* of the lumbering whalers butting their way through the swells and the sleek destroyers on station on their flanks.

One minute before the *Winner* ran up its first signal to heave to for boarding, the admiral broke the silence. "We're in direct radio-telephone communication with the *JFK*, Mr. President. The flag officer understands that his decisions are subject to your—"

"No," said the President. "It's in his hands now."

Later, the Chief Executive would recall only two moments of intense dread—on hearing the flag officer's first order to open fire on the whalers, and his message to the helicopters that one of the ships was beyond salvage. That was the only time the President spoke during the action.

"Can they keep that last one afloat, Admiral?"

"They'll try."

"They must. They must."

The first walkie-talkie report from the boarding party was from the unit sent to the bridge:

"No survivors here. I would estimate no more than six or seven of the dead are torn up badly enough to have been hit by our gun and rocket fire. The rest all have small bullet wounds in the head. It's weird, but they look like suicides to me."

"Thank you, Commander," came the response from the *JFK*. "You're probably correct. We have been able to locate no survivors in the water from the one that's now foundering."

Adams shook his head in disbelief. "It's inconceivable."

"No," said Rand, "they were intending to destroy all evidence—ships and crews. You can't interrogate a dead man."

Minutes later the engineering officer was on the walkie-talkie from the hold of the whaler. "We're up to our hips in water down here but the watertight bulkheads appear to be holding."

"Can you report on the cargo?" was the answer from the carrier.

"There are six long crates and six shorter ones secured against the bulkhead, sir. And there are also a series of depth charges in racks alongside both sides of the hull. If their fusing is like ours, they're set to go off at a depth of thirty feet."

"You're defusing the charges?"

"You know it!"

The engineering officer was off the air only five minutes, but for the President and his advisers it was an infinity.

"We've had a look inside one of the big crates, sir, and it looks like we've hit the jackpot. It's a missile—sixty or seventy feet in length. We're cracking open a smaller crate now. Hold on a minute." There was a short pause. "This one contains what looks to be launcher components, but I'm no expert."

"But you're certain the first one is a missile?"

"Yes, sir."

The President fell back in his chair. "Thank God! Thank God!"

IN LA PAZ the next day a mob broke past police lines to hurl stones through the windows of the Soviet Embassy. In Paris, Left Bank student revolutionaries set fire to the American Library. In Saigon, Vietcong members of the coalition government tried vainly to force through an order expelling all American diplomats from Vietnam, and the pro-American minister leading the opposition was later shot to death over his dinner table by unknown assassins.

In Washington, Secretary of Defense Burgess Rand held a morning news conference in the Pentagon auditorium. More than three hundred correspondents, including those from Communist bloc nations, were first shown a video tape of the engagement at sea which the President had seen live the day before at the National Military Command Center. They also saw tapes shot later by floodlight in the hold of the surviving whaler, showing the long, gleaming missiles, their launching components in the crates and the ranks of depth charges.

When the lights went up, Secretary Rand went to the dais. The transcript:

You have been shown this film to discount, once and for all, the claim of the Chinese commander that action by our fleet units was responsible for the eventual sinking of one of his ships and damage to the other. Adequate signals to heave to were given, as you have seen, and the only action by us before the detonation of their own scuttling charges was a warning shot across the bows.

In addition to the scuttling charges both vessels were carrying destruct charges for the missiles, which the salvage crews aboard the one vessel were able to disarm. The charges aboard the second ship did detonate at the pre-set depth.

Our specialists have identified the missiles you have seen as the equivalent of our own Minuteman. They are sixty feet in length; six feet in diameter; have a weight of sixty-five thousand pounds and a thrust of two hundred and sixty-eight thousand pounds. We can determine from this and from other data an approximate range of six thousand miles. Assuming that each of the vessels was carrying the same number—six—it is clear that had the Chinese been able to position them in Santa Clara, no major city—no major missile site in this country—would have been safe from a devastating surprise attack.

There can be no question that the evidence you have been shown fully justifies our interdiction of the ships and the tactics we were forced to employ. And it further justifies the continuing measures we and the Soviet Union will employ to reduce the risk of a retaliatory response from the Chinese mainland.

I'm ready for your questions now, gentlemen. But I want it to be understood that they must not go beyond yesterday's action at sea. Except to assure the American people that our defenses are in full readiness, I will have no comment on what China's reaction may be or what new steps we and the Soviet Union may be taking to counter that action.

Q. Where's the surviving whaler now?

A. It's under tow toward Pearl Harbor. We expect it to arrive, if sea conditions permit, in three days.

Q. What disposition will be made of its missiles?

A. They will be brought to appropriate installations in the States for examination and study.

Q. Will we let the Russians have one?

A. Whether that would come under our recent agreement with the Soviet Union to exchange intelligence on the Chinese nuclear potential, I can't answer at this time.

Q. Mr. Secretary, could you estimate the number of Chinese seamen aboard the two vessels and confirm that the survivors of our own gunfire were all suicides?

A. We found twenty-four bodies aboard the vessel we were able to keep afloat. I would imagine the other ship had a similar complement. Seven on the ship we were able to board died of wounds

*from our guns and rockets. The rest were suicides. We have found
no bodies from the other vessel and have to presume that the
crew and officers shut themselves in compartments and went down
with the ship. That probably was the plan aboard the ship we did
save. But when it became apparent that our salvage operation
could succeed, they took the other way out.*

*Q. Mr. Secretary, I want to respect the ground rules you've set
down, but would you give us your assessment as to whether we are
closer or further from war than we were twenty-four hours ago.*

A. Your question is not within the ground rules. No comment.

*Q. May I go back, then, to your on-the-record comment earlier
that we and the Soviet Union may be taking new steps against
China? Rather than have us speculate on what they might be,
could you tell us what you would regard as sufficient cause to launch
preventive strikes against China?*

*A. That question is even more out of bounds than the first one.
Good afternoon, gentlemen.*

Palmer Joyce left the press conference and drove immediately
to the offices of Universal Broadcasting on Pennsylvania Avenue.
He first tried to reach Donald Marston at the Pentagon but was
told that the New York executive, although on active duty status,
had not yet been given an assignment. Joyce finally was able to
locate him at his winter residence on Biscayne Bay.

"I'm planning to go with the story tomorrow night, Don. When
can you fly up?"

"Don't push me, Palmer. Grabbing those ships doesn't end the
crisis. We still don't know whether the Chinese are going to unload
on us."

"Look," said Joyce, "you saw the last Harris poll and after today
the President's going to look even better. He can keep this crisis
going for weeks. If we're going to go at all, now's the time."

Marston's tone was almost pleading. "But I've been sworn in.
They'd never let me testify and if I went on the air with you they
could court-martial me."

"Maybe. But you gave me the facts before you went on active
duty. You're in the clear there. And, believe me, if they tried to

keep you off the stand, it would amount to an admission that your charges on my show were correct. It would be just as good as your testimony."

"It's too soon, Palmer. Let's play it by ear a little longer— please."

"You know, I could break this story without you just by crediting it to a reliable Washington source. And once it hits the fan, you'll be out front whether you like it or not."

"You do," said Marston, "and I'll call you a liar. I'll deny every word of it."

Joyce's bluff hadn't paid off. "All right. But remember this. We're less than two weeks away from the election, and it's going to take time and pressure to force Senator Breckinridge to call a hearing."

"Then let's hope the Chinese cave in before then. I gave my word to Senator Grant that I'd do nothing until this passes over and I'm going to keep my word."

That night the *JFK*'s tape of the encounter at sea was shown over all four TV networks. Within hours, a flood of tens of thousands of telegrams were pouring into the White House, commending the President on his courage and decisiveness. But on the West Coast families drew the drapes across their bedroom windows. The fabric might save them from flying glass in their beds if the windows were blown out.

President Jorge Luchengo was forced by the discovery of a second rebel force to the west to abandon his decision to join his troops on the northern front. If Ariella was to come under attack from two positions, he felt that he should remain at the central command headquarters at the Ariella airport.

When the rebels first struck from the arroyo early in the morning, the army was still regrouping to close the gaps left by the departure of its mobile units for the coast. Within the first hour, under cover of a heavy artillery barrage, the guerrillas had forced a mile-long wedge into the federal troops guarding the highway to the port city. A brief counterattack on the rebel flanks was quickly driven back by the accuracy of Jiminez' guns, and there was no action for the rest of the day except for the movement of the rebel artillery into more forward positions and light probing attacks against the federal defense lines.

When night came, convinced both of Jiminez' invincibility and of the ineptness of their own commanders, hundreds of federal troops left their positions either to defect to the enemy or to hide in the hills. The veterans of the first major battle weeks earlier on the slopes of Arroyo Seco had no stomach for another such slaughter.

Colonel William Gruver gave Ambassador Hood a running report on the attack, retreat and desertions and, at midnight, Hood drove from the consulate to the airport.

Luchengo, finally acceding to the orders of his doctors, was in a hospital bed in an alcove in the rear of the command center. When the ambassador first saw him he thought he must be dying. A yellow pallor from the gangrene had crept over the parchment of his face, and his deeply sunken eyes were staring dully at the low ceiling.

Hood was within five steps of the bed when the voice of one of the officers on the northern front came crackling over the radio, reporting the desertion of another of his forward patrols. Luchengo signed weakly to the doctor at the foot of the bed to crank him into a sitting position. He spoke to General Carlos Silvera-Guzman, who was standing with other officers at a battle map on the wall. His voice had surprising vigor.

"There is still no action up the coast, General?"

"None."

"Then do you agree it would be wise to send reinforcements back to the north?"

"I do."

"Then order it." Luchengo's glance fell on Hood for the first time. "Good evening, my friend. Sit down. Sit down." Hood took a chair next to the bed. "My compliments on your victory at sea. I regret that I can report no victories of my own." His head fell back on the pillow. "Why have you come, Ambassador?"

"It is my hope," said Hood, "that the situation will reverse itself—

that you will bring Jiminez decisively to battle before he can reach Ariella."

"But you doubt it?"

"No, but I have to consider the safety of the staff at the consulate."

"You are preparing to leave?"

"Not yet, but one of our destroyers will be lying off the coast if it becomes necessary to evacuate."

Luchengo's hand trembled on the white sheet. "That is most wise."

"I have come," said Hood, "to advise you that if Ariella should fall—"

"May I anticipate you? You have come to tell me that you would also be willing to evacuate me and those members of my government who have been loyal to me." He cast a bitter glance around the command center. "We would not be many, but I must decline."

"A government in exile, Mr. President, could have tremendous influence in mobilizing pressure for intervention against Jiminez."

Luchengo's smile was mocking. "Influence with your own President? Can you guarantee it?"

Hood was silent.

"No, Mr. Hood. I will stay. It is not important whether the *gangrena* or Jiminez kills me." His voice rose defiantly. "But we have not lost, my friend—not yet. I spoke to you once regarding Señora Novarese—the possibility she might join me. I am still convinced that she can accomplish what I cannot—that her presence in the government would persuade your President to act."

"Her answer was no," Hood replied. "The answer of my government was no."

"Ah, but now it is different. Your President is more daring now because circumstances compel him to be. Is he to move to the brink of war against China, a giant, and do nothing against Jiminez who has no power to strike back?"

"I have no answer for you."

Silvera-Guzman came to the bed to report that the first reinforcements for the arroyo were preparing to move. Luchengo gave him only a cursory nod of acknowledgment.

"Mr. Hood, I am going to place you in a most difficult position—

to weigh your affection for the señora against your concern for this republic. I am going to ask you to urge her once more to succeed me as President—to stand by my side in rallying our countrymen to fight for their own freedom. She would be accepting great risks. Jiminez would spare neither of us if we fail."

"Would you agree, Mr. President, to the señora's evacuation if the situation clearly becomes hopeless?"

"I would, of course. I think she would be a far more persuasive President in exile than I. You will speak to her, then?"

"In the morning."

A shuddering chill swept Luchengo's gaunt frame. "Thank you and good night."

Arturo Lara was waiting in front of Hood's car. "The doctors say our president cannot live much longer. But you have been with him. You know."

Hood didn't try to conceal his contempt. "He would appreciate your concern, Lara. Now if you will let me pass . . ."

"It is the belief of the generals and of the Cabinet that all resistance will end with his death—that his successor must take power now."

"Then take it," said Hood.

"You persist in misjudging me," said the Foreign Minister. "Tomorrow morning, Lara, I will speak to Señora Novarese. I will urge her to come into the government—the presidency, if she wants it. Now will you step out of my way, or must I—"

There was a triumphant smile on Lara's face. "I could ask for no more."

Hood shoved him against the side of the car. "I'm asking for Luchengo, not for you. And if the señora agrees, Lara, I'm going to place one condition on my remaining in Santa Clara as ambassador—your immediate dismissal from the Cabinet as a traitor with whom I would not associate myself."

Lara, his face ugly with hate, stood watching until the car was lost in the night.

I T WAS just after dawn when Johnny Partridge saw José's skiff round the breakwater, wallowing in the wake of shrimp trawlers returning from their night's fishing. He had a hasty breakfast and then drove to the fishing pier.

José was eating his breakfast of eggs and chili when he heard the Maserati stop outside the shack and was waiting for Partridge at the door with an envelope.

The American tore it open and read Jiminez' answer. "I have no grievance against those who seek refuge from the imperialists, and I accept your offer. But I must fight the enemy where he is, and if he tries to defend Ariella, I cannot guarantee your safety."

Partridge sat opposite the old man at the crude wooden table and shoved a hundred-peso note toward him. "I want you to move out to the *Mañana* and live aboard. The señora and I may have to move out fast."

"The letter from Jiminez does not please you?"

"Let's just say it won't please my friends at the hotel."

José took the money and jammed it in his shirt pocket. "I will go. For how long, señor?"

"Until we know whether the *federales* can stop Jiminez."

"I tell you now, they will not stop him. Nothing will stop him."

From his window overlooking the waterfront, Ambassador Hood saw Partridge's Maserati outside the shack and was waiting to intercept him at the foot of the pier.

"I'm glad I found you in town, Partridge. I have a message for Señora Novarese I wouldn't want to entrust to that party line at the hotel. Can you come with me to the consulate?"

"You go on ahead," said Partridge. "I'll be there in ten minutes." He then drove a hundred yards along the waterfront to where the

Reina del Mar was tied up alongside the main wharf. His orders to the captain were brief.

"I want you to be ready to sail on an hour's notice."

"*Sí, señor!*" The captain had been away from home too long. "We return to Acapulco?"

"No, not Acapulco. You can be ready?"

"How?" was the surly response. "You have most of my crew guarding the hotel."

"I'll take care of it," said Partridge.

The first-floor corridor of the consulate was jammed with packing cases and files and Partridge had to jostle his way past civilian and Marine personnel loading them aboard trucks in the street. He met Bennett Cullers at the stairway leading to Hood's quarters.

"Moving day, Cullers?"

"Yes, and you and your friends are welcome to join us." A nervous tic belied his facetiousness.

"No, thank you."

Ambassador Hood was having coffee at his desk. His door was open. "Come in, Partridge. Coffee?"

"No, nothing."

Hood was in a cordial mood. "The information you gave me on Jiminez' move to the sea was correct. I want to thank you for it, and if Luchengo knew the source, he would want to thank you for it."

"That artillery fire up north yesterday morning—that didn't sound as if Jiminez was on the sea."

"He's split his forces. The attack could come from either direction or from both simultaneously."

"From all the activity downstairs," said Partridge, "it seems to me that you've already written Ariella off."

"Just a precaution," said Hood.

Partridge lit a cigarette. "You said you had a message for the señora?"

"I do. Luchengo wants her to come into the government, and from what you told me the other night, she might finally be amenable."

"She might. But I'd try to argue her out of it."

"Why?"

"Come off of it, Hood. Jiminez is a winner, and you know it. She'd just be asking for a firing squad."

"If I thought that," said the ambassador, "I'd also try to argue her out of it. No, Luchengo agrees that if he can't save Ariella the señora should be taken out to head a government in exile."

"You're overlooking one small point, Hood. You think that Cassavettes would let her walk out of the hotel—just like that?"

"You told me you had a way out for her and yourself."

"I have a boat hidden in the cove out at the end of the peninsula. We'd have a good chance, but it's still risky."

Hood spread his hands impatiently. "Luchengo wouldn't accept this situation. If she agrees to join him, and they try to stop her from leaving—"

"He'd invade the place?"

"Exactly."

"That's even riskier," said Partridge. "How much time do we have?"

"I told Luchengo I'd speak to her today."

"Let me tell her for you." He saw the skepticism on Hood's face. "It's her decision. I won't interfere." He jammed his cigarette out in the ashtray. "I'm going back to the hotel now. I'm going to tell them you're evacuating—that all hell is going to bust loose here. I think I can persuade them to go back aboard the *Reina del Mar*."

"Then that should do it," said Hood.

"No, the Cassavettes aren't likely to leave the señora and me behind."

"Partridge, I can't believe that if I were to return to the hotel with you now and demand her release they would stand in my way. What rational choice do they have if you explain the alternatives? If she agrees to join Luchengo and they refuse to free her, he won't hesitate to take her out of there by force."

"You're not dealing with rational people, Hood. Leave it to me. I'll try to bring her here tonight."

"And if you can't?"

"Then it's your show."

"Good luck." The ambassador shook his hand. "You ought to

know, Partridge, that we have a destroyer off the coast to evacuate us. You'll be back under American jurisdiction."

"I know that."

"I don't know how much help I could be to you in court," said Hood. "But you have my promise I'll testify to—"

"My good character?" Partridge was smiling.

"Perhaps even that."

Bruno Cassavettes read the message from Jiminez twice, then threw it on the writing desk. The drapes in his suite were drawn against the afternoon sun. The capo glanced scornfully at his son, then at Partridge, both of whom were standing in his presence.

"Jiminez says he will take our money but can't guarantee us protection. That is no way to do business."

"He's just leveling with us," said Partridge. "He can't control whether Luchengo decides to turn the whole town into a battlefield."

The knife scar on the old man's face was a luminous streak against his dark cheek. "You two smart boys—maybe you know what to do next?"

"I don't think we have much choice, Mr. Cassavettes," said Partridge. "The guns we heard yesterday will be moving up. I think we ought to go back aboard the *Reina del Mar* and leave the port until Jiminez or Luchengo comes up the winner. I've already given the captain orders to be ready."

The capo struck the desk with his fist. "I give the orders here—not you!"

"I spoke to the captain only after I found out that Ambassador Hood and the others over at the consulate were moving out. Their information is better than ours, and they're apparently convinced it's no longer safe here."

"So let them run," said the capo. "They have more to fear from Jiminez than we do." His massive head swung toward his son. "The consigliere has nothing to say?"

"I agree with Partridge. We have deals with both Jiminez and Luchengo. We have nothing to lose, whoever wins."

The capo's voice rose shrilly. "Five million dollars! We pay five million dollars for protection, and now you tell me we have bought nothing!" He rose heavily from his chair, glaring at his son. "You will call a council. We will vote." Then to Partridge, "But not you. You are not of us."

They were walking along the sea front, scattering before them flights of gulls and cormorants perching on the stone wall of the promenade.

"And Sam Hood thinks I should?"

"Yes."

"And what do you think, Johnny?"

"I think it's your decision. You told me once that you'd never leave this country—that it's too important to you. But maybe that's exactly the reason you should leave now. Hood could be right. If Jiminez takes over, you could continue the fight against him outside the country."

She stood watching the encroaching tide sweep higher up the beach, driven by a strong breeze that was raising whitecaps beyond the surf line. For her, an alliance with Luchengo was unthinkable. "You must understand why I can't, Johnny—not as long as Luchengo lives. It would be a betrayal of—"

Partridge took her hand. "They're holding a council of the capos up there now, and they'll be voting on more than whether to leave. They'll be voting on my life, Constanzia."

"Then go."

His voice was pleading. "And leave you to Jiminez? All I'm asking, Constanzia, is that we go to the consulate tonight. We'll both be safe there. What you decide after that is up to you."

The wind was brisker now, and she drew her scarf closer around her shoulders. "You said once that you had no place to hide— that wherever you went they would find you sooner or later."

"Better later than sooner."

She gave way. "When?"

"Very late—probably around midnight."

"I'll be waiting."

Partridge saw her to the elevator, then went to the cantina where he knew he would find Mario Cassavettes.

"Have a Margarita with me, Johnny."

"Just whisky and water, thanks." He took the adjoining bar stool. "I don't know how your gut takes it. Bloody Marys all morning—two or three beers with lunch—Margaritas in the afternoon—martinis before dinner."

"You forgot the brandies after dinner, old buddy." He lit a cigarette. "The vote was thirteen to one for shoving off if the town comes under fire. My father was the only one for hanging tough."

"It was the right decision." He paused. "Nothing else on the agenda?"

Cassavettes grinned over the top of his glass. "Your name never even came up—but it would have if I had told them what I think."

"What do you think?"

"That you and the señora are planning to duck out on this little cruise."

"You're wrong."

"Am I? Let's add it up. You've got the hots for her, right? But Jiminez also wants her—and not for fun and games. She might have been against Luchengo, but she's still the last of the fat cats, and one of the first Jiminez will want to splatter against a wall."

Partridge took a sip of his beer. "So?"

"So now we have a better reason for holding onto her than just insurance against your running out on us. Now we have a little present for Jiminez." He slid off the bar stool. "Don't try to con me into believing that you would ever turn her over to him."

Partridge shook his head, smiling. "Would you believe, Mario, that I've never made it with her—never even come close?"

"But you're still in there trying."

"No, I gave up a long time ago. I brought her in just as a front for this operation."

"That's crap. You've given me nothing but heat for locking her up here."

"Only to keep Ambassador Hood off our backs—and Luchengo, if he found out we were holding one of his nationals a hostage.

No, Mario, if it helps us protect our deal with Jiminez, he can have her."

Shortly after midnight Partridge heard heavy footsteps in the corridor outside his suite and, opening his door slightly, saw Mario Cassavettes stagger down the corridor. A half hour later Partridge crept down the hall to the head of the stairs curving down to the lobby. Four seamen off the *Reina del Mar,* armed with carbines, were lounging in chairs near the main entrance. He retraced his steps to the opposite end of the corridor, where a service stairway led to the rear entrance. There he heard the raucous voices of another squad of sailors.

Constanzia Novarese was at her door seconds after his light tap.

"It won't be tonight," he told her. "The place is swarming with guards."

There was relief on her face. "It is God's will that I should not be at peace with the murderer of Luis."

"Is it also God's will that Jiminez should murder you?"

"That is in His hands, not ours."

"You don't mind if I nudge Him a little, do you?"

"Do what you like, but it will change nothing."

CHINA QUITS! PEACE BID
TO MOSCOW ENDS CRISIS
—Headline from the Washington Post

It is the nature of world politics that no nation can admit to wrongdoing—that even in capitulation it must mask its actions in utterances that concede no guilt.

The break in China's menacing silence came on the second day after the clash at sea in the form of two brief announcements over Radio Peking. The first said that major units of China's defense command were concluding routine training maneuvers on its frontiers and would return to their bases in the interior. The second said that the People's Republic would send an emissary to Moscow to arrange for reopening of negotiations on the long-standing Sinkiang and Manchuria border disputes.

In neither was there a reference to the crisis that had shaken the world, but the significance of the announcement was clear. In the face of the greatest Soviet war provocation in two decades of flash-point conflict between the Communist giants, China was backing down. And if her rulers were willing to appease Moscow, it was equally clear that they would not prolong the crisis responsible for the array of Soviet-American power on their borders.

Chairman Borichev was willing to play Peking's game. A one-paragraph news story, buried in the back pages of *Pravda,* said merely that the Kremlin "would welcome the early resumption of frontier negotiations vital to the solidarity" of the two Communist powers.

The American President, however, was bound by no such sophistries. He spoke to the nation on radio and television that night from the Oval Office to announce "an early but cautious withdrawal of American air and sea forces from areas contiguous to mainland China," but "the continuation of high-altitude, early warning reconnaissance of China's missile installations." In his position as Commander-in-Chief, he would regard "new or larger deployments of offensive weapons capable of reaching targets within the Western Hemisphere as an aggressive act calling for swift and appropriate counteraction."

The President said he had spoken to Chairman Borichev earlier in the day "to express my deep appreciation for the coopera-tion of his government and to receive from him the assurance that the Soviet Union's agreement to resume negotiations with Peking would be conditional on China's willingness to desist from further incidents menacing to world peace."

The President was hopeful that "the negotiations will succeed and will presage a new era in which China will recognize that the concomitant of power is restraint—that binding treaties, not blustering threats, are the price of admission to the world councils of responsible nations.

". . . Finally, I wish to express my pride in my fellow Americans, whose calmness and courage in this crisis were just as powerful a warning to China of our strength and determination as the presence of our retaliatory forces on her frontiers."

Palmer Joyce spoke to Donald Marston from Washington later that night, and the next morning the aircraft executive made two calls of his own from his home on Biscayne Bay. The first was to Air Force Secretary James Halverson at the Pentagon.

"Mr. Secretary, I can understand why, for security reasons, you had to rush me back into uniform. But the crisis is over now, and I've got a business to run."

"Marston, I appreciate your holding still for all this. But you're right, it was necessary. I'll relieve you of duty as of now if I have your assurance that you won't repeat one word—even to your wife—of what you overheard during the NSC proceedings."

Marston's story was not what he had heard at the council session, but afterwards. "You have that assurance."

"All right, I'll have your formal discharge from temporary duty in the mail to you today."

"Thank you, Mr. Secretary."

Marston's next call was to Harlan Grant in Washington, where the candidate had been sitting out a voluntary moratorium on politics for the duration of the crisis.

"Do you recall my conversation with you on the plane in Chicago, Senator?"

"I do."

"I think it's time for me to speak up now, but I won't do it without your approval."

Grant chose his words carefully. "I can't give you such approval."

"But, Senator—"

"Nor can I deny it to you. I told you in Chicago I wouldn't touch it, and I still won't. But whatever you decide to do with your information at this point is entirely your decision."

Marston understood. He could go ahead, but Grant could always claim he had nothing to do with it and, to the contrary, had tried to discourage him.

"Then, Senator, I think you should know that I plan to—"

"I don't *want* to know what you plan to do."

"Thank you for your time, Senator."

"Always happy to hear from an old friend, Don."

Ambassador Hood heard the President's address in the communications office of the consulate with members of his staff. There were smiles and handshakes when the broadcast ended, but Hood left the office in a grim mood. Colonel Gruver caught up with him in the corridor.

"Thank God, it's over. You go to the brink too often and your luck has to run out. I thought this could be it."

"It's not over here," said Hood. "The President could have thrown in just one reference to Santa Clara—one warning that he wouldn't tolerate a military victory here won by Chinese arms."

"He couldn't scare off Jiminez," Gruver replied. "He's been up in those mountains too long to blow his big chance now. And Luchengo couldn't stop him on two fronts even if the army was willing to put up a fight."

"You think it's all over then?"

"Don't you, sir?"

The ambassador spent a restless evening alone in his upstairs office, waiting for darkness and the arrival of Constanzia Novarese. Toward midnight he heard a crescendo of heavy gunfire from the north, and Gruver was at his door five minutes later to confirm the worst.

"Luchengo's HQ tells me Jiminez has broken loose. He's pounding the federal defense lines south of the arroyo with mortars and laying his long-range stuff on the army positions up the coast. This looks like the final push."

The ambassador went to the window overlooking the bay. Nothing was moving on its slick, black surface except the patrol launch from the *Reina del Mar,* its searchlight probing the approaches to the Playa del Sol.

"Thank you, Colonel. If there are signs of an actual advance on either front, please let me know."

At three o'clock it was clear to Hood that Johnny Partridge

had not been able to carry off the escape. He took a sleeping pill and went to bed without undressing.

Gruver woke him from a deep sleep four hours later. "It's going badly up north. The army places Jiminez' advance at four to five miles."

Hood was already out of bed, reaching for his shoes. "And up the coast?"

"No advance yet. But the army's mobile units are taking a hell of a beating from the artillery. HQ is monitoring the rebel radio. One of our Chinese friends is pinpointing the coordinates, and he's right on target."

Hood took a fresh shirt from the bureau. "I want from you, Colonel, your most pessimistic estimate of when Jiminez could actually fight his way into Ariella."

"That's tricky. He's under ten miles away both to the north and west. He has no transport of his own. I would think tomorrow at the earliest—even if the army cuts and runs as it has in the past."

"What if he's able to capture troop carriers?"

"If he has wheels," Gruver replied, "and resistance is light, he could be here in a matter of hours."

Consul Bennett Cullers stuck his head in the half-open door. "I think, Mr. Hood, that it might be the better part of valor to move our people onto the trawler."

"Colonel?"

"I would agree. If either front collapses, the army has to fall back on Ariella and Jiminez wouldn't hesitate to open up on the town."

"All right, Cullers, start putting them aboard. But hold the communications officer. I'll have a cable to Washington. And, Colonel, you'll advise the Pentagon of the military picture?"

"Right now, sir."

Hood told Cullers to wait. "I'm placing you in charge of the mission as of now."

Cullers didn't want such responsibility. "Isn't this highly irregular?"

"Not at all. I've been planning to resign for many weeks. I spoke to the President on my last trip to Washington. We agreed I would step down when we had to close up shop here."

"All right, sir. But I know of no precedent for—"

Hood's voice was stern. "There's nothing left to be done, Cullers, except move our people out to the destroyer. I think you can handle that."

The consul left, shaking his head. It was grossly unfair, he thought, that Hood should enjoy the amenities and prestige of the ambassadorship for three years and now walk away from his own failure, leaving it to him to preside over the collapse of the mission.

Five minutes later Hood was downstairs. The communications officer was already transmitting the military adviser's message. The ambassador gave Gruver his own cable.

"You might want to read this and then have it sent."

It was to the Latin American desk.

MILITARY SITUATION REQUIRES IMMEDIATE EVACUATION DIPLO-MATIC PERSONNEL. MOST IMPORTANT YOU ADVISE PRESIDENT MY TENURE AS AMBASSADOR ENDS WITH THIS ACTION AS PER PRIOR AGREEMENT WITH HIM. ASSIGNING CONSUL CULLERS TO DIRECT EVACUATION. I WILL REMAIN HERE.

Gruver threw the cable on the desk in front of the communications officer and ran after Hood. The ambassador was just climbing behind the wheel of a consular car on the street.

"I don't understand, sir. There's nothing you can do here." Gruver was leaning against the car door, his face only inches from Hood's.

"I'll be all right, Colonel."

"I've been taking orders from you for three years, sir. But that cable says you're no longer ambassador—that you're a private citizen. Right?"

"Right."

Gruver forced a nervous smile. "But I'm still an officer in the U. S. Army, and I'm ordering you, as an American national, to climb aboard that rust-bucket with the rest of us."

Hood put a hand on his arm. "You won't rendezvous with the destroyer until late this afternoon?"

"That's correct, but—"

"With luck, Colonel, I'll join you before then. Keep an eye open for me."

Gruver watched the ambassador speed west on the boulevard toward the airport.

A light rain began to fall as Hood drove up in front of the command center and saw that another retreat was apparently under way. Soldiers were hauling radio equipment, sheafs of maps, message boards and other supplies from the headquarters and loading them aboard a truck. The Electra, its engines turning over slowly, was standing by on the landing strip.

Inside, Jorge Luchengo was sitting at a desk, arguing with General Silvera-Guzman. Foreign Minister Lara was standing to one side, taking no part in the exchange. He was in army uniform with holster and sidearm.

The ambassador heard only the end of it. "What you propose is surrender," Luchengo told Silvera-Guzman. "The battle will be here. We cannot direct it from Ciudad Alarcon."

The squat general disagreed. "It is important to protect you—to save the government."

"And abandon our troops here to Jiminez? No, General, we will fight for Ariella *calle* by *calle—casa* by *casa!*" He glanced up and saw Hood at the door. "That is all."

Silvera-Guzman and Lara strode past Hood into the rain. Luchengo rose unsteadily to his feet. His arm was in a sling, but he was more vigorous than when Hood had last seen him. His eyes swept around the barren command center. "Yes, Mr. Hood, we are running again—but not as far as Ciudad Alarcon as my courageous advisers propose." He saw the question in Hood's face. "We are in retreat to the west. And most of the mobile equipment we did not lose by gunfire was taken by Jiminez in raids on our motor depots."

"You are moving your headquarters to Ariella?"

"To the army barracks there. Jiminez can flank and bypass this position. We will engage him in the streets of Ariella and there, perhaps, we can stop him. I would hope that you and your staff will leave the city as quickly as possible."

"The staff, yes. I intend to stay for a time, but not as ambassador. My resignation is already effective."

Luchengo held out his hand and Hood took it. "You have been my friend. You have been Santa Clara's friend."

"I have not been able to serve the interests of either your country or mine," Hood replied.

"But you have tried, and for that you have my gratitude." Luchengo let himself slowly into a chair. "You are staying because of the señora?"

"Yes. But I must tell you that I have not been able to present your proposal to her."

"But she is still at the hotel, is she not?"

"But not available to me. American officials, understandably, are not welcome there."

Hood had given long thought to how much he should tell Luchengo. If he were to inform him of the Mafia's contacts with Jiminez, and that the señora was being held as a prize for the revolutionary, it would almost certainly invite a dangerous over-reaction by Luchengo. The seizure of the *Reina del Mar* to prevent the Mafiosi's flight to safety or an appearance of federal troops in force at the hotel were alternatives for which Hood was unwilling to accept the consequences.

"If you cannot speak to her," said Luchengo, "then I must go to her myself."

It was the decision Hood had been waiting for, and the one he felt had the best chance of succeeding. "I would like to accompany you."

"Of course," said Luchengo. "I would not expect to be able to convince her alone."

At that instant the first shells struck the airport. Hood ran to the open door and saw the high explosives rip deep holes in the runway and send black smoke fuming skyward from oil storage tanks. The Electra began taxiing at high speed toward a section of the runway that had not yet been hit.

Behind him he heard the calm voice of Luchengo. "Come with me, Mr. Hood." The rain was heavier now as Hood, supporting the President, led him toward a staff car just outside the command shelter. Silvera-Guzman and Lara were waiting.

All heard the deepening roar of the Electra's engines as it began gaining speed down the runway. Another shell burst just ahead of it, the white-hot shrapnel ripping into its wing tanks. The flaming plane, racing past them at a hundred miles an hour, shot off the end of the runway and plunged into the sea beyond the surf line.

Soldiers ran past them toward the beach but it was too late. The dark smoke from the burning fuel became clouds of hissing steam as the aircraft slowly sank under the battering of the seas. Luchengo stood watching, his jaw muscles pulsing spasmodically, until nothing could be seen of the aircraft but a wingtip jutting skyward. Only then did he ease himself into the car, his face set grimly ahead.

The driver swerved expertly around the shell craters toward the highway. Lara sat with the driver and Luchengo was between Hood and Silvera-Guzman in the back seat. Hood edged closer to the door to avoid contact with Luchengo's arm. The flesh of the hand projecting from the sling was a deep yellow, and the fingernails were black.

Minutes later they were in Ariella. Hood saw that the trawler was pulling away from the dock—the Americans standing in the rain on the foredeck watching the pall of smoke from the airport. The civilian exodus from the city was already beginning. Women were herding children before them, and their husbands were towing carts full of household possessions. Whining dogs scurried in and out of the procession, looking for the faces of their masters. Among the crowd were priests carrying gold artifacts, and Luchengo, his face grim, saw soldiers who had fled from the barracks to join their families.

The army headquarters, three blocks inland from the boulevard, was a quadrangle of low adobe structures surrounding a small drill field.

Luchengo spoke to Hood as the car came to a stop in front of the headquarters building. "I must first attend to decisions here."

"I will wait, of course."

The latest battle reports could not have been more discouraging. Jiminez was advancing against light resistance on the coastal sector, and his advance patrols were already nearing the airport. To the north, the rebel force had driven four miles into the federal lines. Luchengo issued a general order for his troops to fall back on the outskirts of the city and to defend it to the last man.

It was three hours before the remnants of the army were in their new defense positions and Luchengo was ready to leave for the Playa del Sol. He sent for Lara. "You will come with us to the señora. You may prove to be useful."

A truck carrying an army guard of ten left with them for the Playa del Sol. The artillery fire was closer now.

JOHNNY PARTRIDGE had spent a sleepless night prowling his suite, chain-smoking and listening to the rebel guns pound the federal forces to the north and west. If he had made his move only one night earlier . . . He could admit to himself now that he had been wrong in rejecting Sam Hood's alternatives.

Certainly the señora could be in no worse position if the ambassador had come to the Playa del Sol to demand her release. With a squad of Marines to back him up, he might have been able to carry it off. Even if Luchengo had sent federal troops to the hotel to free her, and there had been resistance, she might still have had a chance. But in Jiminez' hands she would have no chance at all.

At dawn Partridge went down to the lobby to telephone Hood. The ambassador would have to call the shots now. But as he was crossing toward the switchboard, one of the sailors blocked his way. "No, señor—no teléfono."

Partridge removed a hundred-peso note from his wallet. The

guard took it, smiling, then jammed the butt of his carbine into Partridge's ribs. *"No teléfono, señor."*

Partridge went into the kitchen. The one chef on duty was swabbing out the coffee tureen, his back to the cutting block and the array of knives and cleavers hanging over it. Partridge quickly chose a short boning knife. Back in his bedroom he hid it inside the lining of the balcony drapes. He had a shower and was shaving when the opening salvo hit the airport only two miles away, the sound waves rocketing against the hotel under the low, black layer of clouds.

Partridge heard anxious voices in the corridor, then Mario Cassavettes pounding on his door.

"That's too close. We're moving out." He took a cigarette from the package on Partridge's bureau and lit it nervously. "I want you to go into town and round up every taxi in sight. We'll start loading up as soon as you're back—and if you're gone more than an hour . . ."

"I know," said Partridge, "there'll be one less passenger going with us."

"You'd better believe it!"

Partridge drove directly to the consulate to find Hood. The diplomatic personnel, carrying their own luggage, were already leaving. He met Cullers in the foyer. "The ambassador?"

"He's not here."

"Where, then?"

The consul had never been more officious. "I'm in charge here now. You will deal with me."

Partridge held his temper. "The ambassador is expecting me. I have to know where he is."

Cullers was in a hurry to leave. "At the airport, or what's left of it."

Partridge glanced at his watch. He had only forty minutes left, and would be cutting it too fine if he tried to find Hood. He was able to locate only five taxi drivers who, at a thousand pesos each, were willing to delay their own flight from the city. His hour was running out as he sped back toward the hotel. Passing the *Reina del Mar,* he saw smoke spiraling from its funnel and crewman singling up the mooring lines for a fast departure.

Two of the taxis were already in front of the hotel, and Mario Cassavettes was waiting for Partridge at the entrance.

"That's the best you could do?"

"Three more are right behind me. We can handle everything in three or four trips. I'd move the luggage first."

"You wouldn't be trying to buy a little more time?"

"No," Partridge lied. "I spoke to the skipper. He's still fueling. It will be at least an hour before he can shove off—and longer than that if we don't send the crewmen back who are standing guard here."

"All right," said Cassavettes, "but I'll keep a couple around just in case you and the woman decide to cut out for the point." *He knew.*

"Why would we?"

"I took a little walk out there yesterday afternoon and saw a boat down in the cove. You going to tell me you didn't stash it there?"

"You're out of your mind."

Cassavettes slid back his coat to reveal his shoulder holster. "You're going upstairs, Johnny, and you and the señora are going to stay put until I come for you. One more trick and you've had it."

Partridge's suite was a mess. His mattress and pillows had been cut to ribbons. The contents of his bureau drawers and closet were flung on the floor. But the knife was still hidden in the drapes. He then went to Señora Novarese's door.

She, too, had had little sleep. Her face was drawn, but her manner was fatalistically calm.

"I was in town this morning," he told her, "trying to locate Hood."

"Why?"

"Why? Because he's our last chance." He fought back his impatience with her. "But I couldn't find him. He was with Luchengo. If my hunch is right, we can expect them both to show up here —and soon."

"It's not important."

He took her harshly by the shoulders. "You want out of here alive, don't you?"

"Not this way. I am to be in Luchengo's debt?" She broke free of his grasp. "Never!"

Partridge went back to his suite, slid the knife inside a coat sleeve and then fell wearily into a chair to wait. He heard the comings and goings in the corridor and the relays of taxis clattering below his balcony. It was almost noon when Mario Cassavettes came to his door.

"We're the last."

"I'm ready to go." Partridge stood.

"Sit down!" Cassavettes was five feet away and had drawn the automatic from his shoulder holster. "You're going—man, are you going—but not with us."

Partridge gauged the distance between them and bent forward slowly in the chair, setting his feet.

Cassavettes was enjoying himself. "A gutless wonder—remember calling me that? You've been riding my ass since day one, and I held still for it because I had to—because you were Mr. Big in this operation. But we don't need you now, do we, old buddy?" He took a step closer. "Where do you want it? In the head, fast and clean—or in the belly, slow and messy. I think the belly, don't you?"

Partridge came in low at the knees, driving Cassavettes against the bureau. The first shot was high. Partridge seized the wrist of Cassavettes' gun hand, forcing the muzzle upward. Simultaneously, Partridge shook the knife from his sleeve into his other hand and drove it into Cassavettes' stomach with a hard, twisting thrust.

His face a mask of agony, Cassavettes began to slump slowly toward the floor, his trigger finger spasmodically emptying the gun into the ceiling. Partridge stood over him, the knife still in his hand. Cassavettes died slowly, looking up incredulously at his killer.

Partridge was suddenly aware of movement behind him and spun toward the door in a knife fighter's crouch. It was Señora Novarese, staring in horror. Partridge glanced down. His own clothes were dark with Cassavettes' blood. He let the knife fall and took a step toward her.

"I had to—"

But she was still looking at Cassavettes and the stain spreading over the carpet. Partridge took her by the shoulder and led her into the corridor.

"When he doesn't show up at the dock they'll come back for us. We're shoving off—*now*."

Bruno Cassavettes, waiting for his son in the last taxi, heard the fusillade of shots through the open window above. His son was a poor killer, he thought to himself. One bullet or two at the most should have done it. He was watching the entrance of the hotel. When a minute went by and then another and his son and the señora did not appear, Cassavettes knew that it had gone wrong. He dug into a briefcase on the seat next to him and found his own gun. But as he flung open the door of the cab he saw the army staff car and the troop carrier speeding past the guard post a hundred yards away. The cops ran down the steps of the promenade to the beach. He had a clear view of the *Reina del Mar* across the bay and of the artillery blasts now crumbling structures along the waterfront.

J OHNNY PARTRIDGE and Constanzia Novarese were leaving the front entrance of the hotel when the army vehicles came to a gravel-scattering stop. Ambassador Hood was first out of the staff car and ran up the steps.

"I thought we might have been too late."

The señora took a step toward him. "Sam!" He took her gently in his arms, and she clung to him desperately. Then, over his shoulder, she saw Jorge Luchengo emerge from the car, the driver steadying him on his feet.

The señora broke free from Hood and ran back into the lobby to a chair behind the bell captain's desk.

"She's had a rough go of it." Partridge told Hood.

The ambassador, for the first time, saw the blood on Partridge's clothes. "Mario Cassavettes?"

"It was him or me."

"She saw it?"

"Enough of it."

Luchengo was now at Hood's side. "Let me go in first," the ambassador said.

The señora had one hand over her face, the other trembling violently on the surface of the desk.

"You *must* speak to him, Constanzia. Jiminez is breaking into the city. There's no more time for hate or for vengeance."

She let her hand fall from her face. Her expression was cold and implacable. "Nor will there ever be time for forgiveness." The hand on the desk was now a tight, white fist.

"He isn't asking forgiveness," said Hood. "And if it's his death you want, that's almost certain. He intends to fight on here until the end."

A shell struck no more than a hundred yards from the hotel. There was a shattering of windows and the dull thud of shrapnel ripping into the thick walls.

Only minutes before she had heard the shots from Cassavettes' gun—an echo from three years earlier in the courtyard at Casa Castillo. And she knew this moment was hers, not Luchengo's—that the confrontation was inevitable. She stood to face him.

He came forward slowly, holding himself erect against the pain. Hood took two steps to the side and felt Lara's presence behind him. Partridge was still near the entrance with two soldiers who were flanking the massive door.

Luchengo, facing the señora across the desk, spoke slowly. "I have no words for myself, señora. You cannot condemn me more than I condemn myself."

She saw the arm hanging limply in the sling, the almost fleshless face and the dull eyes peering from their dark, deep sockets. But she felt no pity. "Why do you come to me?"

"To ask you to do what I cannot do—to continue the struggle that you and Luis and I began together."

"Luis! You can speak his name to me?"

Luchengo began to waver on his feet. "I govern, señora, a nation of widows. Luis was one man. I have sent many hundreds more to their graves and their widows to the churches to light candles. And for that, only God and my own conscience can judge me."

"No, I judge you! Luis spoke of you as his friend—his brother."

"And he was," said Luchengo softly. "I remember him with love."

Her eyes were blazing. "And you gave him death."

"Yes, señora. But I must ask you this. What would Luis have you do now? Let Santa Clara die because I still live?"

She gave him no answer.

"Is it my death you must have?"

"I pray for it."

"Then you may have it, señora." Luchengo took the automatic from the holster on his hip and laid it on the desk before her.

Hood took a step forward. "No, Constanzia."

But Luchengo put out an arm to restrain him. The gun was heavy, and she had to raise it with both hands, the muzzle only an arm's length from Luchengo's chest.

For three years the memory had never been more than an instant away from her consciousness—Luis looking up to her from the paper he had only to sign to save his life—the defiant Castillo answer on her face—the shots in the courtyard.

Who *was* Luis' executioner? The truth she had always denied to herself she could not deny now. Luchengo was observing her evenly across the gleaming barrel of the gun, and she knew he, too, was reliving that long-ago moment and sharing the guilt with her.

Slowly she began to lower the gun and, at that instant, Hood felt the searing blast of a gunshot behind him and saw Luchengo lurching toward the red tile floor, blood spurting from his throat. Turning, the ambassador saw Lara, the automatic still smoking in his hand, look to the señora for approval of this ultimate act of loyalty. But there were only disbelief and horror in her face.

The two sentries were upon Lara, wrestling the gun from his hand. He fell to his knees on the floor, raising his arms beseechingly toward the señora. But Partridge was already at her side, leading her away.

Hood knelt beside Luchengo, raising his head to try to stanch the flow of blood. But he was beyond saving. Gazing blankly into the ambassador's face, he tried to work his mouth, but no words came.

Other soldiers were now rushing into the lobby, and two of them tried to lift Luchengo to carry him to the staff car. But Hood told them quietly that it was too late. The last shudders shook the President's gaunt chest and his head fell to one side, limply, grotesquely.

The ambassador found Señora Novarese and Partridge on the front portico. She was leaning against him, ashen and trembling. Seconds later the soldiers led Lara past them to the staff car, and it began to move slowly down the road toward the guard post.

The señora sensed the ambassador's presence behind her and turned to him, burying her face in his shoulder. Partridge let her go—for the last time.

As quickly as it had begun, the bombardment of the waterfront ceased. In the sudden silence Partridge heard the deep baying of the *Reina del Mar*'s steam whistle and went down to the promenade with its view of the harbor. The ship was heading toward the opening of the breakwater, its screws alternately churning ahead and in reverse to dodge the flotilla of smaller craft also moving toward the open sea and safety.

Then Partridge saw a convoy of army vehicles moving slowly down the main boulevard from the west, flying the red flag of revolution. There was the rattle of small-arms fire from federal snipers along the route and, at the intersection leading to the army barracks, there was resistance in greater force. The convoy drew to a halt, the guerrillas scurrying for cover until the mobile guns in the rear could be brought up to rake the waterfront buildings the army had chosen as defense points. The staff car, carrying Lara and his guards, swung into a U-turn two blocks short of the intersection and sped back toward the hotel.

Ambassador Hood and Señora Novarese were in the lobby. She was in a chair facing away from Luchengo's corpse, and Hood was leaning over her, massaging her hands.

"Jiminez is already in the town," Partridge told Hood. "We had better start moving."

The ambassador got to his feet, nodding. "We're leaving now, Constanzia." Her gaze fell on Partridge but without recognition, and she fell deeper into the chair. Hood drew her to her feet and led her like a sleepwalker toward the entrance.

Partridge, behind them, saw Luchengo's automatic on the writing desk and stuck it in his belt.

It was a steep quarter-of-a-mile climb up the narrow road leading to the lighthouse. The two men, each holding one of the señora's arms, were almost carrying her.

Partridge heard running steps behind them on the flinty surface of the road. It was Lara, who had broken away from the guards in their return to the hotel.

"You go ahead," he told Hood. "I'll be right behind you."

The ambassador saw Lara stumble and fall, regain his feet and continue the pursuit. He also saw Partridge pull the gun from his belt.

"No!" he said.

"We're not taking the bastard with us?"

"If there's room, why not?"

Lara was only ten yards away when he saw the gun in Partridge's hand. He took a faltering step backward and then another, staring at the gun. And before Partridge could speak, Lara began walking slowly back toward the hotel.

The incline was steeper as the road rose toward the lighthouse, and it was another five minutes before they were at the crest and the head of the tortuous path leading down to the cove.

"We're going to have to give her a little rest," said Hood.

Partridge went to the edge. The Mañana was still at the old jetty, but there was no sign of José. Partridge glanced back toward the town and saw that the lead vehicles in Jiminez' convoy had broken through the intersection and were heading in the direction of the hotel.

Hood left the señora resting against the wall of the lighthouse and stood watching with Partridge.

"Why the hotel? The action's in town."

"Jiminez must have been told Luchengo came here." Hood replied. The lead car was now passing the guard post and they saw Lara waiting for it in the forecourt, raising his hands in surrender. The car ran him down, dragging him under its wheels until it came to a stop. Hood had never seen Jiminez, but it was he who strode to the front of the car and knelt just for the instant it took him to fire a bullet into Lara's head.

Nor did Hood recognize the tall Chinese who was next out of the car, but he knew it had to be General Gi. But there was no mistaking the second Chinese, even in his uniform. Hood had faced that bricklike little man too many times across a tennis net.

Partridge took the lead down the path cut into the rocky face of the promontory, testing the footing for Hood, who was supporting the señora. The going was hazardous, and more than once the ambassador had to grasp at plants or outcroppings of rock to maintain his balance.

When they were fifty yards from the foot of the path and Partridge still had caught no sight of José, he told Hood to wait and advanced toward the jetty in a half crouch. The *Mañana* was rising and falling gently in the swell. The only sounds were the rasping of the mooring lines, the soughing of the sea and, in the distance, staccato gunfire from the city.

Partridge was stepping into the cockpit, gun drawn, when he saw a movement in the water between the hull of the cruiser and the jetty. Although there was little of his torn face left to recognize, it was José, floating face up, one hand clutching a line trailing over the side. Drifting next to him was the weapon—a heavy fish gaff with its steel hook.

Partridge heard a warning shout from Hood and, glancing up, saw the battering ram of a head and the massive shoulders in the entrance to the cabin. Bruno Cassavettes got off the first shot and Partridge felt his left leg crumble. Partridge's shot, an instant later, tore the gun out of the capo's hand, but he kept coming in a bull-like charge. Partridge's next bullet struck him in the temple, but he had too much momentum now. His head drove into Partridge's chest, crushing his back against the stern railing.

The capo, half blind with blood, reacting now only to the instincts of a fighting bull that charges even when its wounds are mortal, took four steps backward, then began another rush. Partridge put two more bullets in his chest, but they didn't stop him.

An instant before Cassavettes was on him, Partridge fell to his broken left knee and drove himself upward. His shoulder caught Cassavettes in the stomach, catapulting him up and over the stern.

Partridge heard Hood running along the jetty toward him, but he was still watching the capo, thrashing in the water like a marlin at gaff. Finally his movements became slower and slower, and in a mist of red spume he began to settle toward the white sand under the jetty.

Partridge's voice was sharp. "For Christ's sake, Hood, will you bring her aboard? They must have heard the shots back at the hotel."

Partridge had the engines running by the time Hood and Señora Novarese were aboard. He told the ambassador to cast off the bow lines and threw off the stern moorings himself. They were fifty yards from the jetty when they heard the first shots.

"Below! Both of you!" Over his shoulder Partridge saw a skirmish line of guerrillas firing from the cliff. He was reaching for the throttles for more speed when a bullet struck the instrument panel, blinding him with flying glass. The next bullet caught him in the back of the head, and he fell against the wheel.

Below, Ambassador Hood was placing a blanket over Señora Novarese in one of the bunks when he felt the *Mañana* lurch out of control. Had he taken five seconds longer to reach the deck, the cruiser would have been on the reef guarding the cove.

He spun the wheel sharply to the left, and they were on course for the open sea, They were out of range now, and the firing ceased.

Hood cut the engines to idle and knelt beside Partridge. Except for the sharp fragments of bone, the back of his skull was mushy to the touch. Hood felt Señora Novarese brush against him, and she fell to both knees. He shook his head. "He's dead."

But she sat mutely on the deck, raising Partridge's head onto her lap, indifferent to the blood, stroking the blond hair back from his forehead.

Miles to the west, Hood saw the low, gray silhouette of the destroyer and, close aboard, the rust-red hull of the trawler and the white gleam of the *Reina del Mar.*

ASSISTANT SECRETARY Edward O'Farrell, who was to write his memoirs a year after resigning from the State Department, gave the title "Black Tuesday" to the chapter recounting the events of that day.

But, driving home at midnight to his home in Falls Church, Virginia, he was still too weary, still too shaken by the rapidly escalating tempo of the debacle to shape it into plausible proportions. It was the more incredible because it had struck at a time when official Washington was basking in an atmosphere of euphoria. No one, not even Harlan Grant, had been able to fault the President's crisis leadership. And implicit in the confident mood of thousands of presidential appointees was the probability—now almost a certainty—that their positions, power and prestige were secure for another four years.

Until that morning O'Farrell himself had been confident of the outcome of the election and was determined to stay on in the department. A second-term President—he cannot run for a third—was freer of partisan political restraints and more likely to look to the judgments of history than to the public opinion polls. And O'Farrell had been certain that he might finally succeed in moving the White House toward a new, if grudging, reform of the nation's bankrupt Latin American policy.

But now he was certain of nothing. It would all depend on Sam Hood.

The day had begun, ominously, with Hood's cable announcing the start of the evacuation and confirming his own resignation. Secretary of State Sterling Adams and O'Farrell spoke to the President on a conference call to decide on the manner and timing of its release to the news media. His orders were that State, not the White House, should announce the evacuation. He gave no reason, but it was implicit that this was not the time to tarnish the President's triumph over the Chinese by attributing to him, directly, the news that a Communist victory in Santa Clara—even after the interception of the missiles—was a distinct possibility.

The President was just as adamant that there should be no mention of Hood's resignation. And to Secretary Adams' demurrer that it was a *fait accompli* that would be dangerous to try to conceal, the President said it would be even more dangerous to announce, simultaneously, the withdrawal of the American mission and the resignation of the ambassador. It would raise too much speculation over Hood's known disagreements with him on Santa Claran policy. The resignation could not become effective without his approval, and he would give it in his own good time.

Harlan Grant was also biding his time that morning. To reporters asking for his reaction to the flight of the mission and the new military threat from Francisco Jiminez, he said that he would have no comment until he had a clearer picture of events.

That picture began to emerge more fully with the first of two cables sent that day by Consul Bennett Cullers from the destroyer U.S.S. *Dale*y to the Latin American desk of the State Department. The first:

ACTING IN RELIEF OF AMBASSADOR HOOD. WISH TO REPORT SUCCESSFUL EVACUATION ALL AMERICAN PERSONNEL. REBEL FORCES ENTERING ARIELLA FROM NORTH AND WEST. WITH FULL COOPERATION OF CAPTAIN OF REINA DEL MAR, MEXICAN VESSEL OF PRIVATE REGISTRY, BOARDING PARTY FROM DALEY HAS TAKEN INTO CUSTODY AMERICAN NATIONALS IN RESIDENCE SANTA CLARA TO ESCAPE CRIMINAL PROSECUTION OUR COURTS. COMMANDING OFFICER DALEY HAS PERMISSION PERUVIAN 'AUTHORITIES TO DEBARK US PORT OF CALLAO. PRESENT WHEREABOUTS AMBASSADOR HOOD UNKNOWN. WILL DELAY

SAILING UNTIL NIGHTFALL IN EXPECTATION HIS ARRIVAL ABOARD DALEY.

Adams and O'Farrell drove immediately to the White House. The President was shaken by the cable and its portent of another major victory for Francisco Jiminez. But he was still determined to isolate himself from the announcement. It was agreed that State should reveal the growing threat to Ariella but emphasize that the capital, Ciudad Alarcon, was still in government hands. Again, there was to be no reference to Hood's resignation or to his disappearance.

The one positive development of the day—the capture of the Mafiosi—was given to the Attorney General's office to announce. Three of the Mafiosi had been shot resisting the boarding party from the *Daley,* but their wounds were not critical. Federal marshals would fly to Callao that night to return the fugitives to American jurisdiction.

The receipt of Cullers' next cable, two hours later, sent Adams and O'Farrell back to the White House for the second time:

AMBASSADOR HOOD ABOARD DALEY IN COMPANY WITH SENORA CONSTANZIA NOVARESE, WIDOW OF FORMER PRESIDENT. HOOD RE- PORTS ASSASSINATION JORGE LUCHENGO BY FOREIGN MINISTER ARTURO LARA, HIMSELF SLAIN BY REBELS. HOOD ALSO REPORTS ENEMY FORCES OVERRUNNING CITY. UNDER WAY CALLAO. ETA 0900 LOCAL TIME TOMORRROW.

Adams and O'Farrell found the President in conference with General Mark Courtland, chairman of the Joint Chiefs. The Chief Executive read the cable twice, gave it to Courtland, then sent for Maxwell Busby. He told the news secretary to announce to the White House correspondents the assassination of Luchengo and the death of his murderer, and to report further that he was con- sulting with General Courtland and Secretary Adams on the military and diplomatic options still open to the administration.

The options Courtland had given the President were discouraging. With Ariella in rebel hands, there could be no early, massive shipment of troops or matériel into the port unless the President was willing to order the devastation of the city by bombing and naval bombardment. Amphibious landings along the coast would be hazardous because of the high escarpments guarding the beaches.

Troops and weapons could be flown into Ciudad Alarcon, but the main enemy force would still be eighty miles to the south, and it could be weeks before it could be drawn into decisive battle. But it was more likely, said Courtland, that Jiminez would retreat back into the Andes, and the President would face a commitment to drawn-out guerrilla warfare in terrain clearly favorable to the enemy. Complicating the picture further was the certainty that Bolivia would supply Jiminez and perhaps commit forces of its own.

There was the same note of pessimism in Secretary Adams' appraisal of the diplomatic options. Despite Moscow's brief alliance with Washington against the Chinese threat, there was no question that the Soviet Union would try to recoup its standing among more militant Communist nations by condemning American intervention in Santa Clara. And its veto in the Security Council would block possible United Nations action against Jiminez. The Organization of American States might, under duress, follow Washington's lead, but only with token commitments of troops. There could be no question, Adams said, that the United States would bear the brunt of the fighting and of world censure alone.

In both Courtland's and Adams' analyses, the parallels with Vietnam were not lost on the President.

For Palmer Joyce, the stage could not have been set more dramatically for his telecast at seven o'clock that evening. Throughout the day newspaper headlines and flash bulletins on television and radio were confirmations of impending disaster for American prestige in Latin America.

But Joyce's own interview with Donald Marston was the stunning climax. The aircraft executive told his story simply: the breakdown of White House security responsible for his presence at the National Security Council session, whose deliberations he could not, of course, reveal . . . the conversation between the President and Ambassador Hood and the President's admission that he had chosen, for fear of the political consequences, not to act upon the ambassador's early and frequent warnings that the Communists were building missile sites in Santa Clara . . . the President's conditional acceptance of Hood's resignation because of long-standing policy disagreements . . . and, finally, Marston's own impressment into the Air Force to silence him.

Yes, said Marston in response to a question from Joyce, he would be willing to appear before an appropriate committee of Congress to repeat his story under oath.

Within half an hour of the telecast, Senator Grant went on the offensive with a demand that the Senate Foreign Relations Committee convene at the earliest possible time to investigate the accusations. He insisted also that Francisco Jiminez be given an ultimatum to withdraw from Ariella and desist from further aggression against the central government of Santa Clara or face the certainty of American intervention. It was inconceivable, said Grant, that the President would risk nuclear war against China and now shrink from the nominal commitment of force necessary to crush China's ally—Jiminez.

There were two responses in support of the President—one from James Mallory, chairman of the National Committee, and the other from News Secretary Max Busby.

Mallory issued a brief statement identifying Donald Marston as New York state chairman for Harlan Grant and suggesting that his credibility was, at best, suspect.

Busby, like Mallory, did not expose himself to questions from the press. Instead, he had one of his secretaries distribute a statement to the White House correspondents to the effect that Grant's demand was both premature and irresponsible and an invitation to another Vietnam. The administration, the statement continued, would react swiftly and appropriately to events in Santa Clara, but only in concert with America's allies.

There was a final conference in the Oval Office at ten o'clock that night. Attending were Mallory, Busby, Secretary Adams and O'Farrell. The President already had spoken to Senator Robert E. Breckinridge, chairman of the Senate Foreign Relations Committee, and had agreed with him that it should convene the following Wednesday to inquire into Marston's accusations. It was, the President told the gathering in his office, the only way to set the record straight. Hood, of course, would be the key administration witness, and the transcript of the telecast should be in his hands as quickly as possible.

O'Farrell was told by the President to send it by State Department teletype to the embassy in Lima for delivery to Hood on his arrival in Callao. He was also to advise Hood by separate cable that his resignation was not yet effective, which would give him greater standing before the committee. The thought struck O'Farrell that it would also give Hood greater immunity from answering questions that could fall within that limitless and forbidden area of national security.

The question no one put to the President was whether Marston's charges were true—and no one ever would.

The U.S.S. *Daley* was gliding through the narrow entrance to the outer harbor of Callao when the chief radioman brought O'Farrell's cable to Hood in the officers' wardroom, where he was having a silent breakfast with Constanzia Novarese.

YOU WILL BE MET CALLAO BY HARRISON BRUSH, FIRST COUN-SELOR LIMA EMBASSY, WHO WILL HAND DELIVER TRANSCRIPT OF PALMER JOYCE TELECAST CONTAINING CHARGES TO BE SUBJECT OF SENATE FOREIGN RELATIONS HEARING OCTOBER 27–28. YOUR AP-PEARANCE BEFORE COMMITTEE IN OFFICIAL (REPEAT OFFICIAL) CAPACITY AS AMBASSADOR VITAL. RECOMMEND YOU AVOID ALL CON-TACT WITH NEWS MEDIA UNTIL YOU HAVE FULL BRIEFING. ACCOM-MODATIONS FOR YOU AND SENORA NOVARESE AT AMBASSADOR'S RESI-DENCE.

Hood read the cable grimly. What could the transcript possibly contain that would force the President to default on their agreement on his resignation and be of a magnitude that would call for a Senate hearing? He glanced up at the señora and tried once more to rouse her from the insensate apathy into which she had fallen since boarding the *Daley*. "A car will be waiting for us. We'll go directly to the embassy. You'll be able to rest there."

She said nothing, and a moment later left him to go out to the deck, staring dully at the destroyer's bow wave rippling across the oily surface of the harbor. She was still wearing the gray smock in which she had fled from the Playa del Sol. But now it bore muddy streaks from her descent of the cliff and the darker stain of Johnny Partridge's blood.

Hood stood behind her, resisting the impulse to hold her in his arms and speak the words—were there such words?—that might bring the tears that could dissolve the terror of the past twenty-four hours.

But he knew her trauma was more than a reaction to the horrors to which she had been a witness. Its source was guilt. Luchengo. Lara. The Cassavettes. Partridge. Could time ever acquit her of complicity in their deaths? Or of the hundreds more dead and dying in the streets of Ariella, or long buried at San Quentin and the Arroyo Seco?

An hour after the *Daley* was under way from the offshore rendezvous the previous afternoon, the commanding officer had sent a message to Hood requesting him to come to his quarters.

"I thought we ought to agree on the billeting of the civilians aboard," the curt young commander told him. "Your Marine detachment and the rest of the official party can have the bunks of my crew members who are on watch. We can move the prisoners and their wives into the petty officers' quarters. They'll have more privacy there, and we can maintain a closer guard. We'll find room for you and the lady here in officers' country."

"Thank you," said Hood. "That sounds all right."

The cabin was silent except for clicking of the gyro compass repeater over the captain's bunk and the rush of seas along the destroyer's fragile hull.

"The dead man," said the officer. "There was no Stateside address among the papers in his wallet. Where do I ship the body?"

Hood had read Partridge's dossier more than once. "I don't know. His only next of kin, I believe, is his mother—and she's in Sicily."

"We can bury him at sea," the officer replied, "if you approve and would be willing to sign a statement attesting to the cause of death."

"I'll let you know," said Hood. He found Señora Novarese

on the signal deck behind the bridge, watching the black pall of smoke over Ariella vanish into the distance, and told her of the captain's proposal. She gave him no sign of approval or disapproval.

An hour later the body, sewn in canvas, was taken to the stern. There was no mustering of the crew. Only the burial party of four seamen, the captain, Hood and the señora were present. The captain spoke the brief ritual: "Almighty God, we consign to the deep the mortal remains of . . ." The body slid from the board into the frothing wake of the *Daley*.

Constanzia Novarese made the sign of the cross but her face was void of expression. Hood led her forward along the rolling deck to her billet in the engineering officer's quarters, and did not see her again until morning in the officers' wardroom.

He was still with the señora on deck when the *Daley* came alongside the Grace Line dock. Among the waiting crowd Hood saw Peruvian military officers, a host of reporters and photographers —and Harrison Brush.

Two busses were on the dock—one for the diplomatic evacuees, the other for the Mafia leaders and their wives. Brush was the first to board the destroyer and was taken directly to Hood. He shook his hand vigorously.

"You had us worried, Mr. Hood. You can't know how good it is to find you safe." Hood, turning to introduce him to Señora Novarese, saw that she had finally broken. Tears were streaming down her face as she saw the Mafiosi leave the gangway in handcuffs. Together with their wives, once again in the severe black dresses they had worn on first arriving in Santa Clara, they had to run the gamut of milling, shouting newsmen and photographers to reach the bus. A Peruvian officer, trying to rush them along, shoved Mrs. Cassavettes, and she fell to her knees.

Constanzia Novarese began to scream, "No! No!" and Hood took her back into the wardroom.

Only minutes later the commanding officer came for them. "Everyone's ashore, Ambassador. Are you ready?"

"Thank you, Captain. Thank you very much for all you've done."

On a signal from Brush, the driver of the limousine brought it to the foot of the gangway, and seconds later the car was edging its way through the crowd. Angry reporters were pounding on the doors, and photographers shot off their flash guns at the windows, blinding the passengers.

Hood threw a protective arm around the señora. When they were out the gate and on the highway to Lima, he tried to withdraw it. But she drew even closer to him.

It was an eight-mile drive from the port to the capital. Brush had no opportunity to hand Hood the bulky envelope containing the Joyce-Marston transcript until the limousine drew up in front of the ambassador's residence.

ARTHUR ASHTON, the American ambassador to Peru, was waiting for them on the steps of his residence on one of Lima's most exclusive boulevards. The long-time foreign service officer shook hands vigorously with Sam Hood.

"You apparently got out just in time, Sam. We've had a report on Santa Claran radio that General Silvera-Guzman is surrendering today. His only condition, already agreed to by Jiminez, is amnesty for federal troops, including himself, presumably."

But Hood's immediate concern was for Constanzia Novarese, who was being led into the residence by Ashton's wife. "Could you call a doctor for the señora, please? She's very close to collapse."

"Certainly."

The reporters and photographers from the wharf were now outside the gates, demanding interviews and pictures. Hood could still hear their shouts as he was shown to one of the guest suites. He read the transcript of the telecast, then put through a call on a secure line to Ed O'Farrell at the State Department.

The Assistant Secretary broke through his opening words. "Thank God you're all right. The report from Cullers that you were missing had us worried as hell. Now, Sam, we want you up here Wednesday night. There'll be a reservation for you at the Mayflower."

Hood's voice was resolute. "I don't think you want me up there, Ed—not unless you expect me to perjure myself."

"You've read the Marston transcript?"

"I have, and the sections relating to my conversation with the President are absolutely correct."

There was a long pause. "You should know that we intend to present evidence that will thoroughly discredit Marston. He's been one of Grant's biggest fund raisers, and we can prove that he met to conspire with Grant in Chicago hours after leaving the NSC session. By the time Senator Breckinridge is through working him over, his testimony is going to smell to high heaven of an eleventh-hour political smear. Grant, of course, will take his best shots at you, but you can always fall back on your immunity."

"No," said Hood, "I have no immunity, even if I did want to claim it. My resignation took effect yesterday morning."

"It takes effect," said O'Farrell, "when the President signs it—and he hasn't."

Hood's anger rose. "The President gave me an absolute commitment that he would sign it the day I had to evacuate the mission. That's in the Marston transcript too."

"It's Marston's word against yours and, by implication, the President's."

"In other words, you expect me to deny that the conversation ever took place?"

O'Farrell had a ready answer. "Let me ask you this. If you had known there was an eavesdropper outside the door, *would* the conversation ever have taken place?"

"Of course not."

"All right. Marston was that—an eavesdropper—trying to recall many days after the event what he *thought* he heard. We're not asking that you deny you had a word or two with the President— just that Marston's recollection of it is faulty."

"We're back to the question of perjury, Ed."

"No, goddammit, we're back to the question of whether we're going to turn this country over to a trigger-happy psychopath like Grant!"

"Or," said Hood, "leave it in the hands of a last-hurrah politician who hasn't the guts to face up to what he is, or to the consequences of his cheap pandering to public opinion. No, I don't believe the choice is all that obvious, Ed—and neither do you. You've been ready to walk out as long as I have."

"There is a choice, Sam, and you know it. I've made it, and when you cool off I think you will too." He paused. "In any event, you have no alternative but to testify. The committee has subpoena powers."

Hood said nothing.

"The embassy there in Callao will book you aboard the Pan Am flight arriving at Dulles at midnight Wednesday. We'll have a suite for you at the Mayflower, and I'll be waiting there for you with Arnold Moscov, one of our brighter legal officers who will serve as your counsel at the hearing. We can discuss your line of testimony then."

"That won't be necessary, Ed."

O'Farrell was becoming impatient. "It's not all that simple, Sam. Marston will appear before the committee Wednesday morning. We'll have to go over his testimony with you. And Moscov will want to explain the ground rules on immunity. You can claim it, for instance, on written and verbal communications to the department and the President, but not on your public statements. You've got to know where you stand before you go in there."

"I know where I stand," Hood replied.

"Are you trying to tell me you don't want me or Moscov?"

"What I'm telling you, Ed, is that I don't want a brain-washing, I can handle it."

O'Farrell gave up. "I'll have a transcript of Marston's testimony waiting for you at the Mayflower. You will read it?"

"Certainly."

"Sam?"

"Yes."

"The whole ball game is riding on you. The President's lead over Grant isn't all that secure, you know."

"I know."

"And you will go along?"

Hood hung up without answering.

Hood and Constanzia Novarese had a quiet dinner with the Ashtons. The doctor had given her a sedative, and she had slept through most of the afternoon, but her face was still wan and her eyes lusterless. The Ashtons, forewarned by Hood, did not allude to events in Santa Clara. The men spoke of old colleagues in the State Department—the women of a shopping trip the next day to acquire a new wardrobe for the señora.

The meal was as brief as it was awkward and Hood took the señora into the garden for a moment alone. There was a rumor of rain in the air, and the silence was broken only by the calls of night birds and the gentle splash of a fountain. They sat on a bench in the far corner of the garden, under a wall heavy with ivy.

"I'll be returning to Washington tomorrow night," he said. "I want you to go with me."

"No."

"But you ought to appear before the UN at the earliest possible time, and then a plenary session of the OAS. And you'll need my help, Constanzia."

She shook her head. "It's too late, and what purpose would it serve?"

"Perhaps none at all—now. But you have to try. You could at least become a rallying point—a symbol of resistance for ex-patriate Santa Clarans in the overseas legations. And you would represent a hope, at least, to your own people that there exists a government in exile—an alternative to Jiminez and the repressions that have to come."

She took his hand in hers. "No, Sam, that is for others to do—for those who are innocent of blame. And I am not." Her eyes met his. "Do you know what I was thinking when I held the gun in my hands—when Luchengo, my enemy, stood before me? I was thinking of that day at Casa Castillo, three years ago, when one word from me—"

"You can't bring Luis back to life," Hood said.

"Nor can I go on deceiving myself that his blood—and the blood of how many more?—is not on my hands. For three years, Sam, I had been praying for Luchengo's death as punishment for his crimes. But yesterday, facing him, I knew that he was the accuser, not I—and that I was guilty. You've always known that, haven't you?"

"That's no longer important. What is important is what you can do now."

Her eyes met his. "As penance, Sam?"

"No, because it must be done."

"Then by others. It would be a lie for me, now, to pretend to be a patriot."

Hood lit a cigarette, and both were silent for a long time, watching the play of lights on the plume of the fountain.

"Then what will you do, Constanzia?"

"I don't know. I want time to myself—Rome, Paris—another world. There is another world, isn't there?"

"There can be. And we might look for it together."

Her lips were warm on his cheek. "Good night, Sam."

After breakfast Hood saw her off with Mrs. Ashton for their round of the stores and spent the next hours listening to tapes of the overnight announcements on Radio Santa Clara and reading dispatches on world reaction to Jiminez' victory.

The guerrilla leader spoke for more than an hour, equating his triumph with the Communist conquests in Bolivia and Cuba, but pledging that he, unlike Fidel Castro, would never betray the revolution to the false hope of peaceful co-existence with the imperialists. Santa Clara and Bolivia, with the assistance and protection of the People's Republic of China, would stand together against invasion and intimidation by their enemies, and would eventually carry the red flag of liberation to all of Latin America. And, until that struggle was won, Santa Clarans would have to accept many deprivations, including the abrogation of many of their illusory freedoms under the constitution.

Orders for the expropriation of Catholic churches and the expulsion of the priests and prelates were among Jiminez' first proclamations. The churches would become schools and Marxism the new religion. Elections eventually would be held, but not until the People's Republic was secure against its enemies.

Peking coupled its fraternal greetings to the victorious government of national liberation with assurances of solidarity and support, and a warning to the United States and its Latin American puppets that China would respond appropriately to aggression against the new republic.

In a more moderate tone, Moscow bade Santa Clara welcome to the alliance of Communist nations and proposed an early exchange of trade and diplomatic missions.

Bolivia was alone among Latin American nations in hailing Jiminez' victory. The other governments saw it as an alarming portent for the peace of the Americas—and a justification for the mass arrest of leftist political leaders.

Finally, Hood ran through the sheaf of wire service reports from Washington—Harlan Grant's demand for intervention; the cautious White House declaration that it was exploring military and diplomatic options with its allies, and the announcement that the Senate Foreign Relations Committee would convene to inquire into Donald Marston's charges against the President.

Hood had lunch alone with Ambassador Ashton.

"Incredible, isn't it—the whole Marston affair? I don't envy you having to testify, Sam. It's unconscionable to involve the career service in politics. But the hearing certainly will discredit Grant and his ambitions—now and in the future. Looking at it that way, perhaps it's worth it."

Hood took a long sip of his coffee.

There was a tap on his door in midafternoon. It was Mrs. Ashton. "She's gone, Sam. We did a little shopping, had a bite, then she was insistent that I take her to the airport. I tried to tell her she was too distraught to travel, but—"

"You don't know what plane she took?"

"No, she left me at the car."

"And no message?"

"I'm sorry, Sam—nothing."

SENATOR Robert E. Breckinridge gave him the oath. "Do you solemnly swear that the evidence you shall give before this committee shall be the truth, the whole truth and nothing but the truth, so help you God?"

"I do."

Hood was at the small witness table in the Senate Caucus Room before a cluster of radio and television microphones. He had nothing before him but a copy of that morning's edition of the New York *Times,* whose headline read: PRESIDENT ON TRIAL IN SENATE CRISIS HEARING.

The ambassador had been in this chamber many times in his sixteen years in government to testify in support of administration foreign policy before the most illustrious committee of the Senate. But if the world had changed fearfully in that time, this forum had not.

Four crystal chandeliers hung from the high ceiling, casting a warm glow on the maroon carpeting and drapes and reflecting more brightly off the marble pillars and the lustrous veneer of the long, dark committee table.

Chairman Breckinridge sat at the center of the table, facing Hood, with the chief counsel at his side and the other committee members to his left and right in order of their seniority. The committee staff sat behind the senators in chairs along a cream wall.

On either side of the room, equidistant between Hood and the committee, were the hulking cameras that were televising the hearing live to the nation, and flanking Hood were portable tables for the more than one hundred reporters. Behind him was the blue-ribbon audience of senators, representatives and government officials. And behind them still another battery of television cameras.

Breckinridge was smiling amiably at his friendly witness. "The committee wants to thank you for your appearance here today, Mr. Ambassador. We appreciate fully the stresses you have been under in recent days, and I, for one, regret the necessity of exposing you to still another. And now, will you please state for the record your full name and occupation?"

"My name is Samuel V. Hood. I have, at the moment, no occupation. But I appear here today as the former ambassador to the Republic of Santa Clara."

Breckinridge, alert to the sudden stirring among the audience and the press, ran a quick hand through his mane of white hair. Senator Harlan Grant, two chairs to the left of the chairman, was studying Hood alertly.

"It is the committee's understanding," said Breckinridge, "that you are here as a State Department witness."

"That is incorrect," Hood replied. "My tenure as ambassador, by agreement with the President, was to end with the withdrawal of my mission to Santa Clara." He saw one of Breckinridge's aides lean across the staff table and hand him a note.

The senator read it, then glanced over the audience. "If Mr. Arnold Moscov is present, would he please step forward?"

"Mr. Chairman?"

"Yes, Senator Grant."

"We have a witness before us now. May I suggest that we hear him before calling another?"

"I am not calling another witness, Senator. It has just come to my attention that there is State Department counsel available to Mr. Hood. And it's the judgment of the chair, in light of the grave national security aspects of this hearing, that he should have the benefit of counsel."

Moscov, young, dark, intense, slid into the chair next to Hood.

"You are Mr. Arnold Moscov?"

"I am, sir."

"And you have been assigned by the State Department to advise Mr. Hood?"

"I have."

"Can the committee then conclude, Mr. Moscov, that the department still regards Mr. Hood as having official rank?"

"It can, sir."

Grant spoke again. "I think it might be proper, Mr. Chairman, to ask the witness if he has objection to counsel?"

Grant's interruptions were a violation of the protocol of Senate hearings in which the chairman calls for questions or comment from other members only after he and the chief counsel conclude their own interrogation.

Hood was smiling faintly. "I have no objection, Senator, although I believe Mr. Moscov will be wasting both his time and his expertise. I am entirely familiar with security regulations."

Another hum ran through the audience.

"I repeat," said Breckinridge, "that it is the ruling of the chair that you shall have counsel." His tone was imperative. "You have had the opportunity to familiarize yourself with the testimony yesterday of a Mr. Donald Marston?"

"I have."

"The chief counsel for the committee, referring to the record of that testimony, will now put to you a series of questions that will give you an opportunity to confirm or deny the very serious allegations—"

Hood bent toward the microphones. "I would like to claim the privilege, Mr. Chairman, of an opening statement."

Hood's interruption of the chair was as clear a violation of protocol as Grant's, and Breckinridge cut him short. "You are here as a rebuttal witness. The issue—the only issue before this committee—is whether there is substance to Mr. Marston's accusations, and I will expect you to limit your testimony to that."

Hood tried to object, but Breckinridge ignored him and spoke to Moscov. "To your knowledge, counsel, has the State Department given its approval to an opening statement by Mr. Hood?"

"No, sir."

"All right, Mr. Addison, you will proceed."

Gerald Addison, the chief counsel, studied his notes for a moment.

"On October 15, this year, Mr. Hood, were you present at a meeting of the National Security Council at the White House?"

"I was."

"Following that meeting, did you have a private conversation with the President in an office adjoining the Cabinet Room?"

"I did."

"I now show you a picture of Mr. Donald Marston, whom I understand you have never met. Will you tell the committee whether this man was at any time within earshot of you and the President?"

The photograph was brought to Hood by a member of the staff. "No, I have never seen this man."

"Your testimony then, Mr. Hood, is that Mr. Marston was not present during your conversation with the President?"

"No, Mr. Addison, my testimony is that I didn't see him. He could have heard the conversation through the open door, as he claims."

Addison, pudgy and balding, ran a handkerchief across his brow. "But that would be speculation on your part, wouldn't it, Mr. Hood?"

The chamber was suddenly silent, and Hood's glance swept the dais—Breckinridge peering at him under shaggy eyebrows, Grant's face a mask, Addison bending across the table, waiting.

"No, Mr. Addison, it is not speculation. Mr. Marston's account of the conversation was correct."

The thud of Breckinridge's gavel was heard only faintly through the uproar. On either side of him Hood was aware of reporters dashing for the door and of still photographers moving in on him for full-face close-ups. Moscov was standing next to him, raising his hand for attention.

It was a full minute before Breckinridge could restore order. "Yes, Mr. Moscov."

"I would like a ten-minute recess to consult with Mr. Hood."

Grant was also on his feet at the far end of the dais. "Mr. Hood is at a critical point in his testimony. The only conceivable point of a recess at this time would be for Mr. Moscov or others to dissuade him from further testimony along this line."

But Breckinridge was already standing. "We will recess for ten minutes or as long as it takes to have order here."

The senator went directly to a small anteroom and put through a call to the President.

"You're watching?"

"I am."

"What the hell is Hood trying to do?"

The President's voice was a hoarse whisper. "You gave him the oath. 'The truth, the whole truth . . .'"

Breckinridge was incredulous. "But he's your witness!"

"I thought he would go along," said the President. "I was wrong."

"There are at least fifty million voters watching this," said Breckinridge. "If Hood's testimony stands, you're dead—the ticket's dead—and that includes me."

"I'm sorry, Bob, I didn't expect this."

"Maybe you've given up, *Mr.* President, but I haven't. When I go back in there I'm going to rough him up good. We can tie him in with that Chink friend of his who was at the missile site. That's treason. We can tie him in with Grant—accuse him of swapping perjury for the promise of a high appointment by Grant."

"No," the President replied, "it won't hold water—none of it."

"Then we can at least go to national security as a pretext for cutting off further testimony."

"It's too late," said the President. "Just wrap it up as quickly as you can and head back to your own state to salvage what you can. You can even take me on if it will help."

"You can concede the election, just like that?"

"I'm conceding that I was wrong, Bob—very wrong—and I got caught at it."

"It is your testimony then, Mr. Hood, that the charges against the administration, which you are sworn to serve, are correct?"

"Yes, but I don't like the implications of your question, Mr. Addison. I have spent sixteen years in public life in the service of

four presidents. And in that time I have had to face many challenging decisions, but none weighing more heavily on my conscience
or my convictions than the one I had to face today."

Breckinridge cut him short. "Your soul searching is of little
interest to this committee, Mr. Hood. The fact is that in the wake
of a momentous crisis, whose impact on our security is still perilously
in doubt, you have chosen to cast doubt on the leadership and the
integrity of a great President to whom you owe your own high
position."

"That," replied Hood, "invokes a question of conscience that
confronts all of us who decide to serve in government. Is it our
ultimate duty to defend the policies of our government whether
we agree with them or not? Or is our greater duty to the nation?
I feel shame here today, Mr. Chairman, not for what I have done, but
for the years in which I chose to remain silent. And I share this
guilt with many other foreign service officers who disagreed absolutely with the policies they had to enforce in Latin America and
Southeast Asia and elsewhere under this and other administrations.
It is not to their credit or mine that we chose to be passive servants
of one man—the President."

Breckinridge was glaring at him under the white tangle of his
eyebrows. "They could always resign."

"And many have, Mr. Chairman, but quietly—without publicly
challenging the policies they found onerous. I elect today to speak
out against those policies—to declare that the considerations of
politics and of economic self-interest are and have been the tragic
guidelines of our foreign policy for far too long. You spoke, Mr.
Chairman, of the momentous crisis we have just been through, and
I tell you it was unnecessary—that a Francisco Jiminez could not
exist in this hemisphere if our policy in Latin America was not a
direct encouragement to revolution. Our only viable effort in the
last two decades to restore stability to Latin America was the
Alliance for Progress. And what is it today? A military alliance in
which we ignore the economic welfare of the civil population in
favor of armaments for their oppressors. We build no schools, no
hospitals—only hate among those millions who could be our friends,
who could and would find democracy a preferable alternative to

Communism. Francisco Jiminez is our creation, not Santa Clara's. And his victory over the forces of freedom in that republic could not have been possible except in the vacuum left by our own indifference—our own political rationale that Santa Clara was not worth saving because it could play no profitable role in our economy or no significant role in our defense. We, as much as Jiminez, must accept the judgment of history, not only for the crisis that took us to the very brink of war, but for the tragic oppressions that will now afflict a country to which we were bound by treaties and our own national honor to protect."

Breckinridge rose from his chair. "Are you quite through, Mr. Hood?"

"Today, yes. But I can assure you, Mr. Chairman, that in the months and years ahead I will continue to speak out against the stupidities and the cynicism of our foreign policy." His glance swept to Senator Grant. "And I will do it regardless of which political party is in power."

Grant gave him the briefest of smiles. Breckinridge's gavel came down hard. "The committee stands adjourned!"

On his way out the door, ignoring the microphones thrust in his face and the barrage of questions from reporters, Hood saw Ed O'Farrell waiting at the head of the stairs curving down to the rotunda. The Assistant Secretary of State came toward him.

"You said you would go with a bang, not a whimper, Sam." He fell in step with Hood. "Lunch? They've got a new seafood chef at the Rotunda and a shrimp poulette you wouldn't believe!"

Television and still photographers were surrounding them on the marble stairway. "Are you sure you want to be in these pictures, Ed?"

"Why not? I gave Secretary Adams my resignation this morning."

"Before you knew what I was going to do?"

"Yes."

The sky outside the Old Senate Office Building was clear and there was a cold nip in the October air. Hood threw back his shoulders, breathing deeply. "Why don't we walk until we find a cab?"

"Fine," O'Farrell replied. "It's a good day for a walk."

EPILOGUE

HE spent the early winter months at Montego Bay in Jamaica, preparing a series of lectures on "Last Chance: a Coherent Foreign Policy for the 1980s." The day following Harlan Grant's inauguration, the first lecture was delivered before the Center for International Studies at the Massachusetts Institute of Technology, to which he had earlier agreed to serve as a consultant.

It was both a critique of past American policies and a warning of the even more parlous consequences the nation could expect from Grant's post-election declarations of neo-isolationism and a harder line towards the Soviet Union because of its near agreement with the People's Republic of China on a non-aggression treaty.

In Paris, Constanzia Novarese read an account of the lecture in the European edition of *Time* magazine and wrote him a brief letter. She had taken an apartment in Neuilly-sur-Seine and was planning to accept an appointment to the United Nations Educational, Scientific and Cultural Organization in the spring. She was hoping he would come to Europe soon.

His own plans took him to London a week later to address the Institute for Strategic Studies, and the following morning he was in

Paris. Ten days later they were married in the office of the mayor of the Sixteenth Arrondissement.

On their last night in Paris they had dinner at one of his old haunts —Brasserie Lipp on the Left Bank. While they were waiting for their check, a party of Chinese came into the restaurant and took a facing table. It was not until the waiter brought her coat, and they were standing to leave, that he saw Han Li-Wong studying the menu. The Chinese glanced up only once to nod and smile, ever so slightly. And a moment later they were caught up in the crowds on St. Germain des Prés.